Praise for Julia London's delightful novels . . .

WEDDING SURVIVOR

"In the glittering first of a new contemporary romance series, London gives us the pleasure of a celebrity tabloid without the guilt. In movie-speak, the novel is *XXX* meets *Legally Blonde*: witty and sweet and full of sparks."

—*Publishers Weekly*

"With delicious digs at Hollywood's excess, nutty trends, killer one-liners, highly amusing characters, and hot, hot, hot sex, London sets her newest series up to be a real blockbuster." —*Romantic Times*

"Julia London is in top form with Book One of the Thrillseekers trilogy. Her trademark sparkling wit, outstanding characters, and dazzling dialogue will captivate your attention immediately and maintain it throughout this clever, sexy story, and will leave you salivating for more." —*Affair de Coeur*

"Julia London brings us a delightful romp that has you gasping, laughing, and yes, thrilling to the entire 'extreme adventure'." —Contemporaryromance.com

continued . . .

MISS FORTUNE

"Read this fun and fast-paced adventure of the heart. It will make you laugh, cry, and believe in the power of love."
—The Best Reviews

"With saucy wit, London brings her delightful trilogy to a triumphant conclusion, and her sharp, snappy writing style is the perfect complement to this deliciously entertaining story of a not-so-ugly duckling who discovers her own true worth." *—Booklist*

BEAUTY QUEEN

"A wonderfully endearing heroine, a delightfully roguish hero, some sizzling chemistry, and writing that sparkles with sexy, sassy charm all come together beautifully in the second in London's fabulously entertaining Lear family trilogy." *—Booklist*

"Another 'knocks your sox off' read . . . funny, sexy, and touching. Julia London's colorful characters and superb narrative make this one of the best books of the year."
—Affaire de Coeur

"Showcases [London's] talent for depicting the progress of intimacy between two equally strong and unpredictable lovers . . . [T]he exchanges between Rebecca and Matt are winningly fresh and funny throughout."
—Publishers Weekly

MATERIAL GIRL

"Great characters, sassy dialogue, and a feel-good ending give readers everything they want in a romance."

—The Oakland Press

"Julia London proves her outstanding writing talents as she goes outside the realm of the historical era to debut her first contemporary. *Material Girl* is a well-written novel, worthy of the hours you will devote to and savor reading it."

—Romance Reviews Today

"Simply irresistible. Precious. A polished gem . . . Julia London has been writing stellar books from the beginning with her historical romances, but *Material Girl* puts the *zing*, *ping*, *bang* on this contemporary romance for her readers."

—Reader to Reader

"[Robin Lear and Jake Manning] are as different as night and day, but go together like whipped cream and strawberries . . . You'll never get enough of them . . . The romance is great, the sex is fantastic . . . A number-one pick for your summer reading." *—A Romance Review*

"*Material Girl* is so much fun, I couldn't put it down . . . Don't miss this extraordinary debut contemporary from a very talented author."

—The Romance Reader's Connection (4½ plugs)

Berkley Sensation books by Julia London

MATERIAL GIRL
BEAUTY QUEEN
MISS FORTUNE
WEDDING SURVIVOR
EXTREME BACHELOR

EXTREME BACHELOR

JULIA LONDON

BERKLEY SENSATION, NEW YORK

THE BERKLEY PUBLISHING GROUP
Published by the Penguin Group
Penguin Group (USA) Inc.
375 Hudson Street, New York, New York 10014, USA
Penguin Group (Canada), 90 Eglinton Avenue East, Suite 700, Toronto, Ontario M4P 2Y3, Canada
(a division of Pearson Penguin Canada Inc.)
Penguin Books Ltd., 80 Strand, London WC2R 0RL, England
Penguin Group Ireland, 25 St. Stephen's Green, Dublin 2, Ireland (a division of Penguin Books Ltd.)
Penguin Group (Australia), 250 Camberwell Road, Camberwell, Victoria 3124, Australia
(a division of Pearson Australia Group Pty. Ltd.)
Penguin Books India Pvt. Ltd., 11 Community Centre, Panchsheel Park, New Delhi—110 017, India
Penguin Group (NZ), Cnr. Airborne and Rosedale Roads, Albany, Auckland 1310, New Zealand
(a division of Pearson New Zealand Ltd.)
Penguin Books (South Africa) (Pty.) Ltd., 24 Sturdee Avenue, Rosebank, Johannesburg 2196, South
Africa

Penguin Books Ltd., Registered Offices: 80 Strand, London WC2R 0RL, England

This is a work of fiction. Names, characters, places, and incidents either are the product of the author's
imagination or are used fictitiously, and any resemblance to actual persons, living or dead, business
establishments, events, or locales is entirely coincidental. The publisher does not have any control over
and does not assume any responsibility for author or third-party websites or their content.

EXTREME BACHELOR

A Berkley Sensation Book / published by arrangement with the author

PRINTING HISTORY
Berkley Sensation mass-market edition / May 2006

Copyright © 2006 by Julia London.
Cover photo by David Vance / The Image Bank / Getty Images.
Cover design by Rita Frangie.
Interior text design by Kristin del Rosario.

ISBN: 0-425-20919-9

BERKLEY® SENSATION
Berkley Sensation Books are published by The Berkley Publishing Group,
a division of Penguin Group (USA) Inc.,
375 Hudson Street, New York, New York 10014.
BERKLEY SENSATION and the "B" design are trademarks belonging to Penguin Group (USA) Inc.

PRINTED IN THE UNITED STATES OF AMERICA

10 9 8 7 6 5 4 3 2 1

PROLOGUE

NEW YORK

ON the day of the last showing for the fabulously successful Broadway play, *Marty's Sister's Lover*, Leah Kleinschmidt, one of the leads, was bouncing off the walls in
Michael Raney's apartment, trying to contain her excitement. After a three-month run, everyone was talking about
her hilarious portrayal of Marty's sister, Christine. The
critics loved her.

As a result, her agent had received several inquiries from
Hollywood and was currently negotiating a development
deal for her. After several long years of working her way up,
Leah was finally getting what she'd always wanted—a shot
at film.

"I mean, okay, a sitcom isn't exactly *film*," she'd said
that morning, waving a toothbrush around. "But it's one
step closer, right?"

"Right," Michael agreed. He was still in bed, watching

her bounce around, talking and brushing her teeth all at once. He wanted to remember her like this always—vibrant and happy, her blue eyes shining as she padded around wearing nothing but one of his dress shirts and a pair of footie socks.

"Can you *believe* it?" she asked him for the thousandth time.

"Yeah," he said, and leaned back, sprawled across the bed. "I can definitely believe it. You're awesome."

She laughed, tossed the toothbrush aside, and gleefully pounced on him. "See? This is why I love you, Mikey. I can forgive your sock problem because you're so wonderful to me."

"Hey," he protested, looking at the ridiculous footie socks she was wearing. "I don't have a sock problem— you do."

"No, I have sock *standards*, which is totally different, and my standard is on your feet, in the laundry, or in a drawer," she said, as she nuzzled his neck.

"But I don't get even a fifteen-second grace period," he complained. "Once they hit the floor, the Sock Nazi appears out of nowhere, demanding I put them in the hamper."

"You're lucky! I haven't said anything about boxers yet," she said, and bit him on the neck.

"What are you doing?" he asked, his hand automatically stroking her back, her bare leg.

"Leaving a mark so you'll know how much I'll miss you when you're gone."

The remark made him flinch inwardly. Leah was used to his absence for a week, two weeks tops, but she had no idea that forever was around the corner. That was because Leah really didn't know much about him at all.

Her head popped up; blond hair whispered across his face, tickling him. "How long this time?" she asked.

He pushed her hair behind her ears, looked into her glittering blue eyes. "I don't know, baby." It was getting harder for him to work around the truth, because his frequent absences for work were becoming a source of contention between them. He didn't like that, for a lot of reasons. He didn't like that he felt guilty every time he left. He didn't like that he had to leave. And he damn sure didn't like having such strong feelings for Leah when he knew that he had to leave her for good.

"More than a week?"

"Definitely more than a week."

She groaned, pressed her forehead to his. "Stupid Austrians! Why can't they just hire someone *there* to look after their finances? Why does it have to be you?"

"I don't know," he said, stroking her back. "Maybe because I'm good at it? And I speak German and English fairly well?"

"I know, I know," Leah sighed. "I just really miss you when you're gone."

"I miss you, too." And he did, he truly missed her . . . but he'd always had a disquieting feeling that maybe he didn't miss her as hard as she missed him, like deep in the gut. But he *did* miss her . . . only he'd get busy and forget the little things. Like how she talked with wildly expressive hands. Or how she would frown when she was trying to make the origami art she had been studying the past year. Or how she wiggled her fingers at him when she said good-bye every morning before disappearing into the bowels of the subway.

"And I miss the orchids," she added as she suddenly sat up, straddling him.

He'd gotten in the habit of having fresh orchids delivered every week just to see her smile, because when she smiled, she lit up like a Christmas tree. She loved the orchids. Many nights, she'd sat at his dining room table, trying to replicate one of the delicate blooms with the expensive origami paper he had given her.

She was not as talented in the art of origami as she was at acting—in fact, she wasn't very good at all. But Michael would never tell her that—he kept buying her paper and ignored her various attempts that now littered his apartment.

"But that's okay," she said, caressing his chest with her hands. "I'll be very excited about the big batch of orchids I'll get when you come back."

He hated the disappointment in her eyes, *hated* it. He tried to smile, but he couldn't, and instead, he reached up and touched the smooth skin of her face. He could hardly stand to be near her and not touch her. They'd been a couple for nine months now, and he just wanted her that much more.

Leah smiled, moved her hands over his chest.

He slid his hands to her thighs, beneath the tails of his shirt, and up, to her breasts.

Leah closed her eyes; he slid his fingers over the tip of her nipple. With a soft sigh, she swayed a little, braced herself against his chest. He sat up, quickly unbuttoned the shirt she wore, and pushed it from her shoulders.

This wasn't what he had planned, not how he wanted to end it, but he couldn't resist her, and began moving his hands everywhere, sliding over her arms, caressing her breasts, her hips, her back. He would miss this, he would miss her body, would miss her laugh, her sigh, her smile.

He took her breast into his mouth, and Leah seized his shoulders to steady herself. He moved a hand to the apex of her legs, his fingers gliding into her cleft.

It was he who groaned this time—she was hot and slick. He put an arm around her waist, tried to pull her off him.

But Leah laughed and resisted. "You said I could be on top this time," she reminded him.

He grinned, easily pulled her off, rolled her onto her back. "I lied. If you want to be on top, you're going to have to earn it."

"*Ooh,* bold talk."

He kissed her laugh, felt himself floating, the feral sensations taking hold. With his mouth and his hands, he slid down her body, leaving a hot, wet trail on her belly. He pushed her thighs apart, kissing them tenderly, spurred on by Leah's gasps and moans. And then he moved slightly, so that his mouth was on her sex.

Leah gasped and clutched at his head. Michael loved that about her—she was a lusty lover—and he slipped his tongue between the slick folds. He held her firmly and casually stroked her, his tongue dipping in and out languidly at first, tasting her, exploring each crevice, moving up to the core, then down again, to where her body throbbed. As her groans and her writhing increased, so did his urgency. He was stroking her harder, his mouth covering her, and Leah began to press against him.

He licked and sucked her into a frenzy of delicious torment until Leah was literally gasping for breath. And then she cried out. He came over her, his hands skimming her belly, her breasts, to her face. Leah laughed as he pressed his lips to the hollow of her throat. "Oh my God," she said. "Oh my *God*." She flung one arm above her head, smiling deliriously.

Michael reveled in the soft feel of her body, the tender pressure of her hand and her mouth on his chin. He had never in his life known lovemaking like he knew it with Leah. Each time it left him spent and powerless and hungry for more.

She began to move beneath him, guiding him to her. "What are you waiting for?" she asked him breathlessly.

Michael laughed, moved between her legs and spread them wider, so that the tip of his erection was touching her, moving slowly against her. "You've never been exactly patient, have you?"

"No," she said, and fumbled for the drawer on the nightstand, grabbed a condom. She quickly tore the wrapper with her teeth, then watched his eyes as she rolled the thing on him, using both hands to do it, both hands to stroke and tickle and make him absolutely crazy. "Watch it," he said with a smile. "You may get more than you bargained for."

"Not at this rate."

"Now you've gone and done it," he muttered, and low-ered his lips to hers as he eased himself inside her, moving his hips in small circles, until he had slid deep into her, moving slowly, prolonging the moment, teasing her.

But Leah was in no mood to be teased. Her fingernails dug into his hips, urging him deeper and faster.

He smiled. "Where's the fire?"

"You mean you can't *feel* it?" she gasped, digging her fingernails into him even deeper. "Come on, Mikey, don't make me beg."

"But I love it when you beg," he said, hoping she'd beg soon, because he couldn't keep the teasing up. He needed to be in her. *Really* in her.

"Please," she said, lifting her head and biting his lower lip. "Please fuck me."

That was all it took, and he lengthened his strokes. They were so good together that Leah instantly began to move with him, her hips rising to meet each surge, her breathing as ragged as his, her knees squeezing him.

Michael was sliding deeper and harder, his hands in her hair, his eyes wildly roaming her beautiful face, driving into her, over and over and over again, until he closed his eyes and found a very hot and very potent release with a strangled cry.

With one last, residual shudder, he collapsed on top of her and kissed her forehead. *"Leah,"* he whispered. He loved her, he knew he did, and the Three Big Words were on his lips, just at the tip of his tongue.

"That was *fabulous*." She kissed him, raked her finger-nails up his back. "You are so sexy, Michael. I just want to eat you up." She wriggled out from beneath him, moving gingerly to dislodge him from her, and stood up. "I've got to have something to drink," she said, and walked across the apartment into the tiny kitchen, completely and glori-ously naked.

Michael rolled onto his side and propped his head on his hands, watching her. The Three Big Words slid off his tongue, back into that place inside him where he'd kept them all these years, all shiny and new, never used.

There wasn't anything he wouldn't do for Leah, but there was at least one big thing he *couldn't* do—he just couldn't seem to be the guy she wanted, the guy who could go the distance. He was like a marathon runner who would make it to within ten yards of the finishing line of full commitment, where he would inevitably peter out, falling flat on his face, gasping for air and wanting a drink.

He told himself he was doing the right thing. His job, his history, and his lifestyle said he was doing the right thing. He was. He just had to keep reminding himself of it.

A half hour before the curtain went up on Leah's last performance as Christine, a bundle of orchids arrived for her with a note from Michael. *Break a leg, baby!* it read. *I need to talk to you after the show.*

Leah blinked and read the note again. *I need to talk to you after the show.* A shiver of delight raced up her spine—what if her best friend, Lucy, was right? What if Michael was going to ask her to marry him?

"Nah," she said with a laugh, as she arranged the orchids on her dressing table. The couple of times she had broached the subject, she had gotten the very serious vibe that Michael wasn't ready to settle down. Maybe because words like *not ready* and *commitment is a big step* had come tumbling out of his mouth on those occasions.

But what else could he possibly want? It wasn't as if they hadn't seen each other quite a lot the last few days. Maybe the tide had turned. It was obvious he loved her, wasn't it? Granted, he'd never actually uttered those words, but what guy ordered orchids once a week? Or had very expensive origami paper shipped to her when he was overseas? Or sat in the front row of her play, shouting *bravo, bravo*? Or made love to her like he'd just crawled out of the desert after being lost for twenty years?

Oh yeah, Michael Raney loved her. He might not say it, but she could feel it.

Of course she hadn't said it, either. Lucy had warned her about that. "The guy has *got* to go first," she'd said. "Otherwise, you come off as needy and end up with egg on your face." Maybe that was true, and maybe it wasn't, but Leah hadn't yet found the courage to say it.

She thought of Michael as he'd been this morning after they'd made love. She was combing through trade papers while he lay sprawled across the bed, sleeping. The top sheet was wrapped around his leg, the rest of him wonderfully naked. His shoulder-length, thick black hair, which he often wore in a ponytail, was covering part of his face. He was beautiful—a strong, square jaw, high cheekbones, and a single dimple in his right cheek when he smiled. And he had beautiful penny-brown eyes with thick black lashes that made her absolutely melt.

But it wasn't just his looks that she—and most every other woman in New York—loved. It was that he was so good to her, so supportive. And witty. And smart.

Leah picked up the note again, which she had put down on a stack of reviews that called her "*brilliant and exciting*" and "*a sure bet in Hollywood*" and a "*genius comedic actress,*" and read his note again. *I need to talk to you after the show.*

Maybe Lucy was right. It had been nine months. They were perfect for each other. And they hadn't talked about the future in a long time. Maybe, she thought with a smile, her career and her love life were reaching new heights. Maybe everything was coming together in perfect symmetry, a gift from heaven.

"In ten!" someone shouted outside.

She still had her last performance, then the strike party. And then, tomorrow when she woke up, she would be headed for a new life altogether.

Maybe they'd get a new apartment, she thought as she

tossed off her dressing gown and did one last check of her costume. Something bigger. Something uptown.

THE play ended to thundering applause, and the cast was brought back for three curtain calls before the lights came up. At the strike party, the cast was aglow—many of them would be touring with the production in the next few weeks.

They were all excited for Leah. "You are *so* going to Hollywood, girl!" one of the crew shouted at the strike party, which prompted an eruption of cheers for her.

Leah felt so alive—she couldn't imagine even sleeping again, much less coming down from the exhilaration. And there, across the room, leaning against a column, was the man of her dreams. He was nursing a drink, watching her as she flitted from group to group, saying farewell, accepting warm wishes and accolades from people who had become her friends.

Michael seemed nervous, Leah thought gaily. Like a man on the verge of a life-changing event. He was usually the life of the party, famous for making men laugh and women swoon—he was *always* flirting—but tonight, he kept to himself, his eyes on her.

He was going to ask her. She just *knew* he was, and she was floating in anticipation of the moment, buoyed by the knowledge that he was The One.

Later, when Michael caught her by the elbow, kissed her cheek and said, "It's getting late . . . do you think we could talk?" she beamed at him.

She grabbed her coat, kissed everyone good-bye, laughed at their calls for her to find a place in her new TV show for them, and left on Michael's arm.

He took her to a coffee shop at the corner, which she thought was odd—but it didn't matter where he asked her. The important thing was that he loved her.

He sat across from her, his penny-copper eyes dark as

he gazed at the orchids she was taking home. "You were wonderful tonight," he said. "You're going to be a huge star."

"Oh God, I don't know," Leah said sheepishly. "I *hope* so."

"You are," he said adamantly, and reached for her hand. "You're great, Leah. Everyone who meets you recognizes your talent. You will be very successful."

"Wow," she said, still beaming. "That's so sweet of you to say."

He smiled, too, but it was a strange smile—a smile like he was dying. "You're going to be so successful that you won't need me."

"Oh, Michael!" Leah laughed. If only he knew that she worried she'd lose him. "I *do* need you," she assured him. "I will always need you. You're my rock."

He sighed and withdrew his hand, then gripped the edge of the table so tightly that his knuckles were white, and Leah's belly did a strange little flip. "What I'm trying to say is that you really don't need anyone—you're great all on your own. The world is your oyster."

"Well maybe," she said with a smile, "but I don't want to be alone."

"But you will be, baby . . . because I'm leaving."

Leah laughed. "I know. We talked about that this morning, remember?"

He looked absolutely miserable. "But this time, I'm not coming back," he added quietly.

Something thick and hard snapped inside Leah. Her mind couldn't process the words, but her heart was reeling. "What do you mean, you're not coming back? That's silly," she said with a flick of her wrist.

"Leah . . . I'm ending it," he said, his voice depressingly soft.

"Ending it?" she repeated dumbly. "*Ending it!* Ending *us*? But . . . but why?" she asked as panic started to rise in her.

He looked away, shoved two hands through his hair. "My job," he said simply. "It doesn't leave room for a . . . a significant other."

This could not be happening. *This could not be happening!* She *loved* him. She adored him, and he'd just chopped the legs out from beneath her. She couldn't seem to find her balance, a center where she could even absorb the words he was saying, much less understand them. "Just like that?" she asked him breathlessly. "No warning, no indication? We made *love* today, Michael! What, is this about the Hollywood thing?"

"God, no," he said, shaking his head. "No, Leah. I *want* that for you. I want you to go on and be as great as I know you are."

"But . . ." She surged forward, reached for his hand. "But Michael, we have a great relationship. Why would you do this? Why would you hurt me like this? I don't understand!"

He grimaced. "I don't want to hurt you. I *never* wanted to hurt you. In all honesty, I should never have entered this relationship in the first place. I'm not the kind of guy to settle down, and I knew, I . . ." He paused there, seemed to be searching for words. "I'm sorry, Leah," he said again. "I am leaving for Austria in the morning. I'll be gone indefinitely."

The words fell like rocks between them, each one heavier than the last. Yet Leah could not believe it. She could not believe that nine months of a blossoming, fantastic relationship, that was, by all accounts, a match made in heaven, was ending so abruptly with no warning, no clue. It was a blindsided blow. "I don't get it," she said, as tears began to well in her eyes. "I thought we were so good together. I had no idea there was anything wrong—"

"There's nothing wrong. You're an amazing woman." He sighed again and looked very pained. "I'm so sorry I have to do this to you. I am sorry I ever let it go this far."

"Let it go this *far*?" she cried, and felt the first tear fall.

"What does *that* mean? You weren't into it, but you just strung me along for no reason?"

"No," he said instantly. "It wasn't like that. But I never thought . . . shit, I don't know what I thought. I just can't commit, baby."

"Who the hell asked you to commit?" she cried.

He reached for her hand, but she yanked it out of his reach. "I can't be with you, not anymore. I have to leave. This is for the best—"

"Don't you *dare* tell me what is best," she snapped, swiping at the tears that fell from her eyes. "Just . . . just *go,* if you're going."

"Let me help—"

"No!" she cried. "Don't do *anything* except get the fuck away from me, Michael!" She turned away, fumbled in her bag for some tissues.

He got up and moved toward her, but Leah wouldn't look at him. She couldn't look at him. Her whole world had just been turned upside down in one stunning blow. He'd stolen her breath, crushed her heart, and now she lay bleeding and gasping for air. She hated him in that moment. She absolutely hated him. She flinched when he put his hand on her shoulder, as if he had burned her. Michael removed his hand, and she listened to his footfalls as he walked out of her life, leaving behind nothing but the ashes of what had been the greatest love of her life.

ONE

SOMEONE hurled an empty beer bottle at the limousine Michael Raney was riding in; it bounced off the back windshield and hit the back fender before crashing onto the pavement as the car eased out of the Shea Stadium VIP parking lot.

"Lemme out," Parker Price said through clenched teeth, and reached for the door, but his brother Jack held him back.

"There's dozens of them, bro. You can't take them all," Jack said.

Parker shoved his brother off and sagged against the plush leather seats, defeated. "It's over. It's so over. I might as well shove my cleats up my ass."

"That's the spirit," Jack said. "And anyway, I don't think it's *that* bad," he added, and rather unconvincingly, considering that it really was that bad. Frankly, Michael had never seen a shortstop play a game as poorly as Parker Price had just done. The Yankees had made the Mets look like a bunch of little leaguers, and the shortstop, for whom the Mets had shelled out one hundred and ten million dollars plus bonuses over seven years to make sure that never happened, was the worst of the lot.

Another beer bottle hit the top of the car. Parker snapped his head up and punched the button that lowered the window separating them from the driver. "Hey pal, if you haven't noticed, angry fans are hurling beer bottles at us—do you think you could pick up the pace a little?"

"Yo, genius, *I'm* not the one who had a hole in my glove you could drive a truck through, right?" the driver snapped back. "I'm going as fast as I can, but there are a lot of vehicles in front of us!"

Parker punched the "up" button, raising the window, and stared morosely at the floor.

"Look at it this way, Park," Jack tried. "If you were hitting well, they'd probably say you'd juiced up."

Parker groaned and dropped his head.

Something else hit the car, bouncing off the top. A baseball, maybe?

"Oh for four," Parker said. "I haven't had a hit in *eight games.*" He suddenly punched the window button again. "We're going to the Essex, Central Park South." He sent the window up again without waiting for an answer from the driver.

That address, unfortunately, was where Michael Raney and Jack Price, two of the four Thrillseekers Anonymous boys, were putting up for this baseball series. T.A., as they liked to call themselves, was the premier private adventure club in the United States, catering exclusively to the very wealthy. They also did some of the best stunt work in Hollywood. In fact, Michael and Jack were taking one last little break in New York, while Eli McCain and Cooper Jessup, the other two partners, were back in L.A., finishing up a new deal for the film, *War of the Soccer Moms.*

Jack had the idea of coming to New York to watch his brother Parker play ball for the Mets. "Private box," he'd said to Michael. "Really good-looking women."

'Nuff said.

But now Parker wanted to come up to their suite, and Michael didn't think that was a good idea. He was giving out all the signs of being a seriously wet blanket, and Michael was ready to go out. He hadn't been to New York in a few years and he was anxious to hit some of his old haunts. Nothing against Parker—he was a decent guy when he was on, but when he was off, he was pretty miserable company, and *man* was he off now.

"You sure you want to come to the hotel with us?" Jack asked in a tone that suggested he was having the same misgivings as Michael.

"I can't go home," Parker muttered. "There's an old woman who lives on my street, and Jack, she's . . . she's *lethal*."

Something else hit the car, but it was a softer thud than before. "Hot dog," Michael guessed.

Jack and Parker glared at him.

The reception at the hotel wasn't any warmer, although they did manage to get up to the room without an incident, which was an improvement over the scuffle they'd had trying to leave the stadium.

Inside their suite, Jack was on Parker's case. "What the hell is eating at you? You used to be so damn good. What happened?" he demanded.

"Okay," Parker said, holding up massive hands. "You'll think I've lost it, but here it is: I think it's that Kelly O'Shay."

"Who?" a clearly perturbed Jack shouted.

"Kelly O'Shay!" Parker cried. "She has a morning radio sports show here in the city, and every single damn day she is *hammering* on me. I think it's her," he said helplessly, and dragged all ten fingers through his hair. "She's really on my case, Jack," he said, sounding like a kid. "You won't find a meaner tomcat than her, I swear to God."

Michael rolled his eyes and tapped up the volume on the boob tube. He wasn't a pro baseball player, but he thought that if he were, and he couldn't hit a slow-pitch softball, then he'd be down at a batting cage somewhere instead of holed up here like some felon, whining about some disc jockey who had it in for him. A *female* disc jockey, for Chrissakes.

Jack, however, was appalled. "Wait, wait," he said, waving a hand at Parker as he tried to process it. "Are you trying to tell me that you can't hit because some . . . some chick is talking trash?"

"She's jinxed me," Parker muttered miserably. "I swear she's jinxed me."

Michael sighed and flipped channels. And as he zoomed past one channel after another, something caught his eye, something so unreal that he suddenly bolted forward, quickly bumped it back a couple of channels, and peered intently at the screen.

Holy shit.

He turned up the volume. *"There are times I just don't feel like myself."* A pretty woman with shoulder-length blond hair, tight low-rider jeans, boots, and a suede jacket was walking down a country lane with her dog. She paused by a wooden fence and leaned against it, looking into the camera. *"Sometimes, irregularity can really put a damper on my day. But then my doctor told me about Fibercil."*

Jack, who had paused in the dressing-down of his brother, chuckled.

"Ssh," Michael hissed at him.

"Just one pill before I go to bed, and the next day, I feel like me again!" She smiled brightly and resumed walking, pausing once to pick up a stick and throw it for the dog, as a male voice intoned, *"Serious side effects may include nausea, fatigue, hypertension . . ."*

Michael didn't hear any of it—he was too mesmerized by the woman. He watched as she strolled along, her corn silk hair shimmering in the sun, her smile content, her stick-throwing abilities pretty lame.

Leah Kleinschmidt.

He hadn't seen her in five years now, and man, she looked . . . she looked so much better than what he remembered. Long blond hair. Fabulous breasts. Legs that went on for miles. Oh yeah, he remembered those long legs wrapped around him as he moved inside her, and his wanker gave him a little nudge. And that warm, million-watt smile he'd carried in his mind's eye, comparing it to all the other smiles he'd seen in those five years, never finding one that could match it.

So Leah had gone to Hollywood. Good for her. He just hoped there was something a little better in her portfolio than a commercial for some constipation product.

"Mikey . . . are you having a problem?" Parker asked, as a male voice continued with the serious side effects.

"Huh?"

"A *problem.* You know . . ."

"No, no," Michael snorted. "No, it's just . . . I know her."

Leah turned and smiled at the camera. *"I can rely on just one pill at night, and I feel as good as new in the morning,"* she repeated sunnily. *"That's great peace of mind."*

"So who is she?" Parker asked.

What a loaded question—she was everything in some respects. And really nothing since he'd dumped her five years ago. "No one," he said. "Just someone I used to know."

Leah's face faded behind a giant bottle of Fibercil. Michael quickly switched the channel to ESPN. Two commentators were discussing the Mets game. *"The problem with major league baseball is there is no accountability. You don't spend that kind of money without being guaranteed some results. If I were the Mets organization, I would be suing for every last dime I'd given Par—"*

"Jesus," Parker moaned. Michael quickly switched again, landing on some movie channel. He handed the remote to Jack, got up, walked to the windows that overlooked Central Park, and stared out, as Jack demanded that Parker explain more about the female shock jock who was harassing him to the point he couldn't hit.

Leah Kleinschmidt. The One Who Got Away.

Well. *Technically* speaking . . . the One He Never Should Have Dumped.

TWO

IN L.A., Leah Klein was dressed in a huge, thick robe and fuzzy slippers. Her hair was sticking up in two Mickey Mouse–like earballs on the top of her head, and she was holding a huge box of tissues stuffed under her arm.

The man across from her cocked his head to one side, studying her face. "Redder around the nose," he said, because he was the director and could decree such things. "A *lot* redder. We want her to look like she's been blowing more than her brains through there. Now she just looks like she's had too much to drink. Let's get this right, okay?"

Apparently, considering they were on what had to be at least the fiftieth take, getting a tissue commercial right was a lot harder than Leah could have imagined. Her agent, Frances, had said, "Just go without makeup. That oughta be good enough."

Leah hadn't quite known how to interpret that, but she had come without makeup and couldn't wait to tell Frances that apparently her bare face didn't look *that* ill.

A girl with two nose rings and a tongue and eyebrow stud suddenly popped up in front of Leah and started dabbing a brush around her face with a vengeance, shoving red powder into her nose and eyes. There was so much powder flying that Leah started wheezing and had to wave her hand in front of her face to get rid of the girl and the powder.

The director leaned in, his face looming large as he studied the newly applied powder and nodded. "Okay, Lisa," he said as Leah blinked several times, trying to clear the cloud of makeup in them, "Let's please try and get this done in this take, okay? Just dig down deep, think back to the last time you had a really bad cold, and let that emotion come out," he said, making a digging motion with his hands.

"Leah," she said, shaking her hands violently in front of her face to help her resist the urge to plunge her fingers into her eyes and wipe them clean of powder.

The director stared at her. "What?"

"Leah. My name is Leah. Not Lisa." The idiot couldn't seem to process what she was saying. "You, ah, you called me Lisa earlier," she said, pointing over her shoulder to earlier. "I was just clarifying."

He blinked, reared back, stabbed his hands high in the air and bellowed, *"Great, Leah!"* He dropped his hands to his waist. "Okay, *Leah*, let's try and get it this time. Could you please try and get it right, *Leah*?"

Wow, he really meant it. Was she that bad? Did her acting skills suck so badly that she couldn't play a sick housewife convincingly? If she was such a bad actress, then why was she here? *WhywhywhywhyWHY* did she keep taking these gigs?

Oh, right. Because she needed money. Needed it so desperately that she really didn't want to lose this commercial—

it was her second national, which meant residuals good enough to maybe get another car, and she was insanely desperate for another car. Her '98 Ford Escort had a bad transmission and started only about half the time.

"Hello! Earth to *Leah*!" the director snapped, startling her out of her thoughts. "I asked you, can we get this done?"

"Yes," she said with a resolute nod, ignoring the smirks of the people behind the camera. Who were they, anyway? Did Fluffy Tissue really need five people to make sure this thing went down? It was a *tissue* for god's sake!

"Fabulous," the director snapped, turned around, and stalked behind the camera. "Okay, places!" he yelled.

Leah jumped up and hurried to her place. Because she was the only one with a place, she gripped her box of tissue and smiled brightly at her director.

"Look *sick*," he said.

She dropped the smile.

"Action!"

With a theatric sneeze into her tissue that would have won her a Tony had she been back on Broadway, Leah looked miserably into the camera. "I don't know which is worse," she said in her best stuffy-nose voice. "To have the aches and pains and the stuffy runny nose that goes with the flu? Or to have really rough tissues?" she exclaimed, shaking a fistful of them at the camera before tossing them aside. "I need a cottony soft tissue!" she cried into the camera, then pulled several more tissues from her box of really rough tissues and blew her nose into them, wincing with pain the whole time.

And then she started shuffling across the stage to a bedroom. When the commercial aired, this was the point someone would be telling the world that there *was* a cottony soft tissue for her tender nose. She had to make the shuffle last fifteen seconds, which meant she had to pause and sneeze twice on her way.

When she reached the bedroom, she picked up a box of cottony soft tissues from the dresser, which was really stupid, because why would her character be complaining about rough tissues when she already had a box of the cottony soft shit? But when she'd asked that during an earlier take, Marty Scorsese over there almost had a seizure. She glanced at him from the corner of her eye; he cued her, and she put one of the cottony soft tissues to her nose and sighed with relief. "Now *that* is a soft tissue!"

She did some more dabbing around her nose, waiting for the director to say "cut." But he didn't say "cut," he just stood there on the other side of the camera, his hands braced on his knees, staring at her. It was so bizarre that she could actually feel the giggles building and began to panic. Why didn't he just *cut*? *CUT! CUT! CUT!* What was *wrong* with this asshole?

"CUT!" he shouted. "Print it," he added, and hitched up his pants like he owned the thirty-second commercial world.

The wardrobe guy was instantly yanking the skanky robe from her shoulders, as if he was afraid she would steal it. Leah leaned over, rolled down the jeans she had worn under the robe, then dodged her way through the crew, tripping over a cable and nearly face-planting in her haste to make her way to the makeup girl's rolling cart of treats. Once there, she picked up a towel and wiped her face as best she could. She didn't even bother with the janitor's closet they tried to say was a dressing room—it smelled awful in there. She tossed the towel aside, grabbed her sandals and her backpack, and walked out into the bright California sunshine.

She paused, looked up through the newly planted palm trees at the cloudless blue sky, flung her arms wide, and cried, "What am I still doing in L.A.?"

Naturally, the heavens didn't deign to answer. They never did.

With a growl of exasperation, Leah marched across the parking lot to her old car.

She'd been asking herself that question since her car's

transmission had started to tank a few months ago. Five years ago, she'd been the hottest actress on Broadway, the one everyone said was "going places." She worked in plays that paid some serious scratch, had a beautiful rent-controlled apartment, loads of friends—her best friend, Lucy, who still lived in New York, was constantly reminding her of that.

But Leah had left all that to come to L.A. to pursue a career in acting because it was what she'd always wanted to do. From the moment she'd been cast as a pussy willow in the first-grade play, she'd had the acting bug. In high school, she'd acted in every production, and when she couldn't act, she joined the stage crew. When it came time to go to college, her parents—who still lived in an upscale Connecticut suburb—said acting was frivolous and they would only pay for her college if she majored in finance or law or even humanities. But not acting.

She was wholly unprepared to make her own way, but nevertheless, Leah stepped off the money train and headed to NYU to study acting. She started doing community theater around New York, then landed a couple of minor roles in Broadway productions, and then began to get good, decent roles. And finally lead roles. Her agent and the critics started talking Hollywood. They said she was fresh and original, that she glittered on stage.

But then Michael Raney, former love of her life and sorry-ass bastard, dumped her out of the clear blue sky. Just when she was riding the huge crest of love and success, he pushed her off the ride, and she'd plummeted to earth. For months afterward, she walked through a very thick and emotional fog. She suddenly hated acting. She suddenly hated New York, because everything there reminded her of him. She hated leaving her apartment at all because she couldn't face the *"Where's Michael?"* question she would invariably hear. She stopped getting calls from her agent. She stopped getting auditions. Everyone worried about her.

And then one day, several months after he'd crushed her,

Leah had had enough. She didn't tell her parents she'd cashed out her retirement, bought a used Ford Escort, and left to find fame and fortune in L.A. until she was already in L.A. To this day, they were still a little prickly about it, especially since fame and fortune had eluded her completely since her fantastic fall from grace. Fast forward five years, and the best acting she'd done had been in a beer commercial. Granted, it was a Budweiser beer commercial, the cream of the beer commercial crop, but still . . .

Now, here she was, doing Fluffy Tissue commercials.

Her stupid car took several pumps on the gas and turnovers before it actually started. She crossed her fingers that it would make it all the way to the rundown bungalow in Venice she shared with another struggling actor, because at least there, she could bum a ride to her job waiting tables at a low-rent Italian restaurant.

"How great is this scene?" she asked herself as she gingerly put the car into reverse. "Education at NYU: $50,000. Current Job: $6 an hour plus tips. Acting Career: So bad, it's priceless," she said, and laughed at her own sick humor.

Unfortunately, it was true. She was almost thirty-four years old. Her chances for stardom were eroding away each day. A few weeks ago, her new agent told her that she needed to start thinking character roles at the same time she told her about a chance she had to land a role in *War of the Soccer Moms*, a studio film about a war between two groups of suburban moms.

"Women reach a certain age, and a good meaty character role is about all they can hope for," Frances had said as they sat in her tiny little beige office and popped chocolate-covered cherries, one after the other.

"A certain age?" Leah had echoed, mildly confused.

"Late thirties."

"Except that I'm not in my late thirties," Leah pointed out, reaching for another chocolate-covered cherry.

Frances adjusted her black, thick-framed glasses and leaned across her desk, her eyes reminiscent of a mutant fly.

"Don't fool yourself, Leah. You're getting close to late thirties, and frankly, thirty-four is not that far from forty in the greater scheme of things." She leaned back. "When you hit forty, forget it," she said, making such a grand sweeping gesture that the fleshy part of her arm created a breeze, "The well dries up, and you are lucky if you can even get an audition anywhere, unless you make a name for yourself doing character roles. You *really* need to do this film." And with that, Frances shoved the casting information at her, stuck a pencil behind her ear, and closed the box of chocolate-covered cherries before Leah could snatch another one.

"Get something soccer mom-ish to wear to the audition," she'd said, waving her heavily jeweled hand at Leah's outfit. "You know, Keds, or something like that. Maybe one of those shirts with flowerpots or kittens on it. Do *not* go looking like a hottie. Soccer moms aren't hotties."

"Okay," Leah said uncertainly.

"Great. Now go be a soccer mom!" Frances said cheerfully, then swiveled around in her seat to her computer. The meeting was, apparently, over.

Leah opened the box and took one more chocolate cherry before she went to pursue a career in character roles.

AT the time, she hadn't been too crazy about the film, but now, as her car hissed and shuddered its way onto Sunset Boulevard, she prayed she got the damn part. She made it all the way home, her car gasping its way into the driveway of the house she shared with Roddick Anthony—or as she'd known him since she met him in an acting class four years ago, Brad.

Brad was home, lounging as he often did. His skinny, lanky frame was barely enough to hold up his boxers, his loungewear of choice. He was sprawled across a plaid rent-to-own couch, eating Doritos, drinking cheap beer, and flipping channels. "Hey, how'd it go?" he asked as Leah dropped her bag in a chair next to the enormous, lopsided,

half-finished peacock, her latest work of origami she refused to part with. She was going to finish it. Really.

"Apparently, I do not possess the acting skills necessary
to portray a sick housewife," Leah said solemnly before
heading for the kitchen.

"Bummer. By the way, your agent called," Brad said,
looking away from the boob tube for a split second. "Something about soccer moms."

Leah stopped midstride and jerked around. "*Soccer
moms*? What? What did she say?" she cried, suddenly
hurtling toward the couch and Brad, who instantly fell back
and raised the remote between them as if he was afraid she
was going to hit him.

"She said to call her, she had good news."

"*Aaaiieee!*" Leah shrieked and twirled around, lunging
for the phone. "*War of the Soccer Moms* is a huge studio
film that Harold Bristol is directing!" she said breathlessly
as she punched in Frances's number. "You know Harold
Bristol, right?"

"Yeah," Brad said, twisting around on the couch. "He
got the Academy nomination for *Red Devil,* right? So what's
the war?"

"It's this, like, war that happens in a suburban neighbor-
hood between these soccer moms. It starts over something
like a cheating husband and then escalates into full-scale
war. They form armies and wage guerrilla warfare against
each other until the government calls out the National
Guard to end it. I had three callbacks for the role of one of
the soccer moms, but then I didn't hear anything, and I figured I was too fat for the role, and—Hello? Hi Verna, it's
Leah! May I speak with Frances, please?"

She twirled around and beamed at Brad. "They have
sixteen parts for women!"

Whatever Brad might have responded, Leah didn't hear,
because Frances was suddenly singing into the phone, "It's
great news, sweetie! They've offered you the role of one of
the soccer moms. They don't know which yet, but it will

almost certainly have lines. It's two months of filming, three weeks of which are on location in Bellingham, Washington. Now the money is—"

"Yes!" Leah shouted. "YES YES *YES!*" she shrieked, thrusting both arms into the air, phone included, before whirling around to face Brad. "I got the part! *I got a part in a studio film!* And it's a *speaking* part!" She quickly returned the phone to her ear. "When does it start?"

"Production starts in four weeks, but listen, I want to talk money with you."

"Okay," Leah gasped, but she didn't hear a word Frances was saying, because she was doing a little happy dance around the living room.

Her troubles were over. She had a part in a studio film. She was back. Leah Klein, once the toast of Broadway was *back.* Who knew where it could lead?

Subject: Soccer Moms!!
From: Leah Kleinschmidt <hollywoodiva@verizon.net>
To: Lucy Frederick <ljfreddie@hotmail.com>
Date: 1:32 am

I GOT SOCCER MOM #5!!! Isn't that fantastic?? I'm in four huge scenes with Nicole Redding, and two with Charlene Ribisi. Or maybe with their stunt doubles—I'm not sure how the battle stuff is going to work out, altho we start boot camp tomorrow. Isn't that a stitch? A three week boot camp to make us into soldiers! Oh, Lucy, this has been so much FUN!! The only downside has been the costumes. I mean, they are sexier than what you'd see on a real soccer mom like in Torrance or someplace like that, but they're still pretty frumpy. And the camouflage uniforms we have to wear for the last two battle scenes are HORRIBLE. *No one* is happy. Those pants make our butts look enormous. It's like my friend Trudy said, "We're an army of asses."

So get a load of this: You know my boss, Henri, at the

Silver Leaf Restaurant? The guy with hands everywhere and nowhere appropriate? I told him I needed a leave of absence for this film. And he was like, *"What ees theees leave of absence? Theees eees not a job to have leave of absence! There are many girls to take your shifts!"* Can you believe him? After how much I have worked for that asshole the last two years? So I said to his bald spot, because he's so short and that's really the only thing you can see when the lights are up, "You know, HENRY (he hates it when we call him Henry instead of ooon-reee), you are absolutely right. I quit!" HA HA. I walked out just before the evening shift started. I know what you are going to say, but I don't need that stinking job, Lucy. I finally have the break I've been waiting for, I can feel it in my bones. Something fabulous is going to happen! I've got *three* auditions this week! THREE!

And guess what? I figured it all out: I will make enough to pay rent and bills, yada yada yada, AND get a new car (I really want a new Thunderbird)!

Okay, enough about me . . . I STILL can't believe you are actually getting married!! GAWD, it seems like just yesterday we were clubbing in search of guys. And then I met Asshole and you met Pete (did he ever move to Atlanta like he promised?). Never mind. That's been a long time ago, and YOU are getting married!!! But I never really thought you *liked* David. Didn't you call him a moron?

Subject: Re: Soccer Moms!!
From: Lucy Frederick <ljfreddie@hotmail.com>
To: Leah Kleinschmidt <hollywoodiva@verizon.net>
Date: 8:30 am

Leah. It has been TWO AND ONE-HALF YEARS since David and I started dating, and that was a full six months AFTER I said he had moronic tendencies with a streak of idiot. Just to put things in some sort of time perspective for you since you are obviously on LaLa time, I will remind you that 2.5 years ago you were going to come back to New York because you hadn't gotten anything but a commercial and had a car that was falling apart and hated your waitress job. And 2.5 weeks ago, you e-mailed and asked if you could sleep on my couch because you were definitely coming back to NY. So let's see—now you've made TWO national commercials, have a car that is falling apart, and quit your job waiting tables so you can be a soccer mom. Okay, I will concede that the Soccer Mom thing sounds pretty cool, altho I don't get why a bunch of soccer moms would have a war, but whatever. You have scenes and lines and get face time with huge Hollywood stars! AND you get a new car! But if this doesn't lead somewhere, you really ought to come back. We have to shop for bridesmaid dresses!

Subject: Re: Re: Soccer Moms!!
From: Leah Kleinschmidt <hollywoodiva@verizon.net>
To: Lucy Frederick <ljfreddie@hotmail.com>
Date: 10:10 pm

You know I can't come to NY before we film. But I will when we wrap, I promise! Did I tell you about Trudy? She's hysterical—we worked together a couple of years ago. Trudy got a speaking role, too, and best of all, she is on my side in the war!!! You'd like her, Luc—she's got dark brown hair and brown eyes and one of the stunt coordinators is already calling us Yin and Yang, because we're the same height but, duh, I have blond hair and blue eyes. The only difference is that Yin got a boob job since I last saw her, and let's just sat Yang is fairly jealous of her perfect breasts. In fact, I was looking around the other day and decided I am about the only one in all of L.A. who has not gotten a boob job yet. Do you think I need one? Be honest!

    P.S. I loved the new 4 Doors Around CD. Have you heard it?

* * *

Subject: The Mess You Got Us Into
From: Jack <jack.price@thrillsanonymous.net>
To: Mikey <michael.raney@thrillsanonymous.net>
Date: 10:10 pm

Get your ass back to L.A. These women are driving us nuts. Jesus, Raney, do you have any idea what you got us into with this movie? I know, I know, you thought twenty or so mostly available women was a gift from the gods, but I don't think you took into account how much twenty some-odd women can *talk*! They talk all the damn time, and I do mean *all* the damn time, and all at once, too, and it doesn't matter, because somehow, they can hear each other through all that chatter. And don't even get me started on the cell phones. We put a ban on cell phones but no one cares. They don't listen to us. They just take the call like they aren't on a job or time isn't money and then the next thing you know, they are telling everyone around them whatever the person on the other end of the line said, and then our whole drill goes down the tubes. It's just damn chaos around here, and we're all remembering that this film was YOUR brilliant idea, even if you did have to draw the straw to lead the volcano hike in Costa Rica (how convenient). So when are you going to be back? I've got a little surprise for you.

Subject: Re: The Mess You Got Us Into
From: Mikey <michael.raney@thrillsanonymous.net>
To: Jack <jack.price@thrillsanonymous.net>
Date: 3:00 am

What's the surprise?

Subject: Re: Re: The Mess You Got Us Into
From: Jack <jack.price@thrillsanonymous.net>

To: Mikey <michael.raney@thrillsanonymous.net>
Date: 6:00 am

Well Raney, it would be a pretty sorry surprise if I told you, wouldn't it? So when are you back?

Subject: Re: Re: Re: The Mess You Got Us Into
From: Mikey <michael.raney@thrillsanonymous.net>
To: Jack <jack.price@thrillsanonymous.net>
Date: 4:00 pm

I'll be on the set Monday morning. That's when I'll show you schoolgirls how to handle a couple of women. Sheesh. You're embarrassing me with all the whining.

THREE

MICHAEL coasted into a parking spot with the new 4 Doors Around CD up full volume to test the speakers of his brand-spankin' new silver Thunderbird convertible. Satisfied that the Bose speakers were adequate for his driving needs, he stepped out, locked her up, and then looked around.

The Downey lot was literally teeming with women. Tall and short; reds, blondes, and brunettes; long legs, great racks, and fabulous derrieres. This film was truly a gift from the gods of Guy Universe—Michael was just glad he'd been able to talk his partners in T.A. into it.

They hadn't wanted to do it at first—what with their extreme sport adventure business taking off so well, the four of them had more on their plates than they could handle. They were already coordinating two action films this year in addition to having booked a half dozen extreme adventures with the extremely wealthy, and the prospect of adding a third film to the mix seemed too much. But Michael reminded them that in addition to the compressed schedule—the studio didn't want a long shoot on location, given the number of actors and costs involved—there would be twenty to thirty women. Twenty to thirty good-looking women. Women who were, relatively speaking, available.

"Why do *you* want to do it?" Jack demanded the day they had discussed it over a plate of nachos and a pitcher of beer. "It's not like you a need a shot at twenty or so women to hook up with one. You have them hanging all over you as it is."

"Yeah, right," Michael said with a snort. "That's why I've been available for so much of the extreme sports work lately. They're not hanging off me! And besides, I just really like women. Don't you?"

"I like women a lot, only one-on-one," Cooper interjected. "Women in a pack? Forget it—they're awful. They gang up on you, and you don't have a chance."

"Okay, forget it then," Michael said with a shrug. "I just thought it would be fun to hang out with twenty good-looking women for a few weeks."

No one said anything for a long moment. For a bunch of guys who didn't have the sort of job that afforded them the opportunity to hang out with women that often, it proved to be an argument none of them could resist—they signed up for the film.

Michael's only regret was that he had earned the lead on the Costa Rica trip and had missed the first week of boot camp. That was one week of being surrounded by women he'd never get back, and if there was one thing Michael Raney loved, it was to be surrounded by women.

There was no time like the present, and as soon as he got through this studio budget meeting Jack had asked him to attend, Michael was ready to go play.

He started across the parking lot, making eye contact with as many women as he could, who in turn gave him a smile, a smile, a smile . . . oh, *ouch*. No smile there. That was a definite glare from ah . . . Linda. Yeah, Linda, that was her name. *Linda* . . . the production assistant, right, right. Or was it Lindsey? He couldn't really recall much about her, other than that he'd been involved with her for a very short time once. She didn't have the looks most guys wanted, but Michael had liked her a lot in the beginning—she had a wry wit. Unfortunately, it turned out that she was funnier in a weird way than a ha-ha way, and he hadn't pursued it.

And as she was still staring daggers at him, Michael looked in the opposite direction.

Well, shit.

He knew that one, too. Jill, perky Jill with the brand-new, perky breasts. Nice perky breasts. Nice perky breasts attached to someone with stalkerlike tendencies.

Okay, so there might be a couple of rough spots in this dream gig, but nothing to worry about. There were still more than a dozen women he hadn't been involved with, and one with golden hair was walking toward him that minute. Michael smiled, slowed his step. "Excuse me, can you point me toward the office?"

The golden-haired woman smiled brightly and offered to take him there herself.

Was America a great country, or what?

THE women gathered on the basketball court to play dodge ball, or as one of the stunt coordinators put it, "practice teamwork."

"I don't know how in the hell we are going to learn team-work playing dodgeball, but whatever," Trudy said on an impatient sigh as she studied her hand through giant black sunglasses she had yet to remove. Trudy was a single mom with a useless boyfriend and an unusual fetish for showy sunglasses. She had more pairs than Leah could count.

At that moment, she was wiggling her fingers at Leah. "So what do you think of this color? I got it from my daughter Aralia."

Leah looked at the fingernails Trudy was wiggling at her. The color was a little too bubblegum pink for her tastes, but looked like something a fifth-grader like Aralia would like. "Fabulous," she lied.

"Don't look now, but here comes the Stud Strut," Jamie said. Jamie and Michele had migrated toward Trudy and Leah early on, and now the four of them were inseparable. Jamie nodded her dark red head in the direction of the door to the basketball court. "Hey, you know what T.A. stands for, don't you?" she asked as they watched two of the three stunt trainer-slash-coordinator hunks, Cooper and Eli, stroll in.

"What?" Leah asked.

"Tits and Ass," Jamie said, and then guffawed. "Get it? They have a thing for tits and ass!" She laughed. Leah, Trudy, and Michele rolled their eyes.

"Ladies, if we could have your attention!" Eli, the one with the sandy blond hair was speaking. He was a quiet guy who Leah thought looked pretty damn good in faded jeans. Hell, they *all* looked good for that matter, from Cooper's dark locks, to Jack and his thick brown hair, and then of course they were all tall and built like a brick shit house.

"We finished up our first phase of intensive gym work," Eli said. "You did good, ladies. Real good."

Several of them cooed like a flock of doves.

"This week, we're gonna focus on team-building exercises. And then next week, we're going to work hard to block those two big battle scenes with the team skills you've learned. We won't lie to you—this is going to be a lot of hard, physical work. But if you do like we ask, and we get those battle scenes down, we've got a little surprise for you."

"I hope the surprise has the name *Gucci* in it somewhere," Leah muttered.

"The studio has okayed us to go on location a couple of days early and do a final weekend of team building on some of the best white water in the country. In other words, we're going rafting."

That was met with a lot of *ooohs* and *aahs,* and of course, one of the Serious Actresses (as they had begun to think of a few of them, as opposed to the young, eager, will-sleep-with-anyone Starlets) began applauding, because she applauded *e-ver-y-thing.* And naturally, once she started, everyone started applauding because no one wanted to be the lone non-applauder. Personally, Leah thought the constant applauding was way out of hand and only gave it a halfhearted effort.

"Okay, all right," Eli said, signaling with his hands for everyone to quiet down. "Before we get to the gravy, we need you to focus," he said, pointing at his head. "When we start shooting in a few weeks, you all need to be fit and ready to go. To get fit, you have to focus, and that means leaving your cell phones in the locker room—"

And that was, of course, the precise moment Leah's cell phone started to ring. She frantically dug in her bag for it as the ringing got louder. She looked at the display— *Frances!* Unfortunately, the whole room had quieted— everyone was looking at her. Eli was looking at her so intently that she flinched a little. "Ah . . . I've really got to, ah . . . take this," she muttered, and flipped it open, whirled around, and whispered, *"Hey."*

"Bad news, sweetie." Frances had never been one to beat around a bush. "You got passed over for the spot on *Desperate Housewives.*"

Leah's heart sank. "Why? They said I was perfect for the part of the preacher's wife."

"I'll put it to you straight. You're too fat. If you lost ten pounds, maybe. But don't worry—we've still got a couple of auditions outstanding."

"But what if I lose the—"

"Ooooh, I really need to take this call," Frances said, and clicked off.

Leah sighed, shut her phone, and turned around. The meeting had resumed. Eli was explaining what the next couple of weeks looked like.

"Ohmigod, he's so *cute*," Michele whispered to Leah as she stuffed the phone back into her bag.

"Question!" Tamara Contreras's hand shot up, as if Eli and Cooper didn't know who'd be asking a question after the two bazillion she'd asked every day. Tamara was an ex-soap-opera diva (killed off by her murderous twin disguised as her ex-husband on a remote island with an invisible and impenetrable barrier, which naturally meant she could not seek medical treatment) who had begun annoying Leah and Trudy on the second day, when she announced she had a problem with perfume. Not any particular perfume, but the amount of perfume that was being worn. It gave her a headache.

The entire cast spent an hour arguing about it. The stunt guys had been so agitated that they'd had to caucus. After fifteen minutes of shuffling feet and a lot of head scratching, they had come back with, "Use your best judgment."

Trudy, Leah, Michele, and Jamie had howled about that over drinks after work. Men could be so stupid sometimes. But they decided that Tamara had so many things wrong with her—perfume sensitivity being the tip of the proverbial iceberg—that she wouldn't last.

"I give her two weeks on set," Jamie had said. Jamie was short and had red hair that in concert with her boob job, preceded the rest of her when she walked into a room. She was a great person, but all Leah could think was, *character roles.*

"I give her two weeks before someone kills her," Michele had responded before wrapping her collagen-enhanced lips around a straw. Michele was really a beauty with long golden hair and big green eyes, plus the requisite fake boobs and lips.

At the moment, Tamara's arm was about to come out of its socket as she tried to get Cooper or Eli to look at her.

"Yes, Tamara?" Cooper finally asked, exchanging a weary look with Eli.

"If the studio okayed the white-water rafting, are they

going to okay the wet gear? The water can be pretty cold this time of year."

"We'll worry about wet gear later," Cooper said.

"Okay, well, I just want to go on record as saying I'll need full-body wet gear," Tamara said, oblivious to the sighs and eye-rolling around her. "I have a low tolerance for cold."

Cooper and Eli looked at one another. "I'll tell you what, Tamara. Let's just make sure we get to white-water rafting first," Cooper said. "So all right, ladies, let's start by breaking up into our armies. West team on that end, East team on this end. We start in five minutes."

"You know what?" Trudy asked casually as the guys began to try, enthusiastically and in vain, to corral them into their respective armies, "I think I am going to have to change my vote for who is the hottest stunt trainer."

It was a question they'd been debating for a few days.

"Don't change your vote until we get a load of the fourth one," Michele advised Trudy as they strolled to the team on the left.

"A *fourth*?" Jamie exclaimed. "A fourth what?"

"A fourth stunt trainer guy. He's coming in later."

Trudy, Leah, and Jamie all came to a stop midstride and looked at Michele. "How do *you* know? And why isn't he already here?" Trudy demanded. "We deserve to have all of them present and accounted for so we can make a fair comparison of who is the hottest!"

"I don't know why he isn't here," Michele said, and glanced over her shoulder, as if anyone could possibly hear her in the din two dozen female voices created in the gym. "But apparently, he's a real player. I heard it from one of the Serious Actresses—seems like a bunch of them know him. Some of them have dated him, too. And get a load of this—they call him the Extreme Bachelor. Isn't that hilarious?"

"Why?" Trudy asked.

"Because he's a serial dater. A *luuuv-ah*," she added dramatically, making full use of her lips.

"When's he coming?" Trudy asked. "I want to see this *luuuv-ah*."

"Later is all I heard," Michele shrugged. "But I'll get some intel this afternoon," she added with a wink. "I promised Katherine Hepburn over there that I would run lines with her."

The four of them glanced at the Serious Actress who they had dubbed Katherine Hepburn, based on her intensity (extreme) and the fact that she studied her script all the time.

"Ladies, *please* split up into your armies," Eli was begging. "East on the left, West on the right!"

"Dodgeball, *yes*!" Leah said with a fist pump. "I love dodgeball."

"How can you *love* dodgeball? The last time I played it was the fifth grade," Trudy said, staring at Leah through her humongous black sunglasses.

"Will you please take those off?" Leah demanded, pointing at Trudy's shades.

Trudy pushed them up on the top of her head and smiled. "Let's decide who we are going to take out first. A Serious Actress or a Starlet?"

"Tamara," Leah said instantly. "If she's even playing. She's probably got an allergy to rubber."

"Oooh, you're so snarky. I love that about you," Trudy said, and linking arms with Leah, Yin and Yang, and Michele and Jamie went off to the left to play dodgeball.

They lined up to wait for some instruction, and when the guys finally got them to all stop chattering like a group of mutant magpies, the song "Like a Virgin" began ringing on someone's cell phone.

"Now come on, you guys!" Cooper cried. He looked close to losing it completely. "We *just* had a chat about this. No cell phones!"

"Sorry!" a brunette called out, but she took the call anyway.

"Okay, attention, everyone," Cooper went on, with a glare for the brunette who held both hands up around her mouth and the cell phone, "I think we all know the game of dodgeball." Eli walked over to a cage and began to toss red rubber balls to Cooper, which he placed on either side of the center line. "Why are we playing dodgeball?" he asked as he laid out the red balls. "Because we're filming it, and we're going to use your movements to craft some of the animation we'll add to the battle scenes."

Everyone instantly looked around for cameras, and spotted one above them, the other at the far end of the gym.

"We play six on a side," Cooper continued. "When I blow the whistle, each team retrieves three balls. If you're hit, you cycle out, and the next person on your team cycles in. You can eliminate a player in two ways—either hit her with the ball, or catch her ball before it hits the ground. Aim for the body—not the head. Anyone aiming for the head will be eliminated from the game and may even lose a job, okay? Everyone get that? Safety first ladies! Remember that—*safety first.*"

He paused, put his hands on his hips, and looked at each team. "If you are taken out of the game, walk over there," he said, pointing to the bleachers. "And sit down. Don't talk. Don't get out your cell phone. Don't get out your nail polish. No stopping to redo your hair like the incident we had yesterday," he said, looking pointedly at a Starlet who batted eyes at him. "These games go pretty fast, and we're going to play a bunch of them until we have each side working together as a team and get enough film to give the animators. But the whole point of this exercise is to work as a unit."

His speech was getting a little long, Leah noticed. Several whispered conversations had begun.

Cooper seemed to know it, too, because he clenched his jaw, then pointed at a Starlet on Leah's team who rarely spoke. "You," he said sternly. "You are the leader for this team." He turned to the other team and pointed to Beth, a Serious Actress who'd been mad at Leah since they ran lines and Leah had snickered at Beth's overwrought, over-the-top performance of a mom out of Twinkies. Well hell, she'd thought Beth had been kidding.

"You're the leader for this team, all right?" Cooper said.

Beth nodded and glared at Leah, who glared right back.

"Okay," Cooper said. "Talk about who you want to target. Talk to each other on the line. Listen to your team leader and just try and communicate."

He and Eli made sure that the teams were lined up properly, then stepped out of the way. Cooper raised his arm. "Ready? Game on."

There was a mad scramble for the balls lying on the center line. One of the Serious Actresses on the other side immediately hurled a dodge ball that hit a Starlet on the leg. *"Out!"* she screeched.

"Hey!" the Starlet cried, rubbing her thigh. "That's not *fair!*"

But apparently it was fair, because the team across from Leah was suddenly and gleefully hurling their balls, accompanied with triumphant shrieks that were lost only in the shrieks of those who were hit.

The quiet Starlet appointed to head Leah's team turned out to be a Commando Starlet, screeching at everyone to pick up their feet and move. Leah was vaguely aware of Trudy getting hit behind her when she cried, "Shit! I *just* had these nails done!" But Leah was moving. She really did love dodgeball, and it was all coming back to her—how to leap to avoid being hit, how to throw on the run, how to stoop to catch a ball.

She nailed Katherine Hepburn on her first throw—that one gasped and looked confused and hurt before slinking off. Leah aimed for Beth with her second throw, just missing her. As she scrambled to pick up more balls, the Commando Starlet shouted at her to *shift left, shift left,* then rushed the line, hurling her ball like a missile at Tamara.

Tamara dodged it, which floored Leah, but then she sang out an uncharacteristic *nanner-nanner* at the Starlet, and therefore missed the red rocket coming at her from the other end of the line. A huge cheer went up from both sides when Tamara took one in the ass.

Within fifteen minutes, there were only three left on each side, and Leah was one of them. She could hear Trudy, Jamie, and Michele shouting at her from the bleachers to stay low. Leah, the Commando Starlet, and a Serious Actress huddled together, ready to leap in opposite directions.

At least that was what the Commando was telling them to do, but Leah wasn't listening—she wanted to take Beth down. Beth had been aiming at Leah since the start of the game, firing off heated missiles like she wanted to see her dead. Leah had to keep racing up and down and diving behind her teammates to avoid being hit.

When Beth picked up two balls and threw them in rapid succession at their little group, Leah seized the opportunity to run down the line, trying to catch a ball as she went. But as she neared the entrance to the basketball court, she caught a glimpse of Jack and another guy standing just inside the door, watching the game. It was only a fraction of a second, but in that teeny tiny moment, Leah thought she'd seen a ghost.

It was enough to take her mind off the game and long enough for Beth to hurl a ball at her. And the ball did indeed find purchase—more like a two-fer sale, actually, because the ball glanced off her shoulder and then hit her in the temple. It didn't hurt at all, but it surprised her, and her feet got tangled, and down Leah went, somehow ending up on her back.

Leah was aware of the shrill protests and boos being bellowed from her teammates, but the fall had knocked the wind out of her, and she laid there, her eyes closed, trying to get her breath back, frantically wondering if she'd really seen a ghost or if he was real.

"Okay, this is what I'm talking about. Your team leader said go right, and you went left." That was Cooper's voice, and presumably, Cooper's hand on her forehead. "You gotta work like a team out there and listen to your leader, okay? Anything broken or sprained?"

Only her pride. Leah shook her head.

"Are you all right, kiddo?"

She recognized Eli's voice. "Yes," she sighed, and opened her eyes and pushed herself up on her elbows.

Jack's face was looming above hers, squinting with concern as he touched her hairline and her temple. "Think we ought to call the nurse?"

"No, no, don't call a nurse," she said quickly, mortified by the suggestion. "I'm fine. I just had the wind knocked out of me." She tried to get up.

"Don't move too fast," Jack cautioned her.

"I'm *fine*. I'm more embarrassed than anything else— who gets hurt playing dodgeball, for Chrissakes?"

"Good question," Jack said.

Someone's cell phone rang. "Hey! No cell phones!" Eli shouted. "This isn't a break! Beth, you sit down over there!"

Leah groaned. "Let me up, will you?"

Jack moved back, and that was when her ghost came into full view. He was down on his haunches at her feet, his face as handsome as ever, his expression every bit as stunned as she felt. He stared at her hard, as if he couldn't quite make her out, and then asked incredulously, "Leah *Kleinschmidt*? Is that really you?"

"*Kleinschmidt?*" someone echoed.

"Oh. My. *God*," she said, squeezed her eyes shut, and wished she'd been knocked out cold.

FOUR

IT was no nightmare, unfortunately, because when Leah opened her eyes again, Michael had come closer. Cooper helped her up and sandwiched her between Michael and himself so they could walk her over to the bleachers and check her over.

As if the whole scene wasn't bone-jarring enough, Trudy's frowning head popped up over Cooper's like a jack-in-the-box. "Hey, are you all right?" she asked.

"I'm fine, I'm *fine*!" Leah said, jerking back from Michael's peering at her head. "This is so stupid! I just tripped and embarrassed the hell out of myself, but that's it," she insisted, swatting Cooper's hand away from her jaw.

"Actually, it looked like you stopped and then tripped," Trudy clarified. "Right over your own two feet."

Leah wished someone would just shoot her now. "Thanks, Trudy."

"You know, someone ought to do something about her," Trudy said, tapping Cooper's shoulder with her finger and pointing to Beth. "That chick was aiming for Leah's head."

"We'll take care of it," Cooper said. "You can go back to your army now. We're going to start another game in a minute."

"You better take care of it, pal, or you're going to have a mutiny on your hands. They're already talking about it," she whispered, nodding fiercely in the direction of some of the Starlets. "Do you want me to stay?" Trudy asked Leah.

"No, really, I'm fine." Leah smiled brightly to prove it, but she wasn't fine, how could she be fine? She felt absolutely ill. A rush of old and long-buried feelings were gushing up and drowning her—hurt, anger, humiliation, to name a few.

Trudy shrugged, handed her a bottle of water before reminding Cooper to do something about that chick, and then disappeared behind him again.

Leah didn't want water, she wanted a giant shot of tequila and a single minute with no noise, no one asking her how she was, just so she could think, because her mind was whirling hard and fast around the unbelievable coincidence that after all these years, Michael Raney would show up *here*, on this studio lot, of all the places in the universe.

It was so unreal that she glanced at him again out of the corner of her eye. His expression was full of concern, and he put a hand on the small of her back the way he used to do a hundred million years ago when they were together and he'd lean over to tell her something.

What made the whole scene outrageously bad was that while she probably had a huge welt on her head where she'd hit the floor, and was wearing gym shorts and a T-shirt and no makeup, he looked so damn good. He still had that sexy thick, collar-length black hair and penny-colored eyes. And he was nicely tanned, too, with little lines fanning out from the corners of his eyes. To top it all off, he had a dark stubble of beard.

That stubble had always been her undoing.

Dammit, had he always been so gorgeous? His lips that full? His jaw that square? This sexy? Her mind suddenly flashed back to a night he'd gone down on her with that stubble . . .

She couldn't look at him. She glanced at the bottle of water Trudy had given her and pretended to read the label so he wouldn't know it was official—that seeing him again after all these years had knocked her completely off her axis. She was spinning off into the universe without a net.

God, she was so unprepared! So self-conscious! The weird thing was, Leah couldn't even count how many times during the years she thought she'd seen him—the way some guy would get in his car would make her think it was him, or she'd see the back of a man on the street ahead of her and *know* it was him. Worse, there were times she'd fantasize about seeing him again, but in her fantasies, she was gorgeous and skinny and fabulously successful and— here was the important part—always with another guy. That was really key to the casual encounter with an ex— she had to at least *appear* to be way better off without him. At that moment, she'd have given her life to appear to be better off without him.

After that awful night in New York when he'd dumped her, she hadn't seen him again. Actually, no one saw him again. He just vanished. He'd gone off to Austria or God knew where and her life had been completely shattered by one simple phrase: *I am leaving and I'm not coming back.*

It had taken Leah a long time to get over him, but she really thought she'd done it—she'd been so *sure* she'd done it—yet judging by the fact that she was having to remind herself to breathe just now, it was impossible, even after five years, to see the man she had once considered the love of her life and not sink into despair with a sick sort of longing.

Seriously, if her heart didn't stop pounding, it was going to pop right out of her chest.

But *waitwaitwait* just a damn minute, she thought as the

world began to take sharper focus. This was totally unfair! How in the hell could Michael Asshole Raney show up *here*? How was it possible he could have made the leap from that successful career of a hotshot financier and ended up in L.A. at all, much less on her first feature film?

She abruptly looked at him again to assure herself that she wasn't hallucinating and that he really was even better-looking five years later. Nope, she wasn't hallucinating. It was Michael alright, and he still had that same sexy, quiet smile that used to reduce her to complete mush. And yes, apparently it was possible to be better-looking five years later.

"I got this," Michael said to Cooper, without shifting his gaze from Leah's face.

"Okay. Just drink some water, Leah, and you'll be fine," Cooper said. "I think I'll go have a chat with Beth."

Cooper walked away, leaving Leah alone with Michael. She stared blindly at the court, taking big sips of water to keep from talking. In the background, she was vaguely aware of Jack talking loudly about teamwork and safety and how it wasn't very nice to fire dodgeballs at other people's heads or something like that, and how Beth wouldn't be playing any more dodgeball because of her disregard for the rules, but the whole thing was fading to background noise.

She was still having serious trouble catching her breath. It felt as if there was a vice around her heart. All the things she thought she'd say if she ever saw him again had vanished into thin air, and the only thing in her head now was one question: *Why?*

She definitely wasn't going to ask him that. *Okay, Leah,* she told herself, *do NOT be a wimp. So what if he is not seeing you exactly at your best? This is YOUR film and YOU can do this, you can do this, you can do this,* she chanted in her head.

She wasn't looking at him, but she could feel him, every single inch of him, strong and hard and warm.

"Leah . . . I don't know what to say," Michael said at last. "I didn't notice your name on the list."

Be fabulously successful! Be nonchalant! Be someone who is glad she moved on! "Oh!" she said, finally forcing a smile. "Well, that's probably because it's not Kleinschmidt anymore."

"No?"

"No," she said, screwing the lid back on the water bottle, her consciousness rousing from its fog of confusion to take hold. She had shortened it because she'd gotten such a bad rap for being a basket case after he'd left her, but that didn't sound very glamorous. "It's Klein. I shortened it for my acting career."

God, that sounded even more stupid than the real reason. She'd been on top of the world when she'd last seen him, and now she could barely get a gig.

"It was a good move," she added, upping the stupid quotient to moronic. *A good move?* she yelled at herself. Jesus, she couldn't even *act* fabulously successful! No wonder her acting instructor said she didn't know the meaning of the word *spontaneous*!

Okay, but it didn't matter, because she didn't owe this man an explanation about anything. Not her name, not her spectacular fall from the Broadway marquee—*Nothing.* If anyone owed anyone any explanations at all, it was him.

"This is so weird," Michael said again with a funny little smile.

"Weird? I wouldn't call it *weird*," Leah snorted. "I mean, granted, it's not every day you run into old, ah . . . okay, all right, you are *definitely* the last person I expected to see here," she admitted. "But it's not *that* weird."

Okay, that was pretty good. Breezy, sort of like an old school acquaintance, nothing more.

Michael chuckled. It was a warm, familiar sound that slid all over her, trickling down her spine, reminding her of how he used to chuckle in her ear when they were fooling around. "You are definitely the last person I thought I'd see, too," he said, and smiled fully, his teeth still white and straight and damnably sexy. "So how are you, Leah?" he asked, peering too closely. He was probably trying to figure out what he saw in her back then.

"Me? Great!" she said, nodding enthusiastically. "Oh yeah, I'm doing *great*," she said, flinging one arm out to emphasize how great, and flashed him an *I'm-doing-great!* smile before turning her attention to the dodgeball game they had just started.

"I always knew you'd end up in Hollywood," he said quietly.

The gentle timbre of his voice dredged up a memory so deep that Leah's heart sank a little deeper. She was instantly transported back to one snowy night high above the streets of Manhattan, when they had lain in his bed after making love, their naked bodies entwined, talking about the future. "I want to be a film actress," she'd said. "Not Broadway. *Film.* Do you think that's crazy?"

Michael had stroked her hair and had said easily, "Not at all, baby. If you really want to be an actress, then we'll move to L.A. so you can be one."

His response had surprised her, and she'd twisted around in his arms onto her stomach, propping herself on her elbows to look at him. "Just like that?" she'd asked incredulously. "You'd really give up your career and move to L.A. for me?"

He'd laughed, had touched his knuckle to the tip of her nose. "I can do my job there. And yes, I'd do it for you," he'd said, and slipped his hand around her nape, pulling her forward. "I'd do anything for you." And he had kissed her until she really believed he would do anything for her.

She wondered if he was remembering the same moment. Probably not. He probably hadn't remembered it a week after he'd said it. Just a lot of bullshit from a player.

She looked at him again, the face that had betrayed her, stunned her, wounded her so deeply that she was almost buried beneath her own bitter sorrow and suddenly blurted,

"Michael, what the hell are you *doing* here? How did you end up here, of all places?" she exclaimed, her hand waving at *here.* "You never said anything about wanting to be in movies! You're in finance, for Chrissakes—so what the hell, you're a stunt guy? Are you the fourth stunt guy now? The *fourth* stunt guy? How is it possible that you are a stunt guy?"

"Well," he said, wincing a little as his gaze dipped to her lips, "It just sort of happened."

"No, no, no, something like that doesn't just sort of happen," she said, stabbing her hands in the air for emphasis. "And even if it did, how would it happen on *my* film?"

"My guess? Karma."

He had to be kidding. He would chalk this up to something as stupid as karma after what had happened between them? Try the devil! Or a hole in the cosmos! Anything but karma! *"Karma?"* she echoed incredulously. "You think this is *karma*?" And did he have to look at her lips like that? "This isn't karma, Michael, this is just . . . just really really . . . un-freakin'-believable."

For some reason, Michael chuckled. "You know what, Leah? You look amazing."

Leah instantly put a hand to her hair. "I usually look so much better than this," she muttered and happened to glance down at her PF Flyers. Oh Jesus, what lame run-into-your-ex shoes. They just screamed *loser.*

Not to mention the T-shirt cropped at the waist that said *Tampa Bay* in cursive letters across her chest. She'd never even been to Tampa Bay—she'd picked this up at a thrift shop along with the PF Flyers.

"I don't know how much better you could possibly look, because you look fantastic."

He said it so sincerely that the warmth of the compliment seeped under her skin, and she couldn't help smiling a little. "Thanks. *Ahem.* So, do . . . *ahem* . . . ah . . . sodoyou."

Now his brown eyes were shining in a way that was making her feel slightly woozy. She wondered how he could possibly have that effect on her after what he'd done to her and after all this time. Yet the pull was powerful enough that she felt a slight panic and abruptly stood up. "So listen, I gotta get back to work."

"Are you sure?" he said, standing, too. "Just take it easy, sit this one out."

"No, really, I'm okay," she said, now suddenly feeling frantic to get away from him. "So thanks for helping me and . . ." *What? And WHAT? And nothing.* There was nothing she wanted to say to him. She gave him a dorky little wave and jogged back to her group, hating him for showing up here after all these years. *Damn* him.

Once again, Michael Raney had ruined everything.

FIVE

SEEING Leah Kleinschmidt knocked Michael flat on his ass—he'd thought so much about her, had lamented leaving her more times than he could count—but this was so unexpected and so shocking, he was not prepared to face her.

Not like this.

Unfortunately, it was too late, because he had seen her, and now he had to get his shit together, because he had to work, and before he did anything else, he had to kill Jack for this little surprise.

Not before he got an explanation of how that asshole had managed to pull *this* off.

Jesus, the moment he realized he was seeing Leah, that it was *Leah* out there hurling red balls and dodging even more of them, his heart had stopped beating and had climbed right up into his throat. When their eyes met, and she was hit broadside with a dodgeball and lost her balance, falling in one ugly sprawl of arms and legs, all he could think about was whether she was all right, and he had rushed forward without deliberation.

Myriad thoughts raged through his head as he'd sat next to her, thoughts he couldn't quite grasp or put into words. All the things he'd wished he'd said the night he'd ended it, all the things he'd wanted to say over the last five years, how incredible it was to see her now. He tried to make conversation, tried to at least say hello without sounding like an idiot, but frankly, when Leah had half-trotted, half-limped away, Michael had felt relieved.

He wasn't ready for this at all. He needed time to get his thoughts together, to figure out how to proceed, but it was proving impossible with her in the same room. Hell, the same *state*. He couldn't keep his eyes off of her, and he watched her at the other end of the gym talking to some women, her hands flying. He wondered where she'd been, what she'd done . . . who she was with now.

His torch for her had never died. The very moment he'd seen her and knew it was Leah, he'd felt a rush of all the loose and fuzzy things that he used to feel for her bubbling up inside him again. It was weird and intense—a feeling he'd only experienced a couple of times in his life. At thirteen, he'd felt it for Candace Flores, who was two years older than him and never noticed Michael at all—except to call him a major geek one day in front of several other kids and then laugh.

After that spectacular put-down, Michael hadn't felt this way again until he'd met Leah at a happy hour one night in New York. There was something about her that felt familiar from the very start, something that had caused the first ribbon of desire to curl around his heart with no more than a hello from her.

And here he was five years later, having been the one to have ruined everything, feeling it all over again.

She looked so good. The image Michael had carried around all these years hadn't done her justice. She'd let her hair grow out—it was below shoulder-length now, but still the color of corn silk. Her eyes were large and crystalline blue, and her mouth still made the man in him squirm. She'd always had that effect on him—when he saw her, the guy instinct in him wanted to be with her, in every way possible.

She was wearing shorts and a tight T-shirt that outlined her near-perfect shape. Her legs were long and athletic, and she looked healthy, not anorexic like so many others in the gym. She looked absolutely fantastic.

Get it together, man, he chastised himself. He couldn't stand at one end of the gym ogling her all day. They had a lot of work to do, and this wasn't exactly the time or place to pick up a relationship he'd broken in half with a single blow to the gut five years ago.

He made himself turn away, made himself work, and somehow he managed to get through the morning session. He took girls aside and tried to teach them how to play team dodgeball by complimenting them and getting them to lighten up a little, to laugh. His efforts, as usual, made him more than one friend among his group.

He even chatted with one of the women he'd once dated, Jill, and had her laughing and looking a little too hopeful at the end of their chat.

He did not, however, look at Leah if he could help it. He just couldn't. If he did, he would want to talk to her, and if he talked to her, he'd want to explain everything, and then maybe even beg her forgiveness, or do something equally wimpish. Besides, he had an instinct that the time for explaining himself had reached its statute of limitations.

But when they broke for lunch, he saw her walking away from him in the company of the three women he'd seen her with all morning.

As he watched them disappear outside, he noticed Jack near the door wearing a rather grand shit-eating grin as Michael came striding forward. "I told you I had a surprise," Jack said with a wink.

"Yeah, that was a surprise, all right," Michael said with a sigh of resignation. "So how'd you do it?"

Jack grinned. "Remember New York?"

Dear God, how could he have forgotten it? It had been his first glimpse of Leah in five years. "What I remember is that your brother couldn't hit the broad side of a barn."

"And I remember you were awfully interested in a certain laxative commercial. Imagine how surprised and delighted I was when you won the Costa Rica gig and left me to sit through three days of casting, only to find a gem of a laxative girl among so many? It was the cherry on top of my sundae."

What were the odds? Seriously, *what* were the odds?

Jack laughed and gave him a good ol' boy clap on the back. "So . . . I was right. She does mean something to you."

"No, no, it's not that," Michael said, and instantly hated himself for trivializing her.

But Jack had known him for a long time and was on to him. "I know, I know, it's never *that*," he joked. "Not for the Extreme Bachelor. Not for our man about town. But Mikey, whoever she is, she's hot."

Michael smiled halfheartedly. "I know."

"That's why I added a couple of your other old flames to the list. You know, to make things interesting. I just want you to have fun," he said with a laugh.

"Why, thanks, Jack. I believe I owe you. And don't forget that—I *owe* you, man."

"My pleasure," Jack said.

The sound of two women laughing caught their attention. They turned to look, and Michael recognized one of them as the production assistant he'd dated a couple of times.

"Gotta run," Jack said, already striding toward the two women.

Michael walked outside of the gym, where he paused and stopped in the middle of the walk, his hands on his hips.

It had to be karma. Marnie, Eli's girlfriend, was always

talking about karma. If they signed a really great gig, she said it was karma. If they turned down a gig, she said it was karma. If they ordered pizza in, she said it was pizza karma. Okay, that was a little overboard, but if *this* wasn't karma, then it sure was one hell of a coincidence.

Granted, the guys were always trying to set him up for a fall, to get back for their chief complaint that he took all the women out of the available women pool. Okay, so he had a reputation, but so what if he'd had a few flings? Variety was the spice of life. And honestly, no one was more surprised than him each time a woman would consent to go out with him. There was still a nerdy little kid inside him, wishing Candace Flores would notice him.

"I hate going anywhere with you and that romance-novel face," Cooper had complained one night when they'd gone clubbing and everyone had been rejected—except Michael. Michael had met a young woman from Kansas who intrigued him and gave him her number. "It ain't right, man. Five women walk up, and all five of 'em are looking at you."

Michael had laughed, but Jack had agreed with Cooper. "I don't know what it is about you, Raney, but you always leave us out in the cold," Jack said. "Women flock to you like flies to a dead cow."

"That's such a touching image, Jacko—I didn't know how you truly felt," Michael had responded with a grin.

"You know what I mean," Jack had groused. "You just need to get your own bar with your own little throne and let them line up around the block. Coop and I will just hang out in pool halls with the rest of the rejects until we die."

Michael had tried to tell these idiots more than once that he found the whole idea of his appeal extremely funny, but they didn't want to hear any of that; they preferred to bitch about it. Nevertheless, it was the God's honest truth that Michael Raney had once been the biggest geek on the planet. A nerd through and through, a stupid little moron growing up in the Illinois foster care system.

He'd passed through six foster homes in all, never truly integrating into a single one of them. His many foster siblings had glommed on to the tough kids and shied away from the science-loving nerds like him. And the foster parents? Forget it—they usually had so many kids to deal with that he'd been lost in the shuffle. He and his Erector set had been left alone.

Yet that wasn't the thing that ate at his adolescent self. What ate at him was that he was essentially invisible to girls, too. He didn't score as much as a kiss until he was nineteen years old. Hell, he didn't get as much as a *look* before he was twenty-four. But then, by some miracle, he had morphed overnight from a nerdy, lonely kid into a man who women flocked to. Why or how, Michael had no idea. It had just happened, and he damn sure hadn't asked a lot of questions. From that moment on, there had been no looking back.

The only thing that had really mattered to him was that it never end, because Michael Raney loved women. Absolutely loved them. Loved the way they thought and talked and walked and laughed. Loved the way they felt under him when he made love. Loved how delicate they were, how they smiled, how they smelled, how they always picked up after him and complained about his empty kitchen.

He'd been lucky enough to date women across the globe. He'd lived with a diplomat in Paris, an artist in Spain. He'd hooked up with a doctor in Ghana and a teacher in Australia. He'd had numerous flings with actresses at all levels, but the little nerd in him never ceased to be surprised when a woman was truly into him.

Now, here he was, coming full circle around to the one truth he'd figured out about himself: He really did want to cherish one woman above all others. He really did want to make babies with one woman and grow old with her. And out of the many women he'd been involved with one way or another, there had been only one who had stood out, only one he still thought of, only one for whom he wished he could go back in time and redo it all.

Leah.

They had clicked from the start—she liked to laugh, liked weird things like off-the-wall indie films, just like him, and Thai food, just like him. She claimed to have morphed from a gangly geek into what she was, just like him. Unfortunately, he'd blown it all in a pretty spectacular way. The night he had walked away from her for what he thought would be forever sat like an ugly scar across his memory. He dreamed of it—in his dream he was always trying to take it back, but he could never catch her to tell her.

At the time, he thought he was doing her a favor. She didn't really know who he was or what he did—their whole relationship had been predicated on a lie. Hell, what he thought he knew of himself hadn't even been the truth. But in hindsight, after five more years of trotting the globe and playing with its women, he had come to another conclusion—Leah Kleinschmidt was the one woman who had the power to push him over the finish line.

He just never thought he'd see her again, and it never occurred to him that he would see her in the flesh, in L.A. On one of his sets.

Now, the Extreme Bachelor had absolutely no idea how to proceed.

His uncertainty added to an already difficult day that got only more difficult after lunch, when they took the ladies out on a ropes course, a series of hurdles designed to test their endurance and their teamwork.

He lost sight of Leah completely during the afternoon, as he had one woman or another in his face constantly. One got rope burn when she fell and did not let go of the rope. One caught her hair on a swing and shrieked so loudly you would have thought she'd been impaled. During a break, several of them camped out around a child's swing set—part of their urban obstacle course—and howled with laughter about something, and when Jack appeared to tell

them break was over, they doubled over with more boisterous laughter, leaving Jack red-faced without even knowing
why.

And moreover, Jack was right—the women *never* seemed
to stop talking. The longer the day went, the louder it
seemed to get. When Michael settled a dispute over a ruined shoe—*"These are Pumas!"* one blonde shrieked at a
brunette who rolled her eyes—he'd had enough. Fortunately, the rest of T.A. felt the same way. Eli, who remained
amazingly calm throughout the day—so calm that Michael
was beginning to wonder if he might have eaten a couple of
elephant tranquilizers over the lunch break to help him
along—called the girls together, gave them a little pep talk,
and sent them home until the next morning.

The women immediately broke into chatter and showed
no signs of going anywhere. It was, apparently, social hour.

"I think we need to talk about that second battle scene,"
Cooper was saying, pulling out a sheet of paper from his
back pocket. "After what I saw on the ropes course, there
is no way in hell we are going to get some of these girls to
jump off a rooftop without killing themselves, and we
can't afford to hire enough stunt women to do it for
them."

Michael watched Leah emerge from the little locker
room, her backpack over her shoulder. She waved good-
bye to her friends, the same wiggly fingers she used to
wave at him at the subway, and walked toward the parking
lot.

Okay, this was it. He couldn't help himself, he couldn't
watch her walk away and not say something. He slipped
away from the very serious discussion of rooftop jumping
and followed her.

Leah was walking fast. He jogged to catch up with her.
"Leah!" he called out when it looked like she might actually beat him to her car. "Wait up!"

She paused; he saw a slight but discernible dip in her
shoulders. But when she turned around, she was smiling. An

odd smile, but a smile nonetheless. "Oh! Hey, Michael . . . ah, listen, I really have to run," she said, jerking her thumb toward an old Ford Escort. "I'd love to chat, but I've gotta be someplace, and you know, the traffic—"

"I just want a minute, Leah. One minute."

She looked at her car, then at him. Her eyes were so blue—he'd forgotten how blue. "Well . . ." She glanced at her watch.

"Listen . . . that was really weird today," he said, wasting no time. "I was blown away by it."

"Oh," she said, nodding, and then her brows dipped a little. "By what?"

She had to ask? "By *seeing* you. I was hoping we could talk a minute."

"Ah. Well. Here's the thing," she said, squeezing the bridge of her nose for a minute. "I've really got to be someplace, and it's just . . . our . . . you know . . . *stuff* . . . I mean, it's old news, isn't it?" She dropped her hand and looked at him, and the expression on her face made his gut wrench. "No offense, but it was really a long time ago."

"Five years," he said instantly. "Look, I don't want to make you uncomfortable, Leah. I just want to . . ." *Dammit, what did he really want?* "I just want to talk," he said decisively. "Just talk. If not today, maybe tomorrow?"

"Tomorrow?" Honestly, she seemed to be debating if she would even be back at work tomorrow. "Yeah, maybe. Okay! So I'll see you tomorrow—"

"Leah, listen . . . ," he said, before she could run off. "I've thought a lot about you over the years. A *lot*."

Leah blinked. "Huh. Well . . . I've thought about you, too."

He could just imagine she had. "But I thought nice things," he said with a lopsided grin. "Great things. Killer things. Things I can't forget, and I'd really like to talk to you. I'd like to tell you that I wish—"

"Michael?"

His name startled him, and he jerked around. Nicole

Redding was staring up at him, her hands on her tiny hips, her lips pursed and her frown deep. "Nicki," he said with a false smile. Why in the hell did she have to show up *now*? He mentally kicked his own ass for ever having slept with her. She'd been trouble from the get-go.

"Well, *hello*, stranger," she said in a tone that made him cringe, and gave Leah a once-over before lifting her face to be kissed.

Michael reluctantly put his hand on her elbow and pecked her cheek, Hollywood-style.

She reared back, squinting up at him in a way that made her multimillion-dollar face look very bitchy. "I didn't know you were in town!"

"Yeah . . . I just got in."

"Costa Rica, I heard."

"Yep." Why was she here? Why didn't she go back to Bel Air where she belonged?

"So what are you doing here? Film? A woman? Or both?" She laughed at her little dig.

Michael didn't laugh. "Neither. But thanks for asking."

"I guess T.A. is doing the stunt work for *War*, huh?"

"Looks like."

"Lucky me," she said with a frown. "I'll get to see the guy who—"

A loud screech startled them both, and Michael turned to where Leah had been standing. She was in her car, backing out, and her car was making an awful screeching sound.

Nicole coughed as the smoke from Leah's tailpipe blasted them. "—the guy who dumped me," she finished.

"Come on, sweetheart," Michael said, waving a hand in front of his face to dissipate the smoke spewing out of the back of Leah's car. "Don't be like that. It was mutual and you know it."

"It wasn't mutual!" she whined, waving her hand, too. "I never once said I wanted to break it off."

"Maybe you didn't say it, but when you started having

those late-night sessions with the director, I didn't think you were exactly committed to our little affair, either."

She tossed her head at that. "Do we have to stand here in that junker's exhaust?"

"No. That junker is leaving," he said, and watched Leah drive away with only one functioning brake light.

"Jesus, they should outlaw those things," Nicole said. "All right, all right, Michael, the car is gone, you can look at me now. God, that's so typical of you. Production hasn't even started, and you're already hitting on some actress."

"I'm not hitting on her."

"Whatever," Nicole said with a dismissive flick of her wrist. "I'm going to go get a drink. You want one?"

Frankly, he could use a drink, and Nicole could be fun when she loosened up a little. "Okay, but no sushi bars," he reminded her.

She smiled. "No sushi, you wimp. Just let me get my things."

She gave him a come-hither look that might have sent a less experienced man to his knees before stepping around him and moving on. Michael turned around, watched Leah's car sputter around the corner, and shoved both hands through his hair.

One ex-lover. One ex–love of his life. So far, not a par-ticularly great start to a film he'd been so damn certain was a gift from Guy Universe.

Subject: Re: YOU WILL NOT BELIEVE!!
From: Lucy Frederick <ljfreddie@hotmail.com>
To: Leah Kleinschmidt <hollywoodiva@verizon.net>
Date: 11:10 pm

Ohmigod, I think I am going to die. Leah, Leah, please do not do anything completely stupid because you know you have a tendency to be really stupid when it comes to guys. You CANNOT talk to him! I mean, okay, obviously you have to TALK to him, but you can't let yourself

TALK to him, TALK to him, do you understand? I hope I don't have to remind you how you laid on the couch for six months after he did what he did. You were a friggin' basket case! You ate an entire box of Fruit Loops in one sitting! Just pleeeease promise me you will remember that he walked out on you, that out of the clear blue, he announced that he was leaving and that was the end of that. He had no regard for your feelings or what you guys had shared for almost a year. I don't care if he is still really hot, he's an asshole! They call him the Extreme Bachelor for Chrissakes!

P.S. When we were on the phone, I wasn't laughing about your humiliating fall. I was laughing at you playing dodgeball. You're too much a goon to play dodgeball.

Subject: Re: Re: YOU WILL NOT BELIEVE!!
From: Leah Kleinschmidt <hollywoodiva@verizon.net>
To: Lucy Frederick <ljfreddie@hotmail.com>
Date: 8:30 pm

Lucy, of COURSE I am not going to TALK to him. Newsflash, but I actually remember what happened. No worries—I am older and more mature and I know what I want and more importantly, I *don't* want to get myself into another toxic relationship, especially with M, because I soooo learned my lesson. Yes, I remember walking around NYC like a freakin' zombie. But for the record—it wasn't *really* out of the clear blue. Every time the subject of long-term commitment came up, which okay, you have to admit it came up more than once, and then you also have to admit I was usually the one bringing it up, M was pretty clear that he wasn't into it. So get a load of this—he called Nicole Redding NICKI. WHAT DO YOU THINK THAT MEANS??? And oh yeah, even in high heels, she still doesn't even reach my elbow, which only added to my general distress for this really miserable day, because there I was looking like a giant gym teacher from some Ukrainian village—but anyway, right when she came prancing up, he had just said, and this is a (nearly) direct quote: "I've thought about you a lot. Great things. Killer things, and I wish—" *I wish!* AUGH!!! What did he *wish*? WHAT DID HE WISH?!?!?!

Subject: Re: Re: Re: YOU WILL NOT BELIEVE!!
From: Lucy Frederick <ljfreddie@hotmail.com>
To: Leah Kleinschmidt <hollywoodiva@verizon.net>
Date: 11:50 pm

Just stay away from him, because that guy will hurt you again, trust me. I always thought there was something not right about him.

P.S. David's mom is really going to drive me NUTS. We don't want more than 200 people at the wedding. Big, but not huge, right? Well David's mom sends her list over, and it's 148 people long!! Like my parents don't have friends they want to invite? What about me and David? By the way, how do you feel about puce? As a bridesmaid color, I mean.

SIX

TRUDY, who had embraced the new Dumpster chic so popular in Hollywood, was waiting for Leah the next morning, dressed in jeans split at the knees, a skirt over the jeans, a camisole, and a poncho, one arm crossed over her middle, the other extended with a smoke dangling precariously between two fingers. She was wearing rhinestone, cat-eye sunglasses today, undoubtedly purchased from Goodwill, her favorite shopping venue, and her lips were pressed together in a little rosebud of displeasure.

Trudy was a hoot. She complained constantly about her kids, but she was fiercely protective. She was very pretty, and wanted to act, but didn't believe in acting classes or trying to improve her craft and told Leah she was wasting her time and money on her classes. "Either you got it or you don't, sugar," she'd say with a wink. Well, Leah didn't have it, apparently, and she was continuing with class.

"Hey," Leah said as she gathered her backpack and locked the one door on her car that would actually lock.

"So why did you run out yesterday?" Trudy demanded, dispensing with her typically enthusiastic greeting.

"I had something I had to do."

"Do, as in shopping? Or do, as in stunt hunk number 4? Because Michele and I saw him take off after you when you left."

"Oh," Leah said, uncertain what to say to the evidence presented to her, and shrugged.

"Shut up!" Trudy cried, tossing her smoke aside and grinding it out with the heel of her very cute sandals. "What is going on with you and that guy? First of all, he's beautiful, and second, do *not* hold out on me! I mean, you obviously know him. He's been here one day! Nobody scores that fast, not even that skank Melinda. Come on, give it up, I'm a single mom with three kids, and this is as close as I get to sex."

"Please," Leah said with a roll of her eyes. "You have a boyfriend. Admittedly, not a great one, but a boyfriend nonetheless—and don't forget you have complained that he wants it too much and you're exhausted. I, on the other hand, *don't* have sex, and damn sure not with the stunt guy." Not that the thought didn't keep crossing her mind, but she wasn't insane. As far as she was concerned, Michael would never touch her again. Ever. "All I know for certain is that he is indeed the fourth stunt guy," she added, and ducked her head, started digging through her backpack to hide from Trudy.

"Ohmigod, I'm so going to kick you or something," Trudy said in a huff. "Why are you being so damn coy all of a sudden? Don't give me, *'he's the fourth stunt guy,'*" she mimicked.

Leah sighed and glanced up at Trudy's cat-eye sunglasses. Trudy took them off and looked at her pleadingly. "Okay," Leah said, relenting. "While it is true that I used to know him, I don't know him anymore."

Trudy squealed with glee and quickly put her arm around

Leah's shoulders. "Do tell, darling, and don't leave out a single detail!"

"Don't get excited. It was years ago."

"He's so cute! Did you date him, or what?"

"I knew him in New York. I hardly remember anything about him," Leah said, figuring that was not a total lie, as some of what they had been together had faded from her memory. *Some.* Not all.

"Damn," Trudy said, clearly disappointed, "I was hoping for so much more. Oh well, it's probably better this way."

"Why?"

"Why? Well, when we saw him walk after you yesterday, Michele almost had a cow. She said you shouldn't waste your time."

"She did?"

"Sweetie, he's the Extreme Bachelor, remember? The lover? And besides, apparently he and Nicole Redding are still an item—I heard the guy dates anything in a skirt and has a particular fondness for actresses."

"Go figure," Leah muttered.

"Well, *yeah*," Trudy said cheerfully. "I mean, he's so good-looking. And nice. He told me he loved my shades," she said, winking at Leah.

So basically, while Leah had not been able to maintain a meaningful relationship since they broke up, *he'd* apparently scored with dozens of actresses, including Nicole Redding and God knew who else. Now she really hated him.

But then again, why should it bother her at all? She and Michael were done and over a long time ago. He was free to sleep with whomever he chose. So what if he was the Extreme Bachelor? What had that to do with Leah Klein? Absolutely nothing. She was here to do a film, not dig up dirt on an old boyfriend.

Still, it didn't seem fair he would show up on this film, and she couldn't get over it. How was she supposed to work while Michael did all the actresses on set?

"What's the matter?" Trudy asked, peering closely at Leah. "You look sort of weird."

"Me? I'm fine!"

Trudy peered even closer, her eyes squinting suspiciously. "How long ago did you say you knew him?"

"A really long time ago," Leah said, and forced a smile. "I love your shoes!" she said, to divert Trudy's attention from Michael.

It worked—Trudy instantly looked down and stuck her foot out. "Thanks! I got these and dance shoes for my son Barton for ten dollars at Goodwill."

With a name like Barton, it was little wonder the kid needed dance shoes.

"You should come with me sometime. They have great stuff. All the women in Brentwood dump their trash there, which, of course, is my treasure," she said, and turned her ankle so Leah could see the heel. Leah pretended to admire Trudy's sandals while Trudy catalogued the other cast-off items she'd snared, but her head was in another stratosphere altogether. She was determined to avoid Michael because she knew herself too well—if she paid any attention to him at all, sooner or later she'd wind up keeping track of his many conquests, and honestly, she couldn't imagine a greater hell on earth. Seriously. Watching him score ranked right up there with forty extra pounds and a fish hook in the eye.

That morning, she managed to stick to her new resolution and kept her distance from him. She focused on the tuck and roll the guys taught them, a skill Eli assured them they would need during the filming. In fact, Leah was so focused on tuck and roll that Eli pointed her out a couple of times as a great tuck-and-roll artist.

Maybe that was something she could add to her résumé. Beer and tissue commercials. Tuck-and-roll artist.

When they broke for lunch, Leah was laughing with Michele and Jamie at how one Starlet could *so* not tuck *or* roll, and Michael surprised the hell out of her by walking right into their midst. Unlike her, apparently, he was not the least bit intimidated by their past or their surroundings. He put his hands on his hips and smiled so charmingly at them that Leah thought Jamie might pass out.

"Good work today," he said to Jamie. "You have a very good roll."

"Thanks!" Jamie chirped, and stepped in front of Michele to get Michael's attention. Only Jamie's head barely reached Michele's chin.

Nevertheless, Michael smiled down at her and said, "You're really a natural. Have you done this before?"

"Me?" Jamie asked, pleased as punch. "Yes . . . I was a gymnast."

Michele snorted.

"It shows," Michael said with a smile and glanced at Michele. "Hey, I know you—you were the blond assassin in *Chechnya.*"

Michele blinked. "Oh," she said, lighting up. "I'm surprised you noticed me."

"Are you kidding?" Michael asked with a sexy grin. "It's not every day you see a beautiful assassin. I couldn't take my eyes off of you."

Michele grinned broadly. Leah wanted to kick her.

"Is it alright if I borrow Leah a moment?" he asked a drooling Jamie and a moon-eyed Michele. "I really need a word with her."

Michele's mouth dropped open and she gaped at Leah. Jamie grinned at Michael, nodding.

That part about him hadn't changed, either, apparently— he was still capable of stopping conversation with a smile and a wink.

"Are you free for lunch?" he asked, looking at Leah, oblivious to Jamie's drooling and Michele's unbridled jealousy. "They have a pretty decent commissary here. I thought maybe we could get caught up."

"Caught *up*?" Michele echoed, and Jamie instantly elbowed her. *"Ow,"* Michele yelped.

Leah wanted to politely thank him and say no, that she had some errands to run, and then wish him a good day. But what came out of her mouth was, "Ah . . . *ahem* . . . I'm really busy today. I don't have time for lunch."

Michael cheated by flashing a smile that could melt a polar ice cap. And apparently two other women standing by her, because they were suddenly gazing at him as if he was the Adonis King of Stuntmen. What Leah wouldn't give to be able to roll up Jamie's tongue and stick it back in her mouth.

"Busy doing what?" Michael asked Leah, the look in his eyes indicating that he didn't believe a word of it.

"Errands," she said, nodding affirmatively, and puffed out her cheeks, looked up at the sky for a minute. "Lots and lots of errands."

"What if I just ride along?"

"That wouldn't be a good idea at all."

"Why not?"

"Why not?" she repeated. *Why not!? Because I don't want to be anywhere near you in a confined area, you stupid, heartbreaking moron!* Leah glanced at her sorry excuse for a car. So did Michele, Jamie, and Michael. "Because . . ." Well, obviously, at least to two of the four people standing here, because she was the biggest wimp to ever walk the earth. But what exactly she was afraid of, she wasn't certain.

Unless it was something really pathetic like falling in love with him again.

Oh *nonononoo*, that was definitely not going to happen. It was dumb to even think it. Like she could ever fall in love with him again. Ha! Like she could ever fall in *love* again! And even if she could, like she could ever get over what he did to her the first time. It was such a sad and stupid notion that—

"Hello?" Michael said, his smile going wider as he looked at her.

Michele's gaze narrowed—she saw right through Leah. And Jamie still had that goofy look on her face as she subtly tried to make her hair look less messed up.

With a sigh of defeat, Leah pushed her hair behind her ears. "Okay, I guess I'll . . . get caught up," she said. "But no more than half an hour," she added, pointing a finger at Michael. "I really have stuff to do."

"A half hour, that's it," Michael said, hands up.

"Bye, Michael," Jamie said longingly.

"Bye, Jamie," he said with a smile.

Leah started walking toward the commissary, not even bothering to look at Michael. She didn't have to—he was right beside her. "Thanks," he said, as they walked out of earshot of the others. "Thanks for hearing me out."

"I am not hearing you out," she said firmly, and stopped so suddenly that he almost tripped over her. She looked up at his gorgeous face and groaned, put her hands to her hips. Then down. Then folded them across her middle and said, "Okay, Michael, the truth is I don't want to relive anything, or take any excruciating trips down memory lane. As long as we're clear on that, I'm cool."

"Relive," he repeated thoughtfully.

"Right. Relive," she said, making a fanning motion with her hand. "I mean, you know, we tried it once, and it didn't work out for whatever reason," she said, making a fast circular motion with one hand, "and it's just a lot of water under the bridge, and its probably just better that we stay friends. Well, not that we're really *friends*," she said, her hand starting to wave, "I mean, since, you know, you *dumped* me in a pretty spectacular way, and it was sort of a bad scene, and then, of course, we haven't even *seen* each other in ages and ages, I don't think we can pretend we're anywhere near friends. But yeah, you know . . . *civil*. Right. *Civil*. That's it. That's the word I'm searching for."

For some reason, his smile just went deeper and his eyes crinkled at the corners, and a little shiver shot down Leah's spine. "You lost me at '*bad scene*,'" he said. "But Leah . . .

it's just lunch. At a *commissary*, for Chrissakes. It's not re-living. It's not tripping down memory lane. It's not any-thing but two people catching up with time."

"Just civil, right?" she demanded suspiciously.

He held up his right hand, Boy Scout fashion. "Just civil."

"Okay. If you put it that way." She looked at her watch. Then at her new aqua trail shoes, which, for some reason, made the price of $89.99 pop into her head, a price that she really couldn't afford. He probably had tons of shoes like this in all different colors. "Okay," she said quietly, nod-ding.

"Great," he said, "I appreciate it." And he smiled. That smile ran down Leah's spine and kicked her square in the butt and took her back what seemed like a lifetime.

She started walking. Michael was right beside her, his hands in his pockets. "You did good today," he said as they walked toward the commissary. "I had forgotten how ath-letic you are."

Ridiculous. He was complimenting her on the tuck and roll. He had obviously forgotten that he once told her that when she jogged, she looked like she was bouncing up and down on a pogo stick. "You're just saying that because I did it right, and half of them can't."

"You're right," he said with a laugh. "After yesterday, I was worried about you. That was a pretty spectacular fall."

It had been a spectacular fall, and Leah couldn't help but smile a little. "Pretty flashy, huh?"

"Very."

She smiled a little more.

"It's great to see you smile. Have I told you how great you look?" he asked, touching the small of her back.

He might as well have burned her—it was an old, famil-iar gesture, one that used to make her feel so safe and wanted. She had a memory of it raining in New York one night, and Michael hailing a cab. When one pulled up, he put his hand on the small of her back, firmly but gently ushering her into the cab so that she wouldn't get wet, and him getting soaked in the process.

Now, she moved a little to her right, so that there was some distance between them and looked straight ahead. "I hope they have tuna."

I hope they have tuna. Sometimes, Leah wondered what alternate universe she was passing through. God, this was a dumb idea! She was already reliving everything in her mind, and they hadn't even begun to talk. He seemed to sense her reluctance—he had always had a strange way of being able to read what was going on with her—because he said, "I just wanted the chance to explain a couple of things."

"There's nothing to explain," she said instantly. "It was a long time ago. Like I said, water under the bridge. We've both moved on, and there really isn't any point in going back to it now, is there?"

"But there is a point," he said. "The point is, for better or worse, you don't know the whole truth about me. You never have."

Oh, great, here came the grand confession. *I was doing an Austrian woman while I was doing you,* or, a real gut-kicker, *I was going to leave my wife, but she got pregnant.* Right, like she hadn't thought of those possibilities a million times over. Why were men so dumb? "Really, Michael, I don't need to know the truth," she said as they reached the commissary.

"But I need to tell you."

"Okay," Leah said, sighing. "But I've probably surmised more than you think, and I already know the truth, but I really don't feel the need to know any more," she said, as Michael got them trays and put one in front of her. She could feel his body at her back. It felt familiar. And so good. And she hated him for it.

He leaned into her, close enough she could smell his cologne and said, "But you *don't* know the truth. You couldn't possibly know the truth." They moved in line behind an actor dressed like a street bum, and Michael straightened up. "What are you having?"

Oh, right, like she could eat now. She chose a tuna sandwich, but had no appetite for it. What did he think she could possibly not know? She'd known where he worked, what he did for a living. What else was there?

"There's a table over there," Michael said, nodding toward the back of the tent. He led the way, as far away from the other soccer moms and actors and everyone else as he could get. He put his tray down and held out a chair for her. "You don't have to do that," she said, but put her tray down, taking the seat he offered, sliding past him, her body brushing against his clothes and feeling that odd jolt of awareness.

He sat across from her, poured some salad dressing on the salad he'd picked up, and forked a mouthful.

Leah, on the other hand, could only sit there looking at him, gripping her sandwich in two hands. After a moment of watching him eat, she put the sandwich down. "Okay, the suspense is killing me," she said, trying to make light of it. "Tell me what I don't know. No, wait," she said, holding up a hand. "Let me start. What I know is that you were not ready to commit. So I guess the only question is why you didn't want to commit to me, and I think we both know it was another woman, but hey, whatever. It's over and done with."

He looked up from his plate, his brown eyes wide. *"What?"* he asked, incredulous. "You think there was another woman?"

Leah snorted. "Well, it's better than another man," she said, and picked up her tuna and took an enormous bite of it. *"That* would have really bugged me."

That gave him a moment's pause, but then he frowned and asked, "How in the hell did you get another woman out of . . . what happened?"

"Are you kidding? How could I not?" she mumbled through the tuna. "Suddenly we're through, and you're gone.

No warning, no sign there was anything wrong. Quite the contrary, in fact. I thought things were pretty damn good. So what else could it be?"

"Leah," he said, putting his fork down, "there was not another woman. *Ever.* I couldn't have done it—I had no desire to be with another woman when I was with you . . . which apparently is another thing you never knew." He picked up his fork again.

If it wasn't another woman, then it didn't leave too many explanations, did it? Other than perhaps that she'd been so pathetic in her desire to marry him and be with him forever that he'd balked, and as *that* was not something she really wanted to hear him say out loud, she blurted, "Whatever it was, it's fine. I mean, I didn't think that then, but look, if I had settled down back then, I wouldn't have come to L.A., and look at me now," she said, lifting her hands, one half a sandwich included.

He looked at her like she wasn't making sense.

Okay, maybe she didn't look entirely liberated, but she was. "You know what, Michael? You did me a huge favor," she said with false levity. "I never would have followed my dreams if you hadn't . . . you know. *Dumped* me."

"Could you please stop saying that?"

"Why? It's what you did."

He frowned at his salad. "Well, it's a relief to know *you* feel okay about it now, because I don't. I've thought a lot about it over the years." He stabbed at some lettuce. "Actually, I've agonized about the way I left things with you."

Don't. Please don't. "Hey, it's all good," she said, flicking her wrist dismissively before taking another bite of her sandwich. Was she kidding herself, or did his eyes sincerely look full of regret? "This is pretty good tuna," she said through a mouthful. "How's your salad?"

He glanced at the salad as if he just realized he had it, but quickly looked at her again, his gaze piercing hers. "You're right about one thing. I . . . I really was afraid of commitment. Deathly afraid of it." He looked away for a moment and pushed a hand through his hair. "It was almost like a mountain I couldn't climb. I'm not sure why, exactly, but I guess it has something to do with the fact that I grew up in foster homes and never really learned what commitment was."

Leah almost spewed her tuna. "Whoa, wait," she said hoarsely. "*Foster* homes? Since when? Now you are being an ass, Michael, if you think I'm going to fall for some woe-is-me-I-was-raised-in-a-foster-home schtick."

He sighed heavily. "It's no schtick. I'm serious."

"Oh *please*!" she exclaimed with an incredulous laugh. "Your parents live in Ohio. Your mom is a homemaker, and your dad has a hardware business, and he called you every Sunday. Don't you remember? You always had to be home by seven so you could take your dad's call."

"No," he said firmly, shaking his head. "I don't have any parents. The man who used to call me every Sunday was my boss."

"Get out," Leah said with a sardonic laugh. She had to hand it to him; whatever he was trying to pull was at least inventive.

"I wouldn't lie about this."

She snorted at that. "Okay, *love* that we're going in a new direction here," she said, wiggling her fingers at the new direction. "But you're missing a couple of important details. For example, why would your boss call you every Sunday? Why would your boss be asking questions about your brother's soccer game? And even if it was your boss, which it wasn't, because it was your dad, why wouldn't you just tell me?"

"That's what I need to explain," he said, and in what was possibly the greatest straight-man role in the history of theater, he leaned forward, his gaze intent. "There was no father, no brother. That was my boss. The talk of a brother was just . . . code."

"*Code.*"

He nodded.

Whatever she had thought, she had not expected this, some fantastic tale of foster homes and code-speak and God knew what else, and Leah burst out laughing. Maybe the other guys had put him up to it. Maybe she was being punked. Maybe he had turned schizophrenic in the last few years and actually believed his delusions. But she wasn't stupid enough to fall for it—he was forgetting that she had been there, every Sunday. That she would answer the phone and his dad would ask how she was doing. That she'd seen pictures of his damn brother!

Michael clasped his hands tightly together. "Damn, but this is really a lot harder than I thought it would be," he muttered, and glanced up again, looking, oddly, very tired. "I couldn't tell you the truth about me. I couldn't tell you that I grew up in foster homes and that I didn't work for an Austrian company, and that I knew, from the time we started dating, until the time I had to leave, that I *would* leave, because that was my job. At the time, I was more committed to the job than I was to you, and that, I think, was perhaps the biggest mistake of my life."

The punch line was coming any minute now. Leah polished off her tuna sandwich, waiting for him to say it, to deliver the big laugh.

But when he didn't deliver, Leah squinted at him. "So? Are you going to tell me what the big 'mystery' job was?" she asked, making invisible quotation marks with her fingers. "I bet I can guess. You were really . . . *Bond. James Bond*," she said in her best British accent, and then laughed at her joke.

But Michael didn't crack a smile, just kept looking at her like his puppy had just died.

"Double-Oh-Seven," she said. "Man of Steel."

"Man of Steel was Superman," he solemnly corrected her.

"Oh."

"But yeah, it was something like Double-Oh-Seven."

Leah choked on a laugh. "Shut up, Michael, you're killing me! Come on, what was it really?"

He leaned across the table and said low, "CIA."

Leah blinked and then burst out laughing. She slapped the table a couple of times in a fit of laughter so loud that several people turned in her direction, and in fact, from the corner of her eye, she could see Trudy's head crane above the others to look at her. "Oh God, that is hilarious," she said breathlessly, still giggling. "I don't know about the game you're playing—and don't get me wrong, I think it's a little sick—but my hat is off to you. That has got to be the greatest excuse ever invented by a guy! It's a classic! I haven't laughed this hard in five years!"

He did not laugh, did not even smile. He reached across the table and caught her hand. "I could not possibly be more serious," he said quietly. "I was an operative for fourteen years. When I met you, I had been called back to New York to consult a foreign government."

He looked completely earnest, but Leah was beginning to wonder if he really was delusional. She quickly withdrew her hand from his. "Stop it," she said sternly. "Do you need to maybe take a pill or something? Something to help you manage those hallucinations you're having?"

"At the time, I wanted to tell you," he said, doggedly continuing his outrageous tale. "But my boss wouldn't hear of it—it would have blown months and months of work. And then I got sent back out."

"Oh. And it naturally flows that because you were a CIA guy," she said, stabbing the air with both hands to emphasize that ridiculous notion, "you couldn't commit?"

His frown went deeper. "My job wouldn't have made it very easy, but it wasn't impossible. I just got cold feet, and it . . . it was a convenient excuse."

"A convenient and a completely whacked-out excuse, you mean," she said, no longer smiling. Frankly, she was seething. "So you basically forced me into this lunch, forced me to hear you out, and you hand me *this* crap?" She pushed aside her plate. "Thanks, Michael!" she said cheerfully. "Thanks for that laugh and clearing everything up for me. Now if you will excuse me, I am going to go and run a few errands before the afternoon session."

She stood up. "Oh, by the way . . . I don't know if you said all that to try and make yourself feel better, or if you really think I am that gullible, or better yet, that I even give a shit after all this time, but that was the best line I have ever heard. And I can't wait to share." She marched off in the direction of Trudy's table before he could respond.

She could not wait to tell them that her extreme ex-boyfriend claimed to have dumped her because he was a big world spy.

Oh God, what a laugh.

Subject: You will DIE
From: Leah Kleinschmidt <hollywoodiva@verizon.net>
To: Lucy Frederick <ljfreddie@hotmail.com>
Date: 11:01 pm

When you hear this, you will fall out of your chair laughing and David will have to resuscitate you. So Mr. Extreme Bachelor corners me and makes me have lunch with him today to tell me that the big reason he broke up with me was because he was . . . drum roll, please . . . a CIA SPY.

BWAHAHAHAHAHAHAHAHAAAA!!!

Subject: Re: You will DIE
From: Lucy Frederick <ljfreddie@hotmail.com>
To: Leah Kleinschmidt <hollywoodiva@verizon.net>
Date: 7:30 am

NO WAY!!! I don't believe you! NO man is that stupid!! Well, except for Dick Dimarco, remember him? Anyway, I am SHOCKED and dismayed! Altho, come to think of it, it might explain why no one ever saw or heard from him again . . . I always did think that was sort of strange. It seems like SOMEone would have run into him or heard from him, but I gotta tell you, I saw Jerry, Joey . . . whatever his name was, the guy that was always hanging out with Michael and that guy Rex? Anyway, I ran into him at a party a couple of years ago, and when I asked him if he ever heard from Michael anymore, he got this really strange look on his face and said no, that no one did, that he was out of commission. What did THAT mean? It's just weird, that's all I am saying.

So okay, I decided against puce. I am now looking into gold. Is gold okay? You didn't seem very excited about puce.

*   *   *

Subject: Favor
From: Michael <michael.raney@thrillsanonymous.net>
To: Jack <jack.price@thrillsanonymous.net>
Date: 4:00 pm

Do me a favor, will you? I need you to corroborate my time in the agency. No details, just confirm that's what I did. Would you just find a time and mention it to Yang? No big, but would appreciate.

SEVEN

LUNCH really hadn't gone as Michael had envisioned. But what had he expected, really? That she'd feel sorry for him? No, she just thought he was nuts. Or worse, a sleazy liar.

Unfortunately, Leah could be stubborn at times and refuse to listen to reason . . . but did she really have to tell her pals?

It wasn't long before everyone in boot camp was making cracks about James Bond, Double-Oh-Seven, and for some real laughs, Austin Powers, International Man of Mystery.

If that wasn't bad enough, some of the production office guys had heard that some of the soccer moms were hot and had started hanging around boot camp. When they started giving him shit—asking if he'd found Dr. Evil, if that was Mini-Me in his pants—Michael had had enough. Every time he walked by Miss Kleinschmidt, she was laughing with about a dozen of her closest friends.

It was time to trot out his corroborator, whether Jack wanted to be trotted out or not.

"Hey, you know it's a rule that we don't get involved with any of your women problems," Jack cheerfully rebuffed him the next morning when Michael demanded his help.

"Yeah, but it's different this time."

"Why?"

"Whaddaya mean, why? Because it is. Because it's the truth, and because she is making a laughingstock of me all over boot camp."

"I know," Jack said with a grin. "It's hilarious. Cooper thinks we've finally got a chance with some of the girls since you've been laughed out of commission."

"Look, I don't care about the rest of them, but I have my reasons for wanting Leah to know the truth. I just think she might believe me if she hears it from someone else."

"Man, I don't know," Jack said with a playful wince. "That's really crossing over to the dark side of a soap opera. I'd need a little something more than just you wanting a favor."

Michael sighed, pulled out his Blackberry. "Okay, Jacko," he said, and punched a couple of buttons. "Lindsey, the production assistant, right?"

"Right," Jack said with a grin.

Michael held up his Blackberry. "You tell Leah that what I told her is the truth, and I hit send, and Lindsey's number will be in your e-mail box before you can take your Blackberry out of your pocket."

Jack glanced across the dirt lot where the women were running an obstacle course. Leah was sitting in one of a dozen captain's chairs, talking with great animation. He glanced at Michael from the corner of his eye. "Let me see the number again."

Michael held up the Blackberry where Lindsey's name and number were clearly displayed. Jack squinted at it, rubbed his nape, and looked across at Leah and her friends again. "Great. Send me to do your groveling. Dammit,

Raney, why can't you just be a normal guy?" he complained.

But he'd started walking in that direction.

Michael hit send and went back to the office to do some work.

When he returned to the obstacle course a little later, several of the production office guys had taken up the captain's chairs, and Nicole Redding was right in the middle of them. Why, Michael could not fathom. There was no reason she should be here at this stage of the game, and didn't big major stars have better things to do with their time than sit around and watch boot camp for the minor actors?

But there she was, in the director's chair, naturally, beneath the large awning that had been erected to protect the fair skin of those with huge egos. Nicole's tiny legs were crossed daintily, her red hair hanging in soft layers around her face, as if a stylist had just arranged it. She was accompanied by a couple of Starlets who had already glommed onto her. They were all having a grand time laughing it up with the production boys.

"Michael!" Nicole called out the moment she saw him, waving him over.

Damn damn damn . . . Michael shoved his hands in his pockets and said, "Hey, Nicki."

"Well look who's here," she said, checking him out with a smile of amusement. "The spy who shags me, and I didn't even know he was an international man of mystery." Her little Starlet crew squealed with laughter.

Smooth. She'd just given the impression that they were still together. There was a reason she was considered one of the world's most successful actresses. "I wouldn't be very mysterious if you knew, would I?" he drawled.

"Oh Michael, you are so funny," she said, her smile brightening. "Why don't you sit down?" she asked, looking at the chair next to her that was inhabited by a Starlet, who instantly popped up. "We haven't had a chance to talk today."

"Yeah, I know," he said, wincing sorrowfully. "But I've got some work that can't wait. I'll catch up with you later, okay?" And before Queen Nicole on her throne could say a word, he walked on.

In hindsight, he had to admit that dating Nicole, however briefly, was not one of his better moves.

A couple of hours later, he found Jack on the edge of the field, going over the obstacles with his group again. When he sent the girls out to run the course, Jack and Michael stood side by side, their arms crossed over their chests, watching five women hop daintily and very slowly through a roped hopscotch course.

Jack groaned when one of them tripped but then righted herself before she hit the ground. "This is never going to work. They run like girls. We are never going to get them to look like they know what they're doing out there. This is going to be the biggest disaster in the history of T.A., man. I feel it in my bones."

"They're fine. So . . . did you do it?"

Jack glanced at Michael, then at the women again. "Just who is Leah to you, anyway?"

"Just someone I used to know. Why?"

"Because when I told her you really were an ex-operative, she said, 'Really?' like she was surprised by it. And I said, yeah, that you really were, and that I knew you then, because I had done some flying for the Air Force, and that we'd worked together."

"Great. So now she believes me."

"Not so fast. She asked if we'd been on any dangerous missions, and I said some of them were dangerous. And then she asked me what you did, exactly, and I said I didn't really know that much, as we were from different agencies, and it was all covert operations, so strictly on a need-to-know basis. Then she asked where you were stationed, and again, I said I didn't really know, that you'd sort of show up when it was time to go, and—you get the picture. There were just a lot of questions. Women ask a lot of questions in general. I dated a woman once, and it was six months of one long question. Where are you going, who were you with, when will I see you—"

"So what happened?" Michael asked, cutting Jack off before he could catalogue all his dating woes.

"What happened is that in the end, she said it was all very impressive, and that she was totally blown away, because she couldn't imagine how we managed, and I asked her, 'Manage what?' And she said . . ." Jack paused there, slanted a look at Michael. "And she said it must have been hard to operate with phones in our shoes, but at least our cameras were in our watches, and that was probably more convenient, and then she laughed and trotted over to her friends and apparently said the same to them, because the next thing I know, they are all laughing at me."

"Shit," Michael said.

"You're on your own, pal," Jack said. "I'm not getting in the middle between you and any of your female acquaintances. *Marian! Pick up your feet and run!*" he shouted at one woman who was strolling through the roped hopscotch.

Michael sighed and peered across the ropes field. Damn it if Leah and her three pals weren't looking at him now. They burst out laughing when he made eye contact, then shot forward at once, their heads together, talking and clearly enjoying themselves.

Okay. No more playing around. Leah didn't have to accept his apology—shit, she didn't even have to hear it. But she had to believe this about him—his pride was at stake now.

He knew what he had to do.

At the end of the workday, Michael walked out to his car, rolling his eyes for every *Bye, Double-Oh-Seven!* and *Where are you going, another Mission Impossible? HA HA*. Everyone was a goddam comedian. He slid into his T-bird, stuck his Blackberry in the hands-free set, and dialed a number he hadn't dialed in a couple of years.

EIGHT

LEAH made it all the way to the 405 before she pulled into a convenience store and pressed her forehead to her steering wheel, her eyes tightly shut. He looked so good, he sounded so good. And every time he looked at her, all she could think of was sex. The really fabulous sex she'd only experienced with Michael. No one else could do it like him.

This was really all so unbelievable—all the times she'd thought and dreamed about Michael, and now here he was, walking around, pretending he'd been some super-secret spy.

What really hurt is that during the day, she'd catch sight of him and see something as familiar as an old pair of pajamas, and her heart would swell, and she would find herself longing for those days.

But then she'd remember that he was trying to convince her that he had dumped her because he was a spy, of all the ridiculous, stupid things he might have said—and she smashed any feelings that were trying to rear their ugly heads like bugs.

She found little satisfaction in the fact that everyone was calling him James Bond and making really crude jokes about his Mini-Me.

It didn't matter, because the bottom line was that whatever was going on with Michael, Leah was going to have to put their past solidly behind her. It was the only way she'd make it through two months of production with him. She *had* to make it. Last night, she had contemplated quitting—but she'd quit because of him before, and it had cost her a career. She had never recovered professionally from her meltdown, and she'd be damned before she'd let him take that from her again.

She lifted her head, pushed her hair from her eyes. "Still . . . it's so *weird*," she said aloud.

She got out, walked into the store, and got a soda. When she returned, she turned the key in the ignition. The engine made a strange chugging sound, then nothing. "Oh man," she muttered, and got out to pop the hood.

BRAD arrived a couple of hours later in his VW van. That was one good thing about having him as a roommate—he did know a thing or two about cars. He had her up and running in about fifteen minutes, and Leah bought a six-pack and brought it home for him. They ended up on the back porch—which was actually a concrete slab in a postage stamp of a yard, surrounded by cinder-block walls. Her lopsided origami peacock joined them, complete with a smoke stuck in its beak, courtesy of Brad, who clearly had no appreciation for fine arts.

Brad had gotten a tiny part in an indie horror film, and was happy that, even though he'd play a spewing ghoul, his face would not be covered with a mask.

To celebrate, Brad put some chicken on a rusty barbeque pit. While the chicken grilled, he went over his lines

with Leah, practicing the spewing ghoul part in the backyard until Leah was laughing so hard she could hardly
stand up. They had just finished the last of the beer and the
chicken when the phone rang. Brad answered and handed
the phone to Leah.

"Who?" Leah mouthed.

Brad shrugged. "Some guy named Rex."

Rex. *Rex.* She'd known a Rex in New York, Michael's
friend . . . wait just a damn minute. Not him, too!

Leah grabbed the phone from Brad and slipped inside
through the patio door. "Hello?"

"Hey Leah Kleinschmidt, it's Rex Anderson. Remember me?"

How could she forget Rex? He had a boat, and she and
Michael used to hang out with him and his flavor-of-the-
month girlfriend off Long Island on the weekends. "Of
course I remember you!" she exclaimed. "How long has it
been? Five or more years?" she asked, in spite of knowing
full well just how long it had been.

"At least that long. So how's it going out there in L.A.?"
he asked jovially. "Do you miss Broadway?"

Leah slid into a chair at the scarred kitchen table. "A little. So I suppose you heard that from our pal Michael,
huh?" she asked, unwilling to discuss the precipitous de-
cline of her career since she'd last seen him. "I'm guessing
you called to tell me that good ol' Mike was a spy, right?
And since it seems like all his friends were involved, I bet
you were a spy too, huh?"

Rex chuckled. "You were always a firecracker. Mikey
warned me you still were. Well here it is, doll—I *did* call
to tell you that Michael was a spy, or as we like to call it,
an operations officer. Me, too. Now the difference between me and him is that Mike isn't a spy anymore. He
left the agency, but I'm still with them. I'm in Langley
now, and if you want to check that out, you can call the
number I am going to give you. It's the CIA, and when

they answer, you will ask for me, and they'll put you through."

Leah snorted into the phone.

"Just try it," Rex said with a laugh. "It's true. Mike and I, we had some close calls in the field. And after a really close one, our cover was pretty well blown, so I came back home and took a desk job. But Mike, he thought the last one was just a little too close for comfort and decided to get out for good. That's when he hooked up with Jack Price."

"What sort of close calls?" Leah asked, squinting suspiciously at a front door desperately in need of paint.

"Now, Leah, those details would just bore you."

"Oh yeah?" she asked, spying Brad's laptop on a chair. She hoisted it onto the table and opened it, then punched the power button. "Just try me. I'm not the least bit bored! In fact, this is the most entertaining conversation I've had in a while. Oh wait, I stand corrected. The *most* entertaining conversation I've ever had was just yesterday, when Michael told me he was a spy. That was classic!"

"I wouldn't kid you, Leah. I have no reason to. And I wouldn't lie for him, either," Rex avowed.

"So let me get this straight, Rex," Leah said as she waited for the laptop to boot. "Do you seriously want me to believe that you and Michael were spies? International covert operatives? And those Sunday afternoons we were sailing on your boat, that you were playing a role?"

"No, of course not. On Sundays, we were pretty much who we were. Just a couple of guys having a good time with a couple of hot babes."

"You mean me and your half-dozen hot babes," Leah muttered as she Googled the CIA.

"Hey—I confess, I have issues," he said with a laugh. "I still do."

"You and your pal both, apparently."

"I can't speak for Mikey."

Leah didn't say anything—she was reading the mission of the Clandestine Service on the CIA Web site.

"You're looking at the Web site, huh?" Rex asked.

That startled her, and Leah reared back, looked at the phone in her hand for a moment before putting it back up to her ear, then suddenly dipped down, looking under the table. "How did you know that?"

"Don't freak out—there isn't a camera anywhere. I heard the Windows music when you turned it on."

Leah sat up and frowned. Was she honestly going to believe this? "So . . . so Michael asked you to call me and tell me that he was really a . . ."—she could hardly say it—"an operations officer or whatever you said?"

"That's exactly what I am telling you. Look, for whatever reason, it's really important to him that you know the truth. Hell, I haven't even heard from him in two years—I didn't even know how to get hold of him. I'm glad he called, because there was some stuff I wanted to tell him, but the point is, you are important enough for him to come out of the closet, so to speak."

For once, Leah was speechless. It was one thing for Michael to hand her some lame excuse, but quite another to rope in a couple of friends. "Okay," she said, nodding. "If I believe you—and I'm not saying I do, but if I did—then what was the story in New York?"

"We'd been out of the country for a long time," Rex said easily. "We got called back to New York to do some consulting. But after being out of the country for a couple of years, New York was like Disneyland. And then Mike met you. I don't think he ever meant it to go so far."

Leah's gut clenched. That's what Michael had said that night in New York. *I am sorry, I should never have let it go this far.*

"But girl, he had you under his skin, and apparently, he still does," Rex was saying. "Unfortunately, at the time, there were some things he hadn't quite finished, and he knew that it was going to break eventually. I guess it took a little longer than what any of us anticipated, but when it did, he had to book," Rex explained.

"But he worked on Wall Street," Leah argued.

"He said he did. But if you think about it, you only saw his office once. Every other time he met you in the lobby. Let's just say he borrowed an office to show you one day, and that was all it took."

Damn. If that was true, that was good—she'd only seen his office once, on a day his secretary . . . "But what about Donna, his secretary?" Leah demanded. "She answered the phone every time I called."

"Calls were routed through Washington."

"What about his boss?"

"Bill. He called every Sunday."

"No, that was his *dad*."

"No, that was his *boss*. Michael doesn't have a dad. At least not one he knows about. He has no family—he was orphaned, grew up in foster homes, and it was his boss that called on Sundays."

Leah obviously needed to go lie down because she really was beginning to believe the spy story. Not that she didn't have some pretty strong doubts—somehow, a huge guy conspiracy was a lot easier to swallow than an outlandish tale of spies. But could Michael really talk two friends into going along with it?

She continued to chat it up with Rex, throwing him a couple of curve questions to catch him in a lie. Rex handled each one flawlessly.

She sat at the table a long time after she hung up, staring at the CIA Web site, trying to absorb this strange little twist in the history of her life. All right, so what if she did believe it? It didn't really change anything . . . did it? Of course it didn't change anything! It was just a curious and unusual turn of events in something that was really ancient history and had absolutely no effect on her now. No matter why he left, she could never forgive the way he left. She just had to keep reminding herself of that.

Subject: Re: Spies and Other Stuff
From: Lucy Frederick <ljfreddie@hotmail.com>
To: Leah Kleinschmidt <hollywoodiva@verizon.net>
Date: 10:34 pm

Rex Anderson! Oh gawd, he was so CUTE! So you really think the spy thing might be true, huh? I guess it could be—if you think about it, there's really no reason three grown men would lie about it, even if they are friends. And there's nothing for M to gain from lying about it—it's not like you're going to get back with him. ROFLMAO!! You're not, right?

Subject: Re: Re: Spies and Other Stuff
From: Leah Kleinschmidt <hollywoodiva@verizon.net>
To: Lucy Frederick <ljfreddie@hotmail.com>
Date: 7:48 pm

God, NO! He could get down on his knees and BEG and still there'd be no way I'd go back. Who cares, anyway? I mean, think about it, he's telling me that he dumped me because he was a spy but he *lied* about being a spy. The obvious question is, what else did he lie about? Maybe the whole damn thing was a lie. Anyway, I do not want to go back there, I really honestly don't, so please let's not talk about it anymore.

So listen, the buttercup yellow dress you attached in your e-mail this morning? You know, the one you said was gold but was so yellow that it made me want a fried egg? If that was supposed to be a joke, I'm dying here . . .

Subject: Re: Re: Re: Spies and Other Stuff
From: Lucy Frederick <ljfreddie@hotmail.com>

To: Leah Kleinschmidt <hollywoodiva@verizon.net>
Date: 10:56 pm

Would you PLEASE adjust the color on your computer
screen? That was gold! Sheesh!

*   *   *

Subject: Men of Mystery
From: Jack <jack.price@thrillsanonymous.net>
To: Mikey <michael.raney@thrillsanonymous.net>
Date: 10:57 pm

Yo, we've got a problem. Nicole doesn't want someone
named Amy on her side and has apparently convinced
the producers Amy should be moved, which means we
have to retrain about four women. Can you show up at 8
tomorrow for that? Other than that, just wondering how
the spy angle is working for ya. hahaha

NINE

WHEN Michael arrived the next morning, he was surprised to see Leah was one of the women switching battlefield positions. She and Jack were already going through some of the moves.

As she ran through a new obstacle course, Michael got Jack over to the side and asked, "Of the twenty women you had to move around, you had to choose *her*?"

"I had to," Jack said, watching her closely. "She's one of the best we have and easiest to retrain, and we have to get one of them trained on the rooftop-to-rooftop leap." He glanced at Michael from the corner of his eye. "Don't worry. I won't let her hurt you."

Michael snorted.

When it came time to do the rooftop-to-rooftop leap— which was really done with cranes and ropes and mirrors for the viewing audience at home—Michael moved to help Leah up.

She gave him a quick, thin smile. "That's okay—I can do it."

"It's not as easy as it might look—"

"Really," she said, cutting him off. "I can *do* it." Michael raised his hands in the air and stepped back, and Leah scrambled up and away from him.

A moment later, she went tumbling off the tightrope, her fall stopped by a harness around her waist and legs. She hung there like a sack, bouncing up and down, her eyes as wide as saucers. Below her, several women had arrived at work and were peering up at her, asking each other what she was doing.

Michael strolled up to where she was bouncing; her head level with his, only upside down. "That's what I was trying to tell you. It's a little harder than it—"

"Shut up, Michael."

He nodded. "Okay . . . but I think you should pull your shorts down. People are beginning to talk."

She almost killed herself trying to do that, squealing and bouncing and twisting while the other women laughed.

Michael couldn't possibly have been more entertained.

"Man," Eli said, walking up to stand next to Michael as Leah bounced. "That really sucks."

Michael nodded and smiled up at Leah, who gave him a murderous look.

"So we've got another small crisis," Eli said as they watched Leah struggling with her shorts. "You know the gal who's always got a problem?"

"Tamara?" Michael asked.

"Yeah, Tamara. She started this thing about how a particular rope fiber—which we just happen to be using—has been proven to cause skin rashes in some people, and the next thing you know, half the soccer moms are up in arms. Someone has an audition for a commercial and can't allow her hands to have a rash, and another one said she is extremely sensitive to certain fibers. Lemme ask you," Eli said, turning to face Michael for a moment. "Have you ever once in your life thought about what kind of fiber is in *anything*? We will never transform these women into believ-able soldiers."

"They aren't supposed to be soldiers. They are supposed to be women who *think* they're soldiers. They're supposed to be a little clumsy."

"A *little*?" Eli snorted. "We're lucky nobody has died yet."

"It's all going to work out," Michael tried to reassure him, but Eli stubbornly shook his head. "Give it a rest, Pollyanna."

"Ex-*cuse* me, is someone going to help me down?" Leah shouted.

Eli sighed and climbed up to untangle her safety ropes. Michael caught her when she came down. She landed a little shakily, grabbing Michael's arm to right herself. But then she smiled up at Eli, one of those beautiful, nut-cinching smiles that only Leah could summon, and she laughed, and her hands were suddenly moving, pointing at the rope ladder and the cranes with both hands as she explained how she had fallen.

That was something Michael had always admired about her—she had that ability to shake off anything . . . or at least he was sincerely hoping she still had it.

After the guys got her out of the harness, Leah trotted over to the awning. Michael followed her.

She obviously didn't notice him—she bent over a cooler, fished out a bottle of water, then stood up and did a weird little backward hop when she saw him. "Oh, hey," she said.

"Are you all right?"

"Me? Sure!" she said, nodding a little too enthusiastically.

Michael couldn't help it—he kept seeing her bouncing on the end of the harness and laughed.

She continued to drink her water for a moment, then lowered it and said, "What?"

"Nothing."

"It's clearly *something*."

He shrugged, tried to keep the smile from his face. "I was just thinking of the time we were in Aruba, and you dove off the boat—"

"Shut up!" she exclaimed, turning red. "You're not supposed to remember that."

"Oh, I remember," he said, nodding. "A full moon rising is hard to—"

"I can't help that a rogue wave took one-half of my bathing suit away."

"A rogue wave? Like a tsunami, or what?"

"A wave! I told you it was a wave!"

"I think it was just sloppy diving," he said with a grin.

She gave a snort of laughter and didn't try to deny it.

"That was some fine rope work out there," he said.

She paused in the drinking of a long draw of water. "Are you kidding? I almost killed myself."

"Maybe so—but you looked good doing it."

"Hey, Austin Powers!" a woman called, and when Michael glanced over his shoulder, he saw Jill, jogging by on her way to the tuck-and-roll clinic. "Where's your groovy sidekick?" she asked, and then laughed loudly, as if that was the funniest thing that had ever been uttered by a human being.

Unfortunately, so did Leah.

Michael sighed wearily.

Leah screwed the lid on the bottle and looked at him with sparkling blue eyes. "So, Austin . . . I had a call last night," she said, pushing her hair off her shoulder. "Imagine, Mini-Me calling me out of the clear blue."

"Imagine," Michael said with a wry smile.

"All right, so maybe you aren't as delusional as I thought," she said. "Maybe you really were a spy—oops, I mean *operations officer*."

"*Senior* operations officer," he corrected her with a bow of his head. "So you believe me?"

She shrugged. "I can't help but believe you—I can't for the life of me imagine why three grown men would make up such a stupid lie."

Michael grinned broadly. He had just cleared the first major hurdle. "That is about the best news I've heard in years."

"But now you've got that little secret off your chest, we can put the whole thing behind us, right?" she said, sweeping one arm behind her. "We'll just be civil, like we said. Right?"

No, not right, not even remotely right, but he thought the better of making his case at the moment and merely nodded. "If that's how you want it. Civil."

Her smile faded. "That's not how I want it. But that's how I can live with it," she said softly.

That stung, and Michael didn't know what to say to it.

"I better get back to work," Leah said, and ducked out of the tent before he could think what to say.

He watched her walk away, her hips swinging just the way he remembered them. He had a peculiar discomfort in his chest, like he needed a drink, or a smoke—and he didn't smoke.

Jesus, this wasn't him, this guy who wanted to smoke or squeeze the life out of something. He couldn't remember the last time a woman had gotten away from him as fast as Leah had just done. But he damn sure could remember what it felt like when a female was repulsed by him, and he didn't like the feeling that gave him in the least.

Leah's aversion to him was enough to make most grown men bow out, to turn around and walk the other way. But it was having a curious effect on him. He was now more determined than ever to win her over—he just needed a better angle. Plan A, in which he had envisioned telling her the truth and watching his second chance at happiness fall into his lap, had been a total bust.

Therefore, it was time to move to Plan B. He'd have to get right on that and come up with a plan.

But luck was with Michael, because he inadvertently got a Plan A-and-a-half later that afternoon, an hour or so after the women were released for the day. He'd stayed behind to talk to the guys about some budget problems that were cropping up, and they hung out for a while, running through some contingency plans. When Michael left, the guys were still talking about something the women had done that day that baffled them, but personally, he didn't want to rehash it—he had other things on his mind.

As he walked out to his car he noticed that, along with the autos of a few production staff stragglers, Leah's clunky old Escort was still at the far end of the lot. The hood was up, and beneath the hood, bent at the waist, wearing a denim skirt and a small T-shirt that didn't quite cover her belly, was Leah.

Michael stopped, glanced heavenward, and grinned at the opportunity that had just been handed to him on a silver platter.

He strolled up to her car, unnoticed by her, primarily because she was talking on her cell phone and poking around under the hood. "Stupid-ass car," she muttered, and bent her head at a funny angle, trying to see something beneath a couple of cables. "Okay, I see the thingie you're talking about. I think," she said, and paused, listening to the person on the other end. After a moment, she said, "I hope you are right, because, dude, there is no way I can afford the cab fare home—huh? The what? Hey, wait," she said, and grabbed something deep in the bowels of the engine and made a strange grunting noise. "I wonder if it's this thing?"

"Maybe I can help," Michael said.

She came up so fast at the sound of his voice that she banged her head on the open hood with a *thump*. "Shit!" she hissed, and emerged from beneath the hood, one hand on the top of her head where she had banged herself, the other still holding the phone. Her eyes narrowed when she saw him. "Oh. Michael," she said, her voice gone flat, and repeated into the cell phone, "*Michael.* Just a guy I used to know."

Ouch. "Looks like you could use some help."

"No, I'm—huh? No, Brad, it's too much of an imposition," she said to the phone, dragging her fingers through her hair. "He's too busy and too . . ."—she glanced at Michael from the corner of her eye, her gaze flicking the full length of him—"*nicelydressed,*" she muttered softly.

Michael ignored her and moved so he could see under the hood. He could smell a mix of sweet soap and perfume as he stood beside her, and wished to heaven that his body wouldn't react so quickly to just a scent. "I can take a look," he said, and leaned over the engine, bracing his hands against the frame of the car.

"You don't have to."

"I want to help."

Leah sighed. "Okay, he's looking," she said into her phone.

Michael had no idea who this guy Brad was, but he wanted to get rid of him as soon as possible. Fortunately, he instantly spotted Leah's problem—a battery cable was loose. A good guy would fix it in about a nanosecond and send her on her way. Too bad for Leah, because he wasn't a good guy—he damn sure wasn't going to fix her car and send her off to Brad. So he didn't say a word, just poked around, inspecting the most obvious parts, and then finally straightened up and sighed deeply.

Leah was standing completely still, like a statue, staring at him and holding the phone to her ear.

"You have a problem," he lied solemnly.

"He says I have a problem," Leah quickly repeated, her eyes widening with terror. "Okay," she said, nodding in response to whatever Brad had said. "Just a second." She lowered the cell a minute. "What is it?"

He made a grim face and looked down at his hands. "Do you have something I could wipe my hands with?"

Leah instantly dipped down and retrieved the backpack she had left leaning up against the tire of her car. She dug inside, pulled out a bandana, and thrust it at him.

Michael took the bandana and methodically wiped his hands. Leah's gaze never left him, watching him closely, as if she expected him to total the car on the spot. Which, if it were up to him, he'd do in a moment. Leah deserved to be driving something better than this piece of shit. "It's the distributor cap."

"Okay," she said, nodding.

"It's cracked." He winced sympathetically.

Leah frowned and looked at her car. "It is? I could have sworn I just had that checked."

"Had what checked?"

"You know," she said, waving her hand. "Caps and all that stuff—oh," she added, obviously getting another message from Brad. Her brows dipped into a V. She squinted at the engine, then at Michael. "But I thought you checked that sort of thing—oh. *Oh,*" she said again, her frown turning into a painful wince as Brad obviously explained to her what it meant if her distributor cap was cracked. "Oh. My. God! You have *got* to be kidding!" she cried into the phone and threw her head back, eyes closed, one palm pressed against her forehead. She groaned, "This is the *worst* news ever!"

"I'll give you a ride," Michael offered.

Leah instantly straightened and shook her head. "No, no, that's okay. Brad will come and . . ." Her face fell. "Oh," she said softly. "Right, right, I forgot. No, it's okay. Really. Not a problem. I'll get home. You go do your thing and good luck. Okay, later," she said, and clicked off her phone. She tossed it into her backpack, then stood with her hands on her hips, frowning at Michael.

"Problem?" he asked, trying to hide the delight in his voice.

"Brad has a meeting with his agent he can't miss."

"That means you're stuck with me. Good news."

"For you, maybe."

"Hey, girl, I already said I'd give you a ride. You don't need to try and flatter me."

"I'm not trying to— *Oh!*" she cried with frustration and glared at her car. "Stupid, *stupid* car!" she exclaimed and then glanced at Michael again. Then she suddenly whirled around, scanning the cars that were left. "Isn't there anyone else here?" she cried. "One of the girls, maybe? All I need is a ride to a bus stop—"

"Okay, now you're just hurting my feelings," Michael said. "Leah, it's just a ride. That's it. I will take you where you need to go, and you can call someone to come haul this away while you're working."

"But how will I get to work?" she asked the sky, arms fully extended. Before Michael could open his mouth to offer, Leah lifted a finger. "Ha! I'll call Trudy. She owes me."

"Okay, great. That's settled. Shall we proceed with said ride and get it over with?" She slanted a look at him. He shrugged. "Just following your lead."

Leah actually smiled a little. "Okay. Let's get it over with."

"I'm just over there," he said, and pointed to his bronze T-bird convertible.

Leah turned to look where he pointed, and her shoulders instantly sagged. "You drive a *T-bird*?" she exclaimed. "*I* want a T-bird. I have wanted the blue T-bird for at least a hundred years. How is it fair that *you* have that car and I don't?"

"Come check it out."

Clearly defeated, she nodded. Michael picked up her backpack, but she instantly took it from him, her fingers brushing his, and shoved the pack over her shoulder. She pivoted away from him and locked the driver's door.

"Your passenger window is down," he pointed out.

"It's broken."

He didn't see any point in locking the one good door, but he said nothing.

They walked across the lot together—a good two feet between them that felt like an ocean—to the passenger side of his car. He'd left the top down, so Leah leaned over the door like she was leaning over the ledge of a cliff and looked inside the interior. "Wow," she said reverently. "It's even nicer than I thought."

"You'll love the way it rides," he said, and opened the passenger door for her. Leah slipped into the seat, one leg after the other, pushed her backpack to the floor between her feet, and yanked at her skirt before folding her hands primly in her lap.

That simple gesture reminded him of another moment so long ago; the day she had found out she'd been given a part in the play, *Marty's Sister's Lover.* She'd sat on his couch, her smile brilliant, her hands clasped together in her lap so tightly that he'd had the sense she was trying to contain her absolute glee at having won the part.

"You're excited," he'd said.

"I've never been this excited in my life. Well . . . except for Saturday night," she'd added with a salacious little wink.

With that memory in his mind's eye, Michael shut the passenger door and strode around to the driver's side.

He started the ignition; 4 Doors Around, the music on his MP3 started up, and he reached to turn it down.

"Hey!" Leah cried, stopping him with a hand to his wrist. Michael froze, looked at the slender hand on his wrist. "Is that 4 Doors Around?"

"Yeah—you know them?"

"Know them? I love them," she said, looking at him. "How did you know?"

Her question confused him for a moment, but then he realized she thought he'd played it for her. He resisted the urge to take full credit for doing exactly that—but there had been enough lies between them. "I didn't," he answered honestly. "I just happen to like them, too."

"Oh." She actually looked disappointed. Her hand slid away from his wrist, back to her lap. "That's really . . . another very weird coincidence."

"Not so weird," he said quietly. "We always liked the same music, remember?"

Leah looked straight ahead.

"Ramona Priest. Radioslave. Borrowed Time," he reminded her.

"The soundtrack to *The September Affair*," she added so softly he could barely hear her.

"Excuse me?"

"You remember? The movie you slept through?"

"Like I could ever forget that," he said with a chuckle. "You played it nonstop for weeks to punish me."

"I did not," she said, lifting her head and smiling at him. "It was just a couple of days. You're exaggerating."

"I don't exaggerate. It was at least a week," Michael said, and smiled as he reached across the console, absently stroked the back of her hand with his finger. "Do you still like martinis?"

Leah's smile faded. "Michael . . ."

He removed his hand. "Civil. I swear to God, *civil*. But where's the harm in a drink?" he asked quickly before she could refuse him. "That's what civil acquaintances do. They have drinks, they talk, they catch up with each other."

"Except that we're not exactly civil acquaintances," she reminded him.

"We're more than that," he said, feeling, strangely, a little desperate.

She shrugged.

"Come on, Leah. You're just as curious about me as I am about you, and don't try to deny it. It's written all over your face." He waited, hoping his ploy would work.

For some reason, of all the things he'd said, *that* made Leah smile. "Okay, I won't deny it. But just so we're clear here, Lucy is far more curious about you than I am, and I have a duty to report."

"Oh my God. Good ol' Lucy, huh?"

"Yes, *Lucy*," she responded, her voice full of warning.

He remembered Leah's best friend, a brash and funny redhead who was totally into Leah's business. Neck deep. Michael chuckled and shook his head. "I swear I can't win. So how is the old girl?"

"About to get married, if you can believe it," Leah said with a funny shake of her head. "I never thought I'd see the day Lucy got married."

"Christ, me either," Michael agreed as he backed out of his spot. "I always had her pegged for the man-eating type."

"She is the man-eating type. So where are we going? No place too dressy, okay? I don't want to sit there feeling more like a geek than I already do."

Thank you God. That was one small victory that had him feeling just one step away from dancing on the hood of his car. But Michael played it cool as he put the car in drive. "There's a great place on Montana Avenue—very casual, very laid back," he said, and pointed the car in that direction.

TEN

LEAH had always suspected she had an unnatural tolerance for suffering. One need only look at her history to see it—foregoing the education her parents would have given her and struggling to put herself through school. Collapsing completely when Michael had dumped her. Subjecting herself to auditions over and over again, only to be told she was too fat or too tall or too blond. And now, hurtling up the 405 with the one man on Planet Earth she never wanted to see or speak to again.

But dammit, he was so good-looking and so earnest, and he smelled so good, just like she remembered, that it had been impossible to say no. But she was on to him—whatever he thought would come out of it, it would be nothing.

They chatted—civilly—about the film as they drove, and while Leah was managing to answer his questions—yes, she did scale the wall today, and no they hadn't started blocking the three battle scenes—all she could think of was how crazy she was, how absolutely stupid to think any-thing good could come of this, and how Lucy was going to absolutely howl when she told her. Only Lucy would be howling with laughter. Leah just hoped she would be able to howl along with her.

And what the hell was he doing in a T-bird, the car *she* was supposed to have? She couldn't help but imagine that if they had managed to stay together back then, she'd be liv-ing in some great place in Brentwood, driving the T-bird, owning tons of great shoes, and hosting dinner parties for big-cheese studio execs.

But they hadn't managed to stay together, which made this ride even more insane.

Then again, just to play devil's advocate—and because she was into suffering, remember—could it really hurt so much to have a chat for old times' sake? Because really, once her mind and heart had gotten over the shock of see-ing him again and had absorbed the fact that she really was talking to him after all these years, and that he had the T-bird and she didn't, it didn't hurt as bad as it had way back then. Now, it was more of a dull, vague ache than the open, gaping wound like the days and weeks and months after he dumped her.

At the great place Michael knew, they sat outside on cushy chairs and ordered martinis. The conversation was a little stilted at first—he asked about her family, she said they were fine. Then without thinking, she asked about his family, and there was an awkward silence.

Then Michael asked her about Brad.

"My roommate," Leah said. "We rent a house in Venice Beach."

"That's great," he said.

"No, not great," she said with a half smile. "It's a bun-galow that's run down and falling apart, and as a result, we rent it for dirt cheap."

"Ah," he said, and sipped his martini. One strand of dark hair fell across his forehead. She had the urge to brush that lock away from his eye like she used to. She sipped her martini and looked around the room.

"So . . ." Michael said casually, "is there anyone else besides Brad?"

"Nope. Just the two of us."

"I mean a guy," he said, sitting up and bracing his elbows on the arms of his chair.

"What sort of guy?"

"A *guy*," he said, smiling at her obstinate response. "A significant other, a fiancé, a husband—*that* sort of guy."

Leah inadvertently snorted into her drink. "Not at the moment."

"Good."

She smiled a little at how firmly he'd said it. "I'd ask the same of you," she said lightly, "but I think I know the answer."

"Oh yeah? So what's the answer, Smarty Pants?"

She shrugged, took a long sip of her martini. "It's not like it's hard to figure out. Extreme Bachelor—need I say more?" *Ha!* Michael actually colored a bit. She hoped he was squirming in his chair. "Your reputation precedes you, *Smarty Pants*."

He laughed uneasily, but his eyes crinkled in the corners, and his gaze, soft and deep and the color of warm molasses, seeped into her. "That's just talk," he said. "I've dated around, but it's not like they make it out to be. The truth is, there hasn't been anyone serious in my life since you."

The warm feeling sank a little deeper—but it also infuriated her. No one since her? He had no idea what that really meant. "Dated around," she said breezily. "Sounds kind of slutty."

Michael almost choked on his olive. "I didn't say I was sleeping around. I said I *dated* around."

"Oh. So you haven't slept around?"

He sighed. "Obviously, I don't know what I am saying."

Exactly. Leah smiled pertly, but she was suddenly

struck with an image of him in bed, having sex with a woman. "So has it always been that way?"

"What way?" he asked, his trepidation evident.

"Did you ever get married?"

"No," he said. "Did you?"

Oh yeah, right. Married, divorced, dating around . . . Leah rolled her eyes. "No. So you didn't marry an Austrian woman?" she blurted, hating herself for even asking.

Michael seemed surprised and considered her for a moment before answering, during which time, Leah realized she was holding her breath. "I didn't have a wife or a girlfriend or a mistress in Austria," he said quietly but firmly. "I was never even *in* Austria—I just told you I was. I was never unfaithful to you, Leah—at least not with another woman. I was unfaithful to you with my job."

Was that supposed to make her feel better? She'd been dumped for a job? She suddenly felt very self-conscious and glanced down, noticed she was almost out of martini.

"I'll get you another one," Michael said and signaled for the waitress before she could respond. That was the way he'd been—always knowing what she wanted or needed before she did.

Ooo-kay, clearly she had to stop this little trip down memory lane, because it was only making her crazy, taking her to the precise place she didn't want to go. *Light and carefree!* she chastised herself. *Definitely disinterested! Be disinterested!* "Don't try and get me drunk and take advantage of me," she said sternly.

"You don't get drunk, remember? Two is your limit," he said with a smile.

Man, he remembered a *lot,* which was making it very difficult to be light and carefree and disinterested. "And you usually don't drink at all," she said, the words coming from that part of her brain that refused to listen to common sense.

"I imbibe on occasion." He suddenly leaned forward, his arms on the table, grinning. "Do you remember the night in Cape Cod? Remember we had that punch—at least we thought it was punch—and we got so bloody drunk?"

"Don't remind me!" Leah protested with a wince, flicking her wrist at him. "All I remember is waking up the next morning with my head hanging off the bed, wishing I was dead."

"Believe me, I wanted to put you out of your misery," he said with a laugh. "I never heard such moaning in my life, and I was feeling pretty miserable myself."

"I was *dying*," she reminded him, tapping her fist on the table to emphasize just how close to dying she'd really come. "And you were *laughing* at me!"

"I wasn't laughing, baby, I was just trying to help."

That small term of endearment rolled off his tongue as if he'd never stopped saying it, and it hit Leah broadside, right upside the head, leaving her speechless. But one look at Michael's face, and it was obvious that not only had he stopped saying it a long time ago, to hear it now had been as bone-jolting to him as it had been to her. "Sorry," he muttered, and shoved a hand through his hair, forcing that lock out of his eyes. "Some habits are hard to break."

She nodded, wished to hell the waitress would appear with that second martini. "So what about the CIA thing, Michael?" she asked lightly, changing the subject. "What did you do?"

He hesitated. "Not a lot. Just some surveillance, that sort of thing."

"Oh come on. Surely you did more than that. I've seen all the Jason Bourne movies, so I know what goes on."

"Those movies are nothing like reality. The truth is, I filed a lot of paperwork and not much else."

"No!" Leah scoffed. "Come on, really—what did you do?"

"Just that. What? Do you want me to say I hung out with opium dealers and arms traders and terrorist types?"

"Yes, I want you to say that. Give me *something* here.

Did you have all the cool gadgets? Talking shoes and camera watches? A gun?"

"No, nothing like that," he said with a grin. "Just me. And a very deep cover. And a lot of paperwork is about all I can say."

"Come on, please don't tell me you dumped me for paperwork."

The smile bled from his face.

"Sorry," she said, holding up a hand. "But you did dump me." She was not going to cut him a break on that front.

"I know," he said, and looked around for the waitress. She was making her way across the room, two martinis on her tray.

"So?" she persisted. "At least tell me where you were."

He smiled enigmatically; it was extremely annoying.

"Can you at least tell me how you ended up in the movie business? I mean, as a casual observer, it doesn't exactly seem like a natural career path. You know, spy," she said, putting one hand down on the table. "Stuntman," she said, putting the other hand down on the other end of the table.

"I met Jack on a mission," he said. "We became friends. And then I reached a point where I was sick of living lies and watching my back all the time. I was ready to end that part of my career, but I figured I would end up at a desk job in Langley."

If only he had. She would have been spared this entire, mind-boggling emotional course. "So why didn't you?"

He shrugged. "Jack and I became friends because we both loved adventure. We'd hang out, doing some crazy things." He paused as the waitress set the two martinis down and thanked her with a smile that probably made her melt.

"Anyway," he said, as Leah took the martini and sipped, "about the time I got ready to quit, Jack had learned to fly anything with wings on the government's nickel and had retired from the Air Force."

"So . . . you guys decided to start your own stunt agency?" she asked, becoming less and less disinterested in what had happened to him.

"They did. I came in later. Essentially, Eli, Cooper, and Jack go way back. They grew up together in Texas and developed a love for sports—football, baseball, basketball, rodeo—whatever sport they could play, they played. But when regular sports got to be too easy, they began to create their own sports. They went swimming in mining holes, created dirt-bike trails through the canyons that apparently rivaled the professional circuit. They made a game out of breaking horses without using a bit, and built motorized conveyances that they would race across fallow cotton fields."

"Wow," Leah said, impressed.

"By the time they finished college, they were into the extreme side of sports in general. They were experts in white-water rafting, rock climbing, canyon jumping, kayaking, surfing, and skiing—a person could name a sport, any sport, and they had tried it. After college, Jack went into the Air Force. Cooper and Eli weren't as interested in flying as they were in jumping off buildings and blowing things up, so they headed out to Hollywood to hire on as stuntmen. They got their start working on some of the biggest action films in Hollywood, and before long, they were choreographing huge action sequences."

"They do know their stunts," Leah said wryly, still sore from yesterday's training.

"They do. On weekends, however, they trekked out to ocean kayak, or kite surf, or helicopter ski—whatever caught their imagination. But it wasn't until they got the bright idea to take a couple of pals along who just happened to be big stars that their outings began to be the talk around movie sets, and the next thing they knew, they were taking the Hollywood bigs along on their adventures. As a result, their adventures got even bigger. But what they did really well was to keep the press and paparazzi out of those jaunts."

"Really?" Leah asked. "Do they still do it? The adventures?"

He nodded. "Cooper came up with the idea of making a business out of their love of adventure. It was expensive to stage, but there were a growing number of Hollywood moguls who wanted the exclusive and exotic outings they offered, particularly if it came with the guarantee of total privacy. So when Jack started making noises about getting out of the Air Force, they convinced him to come to L.A. and join them, like the old days. They figured if they could provide their own transportation and fly their clients to their adventure destinations themselves, they'd be that much more mobile and private. That's when they founded Thrillseekers Anonymous."

"The stunt group?"

"That, and the members-only adventure club." At Leah's look of confusion, Michael said, "The motto is, 'Name Your Fantasy, and We'll Make It Happen.' We cater to an exclusive clientele who want extreme adventure with a lot of privacy and can afford to have both. Whatever they want—helicopter skiing, windsurfing, volcano hiking—we make it happen, and we guarantee their privacy."

That sounded like the coolest job on the planet, yet Leah still didn't understand how Michael had ended up with T.A. She remembered that he liked to ski and surf and golf—all the usual guy things—but she didn't remember that he'd ever been into extreme sports and said so.

"Oh yeah," he said, nodding, "I've always been into extreme sports. That is what I was trained to do."

"So how did you hook up with them?"

"I got out of the agency just as T.A. was starting to get a steady stream of high-profile, highly demanding and privacy-seeking clients, and Jack approached me about becoming a partner. I was reluctant at first—you're right; it wasn't exactly my career path. I was into extreme sports, true, but I'd never done any stunt work. And I was definitely the odd man out with those three—it was obvious they were real tight. But in the end, Jack convinced me I had something they needed."

"Which was?"

He looked a little sheepish. "Contacts. Worldwide contacts."

"They wanted you for your Rolodex?"

"You could say that," he said self-consciously. "I've just met a lot of interesting people along the way. Granted, most of them really were terrorists, or arms traders, or financiers who supported radical governments with the drug trade—but I've also met some solid, law-abiding people who knew how to get things done. Jack and the guys wanted me to bring those contacts to their organization . . . along with the utmost secrecy by which I'd cultivated those contacts."

"What are you saying?" Leah asked, confused. "You know kings and queens?"

Michael laughed. "What I'm saying is, if one of our clients is on a remote-island hike and wants a particular foie gras flown in at a moment's notice, I'm the T.A. guy who actually knows what foie gras is, but more importantly, I know where to get the *best* fois gras and how to get it to that island. Or if we have clients that want to hike some of the greatest red canyons in the Middle East for one of their adventures, I know who to call. Those sorts of contacts."

"Wow," Leah said, in awe. Here was Michael, the guy she'd loved and lost, the same guy she believed had been a very cute financial director with a pocket protector. It was a little hard to absorb that he was, in fact, some globetrotting sports guy with more contacts than Elvis. "Sounds like the CIA trained you well," she said, for lack of anything better to say.

"Yeah," he said. "They did."

Leah picked up her martini and took a sizeable swig of

it. "So is that it? Just the four of you?" she asked, still trying to wrap her mind around the notion that not only had the man she'd been so incredibly in love with been a globe-trotting spy, but he knew who to call in the Middle East if she should ever need a camel. How was that possible? And more importantly, how come she didn't get to know it at the time?

"There's one more person. We were contracted to a do a wedding in conjunction with an extreme sports outing for a couple of high-profile movie stars last year. But none of us knew anything about weddings, so we had to hire a wedding planner. Marnie Banks is her name. The wedding ended up not happening, but she stuck around, mainly because she and Eli ended up stranded on a mountain, and . . . and it's a long story," he said with a slight roll of his eyes. "But now they are talking about getting married."

"It sounds like a great job," Leah said.

"It is." He glanced down at his martini. "So . . . what did you do after I left?"

Talk about throwing a bucket of ice water on the party. What did he want to know? That she'd worn pajamas for weeks until Lucy made her change them? Or that she'd been almost incoherent for a month? That she'd felt like her heart had been ripped from her chest and smashed into pieces so small that she still couldn't find them after five years? Or perhaps he wanted to know how many letters she had written him, some of them begging him to come back, some of them condemning him to a fiery pit of hell?

"Leah?"

The question made her angry—a whole lot of stuff was suddenly bubbling up, all the crap that had taken years for her to lock away. And then he showed up unexpectedly, and it was all erupting all over again. "Nothing," she said brusquely.

"Did you get the sitcom deal?"

She stared daggers at him. A million retorts skated through her mind, but she said only, *"No."*

He looked surprised by that. "So you stayed on Broadway," he said.

"No."

His brow furrowed in confusion. "So . . . when did you come to L.A.?"

"About a year after . . . Look," she said suddenly, pushing the martini away from her. "It's not fair of you to even ask. If you can't tell me what happened to you, then I don't have to tell you what happened to me."

"Okay—"

"No, *not* okay, Michael," she said, feeling, inexplicably, angrier. "None of this is okay! I don't want to go back, all right? You should have left me alone when I asked you to," she said, and abruptly picked up her backpack, suddenly desperate to be out of there. "This was a huge mistake." She thrust her hand into her backpack and found her wallet.

"Why is it a mistake?" he asked as she took out her wallet.

"*Please*—It just is."

"Wait—what are you doing?" he asked as she opened her wallet. He put a hand on hers to stop her, but Leah yanked it away.

"I'm leaving."

"Leah, I am *sorry*," he said, and damn him if there wasn't a bit of exasperation in his voice, as if *she* were the one being unreasonable here. "I didn't mean to upset you. It's just that I've thought so much about you—"

"Right. Well you obviously didn't think enough of me to answer my letters," Leah snapped, and regretted the words the very instant they flew out of her mouth. That had been her problem all her life—speaking without thinking, always popping off before she could think.

"What letters?" he demanded.

"You know what letters."

"No, I *don't* know what letters," he said, and this time,

caught her wrist and held it firmly. Why that should re-mind her of sex, Leah had absolutely no idea . . . except that they had shared a mutual desire for experimentation, and there had been the time that he'd held her wrists high above her head—

"*What* letters?" Michael insisted, yanking her back to the present.

"What does it matter? You wouldn't have answered them. You wouldn't have written me back to tell me why—" Oh shit. Shit, shit, shit, this was her absolute worst nightmare because there were suddenly tears in her eyes. She could not let him see them, could not let him guess that there were times that she still ached for him, so Leah an-grily jerked her hand away from his grip and fumbled in her wallet for money.

"Put your money away," he said in a low, stern voice as he reached into his back pocket and withdrew his wallet.

"No. I'm going to pay."

"*Leah.* Put your wallet away. I brought you here, and I will damn well pay for it," he said, and fished out several bills and threw them on the table. He stood up, put a hand on the back of her chair, but Leah was already standing be-fore he could do one lousy gentlemanly thing to upset her even more.

They marched out of the restaurant, Michael slightly behind her, Leah desperate to get away from him. "I'm go-ing to take a cab," she said, looking up the street.

"Don't be ridiculous. A cab would cost you a fortune from here to Venice Beach."

"I'm not being ridiculous."

"Yes you are. Just relax. I'm going to take you home. I am not going to torture you or ask you a lot of questions, or touch you," he said, and in a complete contradiction, he took hold of her elbow and steered her toward the parking lot.

"Do you *mind*?" she asked, pulling her elbow from his hand.

"Fine," he snapped, and made a grand, sweeping gesture toward his car, indicating she should precede him.

She preceded him, all right, striding forward with the determination of a woman who wanted to end a really bad date. In fact, she didn't wait for him to open the car door, but did it herself, tossing her backpack to the floor and crawling in over it. When she had seated herself, Michael leaned over, his eyes hard. "All good?"

"All good," she snapped, and looked forward.

He got in the car, started it up, pulled out of the parking lot at a speed Leah did not think was particularly safe, but came to an abrupt halt at the street. He sat there, one hand on the wheel, one on the gear shift, staring straight ahead until a guy behind them honked for Michael to move.

He pulled out in a screech of wheels onto Montana Avenue.

It seemed only minutes before they were on Venice Boulevard and Leah was directing Michael to her house. When they pulled into the drive, she took one look at the yellowing grass, the trash can that was still lying on the street from two days ago, the pile of shoes near the front door, and—dear God, how embarrassing—her half-finished origami peacock. Brad had moved it from the kitchen table to the porch, and there it sat in all of its half-finished glory, with a pair of men's briefs dangling from its head.

She wished she could crawl in a hole. She was thirty-four years old, and she lived in the middle of a scene right out of *Animal House*.

"Thanks," she said crisply, grabbed her backpack, and opened the door. So did Michael. "What are you doing?" she demanded as she shut the passenger door and slung her backpack over one shoulder.

He responded by striding around the front of the car to stand between her and the house, his hands on his hips. "I see you are still doing origami. I see it has gotten even bigger."

Her eyes narrowed. "You have a problem with big origami?"

"Not at all," he said. "But you like the small, delicate stuff. That is why you paid a small fortune to take the class with that origami master—to get your scale under control."

"Goddammit, is there *anything* you've forgotten? I was only in that class for a week, and you remember that?"

"You didn't even make it a week. You made it exactly two nights before you decided you were in over your head. But that is what I am trying to tell you, Leah—"

"What, that I am in over my head?"

"No," he said, his jaw tight, his patience obviously being tested. "I am trying to tell you that I remember. I remember *everything*," he said. "I remember the origami, the acting, and how you hated the makeup guy on your last play. I remember how you looked in the morning when your hair was all messed up and how you wore my shirts that just barely covered your lovely butt, and how frantic you would get when you couldn't find your keys."

Her heart leapt, began to beat frenetically. She quickly threw up a hand and held it out. "Stop! Stop it right now! Jesus, Michael, have you heard a word I've said? I don't *want* to remember!" she cried, and dropped her arm, tried to step around him, but he blocked her path and caught her by the shoulders. And in spite of her cry of indignation, he forced her to look up, to look at him. There was a glint in his eyes as if he had no intention of ever letting her go.

"I remember how you used to laugh at my stupid jokes and how we'd make spaghetti and fling it at the wall to see if it stuck, and how I never saw a single Monday night football game the entire time we were together, because there was that stupid cooking show you refused to miss."

"Okay, all *right*," she said, and feeling overwhelmed and angry, she grabbed his wrist, tried to pull it from her shoulder. "You remember. Congratulations! But it still doesn't change anything!"

"I remember," he said, pulling her closer, "how you taste, how you smell, and how you look completely naked." His gaze dropped to her breasts.

She was on the verge of crumbling. "Oh God, please don't do this," she pleaded.

"I remember the little smile you have on your face when you sleep and how you moved all my stuff in the bathroom to the bottom drawer to make room for all your things."

Leah remembered all that, too, and more. She closed her eyes and dropped her head back, remembering what he looked like naked, how hot and hard he felt inside her, the way he moved, driving her crazy. How he'd make her breakfast the next morning and serve it in bed, nibbling on her toes while she nibbled toast. She didn't dare open her eyes, didn't dare look at him, for fear of crumbling completely.

But Michael pulled her a little closer and whispered in her ear, "I remember how we used to make love, baby. I remember how to make you come."

Dammit! Leah couldn't help herself—she opened her eyes, saw the desire swimming in his eyes just before he lowered his head to kiss her neck.

She gasped with shock when his lips touched her skin. He skimmed her neck and face, a whisper on her skin, until he touched his lips to her mouth. It was a sweet, tender kiss, but it seared her like a branding iron. His lips were a salve on an old wound—so soft, so perfect. And then his hands were suddenly on either side of her face, cupping it, lifting her chin so that he could kiss her reverently, tasting her, sampling her. She could smell him, could feel the warmth of his body so close to hers, and she felt herself falling and falling, back to the place they'd once been.

That kiss, so wholly unexpected, so astonishingly desired, knocked Leah into a tailspin, sent her reeling and her heart tumbling off its shelf. His lips drifted across hers, tantalizing her. His arm slipped around her waist, pulling her closer, so that her breasts were pressed against his chest, and his erection pressed against her abdomen. His body, hard and familiar, made her want to sink into him, to feel his arms securely around her and his strength infuse her.

But when his hand found her ribcage and slid up to her breast, Leah mentally tripped and fell flat on her back. Rocked by the sensation of being in his arms again, her heart cried out to her to stop, to protect whatever little piece of her that was left, reminding her how deep and painful the hurt had been, and Leah suddenly recoiled, jerking back and away from him as if she'd been burned.

The smile that registered Michael's surprise was so damn sexy that Leah was astounded she was able to resist the urge to fall to her knees and sob. Instead, she found the strength to peel his hands from her body. "How *dare* you," she said hoarsely. "How *dare* you do this to me now, after the damage you've done?"

"Damage? Come on, Leah. I made a mistake." He touched her cheek with the back of his hand, stroked her chin with his knuckle. "I made a mistake," he said again.

"Me too," she said breathlessly, still feeling his lips on her mouth. "A huge, colossal mistake."

"I didn't mean just now. I meant before. I should never have let you go, baby. I am asking for another chance. I want to start over, Leah. I want to pick up where we left off, keep going and never look back, because I have never stopped wanting you, not once. No woman has ever compared to you, and I realized—too late, but I realized—that I'd been a fucking fool. Give me another chance. I promise you won't be sorry."

She was stunned. What was this? Was he crazy? He didn't mean what he said, he couldn't mean it, and she shook her head, pushed her hair behind her ears, and stepped back, away from him, despising him for the look of abject disappointment in his eyes. "Why didn't you say that five years ago when I desperately needed to hear it?"

she blurted. "We *can't* go back, Michael. Too much happened between us, and too much damage was done, and too much time has passed."

"Damage," he repeated skeptically.

"Damage," she whispered. "I didn't go to Hollywood because I was too devastated to function, did you know that? I was so stunned and hurt and wounded that I couldn't even get off my goddam couch, Michael."

"You—"

"I lost everything!" she exclaimed, interrupting him, throwing her arms wide. "I was paralyzed with grief! I couldn't function, I couldn't act, I could barely form a coherent sentence."

He looked stunned. Horrified. And still it wasn't enough.

"You want to know what happened to me after you dumped me? My agent eventually stopped calling me, and finally sent me a letter severing our relationship. My friends from Broadway went on with their lives and kept their distance because they were afraid I would jinx them somehow. I felt like the whole world had faded from view, and it was months—*months*—before I could face it again. But by then it was too late. I had grieved myself into a black hole and no one would touch me. And now you come prancing back into my life five years later and say you're *sorry*?" A shout of hysterical laughter escaped her. "Save your breath," she said, her voice shaking. "I will *never* go back to you."

He looked devastated and reached for her face. "God. I'm . . . I'm so *sorry*, Leah."

"Sorry?" she repeated, and slapped his hand away. "Jesus, Michael, do you have any idea how much I *loved* you?" she asked, as tears suddenly filled her eyes.

"I loved you, too," he said quietly.

She gasped with shock. "Ohmigod, you would say that *now*?" she whispered tearfully.

"You need to know it."

"What I know is that if it is true, if you really did love me, then what you did is even more insidious."

Michael looked as if she'd slapped him. "Good," she said bitterly, swiping at the tears beneath her eyes. "I hope you feel awful, because God knows you left me to feel much worse than that."

She had to get out of there, get someplace where she could just breathe, and started walking toward the house, unable to look at him, unable to even think.

"Leah!" he called after her.

She closed her eyes, told herself to keep walking, but the masochistic part of her that apparently loved as much pain as he could heap on her stopped and turned around.

He was standing there, his head low, that lock of hair hanging over his eye. "Before you go . . . I have to tell you there is nothing wrong with your car. It was just a loose battery cable."

Her mouth dropped open. "You *lied*?"

"Yes, I lied. I lied because I had to talk to you. I'll send a car for you in the morning and have your car fixed while you're at work." And with that, he turned away, walked around to the driver's side of the car. A moment later, he was backing out of her drive without looking back.

Yet Leah stood in her ugly yard long after his car had disappeared around the corner, her head pounding with memories and feelings and the very strong sense that she had just stepped off the edge into an abyss.

Subject: The Chartreuse Dress
From: Lucy Frederick <ljfreddie@hotmail.com>
To: Leah Kleinschmidt <hollywoodiva@verizon.net>
Date: 12:02 am

Okay, you cannot possibly find fault with the attached dress. I know it's not gold, but I've rethought the whole color thing. And oh, I found THE cutest guaranteed-to-get-you-laid shoes ever! They are three-inch heels, straps that go around the ankles, and very sparkly gold. If you say you don't like them, you are not going to be my maid of honor, because I really really want those shoes! Can't wait to hear what you think.

Subject: Re: The Chartreuse Dress
From: Leah Kleinschmidt <hollywoodiva@verizon.net>
To: Lucy Frederick <ljfreddie@hotmail.com>
Date: 9:15 pm

Dress looks great. Shoes sound fab.

Subject: Re: Re: The Chartreuse Dress
From: Lucy Frederick <ljfreddie@hotmail.com>
To: Leah Kleinschmidt <hollywoodiva@verizon.net>
Date: 12:24 am

Okay, what's going on? The last time you answered with exactly six words, you thought you were dying with that disease you found on the internet. What happened? You didn't do anything stupid did you, Leah?

Subject: Re: Re: Re: The Chartreuse Dress
From: Lucy Frederick <ljfreddie@hotmail.com>
To: Leah Kleinschmidt <hollywoodiva@verizon.net>
Date: 12:40 am

HEELLL-LLLOOOH! WHAT DID YOU DO???

ELEVEN

IT was the worst night Michael had spent in years.

There had been only a couple of times in his life that he'd felt such despair—once, as a kid, being removed from the one foster home where he'd ever felt safe and put in yet another foster home. And then again on his last covert assignment in Spain, when he wondered every single day if they'd figured out who he was and if he might not leave that country alive.

But as bad as those times had been, he'd never cried. He couldn't even remember the last time he cried. But the memory of Leah's face as she described her despair after he'd left prompted big, fat, salty tears of deep, soul-aching regret to slide out of his eyes as he tossed and turned between the sheets, berating himself.

She was right, of course—what he'd done was insidious. What made him think he could just waltz back into her life and pick up where they'd left off? What in the hell had made him think that after dumping her, as she had so succinctly put it—and man, he'd done such a number on his own head that at the time, he honestly believed he was doing her a favor—that she would merrily let him into her life again?

It was a little distressing to discover that, at the age of thirty-eight, he could still be such an idiot.

But idiocy aside, he felt a searing need to prove to her that he really had loved her, even if he'd never been able to bring himself to say it. That his leaving had been the work of a coward—there was no other word for it—and he would never forgive himself for it. In a lifetime of trying, he'd still never make it up to her.

He also felt compelled to show her that he wasn't really an extreme bachelor, which, in her mind, apparently, had been equated to the words *male slut*. She really held him in high regard, didn't she?

Yeah, well, he deserved every bit of her disdain, and he knew it. Nevertheless, he was ready to prove himself to her, to do whatever it took. But that was the problem that had him tossing and turning all night—he really didn't know *whatever it took* meant.

Unfortunately, he didn't have a lot of experience in wooing women. Usually, all it took from him was a little friendliness, a casual display of interest, and the women he ended up dating took it from there. Women who would, after just a couple of dinners and something like an afternoon of sailing, leave him little notes of affection, buy him small gifts to commemorate their dates, and make changes in their schedules to accommodate his. Inevitably, after such few dates, they'd begin to talk about their feelings, and worse, ask about *his* feelings before he was able to reciprocate anything but friendship and general pleasure in their company. If even that.

One of the big cosmic mysteries to him was why women were so eager to do a full belly flop into their relationships. Why did they feel compelled to spill their guts about their dreams and desires after a couple of good steak dinners?

Hey, he loved having women around, loved hanging out with them. But they had a way of making him feel incredibly uncomfortable with four little words: *We need to talk.* There wasn't anything in the entire universe that made him want to run faster or harder than those four words.

How ironic it was that he'd been the one to do it this time. Obviously, he sucked at it. Yet he knew—he *knew*—he could succeed if he proceeded cautiously. He knew that because he knew Leah, and after that kiss, he knew there was something in her yet, a desire or need or whatever it was called—just something she still held for him inside her. He had tasted a certain hunger on her lips that was there for him to sate if he could find his way to her. But to find her, he'd have to step carefully through the minefield of her emotions and hurt and disillusionment and all the things that he'd heaped on her.

What he needed, he realized, was a map.

His mood was not improved the next morning when he arrived at work and found Jack grinning from ear to ear. "What?" Michael demanded irritably as he walked into the ten-by-ten closet they were calling an office at the boot camp.

Jack swiveled around in his chair away from the computer screen to face Michael and leaned back, laced his fingers behind his head, looking way too smug. "Been out to the course yet?" he asked, referring to the mock battlefield they had set up.

"No. Why?"

Jack grinned. "No reason. Just wondered if you'd seen it yet."

"Seen *what*?" Michael snapped. If there was one thing he hated, it was fun and games before his first cup of coffee.

But Jack just laughed, swiveled around in his chair to face the computer again, and said, "By the way, we start blocking battle scenes Monday."

Michael tossed down his satchel and walked out of the

office, striding toward the commissary tent for some coffee.

It didn't take him more than a moment to see what had
Jack in stitches—they were everywhere. Four hundred
dollars worth of orchids—bought at a premium last night
as the flower shop was closing, just so he could get them
into the damn car he'd sent for Leah this morning—were
adorning the ponytails and waistbands of the women as
they warmed up, getting ready for the day.

He'd meant for the four large blooming plants to fill the
backseat of the car with a simple note that said *I remember.* He'd meant them to serve as a reminder of how he used
to send her orchids, every Monday morning. He'd meant
for her to take them *out* of the car and put them in her
house.

So much for his attempts at sentimentality.

"Hey, Michael!" He glanced to his right, saw Jamie and
Michele. Jamie pointed to the orchid stuffed carelessly behind her ear. "You have great taste!" The two of them obviously thought that was hilarious, judging by how they
dissolved into laughter as they walked on.

With a sigh, Michael walked into the commissary tent
and picked up a foam cup.

"What do you think, Michael? Does this flower match
my sweater?"

Great. Michael suppressed a sigh and turned to see
Nicole, who was hanging out around boot camp again. She
had the orchid stuck in her recently purchased cleavage,
which was amply displayed in a tiny little top with spaghetti
straps.

"Love it," he drawled. "Nobody wears an orchid better
than you, sweetheart."

She looked down as she put her hands against her breasts
and pushed them together, making the flower bounce. "It's
nice, isn't it?" she asked with a little laugh. "Just curious,
Mikey—how come you never sent *me* a busload of orchids?"

"Nicki—"

"Oh, don't worry," she said, flicking her wrist at him with one hand as she rearranged the flower with her other. "I'm just giving you the business, baby, that's all. Besides, you sent me roses, remember? Yellow roses. And that's exactly what I told what's-her-name this morning."

The day just kept getting better and better, and it wasn't even nine o'clock yet. "Nicki, what else did you tell her?"

She winked. "Just that every girl has her favorite flower, which is why you have a frequent flyer card at the local florist." She laughed at his sigh of exasperation. "You should really be more original, Michael."

"You're right. I should be." He winked at her and turned away, opened the spigot in the big coffee urn and filled up his cup while Nicole stood there, waiting for him to say something more. When he didn't, she clucked at him. "Don't be like that Michael," she purred. "It's not like I care if you are seeing her. Do whatever you want, I don't care."

He picked up his cup, took a sip, smiled charmingly at Nicole, and touched her flower before lifting his gaze to hers. "While I appreciate your permission, I am not seeing her." And he walked away.

He could almost feel the daggers from Nicole's eyes in his back.

He walked out of the tent, back to the little office, and groaned when he saw that all of T.A. was fully present and accounted for.

Jack started chuckling the moment Michael entered, which made Cooper and Eli look up and around. "What's so funny?" Cooper asked.

"Mikey is having some issues," Jack offered.

"Oh yeah?" Eli asked, looking at Michael curiously. "Not more budget issues, I hope."

"Oh hell no, not budget," Jack said, swiveling around in his squeaky seat again. "Mikey's having issues of a more *feminine* nature."

That certainly garnered Eli and Cooper's attention—simultaneously, they broke into wide, gleeful grins.

"Say it ain't so!" Cooper laughed. "Not *Mikey*. Not our golden boy, who's never had a feminine issue in his whole sorry life!"

"Now Coop, go easy," Eli said, grinning just as broadly as the other two bastards. "Every dog has his day."

In response, Michael slapped Cooper's boots down from the only empty chair in the room so he could sit down.

"So who is it this time?" Eli asked. "The brunette with the big sunglasses?"

"Who, Yin?" Cooper asked, and wrinkled his nose. "That one has as a mouth on her. But I'll give you credit for having picked a looker."

"Actually," Jack said, leaning forward between Eli and Cooper. "It's Yang."

"Yang!" Eli whistled at that. "Now *that* is one fine-looking woman. I'll tell you what, if I weren't otherwise attached, that gal is the one I'd be following around like a hound dog," he said, nodding enthusiastically. "And she's a little more coordinated than the others. That's a plus."

Michael had to wonder about a guy who thought coordination on an obstacle course was actually a plus.

"So what's the deal?" Cooper asked, and leaned forward to clap Michael on the shoulder. "Something we can help you with? A few bedroom tips? New moves?"

Michael couldn't help but laugh wryly at that. "The day I need tips from you is the day I shoot myself." That earned a round of guffaws.

"Come on, Mikey, tell us," Jack urged him. "We're your partners. We're here to help."

"Like hell you are. And besides, there's nothing to tell."

"Who are you kidding? You forget I saw you do that weird little jump in New York when you saw her," Jack reminded him.

"New York?" Cooper asked, squinting at Michael.

"He saw her in a commercial and almost came out of his shorts," Jack happily explained.

Cooper, Eli, and Jack looked to Michael for confirmation. He shrugged his answer, which prompted a round of very loud howls.

"A *commercial*?" Eli gasped through his laughter.

"A *laxative* commercial!" Jack squealed, and the three of them doubled over with laughter again.

Fortunately, Michael had a healthy sense of self. Otherwise, he might have been highly offended. But he knew these jokers and just sipped his coffee until they'd laughed themselves dry.

"Okay, okay," Cooper said, wiping a tear from beneath his eye. "Since when do you fall for the chick in a laxative commercial?"

"I didn't fall for the chick in a laxative commercial," Michael said evenly. "I knew her a long time ago. And I . . ." He *what*? He swallowed hard, but couldn't seem to force the words.

"And you . . . what?" Jack asked, still smiling.

"I ah . . . I . . . *ahem* . . . I guess I had a . . ." He gestured lamely. "Had a *thing* for her," he muttered.

That was met with silence all around—all three men were staring at him as if he'd suddenly sprouted a couple of extra noses.

Cooper was the first to speak. "*You* had a thing for a woman? Like a *real* thing? Like Eli-has-for-Marnie thing?"

With a sigh, Michael nodded. "You could say that."

"I'll be damned," Jack said, leaning back in his seat as Michael took another sip of coffee. "I'll be damned."

"What?" Michael said, suddenly coming to his feet. "What's the big deal? You guys act like you've never had a thing for a woman before."

"Whether we have or we haven't, the fascinating thing is that *you've* never had a real thing for a woman that we know of," Eli said. "So if you do, that's great. What's the problem?"

Everything was the problem. That he was sitting here having this conversation was a problem. He sat back down, braced his arms on his knees and looked at the guys. "The problem is that I dumped her a few years ago. And now she doesn't want anything to do with me."

No one said anything for a moment. Cooper looked at Jack, who looked at Eli. Eli looked a little smug as he stretched his long legs in front of him and shoved his hands in his pockets. "Women. They're a tough crowd."

"You can't rely on them to think rationally," Jack added.

"When it comes to women, you gotta play balls to the walls," Cooper said, "or they will eat you with eggs over easy for breakfast. It's that simple."

"Okay. Here's what you do," Eli drawled. "You gotta make her want you. You gotta make her think you are the only guy out here and the one she has to have."

"Okay," Michael said, nodding. "And how do you suggest I do that?"

Eli shrugged. "Hell if I know."

"Look," Cooper said with great authority. "If you want her to come around, you have to show her you are her friend first, *then* a healthy male wanting in her pants."

"Pull out all the stops," Jack added. "They like big, fancy stuff."

Honestly, these were the last guys Michael needed any advice from, and frankly, between their lame suggestions and the dozens of orchids floating around out there, he realized this was going to be a long damn day.

Subject: Guess What Now
From: Leah Kleinschmidt <hollywoodiva@verizon.net>
To: Lucy Frederick <ljfreddie@hotmail.com>
Date: 6:50 pm

So get a load of this. Michael sent a car for me this morning because my piece of shit car broke down, and it was filled with the most beautiful orchid plants I have ever seen. The car, I mean. Can you believe that? I thought it was so sweet until I got to work and Trudy almost coughed up a spleen. She said that was the sweetest thing she'd ever seen a guy do (and of course we had to listen to how her lousy-assed boyfriend has never done anything nice for her, which obviously begs the question of why she is still with him, to which the answer is—and I know this because I have asked—he pays the rent, basically). But then Nicole Redding comes up (yes, THAT Nicole Redding) and hears the conversation and helped herself to one of the orchids and announces that Michael often sends her yellow roses. Apparently, it is his M.O. Can you believe him?? I guess he thinks I am stupid or desperate enough to fall for it.

Subject: Re: Guess What Now
From: Lucy Frederick <ljfreddie@hotmail.com>
To: Leah Kleinschmidt <hollywoodiva@verizon.net>
Date: 9:59 am

What the hell is going on out there? Last night you wouldn't even talk and tonight you are telling me he sent you orchids?? He's obviously trying to apologize or something. Just let him keep trying, and maybe he'll cough up something really cool, like earrings from Tiffany's. Hold out for as long as you can. But really, girl, don't get sucked in. He'll just crush you again. Leopards don't change their spots.

Okay, back to me. Are you really okay with chartreuse? I thought it was a little too yellow-y.

Subject: Re: Re: Guess What Now
From: Leah Kleinschmidt <hollywoodiva@verizon.net>
To: Lucy Frederick <ljfreddie@hotmail.com>
Date: 7:12 pm

I am SORT of okay with chartreuse. I don't really think it is my best color, but hey, if that is what you want me to wear, I am so going to wear it.

Subject: Re: Re: Re: Guess What Now
From: Lucy Frederick <ljfreddie@hotmail.com>
To: Leah Kleinschmidt <hollywoodiva@verizon.net>
Date: 10:15 pm

So I am thinking about a really pale yellow. Almost cream-colored. I am sending you a picture in the next minute. Look at it and tell me what you think.

Subject: Re: Re: Re: Re: Guess What Now
From: Leah Kleinschmidt <hollywoodiva@verizon.net>
To: Lucy Frederick <ljfreddie@hotmail.com>
Date: 7:29 pm

Okay, I LOVE the color. But I sincerely hope that is not the dress. I can't believe they even make pouffy sleeves anymore, Lucy. Girl, this is the 21st century, so you have to accept it—disco is dead! And so is that dress!

TWELVE

TRUDY, Michele, and Jamie were waiting for Leah Monday morning, all three of them behind new, giant sunglasses.

"What's this?" Leah asked as she walked into their midst. "I didn't get the bug-eye memo."

Jamie lifted hers and squinted at Leah. "Trudy bought them for us at Marshalls. They were having a sale."

"Don't worry, Leah," Trudy said as she flicked a long ash from her smoke. "I have a pair for you, too." She took a drag off the cigarette and blew smoke. "By the way, I don't see anything."

"See what?" Leah asked.

"Flowers. Diamonds. Anything the Extreme Bachelor might have shown up with to lure you into his den of *luu-uuv.*"

Michele and Jamie sniggered. One would think the three of them had laughed enough yesterday, when they had screeched like night owls over the orchids.

Leah waved Trudy's smoke from her face. "After yesterday, I don't think we need to worry about orchids."

"Good thing," Michele piped up. "Nicole Redding was fit to be tied yesterday, and you are on her team now."

"She was?" Leah asked, surprised.

"Mm-hmm," Michele said, nodding with great authority. "Everyone knows she's still got a thing for the Extreme Bachelor. Apparently, *he* broke up with *her,* and Nicole doesn't like being blown off. Can you even *imagine* breaking up with a big star?"

Frankly, Leah didn't want to imagine Michael with Nicole at all. "Well it just goes to show you," she said, adjusting her backpack. "You can't trust a carload of orchids."

"So how do you know him, again?" Jamie asked, her shades back down.

"I knew him a few years ago in New York."

"You dated, right?"

Why did the word *date* sound so trivial? It had been so much more to her, so much deeper. She avoided Jamie's gaze. "Right," she said with a shrug. "It was a long time ago."

"I think he is regretting the breakup, or whatever it was," Jamie said as they turned to walk into the gym. "Orchids are not cheap. It was really sweet."

"Don't let them fool you," Leah uttered, and began walking.

She wouldn't admit it, of course, but that was the thing sticking in the back of her mind, too. Not only were orchids not cheap, but they weren't exactly easy to find on such short notice. And the note. The *note.* It still gave her a shiver, those two little words, *I remember.* She would have kept the flowers, but Nicole Redding had made her feel so small and inconsequential with all her talk of dating Michael, and Trudy had laughed at the whole thing, and Leah had suddenly felt like a chump. That was why she had torn the flowers off the tree and handed them around.

But the rest of the women thought the gesture of orchids was swoon-worthy, judging by the way some of them were surrounding him yesterday, hanging on his every word. She could practically see them drooling when he'd smile and touch the flower they wore in their hair, or make some complimentary remark. *Great,* she thought. *Have at it.*

But this morning, for reasons she did not understand, she was regretting that act. She didn't want any of them to have the orchids.

The four of them walked into the gym and were met at the door by a perky girl who looked like she might be all of twelve, who cheerfully told them they would begin scene blocking today. She asked for their names, checked them off of a list, and told them where to report after changing into scene-blocking clothing, which the four of them took to mean shorts and T-shirts.

Fortunately, Trudy and Leah were in the same group, assigned to the western half of an old empty bay, one street over on the lot. They walked over a quarter of an hour later, pausing between buildings so Trudy could smoke. "I really ought to give up the damn things," she said, grinding the butt out with the heel of her sneaker. When they arrived, there were a handful of soccer moms milling about, one of the stunt doubles, a couple of people in street clothes sitting in chairs—there were *always* a couple of people in street clothes sitting in chairs—and Michael and Jack were standing at the far end, looking at some paper, both of them dressed in knee-length jersey shorts.

Her heart skipped—after the other night, she wasn't ready to appreciate how hot he was in flimsy jersey pants. She hadn't remembered how muscular he was—he had a butt that wouldn't quit, sturdy, well-shaped legs, and broad shoulders. When she looked at his arms, she was reminded of a day they had spent on Rex's boat off Long Island. The winds had been calm, and they had been floating in serene waters. She and Michael were on a deck chair, his arms wrapped securely around her, arms that held her like two bands of steel, and he'd said, *"I wish this day would never end."* Had he known then he'd be leaving soon? Had he truly regretted it?

"Hey, this should be good," Trudy said, her face lighting up as she took in the group. "I'm starting to really like Jack, ya know? He's got that sexy super-stud thang going on," she said, and tossed her tote bag against the wall. "And fortunately for him, I've got that sexy super-chick thang going on," she added with a salacious wink, and sashayed away, her eyes locked on Jack.

Leah hadn't noticed until that moment how *short* Trudy's shorts were.

As for her, she was wearing yoga pants. Since that day she had hung from the harness with her ass on display for all of Los Angeles to see, she'd stuck to clothing with legs.

She looked past Trudy, noticed Michael was talking to a Starlet, his arm braced against the wall, that killer smile shining on the Starlet, who was smiling back like a simpleton. Leah turned away. She didn't need to see that, and walked to the opposite end of the room to stretch a little before they got started. She spread her legs wide and bent over, letting her arms hang, stretching her back. She closed her eyes, practiced some breathing, and when she opened them, she saw, through a curtain of her blond hair, his sneakers. Leah bobbed back up so quickly that she felt a rush of blood leave her head, and swayed a little.

"Whoa," he said, catching her by the elbow. "You okay?" he asked.

Her gaze instantly fell to his lips, which of course reminded her of that fabulous kiss, which naturally reminded her of sex—honestly, she was always thinking of sex when he was around. "Yeah," she said, moving back a little. She put her hands on the small of her back and bent backward. "Actually, I'm *great.*"

"That's good. We have a lot of work to accomplish today."

"I'm ready!" she chirped, shaking one leg, then the other, before bending backward again.

Michael nodded, folded his arms across his chest, watching her as she bent backward, straightened, then bent backward again. "So . . ." he said, as she leaned to one side. "I take it you're not a big fan of orchids anymore?"

Bent to one side, Leah puffed out her cheeks a minute as she considered the question, then released the air. "They sort of lost their appeal," she said, very matter-of-factly. "You know, when everyone started getting flowers."

"Hey," Michael said, holding up a hand, looking damnably sexy. "No one else got orchids."

"Orchids, roses, whatever," she said with a shrug, and leaned to the other side. "Just seemed overdone."

"Okay. But just so you know, *you* were the only one to ever get flowers from me on Mondays. *Every* Monday. And you were definitely the only one who ever got orchids."

"Oh, really?" Leah asked nonchalantly. "I heard you were pretty good about handing yellow roses around, too."

"Nicole," he responded with a sigh.

"Nicole. Jill. Lindsey, the P.A." She frowned thoughtfully. "Honestly, Michael, when did you have time to date all these women? I mean, you're only thirty-eight, and there are only so many days—"

"I only sent Nicole flowers once," he said, ignoring her question. "Yellow roses, it's true—but I sent them because she had been nominated for a Golden Globe award."

"Huh," Leah said, and bent at the waist again, hanging down.

Michael squatted down next to her, cocking his head to see her face. "But I didn't send Nicole Redding flowers because I loved her smile. That was why I sent *you* flowers. And I didn't send flowers to Nicole every Monday because I needed to see that smile to make my week. That was *your* smile that made my day, and I've never seen one that could match it or take its place."

Leah bounced up straight again. She pushed her hands through her hair. "That's really sweet," she said. "But I don't want your orchids."

Michael blinked. "Okay," he said slowly. "So what would you prefer? Roses? Tulips? Larkspur?"

"Larkspur?" she echoed. "No. Nothing." She put her hands on her waist and twisted one way, then the other, because if she looked in his eyes, she'd cave.

"Then maybe you'll let me explain about Nicole—"

"Hey, no need," she said quickly. "I get it." At least she thought she was getting it, and while she wouldn't mind maybe a *little* explanation about what exactly had gone on between him and Nicole, she just kept stretching her arms high overhead and looking past him.

But he suddenly stepped in her line of sight and looked at her suspiciously. "Have you been talking to Lucy, by any chance?"

Leah dropped her arms. "Why?"

"Just a guess," he said with a slight roll of his eyes.

"What's that supposed to mean? Lucy is my best friend!"

"I know. It's just that Lucy has a way of . . . let's just say, coloring things."

"Well," Leah sniffed, and pressed her lips together. She didn't have much to say to that because it was so true. Usually. "Not this time," she said, and looked to where the other women were milling about. "So when do we start?"

"You and me? Hard to say," he said with a warm smile. "I'm hoping we start over before we've wrapped this film. In the meantime, do me a favor, would you? Tell Lucy that I am very sorry, that I am trying to grovel, and I will do anything for a second chance, so if she has any suggestions, I'd love to hear them."

Melting. She could feel herself melting a little. "I'll be sure and tell her all that, and how you are trying to impress me with orchids, just like you try to impress all the girls."

"Okay, now, we covered that," he reminded her amicably.

"I don't give flowers to all the girls, and I only gave orchids to you. And besides, you love orchids. You should be impressed," he added with a captivating grin.

"Aha!" she said, pointing at him accusingly. "But I don't love orchids anymore. That's what you aren't getting."

"Okay," he said, nodding thoughtfully. "Message received and duly filed away."

"Well. *Good.*"

He glanced down, his gaze roaming her body to her shoes and back. "Hope you're limbered up."

"Oh," she said, nodding adamantly, "I'm *limbered.*"

He chuckled as he walked away, and she wondered if she'd really just won the battle. And damn, he did look fine walking away, the tenacious, persistent, charming bastard.

She was still admiring his butt when Trudy joined her and looked in the direction Leah was looking. "What did Lover Boy have to say?" she asked.

"Him? Nothing," Leah said, and turned away. "So how'd you do with Jack?"

Trudy snorted. "I had to take a number. What a dilemma, huh? I want one of the guys, and he hasn't noticed me. One of the guys wants you, but you won't take sloppy seconds . . ." She sighed. "It's enough to make a grown girl come to work without makeup."

"At least you already have a boyfriend," Leah muttered, stealing another glimpse of Michael as he stopped to talk to a Starlet, noticing how his smile lit up the whole bay . . . not to mention the Starlet. Christ, there were a lot of women on this film!

"Please," Trudy snorted. "Rick is easy, that's all. Come on, let's go smoke before they begin torturing us for the day." And linking her arm through Leah's, Yin led Yang out the door.

THE blocking was more difficult than any of the women had anticipated. They worked through tuck and rolls, then diving belly flops onto the mats. And before lunch, they practiced flying backward, with Jack and Michael catching them.

Over and over again, they flew, and over and over again, Michael caught Leah, his arms going around her, holding her tight. Every catch reminded her of being in his arms—in a cab, on the subway, on Rex's boat, in bed. Every bit of contact took her back five years, to a man she loved but who had been a lie. Every bit of her memory was really a phantom, of someone who hadn't really existed, who claimed to have loved her and had left her. That's what made it so painful now—as tempting as his entreaty was, she couldn't trust him . . . could she?

By the time the lunch hour rolled around, Leah couldn't wait to get outside and away from the conflicts in her head.

She grabbed her bag, walked out, and checked her cell. There was a call from her agent, Frances. While Trudy was yakking the ear off of a Serious Actress, Leah walked off in the opposite direction of the commissary and wandered around the back lot, looking for a little peace and quiet to return the call. She finally parked herself on a box and dialed. "Hey, Frances, it's Leah," she said when she got Frances on the phone.

"Oh hi, sweetie. Well, the WB folks want a brunette for the part of Chloe, so they are passing on us."

"But I can dye my hair!" Leah cried.

"There is no need to do that. They are looking for a brunette they like. They just didn't like you that much."

Leah's shoulders sagged.

"Don't take it personally!" Frances said cheerfully. "These things are all about looks first, talent second."

"Did they say what they didn't like?" Leah asked, thinking it might be her delivery, or her hands, something she could work on.

Frances snorted. "Sweetie, they didn't like *you*," she said. "I have to run—the other line is ringing," Frances said, and clicked off.

Damn. It was a little hard not to take it personally when a casting director just didn't *like* you. Leah sat on the box, her chin on her fists, thinking for a long time until the rumbling of hunger in her belly could no longer be ignored. She got up, started walking, heavy-footed, to the commissary.

As she made her way, a man with the dark, sexy look of an Hispanic or Italian actor stepped out from between two buildings. "Pardon me, pretty lady, but have you a light?" he asked with a lovely smile.

"I don't smoke," Leah said, wishing that she did in this case, and continued on.

But the man was quickly at her side, walking with her. "Neither do I smoke. Very ugly habit."

"Then why did you ask for a light?" she asked laughingly, looking up at him. He was definitely handsome—square jaw, jet-black hair, deep brown eyes, olive skin. "And why do you have a cigarette behind your ear?"

"No!" he exclaimed, his eyes wide. "There is a cigarette on my ear?" He reached up, grabbed the smoke and tossed it aside, then swept his arm wide. "There. You see? I do not smoke."

She laughed. "I think you do."

"Ach," he said, with a dismissive flick of his wrist. "I do not make the line very well."

"Make the line?"

"Si, si, the line, the line. The man has a line for the woman."

"Oh," she said, catching on. "That was a *line.*"

"Yes," he said, smiling charmingly and proudly. "Do you like it?"

She smiled. "I have to be honest. It wasn't very good."

"No?" he asked, wincing.

"No," she said, smiling. "Smoking isn't sexy."

"Aha. Then you tell me the good line. I will learn it."

She laughed. "I don't know any pickup lines! That's strictly a guy thing."

"Then how shall a poor man have a beautiful woman like you?"

"Maybe by cutting the crap," Leah said with a laugh, and veered off on a path to the right that led to the commissary.

"No, no, *señorita*, do not go!" the man called after her. "I have not provided my name to you!"

Leah turned around, walking backward. "What's your name?"

"Adolfo! Adolfo Rafael!"

"Nice to meet you, Adolfo Rafael," she said, gave him a little wave, and turned around, walking away from him.

"Wait, wait!" he cried. "You did not provide your name!"

Leah laughed, waved over her head, and kept walking.

Subject: Re: Him Again
From: Lucy Frederick <ljfreddie@hotmail.com>
To: Leah Kleinschmidt <hollywoodiva@verizon.net>
Date: 12:12 am

I can't believe he said that about me! Hell if I know what it means, other than maybe, he knows that I know what I am talking about, and how maybe you don't, so he knows if he wants to get through to you, he needs to get me on board.

Subject: Re: Re: Him Again
From: Leah Kleinschmidt <hollywoodiva@verizon.net>
To: Lucy Frederick <ljfreddie@hotmail.com>
Date: 9:25 pm

Maybe that's what he meant. But maybe he meant that you tend to put a different spin on things. Sometimes not a favorable spin. Remember that whole thing with you and him at the sushi bar? Who could forget that?

Subject: Re: Re: Re: Him Again
From: Lucy Frederick <ljfreddie@hotmail.com>
To: Leah Kleinschmidt <hollywoodiva@verizon.net>
Date: 12:42 am

Excuse me, but can't a person make a mistake without fear of being persecuted for the rest of her life? I'll have you know I haven't had sushi since then! You tell Mr. Extreme-Bachelor-Can't-Let-Anything-Go that I am just calling a spade a spade! What's wrong with that? Whatever. Let him bring you orchids and remind you of all the great sex you had and tell you he's sorry for the way he treated you, and that he screwed it up really bad, and that he's changed. But do NOT come crying to me when he turns out to still be a spy or something like that. And anyway, this is supposed to be about me!! MY WEDDING IS ONLY FOURTEEN MONTHS AWAY!! Do you realize how much there is to be done?!?!

THIRTEEN

THE week ended uneventfully—Leah didn't see much of Michael after that afternoon of tuck and roll. He wasn't hanging around the blocking of the first battle scene, and the soccer mom network (a formidable gossip loop, in spite of the rift between Serious Actresses and Starlets, which Michele said just went to prove that women love to talk trash), said there was some big issue with the studio and the film's budget, and that Michael and Eli had been holed up in meetings with the director, trying to sort it out.

That was just as well. Leah could actually focus on her job when Michael wasn't around.

Friday night, Leah, Trudy, Jamie, and Michele went out for a drink and ended up at a club where a bunch of really cute guys who said they were actors—wasn't everyone, really?—bought them drinks. They danced all night, something Leah hadn't done in ages and ages. But it was funny—with each guy that asked her to dance, and each guy who bought her a drink, all she could think of was Michael.

She combated his image in her mind's eye by trying to like each guy who approached her, but by the end of the evening, she was very disheartened. She thought she was so over Michael, so way past comparing him to every guy she'd ever met. But from the look of things on that sorry Friday night, she would never be over him.

Late Saturday morning, a morose Leah was sitting cross-legged on the floor of her living room, staring at the lopsided and unfinished origami peacock, sipping a cup of coffee. Her interest in origami, like her interest in Michael, had been renewed, and as she studied that godawful peacock, she decided she should figure out a way to un-lopside it. It deserved better.

While she was wondering exactly how she'd managed to get it *that* lopsided, Brad stormed into the room, on his way out. He shoved one arm into a V-neck sweater. "Hey, did you see the package for you?" he asked as he pulled the sweater over his head, and nodded toward the kitchen table as he wrestled his other arm into the sweater.

Leah glanced over her shoulder, saw a small gray box. "Where did that come from?"

"Don't know. Some driver in a suit delivered it yesterday while you were at work. Okay, I'm gone," Brad said, and left Leah alone in the house.

Still cross-legged, she inched her way around and stared at the box as she sipped her coffee. She had a pretty good idea who it was from and frowned, because that little shiver of anticipation that ran up her spine was ridiculously short-sighted. She was a fool to trust him. Regardless of the fluttery feelings she got every time he so much as smiled, what he'd done to her five years ago was no small thing.

Okay, so he was sorry for it. What was to say he wouldn't do the same thing again?

Whatever, curiosity was killing her, so she put her coffee cup aside and hopped to her feet, padding across the wood floor to the kitchen table. She hesitated only a moment before picking up the box.

Van Cleef & Arpels, it said in cursive, silver letters. She slipped the silver ribbon from the box and lifted the lid. There was a note on top—she picked it up, saw that beneath it, there was a small bottle of Van Cleef French perfume—*real* perfume. She could not help grinning. She knew that perfume.

Leah opened the note first.

Remember the night we went to see Phantom of the Opera? I will never forget how you looked and how you smelled. You wore a slinky long black dress and your hair up. Your favorite perfume was Van Cleef. You never were more beautiful than you were that night. M.

Her smile deepened—she remembered, all right. Michael had surprised her with box seats and dinner at Pierre Au Tunnel, a swanky New York restaurant for her birthday. She'd worn a simple, floor-length black gown that he later removed so that he could have his leisurely way with her.

That memory prompted another delicious shiver as she extracted the bottle from the box. She removed the stopper and inhaled. It was heavenly, just as she remembered. This was her favorite perfume, but she hadn't been able to afford another bottle since she left New York. The fact that he remembered that it was her favorite was astonishing.

Goddammit, his crap was beginning to work. She could feel herself softening, could feel the ironclad grip she held on her fragile heart starting to ease. She picked up the card again and turned it over. Smart boy. He'd left his cell phone number on the back. She'd once complained about people leaving cards with no cell phone numbers and then never answering their landlines. It had been a running joke with them, checking every business card for a cell phone number.

She dialed the number, but it went to voice mail, for which she was really not prepared, and she started waving her hand, trying to think what to say while Michael's sexy deep voice instructed her to leave a message and he'd call back as soon as he could.

When the beep sounded, she still wasn't ready, and said, "Ah, hey," like a dork. "I ah . . . I—this is Leah, by the way. I ah . . . I got your gift." Okay, well *that* was obvious. She waved her hand harder. "That was really nice." *Nice.* That's what she said when Grandma sent her panties for her birthday. "And I, ah . . . I remember, too," she said, and squeezed her eyes shut. "So . . . thanks," she added, and quickly clicked off.

She opened her eyes, looked at the phone in her hand. "Great, Leah. You've just made an ass of yourself. *I remember, too,*" she mimicked herself. *"So thanks,"* she added with a huge swoon, and with a groan to the rafters, she put the phone down and took her real perfume to her bedroom to try on.

MICHAEL didn't get Leah's message until he returned from Malibu, where he'd spent the day with Jack and Lindsey, the production assistant, and one of her closest friends, Ariel, on a yacht Jack had scrounged up somewhere. Michael had only done it as a favor to Jack—he'd called up, sounding desperate. "Hey, I need a favor, and I can't find Coop," he'd said, dispensing with any greeting. "I've got a yacht lined up, but Lindsey won't go unless her friend goes, too."

"Okay," Michael had said, in the middle of some budget work. "Take the friend."

"Don't be a jerk, Mikey. I need a hand here. Come on, come with."

"What is it with women?" Michael had sighed.

"Who the hells knows?" Jack responded with exasperation. "Just come on. You love this sort of thing."

Normally, Michael did love that sort of thing. But for the first time in many years, his heart was not into being surrounded by beautiful women on a glorious, sun-drenched day.

But he went. And it was torture—all he could think of was Leah. He cursed himself for not thinking to take his cell along to Malibu—although it would have been awkward to receive her call on a yacht while some other young woman was smiling with big moon eyes at him—at least he would have had an opportunity to talk to her, maybe coax her into a date. He took some solace in the fact that she seemed receptive to the perfume, which gave him another idea.

The next morning, Michael was up early, driving to Laguna, where he hoped a little shop he knew of was still in existence. By one o'clock, he was in his T-bird, headed back to L.A. and Leah's house.

When he pulled up in front of Leah's house, there were two cars in front of the house, both junkers, but Leah's car definitely taking top prize. He got out of his car, took a deep breath as he smoothed the crease of his khakis, and walked up to her door.

Michael presumed that the guy who answered his knock was Brad. Brad was wearing pajama bottoms but no shirt. His hair was sticking out in several different directions, as if he'd just gotten up, and he scratched his bare chest as he took Michael in. "Yo," he drawled, and Michael had the impression that he was as high as a kite.

"Hey," Michael responded, suddenly questioning his wisdom for having come here. "Is, ah . . . is Leah here?"

"Leah?" the guy echoed, as if he had to think of who Leah was, then shrugged. "Let me check." He disappeared from the door, leaving it wide open, but not inviting Michael in. That was just as well—from where he stood, Michael could see into the living room. The most remarkable feature was an enormous, big-screen TV in one corner.

As he stood there waiting for Brad to come back, a small, dark-haired woman poked her head out from the kitchen. She was wearing a tiny T-shirt and very short shorts. She, too, looked like she had just rolled out of bed.

"Hey," she said, lifting a spatula. "We're making pancakes. You want some?"

Was she kidding? "Ah, no . . . thanks," he said.

Brad reappeared, still scratching. "She booked, dude," he informed Michael.

"Oh. Okay." He glanced behind him, to her car. So did Brad. "Hey, sweet wheels," he said.

"Any idea where she might be?" Michael tried again.

"Nope."

The woman appeared from the kitchen again, this time holding a plate of pancakes. "I think she went for a run."

"A run?" Brad asked, then laughed. "Since when does Leah *run*?"

Since New York, Michael wanted to tell him. Even when he would tease her, telling her she looked like she was bouncing on a pogo stick when she ran, she would get up at dawn, walk the two blocks up to Central Park, and run.

Brad shrugged and looked at Michael. "So you want me to tell her something?"

Michael had no hope that this guy would remember he'd even been here, much less any message he might give Leah. "Ah, no . . . no thanks," he said. "I'll catch up with her later."

"Sure."

"Come *on*, Brad! I made like four dozen of these things!" the woman shouted from the living area.

Brad smiled sheepishly. "Gotta run."

"Right," Michael said and stepped off the porch. "Thanks."

"No prob," Brad said, and shut the door.

Michael sighed, turned on his heel, and walked back to his car.

He pulled out onto the street, drove down to the intersection, and took the first parking spot he could find. This was undoubtedly a useless exercise—Leah had probably gone another route, or if she hadn't, maybe she'd already been by here. But it was a gorgeous day, and as long as he was in the area, he figured he had nothing to lose by waiting a little while.

As luck would have it, about a half hour later, he spotted her down the street. She was at a crosswalk, her hands on her hips, waiting for a light to change. Her hair was pulled back in a ponytail, and she was wearing tight running pants with a jacket tied around her hips, and a form-fitting sports bra.

When the light turned green, she strode purposefully into the crosswalk, her arms and her ponytail swinging. As she neared him, Michael got out of his car, walked to the front, and perched himself on the bumper. Leah kept walking, was about to stride past him when she saw him, and caught herself just before she walked into a light pole.

"Hey!" she said, and smiled. She *smiled.* A beautiful, almost-happy-to-see-him sort of smile. "What are you doing here?"

"Looking for you."

"You're kidding! How did you know where to find me?"

"Your roommate made a good guess. Come on, I'll give you a ride home."

Leah laughed. "But I live like a block away."

"I was going to take the long way around. By Santa Monica, and Malibu, on up to Oregon, and back. Maybe."

She grinned, cocked her weight to one hip, folded her arms across her middle, and eyed him curiously. "You must have met Brad. Everyone wants to run to Oregon when they meet him."

"I got a pretty good look at him, yeah."

"Sort of goofy, isn't he?" Leah asked with a wrinkled nose. "But then again, I guess most actors are."

"I guessed doper," Michael said.

She laughed again. "He's a Sunday doper—it's his weekend ritual. And the woman he is seeing these days—Alice—she loves to cook. It's a perfect arrangement for the two of them."

"Aha. That would explain the four dozen pancakes,"

Michael said dryly. "So is it a perfect arrangement for you?" he asked, wondering how long she had lived with Brad, how long she could keep on living with him, and how she deserved to be living in Bel Air or Brentwood instead of a Venice Beach rattrap.

But Leah shrugged nonchalantly at his question. "Brad and I wound up in L.A. at the same time, in the same acting class, and we've been friends ever since. But I keep different hours. I like the daytime."

Michael smiled, privately appreciating how pretty she was, how genuine her smile. His casual perusal seemed to make her self-conscious; she suddenly lifted a hand and smoothed her hair. "So hey, listen . . . thanks for the perfume," she said. "I don't know why you are going to all that trouble, and I really should give it back—"

"No, I—"

"But I'm not going to," she quickly interjected. "Because it is my favorite perfume, and I ran out two years ago and couldn't afford another bottle. I figure if you are fool enough to buy it, then I am just fool enough to keep it."

Sweeter words were never spoken. "Good, because I want you to have it," he said. "Even if you don't want to talk to me, or if you find another way to make me the laughingstock in front of the cast, or if you tell me you never want to see me again, I want you to have it."

"Thank you," she said, bowing her head graciously. "That's really very sweet. And I'm not going to make you a laughingstock. That was fun for the week, but I'm over it."

"Great news," he said, standing up from the hood of his car and dropping his hands. "I think we're making progress here. What about seeing me again? Have you decided that?"

She half-laughed, half-groaned, and clasped her hands behind her neck for a moment before peeking up at him. "I'm not going to see you again."

"Damn," he said. "Isn't there anything I can do to convince you that it would be the best decision of your life?"

She dropped her hands, smiled up at him. "You could try feeding me."

His heart nudged him, and he felt the first real glimmer of hope since he saw her on the gym floor, eyes closed, brought down by a dodgeball.

"That wasn't exactly what I meant, but okay, what would Soccer Mom Number Five like to eat?"

With a grin, she put her hands to her hips and rose up on her toes. "Hamburgers," she said, and her blue eyes lit up with pleasure before sliding down to her heels again. "Please don't tell me you've gone all California and will only eat sushi, because I want a hamburger. A big, juicy hamburger. With cheese. And fries. And maybe even a milkshake. And I know the best place in town to get it."

Michael laughed and gestured toward his car. "Hamburger it is, then. Your carriage awaits."

With a pleased-as-punch smile, Leah got in.

FOURTEEN

MICHAEL followed Leah's directions to a hole-in-the-wall burger joint near Venice Beach. They ordered cheeseburgers with fries and a couple of beers instead of milkshakes and sat out on the wooden deck overlooking a parking lot.

Michael was a wealthy man. Personally, he was not accustomed to this sort of joint, but it was clear to him that Leah was. And as he listened to her talk about how she and Brad had found that wretched little house, he couldn't help but wonder what path their lives might have taken—together—had he not done what he did five years ago. It made him feel a little ill, and he left half of his burger uneaten.

"So what sort of acting have you done since you came to L.A.?" he asked when Leah had exhausted the subject of Brad, thank God.

She snorted, shoved a fry into her mouth. "Nothing great. A couple of national commercials. A ton of regional ones," she said with a weird little flip of her hand. "A few theater gigs, and now, *War of the Soccer Moms.*"

So . . . nothing but bit parts and commercials, and no big breaks. He felt even worse.

"Which reminds me," she said, lifting her gaze and pointing a fry at him. "What's the truth about this film? I mean, how is it we ended up working together? Don't tell me it's a coincidence, because it's too freaky. Be real, Raney—how did we end up here?"

Ugh. He preferred having her believe that it was one big coincidence, but he wasn't about to lie to her anymore. He reached across the table and snagged one of her fries, because he knew she wouldn't eat them all. "Well," he said thoughtfully, "it's sort of a long story."

"I'm all ears," she said, sitting back, focusing on him instead of her food.

"Okay . . . Cooper and Jack and I were in New York a few months ago, and while we were there, I happened to see a commercial." He looked up at her. "A laxative commercial."

"Oh," she said, coloring slightly, and gave him a lop-sided smile. "We do what we have to do."

He smiled thinly. "I saw the commercial, and it was the first time I'd seen you in almost five years. So I guess I sort of reacted, and Jack took notice. He asked me what the deal was, and I said I used to know you. So when they were doing the casting for *War*, Jack was sitting in for T.A. He saw your audition and remembered that night in New York, and added you to the list. He did it as a little joke on me, I guess—but he had no idea who you were or what you meant to me."

"Wait a minute," Leah said, suddenly sitting up, planting her elbows on the table, her eyes narrowed suspiciously. "Are you saying I got this role as a *joke*?"

"No, no," Michael said, instantly waving his hands and smiling reassuringly. "The casting was a decision by committee. T.A. had one vote out of five. It's legit, Leah, I swear it."

That seemed to appease her; she leaned back, folded her arms again, and said, "Go on."

He laughed. "What else is there? You got the part, I came back from Costa Rica, and there you were."

"How many times have you been in New York since then?" she asked.

"Since . . . a few months ago?"

"No, since five years ago—since March 18 five years ago, to be exact."

With a mental groan, Michael picked up another fry. "I didn't go back until two years ago."

"Did you look for me?" she asked, her eyes narrowing.

Being totally and completely honest was shaping up to be a real bitch. "No," he said quietly. "I didn't think there was a point. I thought if you were still there, you wouldn't see me. And I thought you were probably with someone else, probably even married. Either way, I didn't want to know."

She frowned. "So what made this different? Why is L.A. the place you've decided to unearth it all again?"

"Because I saw you," he said instantly. "From the moment I saw you on TV, I didn't care who you were with, I wanted to talk to you. And when I saw you lying there on the gym floor—"

"Okay, okay," she said, motioning with her hand for him to speed past that part.

"When I saw you, I couldn't help myself or the rush of all those feelings I still had for you."

She looked skeptical. Michael pushed the baskets away and extended his hand, palm up, silently asking for hers. She didn't take it at first, just stared at his hand until he said *please*, and then she very reluctantly put hers in his, and he folded his fingers over hers, holding her tightly.

"I made a mistake, Leah. I don't know how to impress

on you how sorry I am for it. I would bring down the stars one at a time and hand them to you on a silver platter, and it still wouldn't be enough. I've known for years that it was a mistake, almost from the moment I left, even when I was working to convince myself it was the right thing to do. Unfortunately, as time went on, the more I realized how bad the mistake was. I loved you, and I made a huge fucking mistake and I didn't know how to make it right. But then I saw you—"

He paused, looked heavenward for a moment, trying to put a word to all the emotions he'd felt that morning when he saw her. Hope. Dread. *Love.* More hope, and a strange twisting in his heart, like the thing was cranking up after five years.

He lowered his gaze to her crystalline blue eyes and said softly, "It's just that . . . I never lost your taste in my mouth. I never lost your scent. I never lost the feel of your body on my hands," he said, lifting his palm up to her. "And when I saw you that morning, more beautiful than I remembered, your smile more golden than it had ever been, I knew I had to try. I had to do it for me, because I knew—*know*—I won't ever feel this way for another woman again in my life. And even though the odds are stacked against me, I have to try, because I still love you. I always have."

She didn't say anything for a long moment, just held his gaze, her eyes full of myriad emotions and tears. "Why didn't you ever tell me?"

"I never had the guts to say it before," he confessed.

"It's hard to know what to say," she admitted. "What happened that night was the worst thing that has ever happened to me in my life. I wanted to die. I felt like I'd lost a physical part of me. I felt like a fool, like I'd been used, like I didn't matter."

Those words burned like acid, and he sagged backward against the back of the chair.

But Leah sat up, leaned toward him. "The thing is, there

was a time . . . a long period of time . . . that I would have
fallen on my knees and given everything I had for you to
take me back. But . . . but you disappeared, and I didn't
have that option, so I had to bury it," she said, gesturing to
herself. "Just . . . *bury* everything, because everything had
died. All the love and trust and faith I had in you just died,
and I buried it, and I can't resurrect it now. I don't think I
have the strength to even try. It's really asking too much
of me."

That was it, then. He'd hoped, and he'd lost. "I understand," he said wearily. With another sigh, he reached
down to the small bag he'd brought inside, and put it on the
table between them. "I got this for you." He shoved the bag
toward her. "Just a small reminder . . . that I love you." His
voiced trailed off, and he leaned back, unable to finish his
thought. Now everything seemed like a reminder of how
he'd ruined her life.

Leah took the bag and opened it. Her face lit up at the
sight of the little origami bird, and she carefully extracted
it from the bag and put it on the table. "Oh my God," she
said softly. "It's beautiful. Where did you find it?"

"It doesn't matter," he said sullenly.

She leaned forward, examining the intricate folds. She
spied the rolled-up note he'd lodged beneath the bird's
wing, and carefully extracted it. Now Michael groaned—in
a flush of dreamy love, he had penned a godawful poem,
just like he used to do. It was a joke between them. He'd
write awful poems and leave them on Post-It notes around
her apartment and his, or call up and recite them into her
voice mail. In hindsight, it seemed completely moronic.

She unrolled the note and read it, and Michael winced.
*Roses are red, Violets are blue, I would walk over fire to
come back to you.* God, how lame. He honestly had not realized he could be such a sentimental jerk. He turned in his
chair and looked out over the parking lot, unwilling and
unable to see her laugh or roll her eyes, whatever she did
when she read that lame note. He was five years too late for

this crap, and as soon as he figured that out, they'd both be a lot—

"Michael, it's so sweet," she said.

Wait a minute. That was sincerity in her voice. He risked a look at her from the corner of his eye. She was holding the origami in her hand, admiring the craftsmanship. "It's beautiful," she said. "Absolutely beautiful." She put it down and showed him the rolled up note, which she tucked into her sports bra. "You always did know how to make me smile," she said, and smiled fully then, knocking him back on his heels with the force of it. "Okay, look. I don't want to go back . . . but maybe we could at least be friends?"

Whoa. Was she serious? Hope picked itself up, brushed itself off, and spoke carefully. "Maybe we could try and hang out a little? Just a little. And if it's too uncomfortable, or it looks like you can't find your way back . . . then at least we can say we gave it a shot."

She thought about it a moment, and after what seemed hours rather than moments, she nodded. "I guess we could try that."

He felt a wave of relief. "How's this," he said, his heart pounding with sheer delight. "We could start with a really good date. One date. There is a movie premiere Friday night, which is a little unusual, but they are accommodating James Cameron's schedule."

Her eyes widened. "James Cameron? *The* James Cameron, the director?"

"Yep, the same James Cameron. We worked his film, *The Hero.* So I'd love to take you to dinner and a movie premiere."

"Oh, wow, Michael!" she said, smiling broadly. "That's great . . . but I don't have anything to wear to a movie premiere."

"I have something for you to wear."

"*You* have something for me to wear?" She laughed again. "You've changed in ways I hadn't imagined."

"I have a friend who does costuming for major motion pictures. She has several gowns, clothes that didn't make the movie for whatever reason. I know she could put you in something that would knock L.A.'s socks off."

"Really?" she asked, her eyes lighting up at the thought of it. "Oh man, I don't know," she started, but he reached across the table and grabbed her hand.

"Just . . . just give me a chance, Leah. Give me a chance to prove to you how much I want you."

Her eyes roamed his face, and then a slow, but definite smile spread her lips, and for the first time in five years, she squeezed his hand. "Okay."

For a moment there, Michael believed he could soar.

They talked about movie premieres and stunt work as they polished off the last of the fries. Michael took Leah home after that, and felt like he was walking on air, or had just shot down class-V rapids, or had leapt from a plane into thin air.

When they reached her house, Michael walked around to her side of the car, slipped his arm around her waist like old times, and walked her to the door.

"You want to come in and officially meet Brad?" Leah asked.

He smiled, touched her nose with his knuckle, and shook his head. "It's probably best we do this one step at a time."

"You're probably right. That's a little too much for one day—reconciliation, Brad, and a stack of pancakes." She laughed.

Michael did, too, but before she could step away, before she could speak, he touched his lips to her cheek and heard her catch her breath. He kissed her forehead, the bridge of her nose, and then lowered his head to kiss her lips.

Leah turned her face up to his. He slid his arm around her waist and pulled her into him, smoothed a strand of errant blond hair from her temple, and then slipped two fingers beneath her chin, forcing her gaze up so that he could see her, could see the glittering eyes that had haunted him for five long years. Leah smiled, touched her hand to his cheek, and whispered, *"I remember, too."*

Michael spread his fingers across her cheek and lowered his mouth to hers. Her body instantly curved into his, and his blood rose up, making his arousal almost instantaneous as a familiar sensation of carnal pleasure began to build in him. It was all he needed, to feel her in his arms, to taste her lips.

He could feel the tension slip away from Leah's body and touched the corner of her mouth.

He slipped his tongue inside her mouth, tasted a little bit of salt and sweet breath, which aroused him even more—desire was spreading through him too quickly. But he had so longed to hold her, so longed to feel her in his arms that he could hardly stand it now that he had her. With both hands he cupped her face and deepened the kiss, his tongue slipping over her teeth, against the soft skin of her mouth, twining around her tongue.

Leah pressed hard against him. Her hands slid up his arms, to his shoulders, into his hair, down his back. That loose strand of hair fell again and caught between their mouths, but neither of them cared. Michael was lost in the moment, lost in the erotic pleasure of that kiss—

The door suddenly flung open, and Brad the Pothead said, "Oh, hey. I didn't know you guys were out here. Sorry."

Leah's body fell away from Michael's; her hands fell away from his shoulders. "Hey, Brad," she said.

"Okay!" Brad said, and shut the door.

With a laugh, Leah dropped her forehead to Michael's shoulder. But his body was raging, and he buried his face in her neck. "Come home with me. Come home with me right now," he breathed.

She lifted her head and brought her hands up between them, forcing his head up. Her eyes were shimmering with pleasure and delight, a look that could entice a man to move mountains. "I'll see you later," she said, and moved out of his arms.

As she opened the door and stepped across the threshold, she looked back at him once more, waved fingers at him as she closed the door.

Michael stood on that porch, staring at the scarred door for what seemed like ages before he finally made himself turn and walk to his car.

FIFTEEN

CONTINUING problems with the film's budget kept Michael away for the first couple of days of boot camp that week. Leah saw him in the mornings, when he would invariably greet her at her car with a big smile and a bagel. He confessed to being worried that she had enough fuel for the paintball practice. And they chatted on the phone one night when Michael wasn't swamped and could talk about planning an extreme hiking adventure to the Peruvian Andes for a group of Italians.

Leah regaled Michael with the ongoing tales of boot camp, the highlight being when Jamie single-handedly brought paintball to a grinding halt by screaming when she accidentally got her finger stuck in the trigger of the gun.

"Did it hurt that bad?" Michael asked, astounded.

"It didn't hurt at all. But it ruined an appliqué on her nail she'd paid big money for, and *that* hurt."

Michael sighed. "The guys were right. Women and war don't mix."

"Just wait," Leah predicted. "When we start shooting, we will be one well-oiled machine." She didn't believe it for a minute. And she didn't tell Michael about Nicole Redding. Everyone loved Charlene Ribisi, who had come for the required paintball practice, but they all agreed Nicole was a pain in the ass, unwilling to carry her own weight.

Michael also was true to his word and hooked her up with his friend, Beverly, the costumer, and arranged for Leah to visit Beverly's studio Wednesday at lunch.

Leah talked Trudy into going with her—but not before Trudy made her come clean about her relationship with Michael.

"Dammit! I *knew* it!" Trudy shouted, hurling her straw cowboy hat to the ground and punching her hands to her hips. "*I* wanted him! He's so hot, and he likes my style! But girl, I have to be honest—I have a sixth sense about these things. You really shouldn't lie to your best friends."

"I didn't *lie*," Leah said with a laugh, and stooped down to pick up Trudy's hat. "It really was a long time ago. I haven't seen him in years."

"Oh yeah? So how do you go from not seeing some guy for years to being an item?"

"Well . . . apparently he was thinking about me all that time," she said as a sheepish but gleeful little grin curved her lips.

Trudy suddenly thrust forward, her face in Leah's. "And just what was he thinking?" she asked with a salacious grin.

"Shut up," Leah said, pushing Trudy when she handed her the hat.

"I won't shut up. Come on, come on, tell me!" Trudy pouted. "You know I live vicariously through you! The only thing Rick ever thinks about is what he's going to eat and when he's going to get laid, in that order," she said, swiping the hat from Leah's hand.

"Well . . . he said that he can still *taste* me, and he can still *smell* me, and *feel* me, and that basically, he would walk through fire to come back to me. But a lot more eloquently than that."

"Oh. My. God!" Trudy shrieked, and bent backward so far that Leah was afraid she'd fall before bouncing back up, her brown eyes blazing. "That incredibly gorgeous man said that to *you*?" she cried.

"Hey! Don't sound so shocked."

"Oh girl, I am shocked right out of my shorts, but worse, I am also pea green with envy! Tell me more."

"Well . . . he's taking me to the premiere of *The Hero*. And he has given me the name of a costumer who will put me in a dress for it. And that's where I am going now, and you are invited . . . if you want to come."

Trudy's eyes went wide, and then she let out a *whoop* and linked her arm through Leah's. "Are you *kidding*? Of course I want to come! Good for you, sweetie—you deserve this. Everyone should have one great love in their life. So let's go. I want to see what you're going to wear!"

Leah hadn't actually said anything about one great love. She was privately afraid to say anything like that, afraid of putting labels on the white flag she'd held up to Michael. Nor did she want to be too hopeful, or disinter any intense feelings of love. Even if she managed to do it, and she wasn't certain she could, she wasn't sure she could trust Michael. And if something awful happened, she was one hundred percent sure she could not survive emotionally. Best not to go there at all. Best just to take this one baby step at a time.

Starting with a fabulous new dress and a Hollywood premiere.

So she let Trudy drag her to her car and drove to the workshop, where Michael's friend was expecting them.

"Hi, I'm Beverly," she said as Trudy and Leah opened the door and stepped in. "You must be Michael's latest, right?" she asked cheerfully.

That was such an odd thing to say that Leah didn't know how to respond. So Trudy did it for her. "She's Michael's *last*," she said with great authority.

"Oh," Beverly said, and the fact that her eyebrows nearly reached her hairline did not give Leah a good feeling. But Trudy was dragging her into the middle of the studio and a rack of clothes.

"Ohmigod, these are gorgeous!" she exclaimed. "Do you sell them?"

"Not really," Beverly said as she walked over to stand next to Leah. "Every so often I will. I usually end up using them on a film somewhere." She looked at Leah. "So are you Michael's fiancée?" she asked with a twinge of incredulity in her voice.

"Oh no," Leah said, and shook her head, laughed as if that was hilarious. "I'm really just a . . . ah . . . a friend. My name is Leah."

"Nice to meet you, Leah. You're lucky. Michael doesn't usually do this for his friends."

What did *that* mean?

"Help yourself. This rack over here probably has something more appropriate for a major studio premiere," she said, pointing to the corner.

Leah and Trudy instantly made their way to the rack Beverly had indicated and started sorting through beautiful dresses and gowns.

"Why can't I ever get a role where the character wears this sort of thing?" Leah sighed as they looked through. "Why do I get the role where I have to wear camouflage gear or bathrobes?"

"At least you have a part in a movie," Trudy said. "Think of all the poor schlubs in America who never get to come to a shop like this. Are we lucky, or what?" She picked up a floor-length yellow chiffon number and held it up to Leah.

"That was made for Nicole Redding for a scene in *Washington Square*. But it ended up on the cutting room floor."

Trudy wrinkled her nose and very carefully stuck it back on the rack. "Oh! Look at this," she said, and withdrew a knee-length, turquoise blue sheaf from the rack, held it up to her body, and twirled around to the mirror. "This is *gorgeous*. And this would look absolutely fabulous on me!"

"Actually, it would look fabulous on her," Beverly said, and gingerly took the gown from Trudy and handed it to Leah. Leah had no compunction about stepping directly in front of a gaping Trudy at the mirror and ignoring Trudy's protest that she found the gown first. She held it up to her. It was beautiful. She could just imagine Michael's face when he saw her in this, the little smile lines around his eyes, his eyes going dark—

"Try it on," Beverly urged her, and pointed to a curtained area.

"I don't think I could fit into that in my wildest dreams."

"You *are* a little big through the hip," Beverly said, eyeing her critically, but then she smiled. "I can alter it. Just try it."

For the chance to try it on, Leah could ignore the hip comment, and stepped behind the curtain Beverly indicated and started peeling off her clothes. But as she was struggling to pull the gown up over her hips (she *did* seem a little big through there), she heard Beverly ask Trudy how long Michael and Leah had been an item.

"Oh, I don't know," Trudy said. "They used to be in love, and they broke up, but then they found each other again, completely by accident, and its love again. Isn't that wild?"

"It's *really* wild. The last time I spoke to Mike, he was seeing Nicole."

Great, *that* one again, Leah thought. Trudy must have given Beverly a look, because she quickly said, "Oh, I don't mean anything. It's just interesting, because Michael . . . well, he's a good friend of mine, but let's just say he gets around. And they always think he's the one. I think even Nicole thought he was the one."

"Huh, that's interesting," Trudy said, and Leah could tell by the pitch of her voice that she was uncomfortable, "because Leah *is* the one. He told her so."

Oh nononono, Trudy, don't do that! Leah silently begged her. In some respects, L.A. was a tiny little town, and remarks like that got around.

"I'm not saying she isn't," Beverly graciously agreed. "It's just that he's such a great guy, and he's so charming and handsome, and I was just making a point that a lot of his dates think that it's a bigger deal than it is."

"Well, this is the real deal," Trudy said emphatically.

"That's great!" Beverly responded, and it seemed to Leah that she was getting a little irritated with Trudy.

Leah managed to get the dress on and zipped it up as far as she could before flinging the curtain open. "Ta-da!" she sang.

Trudy squealed with excitement. "It's *gorgeous!* You're gorgeous!" she cried.

"Can you zip it?" Leah asked, hobbling around in the skin-tight sheath.

Beverly tried with a lot of huffing and puffing and finally said, "I can't zip it all the way. I'll have to alter it."

Leah took a deep breath and, holding her arms wide to keep herself from teetering over, turned around.

Both Trudy and Beverly stood back and nodded.

"Perfect," Trudy said.

"The dress was made for Renée Zellweger, but you're a lot bigger than her. You might want to think of losing a few pounds," Beverly added.

"Thanks," Leah said.

Beverly grinned. "So what do you think? Do you like it?"

What Leah thought couldn't be put into words. She felt transformed. The dress was absolutely beautiful. It had a plunging neckline, open to the waist, and a bare back. It was belted at the waist, and a slim sheath hugged her to the knees. It was definitely movie-star fantastic, and Leah felt like a million bucks in it.

"Let me make some quick measurements, and we'll get you some breathing room," Beverly said, and walked away, leaving Trudy and Leah alone.

Trudy smiled broadly, nodding her approval. "Girl, you are going to knock his socks off."

Leah smiled.

"Don't worry about *Beverly*," Trudy whispered. "She's jealous."

Beverly reappeared with a yellow tape measure and a bit of chalk. She made several marks on the dress then promised to have it ready by Friday afternoon, just in time for the premiere.

"Thank you so much," Leah said, shaking Beverly's hand.

"It's my pleasure," Beverly said. "Michael is such a good friend."

As they walked outside, and Trudy paused to light up a smoke, she said, "I have the distinct impression that Beverly wants to be *really* good friends with Michael."

"You're just saying that to make me feel better."

"I am not."

"You are."

"Okay, so what if I am? You just look so gloomy. But hey, who's getting the dress? And what shoes are you going to wear with that? Okay, here's what I am going to do for you. I am going to take you to Goodwill to get some shoes—"

"*Goodwill?*" Leah cried as they got in the car.

"Yes, Goodwill!" Trudy replied, clearly affronted. "Do you have any idea what the fine ladies of Brentwood and Bel Air toss out to Goodwill?"

Actually, Leah had no idea.

THAT afternoon, the women suited up in camouflage again (with a lot of grousing at the wardrobe guy about how fat they all looked), took up empty paintball guns, and walked through the blocking. Tomorrow, they would take the blocking into an old back lot set that had not been struck and still had housing facades up from the last film.

When they broke for the day, Trudy stopped to talk to Michele and Jamie, and Leah walked back to the locker room. As she neared the commissary tent, a familiar face stepped out into the sunshine, grinning broadly, his arms wide. "There you are, the flower without the light for the cigarettes."

"Hello, Adolfo. Still lurking about looking for a light, I see."

"No, no, this is not true. I am waiting for *you*."

"Me?"

"*Si*. You do not recall? You did not give me your name."

Leah laughed, put the tip of her gun to the ground, her elbow propped on the butt. "I don't know if I should give you my name. What are you going to do with it?"

He smiled—a very lovely smile, in all honesty—and said, "You will not give me your trust, no? Ah, but if I have your name, I will do nothing but whisper it to the stars when I wish for you."

"And you said you weren't any good at lines!" she exclaimed with a laugh.

Adolfo looked positively wounded. "You do not believe me. Why is this? Do you not believe a man can see a woman as beautiful as you and wish for her to be his?"

Leah couldn't help smiling. Cheesy? Absolutely. Flattering? Hell, yes. "I think that when a man sees a woman, he's usually interested in something else."

Adolfo grinned at that. "I did not say that I am not interested in this something else as well, sweetheart." He winked.

Leah had to laugh. At least the guy was honest, she had to give him points for that, and he had a way of saying *sweetheart* that could turn a grown woman to jelly.

"If I may, nameless one . . . why do you have this gun?"

She glanced down at her firearm and picked it up, pointed it directly at Adolfo's chest. He instantly threw up his hands, his eyes going wide. "If you aren't careful, I will spray you with red paint."

"You may spray on me whatever you wish," he said, slowly lowering his arms, and took a tentative step forward and casually reached for the gun, took it from her, and turned it around, pointing at the tent. He brought it up to his shoulder as if he meant to fire it, looked through the site, pulled the trigger—and of course nothing happened. He laughed and lowered it. "This is useless," he proclaimed.

"I should hope so. It's a prop."

"Prop? What is prop?" he asked, handing the gun back to her.

"An inanimate object used on a movie set," she said, and cocked her head to one side. "What did you say you did around here, again?"

"I did not say. But now that you have expressed such keen interest, I shall tell you. I am the person with lights," he said, and gestured heavenward.

"Lights?"

"Yes, lights. The things that hang down from the sky while you make the movies."

"Ah," she said, nodding. "Which film are you working on?"

Adolfo smiled. "Which film? Many, many films. And which film are you?"

"War of the Soccer Moms."

"Ah," he said, nodding. "A very fine film. You are the star, no?"

She laughed roundly. "No."

"No? How is this possible?" he asked, and touched her chin with his fingers, admiring her face. "You must be the star."

"Believe me, I have asked myself the same question many times. Why aren't I the star?" she joked heavenward, flinging her arms wide.

Adolfo clucked his tongue, dropped his hand, and looked away. But then he shifted a sparkling brown gaze to her from the corner of his eye. "I should very much like to give you wine."

Leah laughed.

"I mean this. I should like to give you wine and learn your name."

"My name," she said, smiling up at him, "is Leah."

"*Leah*," he said on a long sigh. "The name is nectar for my lips."

She couldn't help but laugh again. "But I can't have wine with you, I'm afraid."

Adolfo frowned and demanded, "Why? Why, why, why, Leah? I adore you, I seek you out, and yet you barely give me a name by which to call you. Do you find me repulsive?"

"Not at all," she said with a smile. "But I don't know you, Adolfo. I don't go out with men I don't know."

"But how shall you ever know me if you do not let me give you wine?" he protested.

"I don't know," she said with a cheerful shrug. "Maybe I'll see you doing the light thing when production starts," she said, drawing an invisible light thing in the sky before picking up her gun. "I'd love to stay and chat, but this uniform is really hot, and I've got shoes to buy."

"*Hasta luego*, Leah. I shall whisper your name to the stars," he said, gesturing poetically to the clear blue sky. And he smiled so warmly that she actually felt her skin tingle a bit. She waved at him, and slinging her fake gun over her shoulder, she walked on, laughing skyward when she heard him begin to sing her name to the stars.

Subject: My First Movie Premiere
From: Leah Kleinschmidt <hollywoodiva@verizon.net>
To: Lucy Frederick <ljfreddie@hotmail.com>
Date: 7:15 pm

So guess where I'm going. Okay, okay, you can tell from the heading. Can you believe it? It's the premiere of *The*

Hero, and you will not believe the dress I am wearing. It's turquoise blue, and I found these really fabulous CFM shoes (you will NOT believe where) that are almost the exact same shade. Isn't that cool?

Subject: Re: My First Movie Premiere
From: Lucy Frederick <ljfreddie@hotmail.com>
To: Leah Kleinschmidt <hollywoodiva@verizon.net>
Date: 10:20 pm

Okay, start with where you got the shoes, then at least tell me how you are managing an actual movie premiere (and isn't Ewan McGregor in that movie? I LOVE LOVE LOVE him!). And when you get through telling me all that, then maybe you can explain why you can suddenly decide on a color for your stupid movie premiere dress, but you can't seem to help ME settle on a color for the brides-maid's dresses! Speaking of bridesmaids, when I take into account my cousins, and my friends from Holyoke, and a couple of women I work with, who I cannot leave out, that gives me 10 bridesmaids, including you. What do you think? Is that enough?

    Oh yeah, BTW, just in case you think I'm an idiot, I am not. I know that because you are skirting around the central question of HOW you are going to the premiere, it can only mean one thing: Michael. Leah, have you lost your mind? How can you not see that you are setting yourself up for a huge fall?

Subject: Re: Re: My First Movie Premiere
From: Leah Kleinschmidt <hollywoodiva@verizon.net>
To: Lucy Frederick <ljfreddie@hotmail.com>
Date: 8:21 pm

Thanks for understanding. Did I tell you he says he loves me? ☺. Don't bother writing back to tell me how crazy I am because I already know it. Anyway, I have to go. I told

Brad I'd go with him for pizza to celebrate his getting a
commercial today. It's regional, but it will definitely pay
his share of the rent, and frankly, I was beginning to sweat
that. Check you later, L.

P.S. I was just kidding about the turquoise. I am fine
with whatever color you choose.

SIXTEEN

MICHAEL was growing increasingly exasperated. Budget woes and problems with the location where they would be shooting, and even bigger woes getting visas for the Italians to do some extreme hiking in the Peruvian Andes, were keeping him from boot camp and Leah.

He and the rest of the guys worked late into Wednesday night, so he never saw her around camp that day. But he called her on his way home.

She picked up on the third ring, and her sleep-heavy voice said, "Hello?"

"Leah," he said, sighing into the phone. "Did I wake you?"

"No. Maybe a little," she admitted groggily. "What are you doing?"

"I just finished up with the Peru thing," he said. "I'm sorry I missed you today."

"Oh, that's okay," she said through a yawn. "I was

pretty busy learning how to avoid getting hit by paint. And might I add, that paint *hurts*."

He smiled into the phone. "I know. Go back to sleep, baby. I just wanted to say hi. Are you ready for the premiere Friday?"

"Are you kidding?"

"I'll pick you up around six."

"Okay. Bye, Michael," she said sleepily, and hung up.

He clicked off the phone, tossed it into the passenger seat, and drove up Santa Monica Boulevard, remembering one night in New York when he'd come home late from work to find her snoozing away on his couch. She had let herself in, obviously intending to surprise him by donning some of the sexiest lingerie he had ever seen. But she had fallen asleep waiting for him, and by the time he came home, she was laying half on and half off the couch. One foot was missing a stiletto, and the gauzy little teddy had twisted around her body, leaving several delicious parts of her uncovered.

Personally, he'd never seen a sexier woman in his life.

Thursday, he at least got to have lunch with her and then worked with her team during paintball training. Thursday night, Leah trotted off to acting class, and Michael was going to turn in early, but Jack called him, begging him to come along on another date with Lindsey and her friend Ariel.

"You're kidding," Michael said flatly. "What is this, middle school?"

"I don't know. Look, just do it, will you? Lindsey is taking it slow."

"Tell her to take it slow with someone else," Michael said irritably.

"Mike, I really like this woman. Come on. It's the last time, I promise."

With a weary sigh, Michael agreed.

On Friday, one of the Starlets broke her leg during the

paintball training. The poor girl just tripped and fell and broke her leg. He spent the rest of the day at the hospital, on the phone with OSHA and studio people who were not very happy (particularly with the over-bloated budget situation), and then with the casting agent, trying to find a quick replacement for Soccer Mom #8. They lost an afternoon, which prompted an all-call for Saturday morning to make up for lost time.

Michael barely made it home in time to change for the premiere.

He arrived at Leah's house in a stretch limo promptly at six the next evening. He stepped out, walked to Leah's door, and hoped like hell that Brad didn't answer.

Of course Brad answered. But at least the dude was fully clothed this time, dressed in dirty jeans and a dirtier T-shirt that said *Rock On* across the chest. "Dude," Brad said, his eyes widening at the sight of Michael in what was a very expensive tux, purchased a couple of years ago for occasions such as this. "Nice threads!"

"Thank you. Is Leah here?"

"Yeah," Brad said. He stepped back and shouted "Leah!" as he motioned for Michael to come in.

This had the feel of prom night, Michael thought uneasily. He stepped into the foyer, glanced around the house. Someone had picked things up a little. There was a pile of clothes on the end of a worn couch, and the peacock had been moved to stand below the massive TV. It had lost the boxer shorts and was wearing an L.A. Clippers hat. The kitchen table was stacked high with papers and a couple of scripts.

"You want something to drink?" Brad asked.

"No, but thank you," Michael responded, and shoved his hands into his pockets.

"Suit yourself," Brad said, and padded across to a cabinet on a windowless wall. He squatted down, opened the doors, and surveyed a litter of liquor bottles, finally selecting Smirnoff vodka.

Brad stood up, turned around and gave Michael the once over. "What's your name, anyway?"

"Michael Raney." He extended his hand to Brad, who padded across the floor and took his hand in a surprisingly firm grip.

"I've been wondering about you," Brad said.

"Oh?"

"You don't know much about cars, do you?"

"I don't?"

"There wasn't anything wrong with her distributor cap."

Michael almost laughed. "You're right, I'm not big on cars."

Brad nodded, took the vodka to the kitchen, got a small glass, and then adjourned a full three feet away, onto the couch. "Wanna watch some baseball?"

"Ah . . . well no, we've got to be some place." He glanced over his shoulder at the empty hallway, then back at Brad. "Are you sure she heard you?"

"She heard me."

And as if to confirm it, Michael heard the click of her heels on the hardwood floor. He turned around, his heart skipped a beat.

Leah looked absolutely stunning. She was wearing an ass-tight turquoise dress, the color of it reflected in her eyes. Her hair was pulled back and done up in a very artistic coif at the nape of her neck with thick strands of blonde curling in and out, making it look like an elaborate love knot. She was wearing teardrop crystal earrings, and her shoes, glittering with turquoise rhinestones, were just about the sexiest thing he'd ever seen.

He must have been staring, dumbstruck, because Leah started to laugh. "You remember me? Leah Klein? Your date for the evening?"

"He's speechless," Brad helpfully pointed out.

Leah beamed a smile at Brad that Michael wanted all to himself. "You're beautiful," he said low, dragging that smile to him. "More beautiful than ever."

"Really?" she asked, and twirled around for him. "Do you like it?"

He glanced at the dress again—the plunging neck and back line, the sheath of a skirt, the long, shapely legs beneath that. "Yeah," he said quietly. "I like it a lot."

"I really owe your friend Beverly. She wouldn't even let me pay her."

He certainly hoped not, as he had paid Beverly handsomely for the privilege of putting Leah in her dress.

"She even lent me these," she said, flicking one of the earrings with her finger. "So are we ready?"

Was she kidding? Michael couldn't wait to get her out of that dump of a house, to put her somewhere where the world could admire her as she deserved to be admired, and immediately moved to her side, his hand possessively on her waist.

Leah grabbed a small silver bag from a console near the door and looked over her shoulder at Brad. "Bye, Brad! Be sure and tell Alice how fabulous I look!"

"You bet!" Brad responded without taking his eyes off the TV.

Leah shifted a sparkling gaze up to Michael, who opened the door, guided Leah through it.

She stopped on the porch and gave a squeal of delight. "A *limo*?" she gasped, twirling around to Michael.

"Of course. Nothing but the best for you, baby."

Her hand flew to her throat. "I feel like Cinderella," she said wistfully, and then grabbed his hand, pulled him toward the car. "Let's go!" she said eagerly.

Inside the limo, Leah took in the various bottles on the mini bar, the console TV, and the velvet seats. "This is so damn cool!" she said excitedly.

"Have you been in a limo?"

"Yes—exactly twice, the same number of times I've been a bridesmaid. But those limos had blue shag carpet and cheap scotch. *This*," she said, reaching for the bar and lifting up a small bottle of Grey Goose vodka, "is *really* uptown."

"Would you like a drink?" he asked, shifting forward.

"I think I would," Leah said brightly. "Something to settle my nerves."

"Don't be nervous," he said as he got a glass, some ice, and mixed her a vodka tonic, just like they'd never been apart. He handed her the drink. "All eyes will be on Vincent Vittorio and Ewan McGregor. Kids like us will be a bunch of background noise. It'll be fun to watch."

"It's already fun—I don't have many opportunities to wear a dress like this. Actually," she said, looking down at the dress, "I'd say I've had zero opportunities to wear a dress like this."

"You should wear dresses like that every day," Michael said sincerely. "You should have the best of everything. I never thought you would be even more beautiful to me than you already are, but Leah, I'm absolutely breathless." And he meant it. She looked like a star in that dress. Her carriage, her smile—everything about her. "I wouldn't be surprised if one day, red carpets and dresses like that are a normal part of your life."

"Oh stop," she said with a roll of her eyes, then quickly slanted him another look. "You really think so?"

"I think so."

Her cheeks turned a very appealing shade of pink, and she looked down. "Well hey, *you* look pretty good, too, Raney. Some men are born to wear tuxedos, and you are definitely one of them. The photographers will think you are one of the stars."

He laughed. "I don't think so. And anyway, men are meant to fade to black when women appear, and that's just as well by me," he said. "I'd much rather do the admiring than be the admired."

"Then you should have been born with a different face." She abruptly reached up, laid her palm against his cheek.

A kiss wouldn't have felt as tender as the touch of her hand. He covered her hand with his own, moved his head, kissed her palm.

Leah laughed and held up her drink, offering him a sip, holding it to his lips. He took a sip, then settled back, her hand still in his. She was changing, the hurt and anger peeling off, a little at a time. Everything felt right in the back of that limo, like this was where he was supposed to be—here, with her.

The press was out in force in front of Mann's Village Theatre, as was the crowd, held back by police barriers. There was a bit of a wait as they queued in line with other limos, but Leah spent the time straining to see who was there, calling out the names to Michael. There was enough star power—A-list actors, directors, and movie moguls were all over the red carpet, speaking to the fans lucky enough to have snagged a position right behind the barricades.

When Michael's limo pulled up at the entrance, and the driver opened the door, he stepped out first, reached down, and caught Leah's hand to help her out.

She paused in front of the open door to straighten her dress, but then gave him a huge smile, and together they walked down the red carpet, into the premiere, Michael whispering in her ear who several people were, Leah smiling and waving when any member of the press—fearful of missing anyone important—would call out to her to smile.

When they at last made their way into the theater, they settled down just behind Ewan McGregor, which made Leah giddy with excitement. The movie was an epic hero's journey, complete with swords and horses and spectacular special effects. What Michael remembered was filming during an unusually cold fall in Poland, where the ground was always muddy and the stunts always impossible to perfect. But when the lights came up and the crowd applauded wildly—of course they did, they were all movie people—Michael felt a sense of accomplishment, like he always did when they finished a film. He supposed he had found his true calling.

They were leaving the theater for a studio reception at a nearby restaurant when Michael felt his cell phone vibrate in his pocket. "Damn," he muttered.

"What is it?" Leah asked him, her eyes shining brightly.

Michael just smiled and shook his head. "Cell phone. I'll turn it off." When Leah happily turned around to do more stargazing, Michael slipped the phone out of his pocket and looked at the caller ID. Rex.

That was weird. He hardly ever spoke to Rex anymore. He figured Rex wanted to know what his little chat with Leah had done for Michael. He turned off his cell and put it back in his pocket. He'd give his old friend a call later and fill him in, but right now, there was nothing or no one who was going to interrupt his evening with Leah.

At the reception, Leah seemed to take wings. She moved gracefully around the room, talking and laughing to whomever struck up a conversation, and frankly, it seemed to Michael like there was a long line of guys waiting to do just that. He could hardly blame them—in his eyes, Leah was far more beautiful than Maria del Torro, the costar on *The Hero.*

He was content just to watch her, his happiness derived purely from hers. He loved the way she smiled, the way she seemed to shimmer beneath the lights. He loved how men and women alike looked at her, wondering who she was, admiring her dress, her lean, tall form. And he loved, he absolutely *loved* the way she looked at him.

It was a look that he remembered well, a look that used to make him feel like the most adored man on the planet, and tonight, it put him over the moon. He would have been content to just stand back and watch her, but he couldn't—he knew too many people. Cameron introduced him around, and Michael found himself at the center of three women's attention. He did what he always did in that case—he flirted and charmed. But he kept one eye on

Leah the whole time, counting off the minutes when they could leave the reception and he might have her all to himself.

After a couple of hours of hobnobbing with stars, he couldn't wait any longer. He tossed aside the phone number one female producer had given him under the guise of exploring some stunt options for her next project and made his way to Leah. "Are you hungry?" he whispered into her ear.

"Famished," she whispered back. He took her hand in his, led her from that room of admirers, a few of which, he noticed, gazed at her all the way to the door.

They dined at L'Orangerie, a French restaurant renowned around L.A. for its sophistication and romantic atmosphere.

They were seated at a table nestled between two huge vases filled with fresh flowers. Michael recognized the quality of the table linens, as well as the china and silver—he'd seen something comparable in a Middle Eastern prince's palace once. At the center of the table was a box of fresh-cut roses, their scent still strong.

Leah seemed to be mesmerized by the place—she kept looking around, touching the silver, the flowers, and the silky linen table cloth, admiring the nineteenth-century French paintings that adorned the walls, and the woman playing a soothing tune on the grand piano.

The first of many waiters appeared and handed Michael a wine list that resembled the L.A. phone book. He ordered a very expensive Châteauneuf-du-Pape wine for them and loved the way Leah's face lit up as he did so.

"You remembered," she said.

"Of course I remembered." He'd given up trying to forget her long ago.

They perused the menu, settling on a tasting menu, which included a foie gras crème brûlée as an appetizer, Swiss chard ravioli, and filets of John Dory, among other things.

They chatted about the premiere through the first course, and then their talk turned to the reception.

"Ewan McGregor is so nice," Leah gushed. "He spoke to me like we were old friends."

"Did you meet Vincent Vittorio?" Michael asked, having worked on *The Dane* with him—not to mention his disaster of a wedding.

"I did," Leah said wrinkling her nose a little. "He's really short."

"Yes, he is," Michael said with a laugh.

"I think he's about boob-level, and I had the distinct impression that he likes it like that."

Michael laughed. If there was one guy in this town who loved women more than him, it was probably Vince Vittorio.

"And I met the producer and Mr. Cameron, and they were so *nice*." She glanced up at him through thick lashes. "Especially after I told them I was there with you. You know what the producer said then?"

"No, what?"

"That he would love to have a look at me for a part in an upcoming film, so I gave him my card. Michael—" She suddenly leaned forward, her eyes blazing with excitement. "Can you believe it?" she whispered. "I've been trying to get film roles for five years, and all I had to do was go to a premiere. And mention your name." She sat back and laughed at that. "If I'd known that was all it took, I would have . . ." She paused, thought the better of what she would say, and waved her hand. "You know what I mean," she said cheerfully.

Unfortunately, he did.

But she remained bubbly, and he loved it. Every dish she tasted she said was divine, every sip of wine was heavenly. By the time the waiter had cleared their plates, Leah had talked herself nearly to death and proclaimed herself stuffed. And she had a delightful glow of having drunk a little wine.

"What are you thinking about?" she asked him pointedly as he gazed at her.

"You really want to know?"

Her eyes narrowed with suspicion, and she leaned forward as her fingers drummed lightly on the stem of her wine glass. "Yes," she said. "I really want to know."

Now it was Michael's turn to lean forward. He took her hand from the wine glass and held it in his. "Remember the night we went to the opera?"

"Yes. I'll never forget those box seats," she said with a wink.

"Is that all you remember? Or do you maybe remember what happened at home afterward?" he asked, one corner of his mouth turning up at the thought of it.

Leah glanced around the tables near them before whispering, "How could I forget that? It was fabulous."

"Well that's what I was thinking about. Only this time, I think I'd tie you up," he said, looking at the top of her blond head, "and lick you down," he murmured, his gaze sliding languidly to the revealing décolletage of her gown.

"Michael," she said. "We're friends, remember?"

"We had a great sex life, didn't we, baby?"

She sighed with a bit of exasperation, but then cheerfully acknowledged, "We did."

"You're squirming," he noted, squeezing her hand affectionately.

"Hey, we all have our memories."

"So what do you remember?"

She smiled wickedly. "I remember how you always liked me to put my tongue in a particular place—"

With a laugh, Michael broke her gaze and looked away a moment. When he glanced at her again, she raised a brow and smiled knowingly. "*Now* who is squirming?"

He grinned. "Leah . . . would you like to see my place?" he asked.

"No," she said instantly. "Well . . ." Her gaze didn't waver, but she was clearly debating it behind those blue orbs. And after several moments of what was obviously an internal debate, a lovely smile spread across her lips. "Yes. I would like to see your place."

He could not have been more elated if he had just been handed a wad of cash and a Porsche. "Great. Let's blow this place."

"Wait, are you kidding?" she exclaimed. "Before the soufflé with Grand Marnier? I don't think so, pal," she said, and withdrew her hand from his, picked up her wine, and leaned back, watching him smugly, with clearly no intention of going anywhere until she had dined on every last morsel. That was his girl—never one to pass up good food or good wine or good sex.

"I'll ask for a doggie bag," he said, and although it was obvious Leah thought he was kidding, he was not. He couldn't get the check or the Grand Marnier soufflé out of the head waiter fast enough, but by the time he had finally invested a full $600 in L'Orangerie, he had what he wanted. He helped Leah up then walked closely beside her out of the restaurant, very aware of the many male heads swiveling around to have a look.

Leah, however, seemed oblivious.

In the limousine, she took the gold box with the soufflé from him. "I'll hold that," she said briskly.

"You don't trust me?"

She laughed. "Clearly you haven't heard a word I've said in the last two weeks," she said, tucking the box on the other side of her body. "I don't trust you in the least."

"Yeah, well, we're going to change all that."

"Don't be so sure. And don't get any grand ideas, Mikey. We're just checking out your place. We're *friends*," she said again.

He smiled, settled back. Maybe she didn't trust him, and maybe she thought they could pretend to be just friends, but there was one little detail she had forgotten— Michael knew how to make her come.

SEVENTEEN

HE didn't tell her that he lived in one of those ornate downtown loft complexes, where fabulously wealthy and famous people now lived. It was the sort of place built around what was supposed to look like an Italian piazza, and had better furniture in the lobby than most middle-class homes across America.

And Michael certainly didn't tell her that he owned a loft on the top floor with its own private terrace, overlooking the L.A. skyline and the Hollywood Hills.

"Wow," she said when the elevator opened onto his living room. It was enormous, like a house without walls. Big floor-to-ceiling glass windows formed two walls, and sheer drapes lifted with the night breeze. The room still had the look of the warehouse from which it had been converted—exposed ventilation in the ceiling, four big columns, and scored concrete floors. There were no walls between the kitchen and the living area, and the only evidence of a bedroom or bathroom was a single door at one end of the room.

In the middle of the enormous living area was a thick shag rug, buttery leather couch and chairs, and a distressed coffee table topped with several books and magazines.

"Great place," Leah said as she walked into the room. "Great rug," she added, looking down at her feet. "I don't think this one came from the Discount Barn."

Michael laughed as he shrugged out of his jacket. "It came from Turkey. A friend owed me a favor."

She could only imagine what sorts for favors people owed an ex-CIA operative. Best not to think about it at all—those sorts of questions only led to more questions. Leah walked to one of the windows, pushed aside the sheer drape, and looked out at the skyline. "I guess you guys do pretty well in the stunt business," she said. "This is prime real estate." Real estate that made her bungalow in Venice Beach look like a shack.

"We do well," he said. "But I've also invested wisely."

Another couple of questions popped into her head. Where he'd gotten the money to invest. What did he invest in, and did it have anything to do with his former line of work? Just the usual sorts of things one thought of when standing in James Bond's very expensive and very chic loft apartment.

"Would you like a drink?" he asked from somewhere behind her.

Leah ran her fingers down the sheer drape. "I'd love one." *What in the hell was she doing here?* Curiosity to see how he lived, okay, she'd admit to that. But there was an unspoken expectation, and no matter how much she pretended they were only friends, she was skating out onto some extremely thin ice.

It was a foolish thing to have done, and she would blame the wine . . . but there was something else, wasn't there? He looked so damn good, so sexy, and in spite of her deep misgivings, she was having a bit of a problem—she couldn't stop thinking about sex in his presence. Raw, hot, and very ambitious sex.

She really missed that.

She really missed *him*.

She really missed being loved, although technically, she wasn't being loved at the time, or he never would have left her, but there she went again, trying to sort out what happened five years ago, letting it mess up an otherwise perfect evening.

Michael touched her shoulder, bringing her back to the here and now. She turned around, and he handed her a cognac. "I don't have any cigars," he said with a smile. "But I hope you can still enjoy it." He was referring to a night they had spent in Boston. He'd had to go for business—*what* business, she wondered—and she'd accompanied him for a chance to see the Red Sox play. After a particularly lusty romp between the sheets, they had sipped cognac and smoked cigars. Sort of. Neither one of them were smokers, but it had seemed like decadent fun.

She smiled and lifted the glass to her lips. "I think I can manage," she said, and tasted it. It was smooth and rich— an excellent vintage, she assumed. Michael turned and walked back to the small bar. His tuxedo fit like a glove, she couldn't help noticing. There was that thought of sex again, only this time, it wasn't just an idea that sprung into her head, it was a jolt to her groin.

Maybe she could get over the past and start over, fresh, just like he'd said. Maybe he really meant all the things he'd said. Maybe he really regretted what happened. Maybe, this time, it could be even better. And besides, she'd suffered through a sexual dry spell recently, and he *was* an excellent lover. Sex didn't mean forever. It didn't mean she was naive or going to make the same mistake again. It just meant . . . *sex*.

Leah abruptly followed Michael, tossing her evening

bag onto the couch. "What did you do with the soufflé?" she asked, looking around.

"I put it away," he said and picked up his snifter, strolled toward her.

"We could have a taste of it with our cognac."

"No," he said with a shake of his head. "Don't think so."

"Why not?" she asked as he reached her.

"Because . . ." He leaned his head toward hers and breathed her in. A little shiver of anticipation shot down Leah's spine. "You have to earn it," he murmured as he moved around behind her, slowly circling her. It was a little joke between them, something he used to say when he wanted to be decadent with her body.

She smiled, turned her head away from him to better feel his breath on her neck. "What exactly do I have to do to earn it?"

He brushed his lips against her ear. *"You have to come."*

If that's all it took, he should just touch her, because she was fairly certain if he kept this up, she could come standing. "That's not on the agenda, remember?"

"Isn't it?" he asked low as he put aside his snifter and touched her shoulder with the palm of his hand, slowly caressing her bare arm down to her hand. And up again. And then he was standing in front of her, his eyes gone so dark they were almost black, his smile soft and terribly enticing.

"What do you think, baby?" he asked, taking the snifter of cognac from her hand and putting it aside, too.

"I think you're nuts?"

He shook his head. "I'm not. Neither are you. So tell me," he said, his eyes dark, his hand moving softly from her shoulder to her neck. "Tell me you want me to make you come," he whispered as he touched his lips to her neck.

Oh God, she did. She really, honestly did. The ground felt like it was melting away beneath her feet, and she clutched his arm, let her head drop back, and against all common sense, she whispered, "I want you to make me come."

He made a guttural sound deep in his throat and slipped an arm around her waist, pulling her into his body as he lowered his mouth to kiss her. Leah's heart began to pound in her chest as his lips moved from her mouth to her neck, then her earlobe, and across her jaw to her mouth again. But then he abruptly spun her around and pushed her up against one of the columns, pressing his body against hers, as his tongue dipped hungrily into her mouth.

Her heart leaped to her throat as his hands flit down her arms to her hips and up again, reaching her breasts. But then he lifted his head, braced his arms on either side of her head. That lock of black hair had fallen over his eye, and he smiled roguishly, just like a man who knew he was in control and on the verge of having fabulous sex.

This would go his way—he would do what he wanted to her, and something about that sent another shiver of delight through Leah.

Michael's gaze roamed her figure, lingering on her neckline. He touched her collarbone with the back of his hand. "I've thought about making love to you for years," he said, his voice low. His hand dipped to her cleavage, from where he drew a line up to her neck again. "I've thought about all of the ways I would touch you."

Leah sucked in a breath.

"I've thought of where I would touch you. If I would use my hands," he said, his fingers flicking over her breast, "or my mouth," he said as his hand dipped down to the apex of her legs, "or my cock."

This was going to be good. This was going to be so good that she could hardly contain herself, and she bit her lower lip to keep from trembling like some blasted recluse who hadn't had anything but mediocre sex in five years— okay, so she hadn't—and would, at that moment, kill the doorman if that's what it took to have fabulous sex.

"I've thought of how you would respond," he added, reaching for his tie and pulling it free of its knot. "Especially if you were my captive audience."

"Oh, Jesus," she whispered. She felt damp, intoxicated, her body turning to mush, and he'd really done nothing more than talk. The effect was so overpowering that she pressed her hand against the column behind her for support.

Michael knew her too well, though, and he knew that she had jelly knees. He laughed a low, dangerously seductive laugh that sent an electric charge through her. "Would you like that, baby?" he asked, and pressed the palm of his hand against her cheek.

"Yes," she said instantly, unabashedly. She wanted to be his captive audience. She wanted to be his captive audience *right now.*

Michael wasn't laughing as he pulled the tie free of his neck and held it up for her to see. "Give me your hand."

She did it without question, holding it up to him. He tied the black silk tie around her wrist, made a knot, kissed her palm, then stepped back and pulled her away from the column. "I am going to make you scream." He dropped her hand and stood back. "Undress."

Leah hesitated only a moment, then slowly turned and presented her back to him to unzip. When he had lowered the zipper, he pushed the dress from her shoulders, down to her elbows, then dropped his hands. "Turn around."

She turned, pushed the turquoise sheath from her body, stepped out of it, and handed it to him. He tossed it onto the couch behind him without a glance, watching her, his gaze taking in her lacy bra, the thong bikini panties she was wearing, the high heels. Her only other accessory was the black silk tie dangling from her wrist.

"Go on," he said, and watched as she reached behind to unfasten her bra, then slide it off her arms. She held that out to him, too. That, he pitched over his shoulder. When she put her hands on the panties, Michael shook his head.

"No," he said. "I want you to wear those." And then he was the one to take a steadying breath.

"Jesus, you're beautiful," he said at last. "You're so

beautiful." He reached for her breast, his fingers sliding beneath it, feeling the weight of it, then the other. "I've thought of you like this so many times." His gaze was so dark, so hot, so intense that Leah began to reach for him, but Michael surprised her by abruptly grabbing her around the waist and lifting her off her feet with one arm. He moved two steps forward and dropped her roughly against the column.

"Beautiful and free," he said with a wink. "We can't have that." He took her hand, pulled it back around the column, then stepped around it and took her other hand, and using the end of his tie, bound her hands securely behind the column. She was tied with her back to the column, her breasts jutting out.

Michael walked around to stand before her and peruse his handiwork. He was smiling as he touched her breast, her lips, and then traced a line from her jaw all the way down her body to the top of her legs. He watched her eyes as he slid his finger between her legs, moving back and forth over the fabric of her thong. "You're wet," he murmured. "You want me to continue?"

Oh yes, hell yes, she wanted him to continue, and nodded.

"I can't hear you."

"*Yes*," she whimpered, and closed her eyes, focusing entirely on his hand and fingers and the wild burst of sensual pleasure that was erupting in her. Michael slipped a hand behind her and pressed against the small of her back, forcing her into his body as his fingers worked against the silk fabric of her panties, going deeper into the slit of her body, twirling suggestively around her clitoris. His mouth moved on her lips in rhythm with his hand, gliding over them so delicately that her lips began to tingle savagely with the whisper of each kiss.

And just when she began to breathe heavily, about to come, Michael withdrew his hand and stepped away from her. "Not so fast, baby," he said, and casually removed his vest, tossing it aside. "I've only begun to play."

He unbuttoned his shirt, laughing a little at how hard she was breathing as he shrugged out of it. The man was magnificent—hard body, sculpted, strong. He put his hands on her arms, caressing her skin as he nuzzled her neck. Then he slid down her body, to her bared breasts, and took one in his mouth, his teeth nipping at her hard nipple.

Leah felt dangerously close to falling and moaned, but that only made Michael suck harder, his teeth grazing her, drawing sensation from deep in her groin. Leah was floating now, on a cloud of pure sensation, buoyed by his assault on her senses and his firm grip of her body. With his mouth and his hands, he slid down her body, to his haunches, his mouth leaving a hot, wet trail on her belly. When he reached the thong, he grabbed the tiny string of it with his teeth and jerked, tearing the fabric. With his mouth, he pulled her panties down her leg so that now she was completely bare to him.

"Ah . . . sweet," he said. "So sweet," he said, his mouth just an inch from the curly hair. "I remember the way you taste." His tongue dipped in between the curls, and a hard shiver of delight coursed through Leah.

He glanced up, ran his hands up her sides and to her breasts. "How do you feel?"

Leah looked down at him, panting. "I'm burning up."

"It is a little warm," he agreed with a salacious grin.

"Untie me, Michael. Untie me so I can touch you, too," she begged him.

"No way," he said, and roughly pushed her legs further apart. "This is all for you."

"No, Michael, let me—"

"Shut up," he growled, and flicked his tongue against her.

Leah sucked in her breath; Michael gripped her hips firmly and began to lick her, his tongue dipping deep into her slit, tasting her, exploring her, teasing her at the core of her desire, then sliding down the slick pathway again, to where she throbbed for him.

Above him, Leah's chin dropped to her chest, and she moaned with the thrill of it. This was just as she remembered it—the man was a master. He knew how to interpret her moaning and heavy breathing; the stroke of his tongue became urgent and harder, his mouth covering her, sucking her as she moved, shamelessly grinding against him, seeking her fulfillment. She was so close, so *close*—

But Michael suddenly fell back, stumbling a little before straightening and dragging the back of his hand across his mouth.

"Michael!" she gasped.

"Not yet," he said with a laugh. "Not until I've made you absolutely insane with desire."

"You win, you win! Please don't stop now!" she cried.

"Oh, I'm not stopping," he said and grabbed her chin, pushed her head back so that her face was tilted up to his, then plunged his tongue into her mouth, kissing her until she was panting for breath. He lifted his head; his gaze roamed her face, and he stroked aside a strand of blond hair. "You've got a long way to go before I'm done with you." And with that, he reached behind her, felt for the slipknot on her wrist and yanked it free. Her hands instantly came up to his shoulders.

Michael lifted her up and pushed her against the column. Leah instinctively wrapped her legs around his waist, felt his erection hard and hot pressing against her, and kissed his face, his lips, his ears, but then he dropped her down and let go.

"Stand there. Don't move," he ordered her, and as she watched, he quickly shed his shoes and clothes. His erection was enormously thick and hot, a drop or two of moisture at the tip an indication that he, too, was almost there. Leah tried to take him in hand, but Michael caught her by the arms and roughly turned her around, so that she was facing the column.

Behind her, he kissed the nape of her neck, caressed her back and her hips, then grabbed her thigh and lifted her leg. "Touch yourself," he demanded in a whisper.

Leah dropped her head back to his shoulder, slid her hand down between her legs, and began to rub her fingers against herself. She could hear Michael's breathing quicken, could feel his hand on her breast, his mouth in her hair, his cock rubbing against her hips.

She was so revved up, so ready to release the years of sexual frustration that had followed her after they had split up that her hand began to move faster. But then Michael's hand joined hers, moving hers aside, and slowing the rhythm as he dipped down and eased himself inside her.

"Ah hell," he muttered as he slid deep into her. "Ah, baby," he said as he began to move inside her, matching the work of his hand.

"Don't stop," she begged him, lifting her hips and pressing against him. "Please don't stop."

Michael groaned like an animal and began to move faster, plunging deep inside her, his hand teasing her to the climax he had twice denied her. Leah could hardly catch her breath; she clung to the column, moving with Michael, meeting each of his strokes, gulping for air as she sank into that sexual bliss that surrounded her.

He slid deeper and harder into her, pushing her toward release with his body and his fingers. Leah could feel her release nearing the surface, could feel it on the verge of eruption.

When it did, she cried out with ecstasy and fell headlong into a sea of pure pleasure. She crested in that wave, heard Michael's guttural moan as he found his release.

He collapsed on her, his dark head on her shoulder until he could get his breath. When he had, he pulled her down onto the carpet with him. They lay together, their limbs tangled in one another. Leah pushed her fingers through his hair as they quietly waited for their breathing to return to normal.

It was just like old times. That burst of excitement and fulfillment and love trickling into every pore. It was several minutes before they had the energy to untangle themselves from one another, but still they lay on the carpet, stroking one another, each of them lost in their private thoughts.

Leah felt alive for the first time in years, and while she was afraid to think it, she was quietly wondering if this could really be, if she really could go back in time and pick up where they'd left off.

After a moment, Michael asked, "What are you thinking?"

She looked into his handsome face and smiled at the odds stacked against them. At that moment, she thought she could gladly live with the odds. "I was thinking about the soufflé," she said, and laughed when he groaned and pressed his forehead to her bare belly and made a remark about her irrepressible appetite.

EIGHTEEN

AT some point in the night, Michael enticed Leah into his bedroom, where they made love again, only this time, he allowed Leah to do some of the touching, too. They'd fallen asleep in the midst of an argument about where their favorite New York restaurant was—on the corner of 74th and Columbus? Or 75th and Columbus?

The following morning, however, Michael woke up to an empty bed. But she'd left a note:

Hey Raney, you gorgeous man, some of us actually have to show up at work on time. You looked so damn good sleeping there that I just let myself out. Don't worry, I called a cab. I'll see you later. L.

P.S. I had an AWESOME time. Awesome, awesome, awesome. Absolutely, 100% awesome, especially here in your crib. Seriously, it couldn't have been better even if you'd turned out to be Prince William, heir to the throne. Kidding! That would have been a whole lot better, haha. You made me feel like a queen. Can't wait to see you again. Leah ☺

He smiled. It *had* been awesome. That was some of the best sex he'd ever had, and he was getting hard again just thinking about it. He couldn't wait to see her, either. And he got up, headed for the shower, anxious to get to work.

THE guys had the soccer moms down at the paintball course for the Saturday morning makeup training session, putting them through the paces with the real stuff while Michael was stuck in the office with a couple of studio people, who were now worried about the schedule as well as the budget. He spent a good part of the day in one long, mind-numbing meeting, going over the sequence of scenes they would shoot, making sure that T.A. would have the time necessary to set up for each stunt, of which, he was beginning to note, there was a huge number. How would they ever pull it off?

The only bright spot was that at midday, when they broke for the weekend, Leah was waiting for him at his car, wearing a short little halter dress, sunglasses rimmed with sparkly rhinestones, and a huge smile.

"Let me guess," he said peering at her shades as he walked up to his car and tossed his briefcase behind the driver's seat. "Trudy."

"Right on. And if you play your cards right, I think I can get you one of the Siesta shirts she bought in bulk."

"Why would she do that?" he asked, curious.

Leah shrugged. "Who knows with her? I'm just thankful I don't have to take one."

"So what are you doing?"

"Me?" She tossed her hair over her shoulder and coyly looked away. "Waiting on a guy."

"Excellent. Would that guy happen to be me?"

"No," she said with a laugh. "You're not the only one with passes to movie premieres, you know."

"Wait a minute," he said, putting his hands on his hips, "Don't tell me one of my partners is trying to score with you on *any* level—"

"God, no—"

"That's good, because I'd have to kill whoever tried it."

"No, your partners actually look annoyed most of the time I see them. The other guy happens to be someone with the lighting crew. And he doesn't have tickets to a movie premiere, he only has tickets to a movie. Very pedestrian."

Thank God, he thought. "I hope he was at least offering dinner with the movie."

"Oh yeah, he offered dinner." She wrinkled her nose. "Mexican food."

"Idiot," Michael opined with a grin. "So let me take you to dinner instead."

"Okay. Where are we going?"

"Mexican food," he said, and Leah laughed.

THEY spent the remainder of the weekend together, walking along the Third Street Promenade, bodysurfing at Malibu, and eating all the seafood they could possibly stomach at Gladstone's, a popular joint in Malibu. When they weren't eating, they were in his loft, making love.

Somewhere in the course of the weekend, the years started to move away from them, drifting like little clouds out the expansive windows in his loft. It began to feel as if they'd never missed a moment—they fell into a rhythm that seemed so natural and real and completely unchanged in the years they'd spent apart. If Leah was harboring any lingering misgivings about him, he was not seeing it or feeling it.

But the love affair they shared was snake-bit from the

start, or so Michael would soon come to believe, because by Tuesday of the following week, when the women were being outfitted and meeting with production staff and the director, running lines, and practicing the war scenes, the replacement for the soccer mom with the broken leg showed up.

That wasn't a big deal—she was athletic and eager to please and learned the stuff so fast that the guys bemoaned the fact they didn't have fifteen more just like her. What *was* a big deal, however, was that the woman—Ariel—was known to both Jack and Michael. She was Lindsey's friend. The same Lindsey Jack was trying so hard to date, and the same woman Jack had talked Michael into accompanying on two dates.

Now Jack had finagled a role in the film for her as a favor to Lindsey.

Not that any of it meant anything in the greater scheme of things—nothing had happened between Michael and Ariel, and in fact, he'd found her to be young and sort of goofy. Of course he said hello to her. He even shared a laugh with her, and chatted about their afternoon in Malibu. He thought nothing of it; he had given her no indication that he was the slightest bit interested, and considered her just another acquaintance. But it obviously meant something to Ariel, who heard about the *Spy who Loved Them* from the other actresses and felt compelled to mention that she had "dated" Michael a couple of times.

She also mentioned that she had "dated" Michael as recently as last week, which, when pressed by Trudy, who had overheard the conversation, Jack agreed that she had.

Michael knew all this courtesy of Trudy. By Thursday afternoon, he couldn't seem to catch Leah anywhere on the lot, but he caught up with Trudy. "Hey, kid," he said, putting an arm around her shoulders. "You're mean with that paint gun."

Trudy removed her sunburst sunglasses and smiled up at him. "Ya think?"

"Absolutely."

She smiled, clearly pleased with his praise.

"So where's the Yang to your Yin?" he asked.

"Oh honey, who cares? Wanna get a drink? I can show you other tricks I can do with paint guns," she said with a wink.

He laughed. "I'd love to, but I can't. I just need to talk to Leah."

"She went somewhere with Adolfo."

"With *who*?" he asked as a couple of red flags quickly popped up in his brain.

"Adolfo," she said with a shrug. "Some friend of hers."

A few more red flags and a couple of orange cones popped up. "I didn't know she had any friends on set besides you."

"She does. And you should have one, too," Trudy added, sidling up to him and touching the button of his shirt.

With a chuckle, Michael grabbed her hand and smiled. "I'm tempted, gorgeous . . . but I really need to talk to Leah."

Trudy sighed. "She's not going to talk to you, Michael."

"Why not?"

"Because, silly, she knows about your other date."

"What other date?" he asked, his confusion raging. "I don't *have* another date."

"Ariel?" Trudy said with a slight roll of her eyes.

"Ariel?"

"Ariel. The new girl." At Michael's baffled look, Trudy sighed and said, "The one you went out with just last week? At least she told everyone you did."

The light suddenly went off. "Oh," he said, nodding unthinkingly. "Ariel. But wait, Trudy—I didn't go out with her like *that*."

"You'll have to convince Leah of that. And Nicole."

"Oh shit," he muttered.

Trudy laughed, punched him playfully on the shoulder. "But you don't have to convince *me*."

He smiled, took Trudy's hand, and kissed it. "I adore you, Yin. Thanks for the heads up."

Trudy sighed and looked at her hand. "God, you're good," she said, and smiled after him as he walked on.

ACROSS the studio lot in the commissary tent, Leah was smiling at Adolfo, but she wasn't really hearing anything he said. He was talking, she thought, about surfing. She smiled, picked up her bottle of juice, and drank, put it down again, and smiled.

Adolfo suddenly paused in whatever he was saying and cocked his head to one side. "What is this frown?" he asked.

"Frown?" she echoed. She'd been trying so hard to smile.

"No, no," he said, shaking his head as she tried to smile harder. "This is not a smile. This is a frown that is . . . how do you say . . . upside down."

So busted. "I'm sorry, Adolfo," she said with a sigh. "I guess my mind is just elsewhere."

"Where is your mind?" he asked in all seriousness.

She sighed, thinking back to what Ariel had said at lunch today, bragging about the luxury yacht Michael had taken her on the same weekend Leah was trying to call him and thank him for the Van Cleef perfume.

Adolfo was looking at her expectantly.

With a slight grimace, Leah spread her fingers across the table and tried to think of a tactful way to tell him she was thinking of another guy.

"It is with a man, eh?" Adolfo surmised, startling her.

"How did you know?"

"How do I know! It is obvious, *mi amor.* Men can be very mean to their women."

She laughed at his quick intuition.

"Tell me," he said, leaning back in his chair.

"I'm not a whiner."

"Yes, you do not like wine, this I know. Now tell me," he said with much authority.

"Okay," Leah said, suddenly sitting up and propping her elbows on the table. "There's this guy that I knew five years ago. We were a couple, you know, and then one day, out of the clear blue, he breaks it off. He basically says he's in a place that doesn't include me."

"Bastard," Adolfo spat.

"Right," she said, nodding. "So then, I run into him five years later," she continued. "And he tells me that he made a huge mistake and that he has thought of only me—"

"Liar," Adolfo cried, jabbing a finger in the air.

"Well, he *did* show me all the things he remembered about me, and it was pretty much everything, and he did seem very sincere—"

"Sincere? What is sincere?"

"Honest."

"Ah," he said, and made a circular motion with his hand. "Continue."

"He was bringing me gifts and telling me that he'd had this . . . this *job* that had prevented him from being with me, but he didn't have that job anymore, and he begged me for a second chance."

"What job?"

Leah rolled her eyes. "Spy," she muttered.

Adolfo leaned forward. *"Que?"*

"SPY."

Adolfo blinked. And then he burst out laughing. A very loud, very boisterous laugh that filled the entire commissary tent. "I am sorry, I am sorry," he said, holding up a hand. "But this line is very good! Bravo, bravo! And what does he spy upon? Cows in the field? Beautiful women?"

Leah was beginning to feel like a naive little idiot. "Terrorists," she said wearily. "Arms dealers or something."

"Aha! And where are these terrorists?" Adolfo asked gaily. "Do they star in Hollywood movies?"

"I don't know. Austria, maybe?"

Adolfo laughed roundly again. "Austria!" he scoffed to the ceiling. "And does he prove this? Does he show you something to make you believe? A key, perhaps?"

"A key?" Leah echoed, confused.

"A key! Something!" Adolfo said, waving his hand at *something*.

A bit of a language barrier. "No," she said, shaking her head. "He didn't show me anything. It sounds completely stupid and made up, doesn't it?"

Adolfo smiled sadly, as if she was a poor, young, imbecile. "This . . . this *man* and his lies and his wild sayings hurt your heart," he said kindly.

"Oh no," she lied. "Not really. It was a long time ago. But this time, I wasn't that into him."

"He is not worth the dirt on your feet," Adolfo said strongly.

"I think you mean *beneath*," Leah said with a smile.

"Beneath. He does not deserve to have the same air you breathe," he added with a grand flick of his wrist, and then he leaned forward, pressed his finger to thumb and said, "He does not deserve to live on the same earth."

Leah shrugged.

"If I had you, beautiful woman, for *my* woman, I would treat you like a princess, shower you with gifts and flowers and kisses. And I would never allow this worry to be in your eyes, no? I would kiss it all away."

"*Oh,*" Leah said, moved a little by the passionate way he made his case.

"And if my woman ever look at this bastard or another man, I cut her," he said with a snap of his fingers and jerk of his hand.

She instantly reared back. She had the distinct impression that he really meant it.

But Adolfo smiled sexily and reached for her hand, taking it into his palm and then stroking her knuckles with his thumb. "Ah, *mi amor*, you look very sad."

"I'm fine."

"Allow me to make you happy—"

"Thanks, Adolfo, but we're just having a guava juice."

"Yes, but I can give you more than juice," he purred.

Leah pulled her hand from his and pushed back. "I have to go."

"No, no, do not go away from me," he pouted.

"I've had a long day and I have to be back very early in the morning."

"Here!" he proclaimed, gesturing to the table and the seat. "You will find me still sitting here, still thinking of you."

"I'll be sure and wake you up," she said with a wink, grabbed her backpack, and walked away.

"Do not dream of this bastard, Leah!" Adolfo called after her as she walked away. "Dream sweet dreams! Dream of Adolfo!"

She smiled at him over her shoulder, but she had no hope of sweet dreams.

MICHAEL scoured the lot, looking for Leah, and finally gave up. He was walking to his car when he saw Nicole Redding coming out of the production offices. She instantly lit up when she saw him and started strutting toward him.

Not now, he thought miserably.

"Well, International Man of Mystery, you're still here," she said.

"So are you."

"I'm actually *in* the movie. What's your excuse?"

He smiled, thrust a hand through his hair. Nicole put her hands on her hips and tipped her head back to look up at him, the smirk still on her lips.

He casually touched her shoulder and pulled a loose strand of hair from her shirt. "What is it now, Nicki?"

"I was just thinking that I never realized how much you got around. You're really quite the ladies' man, aren't you?"

"Am I?"

"Don't be coy, Michael. It really pisses me off."

She looked as if she was on the verge of a major pout. Michael smiled, touched her chin. "I'd bet not as much as an inquisition generally pisses me off," he responded cheerfully.

Her eyes narrowed, and she pursed her lips, which really was not a good look for her—it definitely made her look like an old hag. "Does it even *matter* to you that I have a public profile? I don't like being made a fool of in public."

A number of retorts flashed across his mind, but Michael was a gentleman, and he shoved his hands in his pockets and smiled. "How am I making you seem a fool, sweetheart?"

"People still think we're an item—"

"Only because you keep perpetuating the idea. But we're not, and we haven't been in a long time."

"It hasn't been *that* long. But here's the deal, Michael. You bring your skank girlfriend on the set—*after* you try and get in the pants of that soccer mom."

"First of all, Nicki, I didn't bring a girlfriend on set. I've only met the woman a couple of times and can hardly remember her name. Secondly, I wasn't trying to get in the pants of a soccer mom. I was trying to mend some old fences with the only woman I have ever loved. And still, Nicki, I'm trying to figure out how exactly any of that impacts you—unless, maybe, you've got some idea that by hanging around here and dogging me, you might convince me to get together again?"

He thought that would make her mad, make her turn on her heel and walk away—but it had the exact opposite effect. Nicole suddenly moved toward him, put her hand on his chest and batted her lashes. "Would that really be so bad?" she murmured. "We were so good together, Mike. You thought so, too."

"Nicole," he started, but she grabbed his shirt before he could step away.

"Don't say no. Just think about it. Think about how great we were in bed and how great we could be still."

He sighed, reached up for her hand, but she would not let go, so he covered it with his, trying to loosen her grip. "Baby, we weren't that good together. We argued all the time, and you weren't exactly faithful, and the sex wasn't that great. We really oughta hang it up, don't you think? You'd be so much better off with a guy who made you happy. I don't make you happy, I piss you off."

"Why don't you want me?" she asked, leaning into him, tilting her head back. "I'm a movie star! There are a million guys who'd want to be with me!"

"I know," he said and impulsively kissed her cheek as he removed her hand from his shirt. "Why don't you want to be with a guy who wants you more than the air he breathes, Nic? You're right—there are a million of them. So why beat this old dead horse?"

Nicole sighed and lowered her lids so that she could just barely see him. Michael imagined some director had once told her that looked sexy, but it looked stupid as hell.

"It's not a dead horse. I still love you."

"Nicki, you never loved me," he said, and smiled tenderly, for even though she was making an ass of herself, he felt a little sorry for a woman who was a mega star and had to go about getting a guy like this. He started to tell her she should look beyond the movie business for love, but a movement caught his eye, and he glanced up.

There, across the parking lot, was Leah, looking a little dumbfounded and a whole lot pissed. He tried to step away, but Nicole was determined, and grabbed his shirt again. "Wait," she pouted. "Let me just say this . . ."

It was too late, anyway. Leah was already in her car. And as Nicole made her case to Michael, Leah drove away, surely believing now that not only did he have a thing with

Ariel, but still hadn't managed to get past the one with Nicole, either.

And exactly when was it that he thought being the Extreme Bachelor was a *good* thing?

Subject: Okay. You were right.
From: Leah Kleinschmidt <hollywoodiva@verizon.net>
To: Lucy Frederick <ljfreddie@hotmail.com>
Date: 6:10 pm

There is nothing that makes me want to jump off a building more than this, but okay, I have to admit it, Lucy—you were right. Michael is an asshole and all I did was set myself up for a humongous, body-splattering fall. Granted, it was a fall through a very cool movie premiere and some of the best sex I have ever had in my life, but spectacular nonetheless. So get a load of *this*: he was on a date with someone as recently as last week. LAST WEEK!! And as if *that* wasn't painful enough, I see him in the parking lot today with his tongue practically down Nicole Redding's throat. Oh Jesus, please tell me why I am such an idiot? I will believe anything! I am so going to get a huge bottle of vodka right now and drown myself.

   P.S. Thanks for finding the turquoise fabric for the bridesmaid's dresses, but after what I just went through, I hope I never see the color turquoise again. I will not wear turquoise jewelry or admire it in the ocean or even admit it exists as a color.

Subject: Re: Okay. You Were Right
From: Lucy Frederick <ljfreddie@hotmail.com>
To: Leah Kleinschmidt <hollywoodiva@verizon.net>
Date: 9:19 pm

I TOLD YOU SO. Don't jump, just remember that I am always right, and your life will be a lot easier. Damn, that makes me so MAD. I KNEW he was going to screw you over, that bastard!! But hey, what's done is done. I'm sorry, kid. I always thought there was something totally untrustworthy about him, but I can't believe he turned out to be an asshole. Chin up. Don't drink yourself to death.

NINETEEN

OF course Leah didn't answer her phone when Michael called several times through the last week of boot camp, and of course she found reasons to leave the lot early each day, too, so she wouldn't risk running into him.

And of course he came to her house. She expected it. She also expected Brad to remember her admonitions to keep him at the door, but Brad invited him in for a beer like they were old college buddies. They even watched some hoops, according to Brad, who, when confronted by Leah after Michael had left, very cheerfully confessed it all.

"I like him," Brad said, tipping his beer toward Leah. "Cool guy."

"Yeah, he's cool all right," Leah muttered, and stomped back to her bedroom, pissed at her roommate. "Thanks a lot, Brad!" she yelled at him, and Brad just waved at her over the top of his head.

Michael showed up when she was packing a few things

for the trip to Bellingham, Washington, later that week and knocked lightly on the doorjamb of her bedroom. He would have knocked on the door, but it was open, and Leah was standing in the middle of her room, wearing shorty gym shorts and a cropped T-shirt, trying to decide if she needed two black skirts or just one. When she heard the knock, she expected Brad, and groaned when she looked up, turning away from the sight of him.

"Hey, baby," he said.

"Hel-*loh*, Michael," she said in a sing-song voice that was totally sarcastic. "I see Brad not only forgot that I didn't want to see you, but he also offered you a beer."

Michael looked at the beer in his hand. "He insisted. I mean, he *really* insisted."

That was Brad, all right—party on, with whoever was available, whether he knew the person or not.

"He, ah . . . he pointed me back here," Michael said.

Great. Now Brad was directing traffic back to her bedroom. She seriously had to have a talk with him. She angrily folded a T-shirt and threw it into her suitcase.

"I realize you're upset—"

"No! I'm not really *upset*," she baldly lied.

That seemed to surprise him. He actually looked a little hopeful.

"I'm *furious*," she said with the same smile. "See how my teeth are bared? And my knuckles are white because I am trying so hard not to punch you?"

"Oh Christ—Leah, I didn't *date* Ariel."

"Right," she said, and threw some underwear into her bag like she was trying to knock a hole through it. "You just hung out with her, I guess?"

"Sort of," he admitted with a sigh.

Sort of? He was supposed to say *no*, he never saw her, never talked to her, never—She turned a murderous look on him, and Michael tried to smile, but he couldn't make it happen and just shook his head.

Leah turned back to her Rambo packing.

"Jack started seeing a woman who won't go out without a pack. You know how women are."

"I know how women are?" she echoed incredulously, folding her arms over her middle.

He had the decency to look chagrined. "I just meant . . . you know how some women have that pack mentality . . . never mind," he said quickly, after seeing her expression. "Just leave it at Jack dating a woman who won't go unless her friend goes, too, and so Jack begged me—*begged* me, Leah—to ride along. The first time I went, you were hardly even speaking to me, and even so, I just sat there like a bump on a log, making small talk, just for Jack, because all I could think of was you. The second time I went because Jack really likes this chick, and he practically got down on his hands and knees to beg me. He promised me it was the last time. And it was. And again, nothing happened—we had a few laughs, but that was it. It was *nothing*. It was such a nothing that I don't even remember it."

"Really? You don't remember you were out with her just last week?" Leah asked, fuming. "Between your dates with me?" she added, wiggling her fingers between dates.

"We had dinner, the four of us. I never touched her," he said, moving deeper into the room. "It was just a favor to a pal—go out, keep her company while he tried to make some headway with the woman he wants to get to know. It didn't mean I was *dating* her. Regardless of what she says around work, she knows it, too."

Leah nodded, then stooped over, picked up a pair of shoes. "Then why did you give her a job?" she blurted, throwing a shoe into her suitcase and holding the other one, heel out, aimed right at Michael.

He looked at the shoe and held up his hand. "I didn't give her a job. Jack did. And without my knowledge."

She was still skeptical. "I can't speak for Jack or how he reels them in," he said, looking boyishly distressed.

Leah tossed the shoe into the suitcase, put her hands on

her hips. "So what about Nicole Redding? That was quite an intimate moment you were having a couple of days ago."

He groaned again, shoved a hand through his hair. "Don't get me started on Nicole," he muttered, but then looked at Leah sidelong and shook his head. "Nicole and I were an item a few months ago," he admitted. "We were together for about two months." He frowned slightly, as if the memory was unpleasant. "She was also seeing some director at the same time, and when I found out about it, I ended it with her. Frankly, I was looking for an excuse—I wasn't that interested."

"You had to go out with her for two months to figure that out?" Leah asked disdainfully. "So what was that little tête-à-tête about?" she asked, motioning with her hand.

"Well, to put it bluntly, Nicole appears to be between lays. And she's hoping to hook up again."

"Wow," Leah said. "That's like . . . horribly honest." She turned away, picked up a pile of clothing—dirty or clean, she had no idea—and dumped it carelessly into her suitcase. Nicole Redding, a huge movie star, was jonesing for her guy. How bizarre was that?

"I told her to forget it," he added quietly.

Leah snorted. "That's great, Michael. I hope for your sake she forgets it."

"Leah—"

"Just out of curiosity," she asked, turning to face him again, "when you guys were together," she said, making quote marks with her fingers, "how did you keep from crushing her? She's just a tiny little thing, and it seems like there would have been a danger of *hurting* her—"

Michael closed the distance between them, put his arms around her in spite of her throwing up her arms to stop him, and held her tightly in his arms.

"I guess, though, if you're the Extreme Bachelor, you must have worked those tiny details out," she mumbled into his shoulder.

"Stop," he breathed into her hair, and put his hand on the back of her head. "I didn't lie to you, baby. I love you, and I've loved you all these years. Granted, I haven't been a saint, but I haven't *lied* to you. There is no one else. There is no Ariel, no Nicole, no one but you."

Instead of soothing her he was making her angry— she'd heard this song a few times too many now and was getting sick of it. She shoved against him, breaking his grip on her and making him spill his beer on the carpet. He moved to get something to clean it, but she threw a towel down and stomped on it, grinding it into the carpet. "Just tell me how many other women are going to come crawling out of the woodwork and claim some sort of relationship with you?"

"What does it matter? There is no one else, and there won't be now that I have found you again."

"It matters! What am I supposed to do, just pretend like none of it bothers me? Like it doesn't hurt all over again? Or make me feel like an idiot for believing we could go back?"

"Did you believe that?" he asked, surprised.

Her hands curled into fists. "*Yes,*" she said bitterly. "For a moment, one single, solitary moment, I believed it. But I didn't know you jumped back into the dating pool with both feet. Not me. It took me *years* to get over you! It took me years to get up the nerve to date again, because I didn't think I could ever love anyone like I loved you, and if by some miracle I did, I couldn't stand to go through it all again and risk being dumped like a bag of garbage one day. So it's not exactly easy to keep running across all these women you've dated and been with and try and act like it doesn't bother me!"

"What do you want me to do?" he asked angrily. "I can't turn back the clock; I can't do anything but tell you there is no one else. The fact that there are so many of them cropping up all of a sudden should be more evidence that I could never manage to maintain a relationship for more than a few weeks! They weren't you, Leah."

She glared at him. Michael glared back. She kicked her suitcase shut. He tossed the beer into her trash can.

"So?" he asked.

"So?"

"So where does this leave us?"

She gave him a petulant shrug and looked at the floor. "I'm not sure."

"Maybe it leaves us with dinner."

"Maybe it leaves us with a gash too deep to heal, Michael."

"Come on, baby," he said, moving closer, stroking her cheek with his knuckles. "Trust me. Believe me."

Bite me, she thought bitterly. "I don't know. I honestly don't know if I can."

"Okay, look," he said, just as wearily. "We can't expect to fix everything gone wrong between us in a matter of days, right? So let's just have some dinner and see how it goes. What do you say?"

He was right—old, deep, gaping wounds took time to heal. She just had a funny feeling that she hadn't quite found all her wounds, or knew how deep they ran. "All right," she said. "Just let me change."

He nodded and walked out, leaving her behind, the space between them opening up like a gulf.

Dinner did nothing to improve their mood. Michael tried to talk about work and how he was looking forward to finally getting to Washington and the actual filming. His talk of Washington reminded Leah that Jill, yet another woman Michael had dated at some point in the last five years, had told them when Michael had showed up to boot camp that they had gone white-water rafting with the other guys a couple of years ago in Washington.

Leah could picture herself at dinner parties and Holly-wood affairs with Michael, meeting woman after woman

Michael had once dated, or taken white-water rafting, or flown to Paris, or whatever. She grew more sullen. He grew more exasperated with her sullenness, professing an inability to understand why she couldn't just accept what he was saying, and that made her angry all over again.

"So what you're saying is that basically, I shouldn't have any feelings about the women you've slept with, is that it?" she snapped.

"Hey," he said low, looking at her darkly. "I told you, I didn't sleep with all those women."

"You slept with *some* of them. You dated *all* of them."

He said nothing, but clenched his jaw tightly shut.

"And could you please just explain to me why they all have to end up on this film?"

He drove his fork into his food. "I told you that, too, Leah," he said sharply. "Jack thought it would be funny."

"Ha ha," she said, and pushed her plate aside.

"Jesus, will you stop persecuting me?" he asked, dropping his fork. "I can't change the past. I can't make it go away."

"Right," she said nodding furiously. "And maybe you shouldn't try. Maybe I shouldn't either. Maybe we should just let the past lie."

"Oh for Chrissakes," he said, and pushed his plate away, too. He started looking around for a waiter. "This is going nowhere. Let's just get the hell out of here."

"Fine with me," she snapped.

They sat in stone-cold silence until the waiter came and gave them a bill. Michael tossed a few bills on the table and stood up. So did Leah. And together, they marched out of the restaurant, the gulf that had started to creep between them spilling into an ocean by the time they reached the car.

Michael drove like a maniac back to Leah's house, clearly ready to be rid of her, and the feeling was entirely mutual. At that moment, Leah didn't care if she ever saw him again. But when they pulled into the drive, and she reached for the door, Michael put a hand on her leg. "Leah.

We can leave it like this. Or we can agree that it's something we're going to have to work through if we want to be together."

She hated logic. "Or, we can just call it a day and move on," she said, her hand falling away from the door.

"We could. But I don't want that. Do you really want that?" he asked as his hand sought hers.

"I don't know what I want," she said morosely, and let him twine his fingers with hers.

"I understand that. But please don't jump off the deep end on me, baby. Give me a chance."

Leah looked at the brown eyes so beautiful they almost made her weep, at the chiseled face, the sexy five o'clock shadow, and as always, that thick strand of black hair across his brow. No, she wasn't ready to give up. She didn't know what to think or what to believe, or what really was bothering her, but she wasn't ready to quit.

Michael, like always, seemed to know what she was thinking and leaned across the console, touched his lips lightly to hers. His hand fell on her cheek, his fingers spreading across her face. Leah gripped his wrist, clinging to him, feeling the power of his desire seep through her skin. She didn't want to let go, she wanted to believe him, but she couldn't seem to swim past old, hurtful feelings that kept surfacing. Mixed in with the joy of having discovered her one true love again were bits of anger and distrust and that dreadful feeling that she was headed for the biggest fall yet.

So she pushed back from him and turned away, looking blindly out the window. "I'll see you tomorrow," she said softly, and got out of the car, shut the door, and hurried to her front door without looking at him, without seeing that expression in his eyes that could make her forget herself.

Michael waited until she was safely inside, then put the car in reverse, spinning out of her drive and getting the hell out of dodge.

Frankly, he was beginning to wonder if a man could

ever go back again, or if it was always just too late. He
loved Leah, more than anything. But he didn't relish the
thought of apologizing for his past all the rest of his days.
At some point, if she wanted to be with him, she had to accept what had happened and move on. Or, if she couldn't
let go of her grudge, she could just simply move on now,
like she said. Without him.

Either way, at the moment he didn't give a shit what she
did, because he had a splitting headache.

Subject: Old Times
From: rtj0431 <rtj0431@dc.rr.com>
To: Michael Raney <michael.raney@thrillsanonymous
    .net>
Date: 4:32 pm

Yo, bro, been trying to get hold of you. Rex here—
remember your old pal? The one who is actually trying to
save your ass? Listen, you'll want to hear what I have
to tell you. It concerns an old friend of yours who is no
longer in the place you left him. Give me a call on the
usual line, but call soon.

TWENTY

LEAH was exhausted when she showed up for work the next morning, having spent yet another sleepless night, courtesy of Michael Raney. What happened to that vow she'd made to herself one hundred years ago that she'd not lose one more moment of sleep because of him, anyway?

As Leah marched across the parking lot, backpack in hand, Trudy, who was waiting at the gate, lifted her psychedelic shades and peered closely at her. "What's the matter?" she asked when Leah reached her.

"Nothing," Leah said. "I just didn't get much sleep last night."

"Oh no," she said knowingly, and hands on hips, she nodded sagely as she sized Leah up. "Oh, honey," she said, with a sympathetic shake of her head. "You look like shit. That's the deal with these movie guys—they'll say anything to fuck you. So what did he say this time?"

What hadn't he said? Leah shifted her backpack from one shoulder to the other. "Nothing, really." She didn't want to rehash it all again—she'd just spent the better part of one night rehashing it over and over and over, until her head felt like it was literally going to explode off her shoulders. "So don't we have a meeting with the director this morning?"

"Yeah," Trudy said, and put her arm around Leah's shoulders, squeezing her tight. "Let's go show him that Yin and Yang are the best he's got."

Leah let Trudy pull her along.

They rehearsed the battle scenes all morning with the director and Charlene Ribisi and Nicole Redding, who, Trudy pointed out in a stage whisper, couldn't carry her cell phone if the director asked it, much less the scene. Charlene Ribisi, on the other hand, was a professional and about as buff as any woman Leah had ever seen. In one scene, Charlene had to push her down, and for a woman weighing all of 110 pounds at 5'10", she sure packed a punch.

The most telling part of the rehearsal came just before they broke for lunch, when the director, looking through a camera lens, shook his head and yelled cut.

"Were we filming?" Nicole asked, clearly annoyed.

"No. And it's a good thing we weren't," Harold said. "Honey, you're going to have to lose a few pounds in the next week. You've got a couple of places that aren't coming across very well."

Next to Leah, Trudy gasped. Leah was shocked, too— Nicole was so tiny that she was hardly even there. Not in particularly great shape, but tiny nonetheless.

Nicole apparently thought the same thing, because she said, "*Me*? I'm the smallest one out here! Why doesn't *she* have to lose any weight?" she cried, pointing directly at Leah.

Leah instantly looked down; Trudy gasped again.

"Because she's nobody. You're the star, Nicole, and you need to drop a few L.B.'s, or it's going to look like we've got Attila the Hun lumbering through these scenes."

"Shut up, Harold," Nicole said, and flounced off.

"Her ass *is* looking a little large," Trudy whispered.

But Leah was mortified. "What does that make me? How huge am I?"

"Not to worry, hon," Trudy said confidently. "You probably won't have that much time on screen anyway."

Talk about going from bad to worse. By the time lunch rolled around, Leah was really in a foul mood. She begged off lunch with Trudy, Jamie, and Michele, who were intent on shopping for rafting clothes. "What are rafting clothes?" Leah asked.

Trudy's mouth dropped open. "Are you kidding? Cute little bathing suit tops and shorts."

"And don't forget the sandals," Michele added. "I am definitely getting some of those new all-terrain sandals. You can run in them, too."

Right, like Michele was ever going to run after they wrapped this film.

"Thanks, but I'm going to pass," Leah said. "I don't know if they carry size jumbo where you're going. And besides, Jumbo is really hungry."

"Don't do that to yourself," Trudy said, shoving her psychedelic sunglasses on her face. "You're beautiful! But maybe just a salad," she suggested.

"Come on you guys!" Jamie cried. "We've got to be back in an hour and a half, and the outdoor gear store is across town!"

Leah watched them run across the parking lot to Jamie's car, then made her way to the commissary, where she intended to have a salad of lettuce, period.

Later she was sitting at a table near the back, her lettuce leaves consumed and leaving her wanting more, reading a novel she'd started months ago, when someone jostled her table by falling into a seat across from her.

Leah glanced up; a smile instantly curved her lips. "Hi, Adolfo."

"*Mi amor*, my heart is warm now that I see you," Adolfo

said, and took her hand, brought it to his lips, and with his gaze on her eyes, he kissed her knuckles lovingly.

Leah laughed and tugged her hand free. "So what are you up to, today, Adolfo? Trolling the commissary tent looking for women?"

"Women! I have no need of women!" he said dramatically with an incongruent wink. "It is only you I wish to see, *mi amor.* Only you who fills my dreams with smiles," he said, his hands doing a flowery little flitter. "Only you with the nectar that lures me to you."

"Nice," she said, nodding. "Your lines are getting better all the time."

"Gracias," he said, inclining his head in acknowledgment of her compliment. "I do it all for you."

Leah snorted, resumed reading.

"You don't believe me?" He looked wounded. "Look, then, look what I have brought for you." He pulled a brown paper bag from his back pocket, removed a small picture frame, spread the bag flat, and placed the picture on it, turning it so Leah could see it.

She leaned over to look and blinked with surprise. It was a picture of her. She recognized the setting—she was wearing camouflage, and it was the day they had been fitted. She was standing with someone else, who had been cropped from the picture, and she was laughing. Her eyes were crinkled, her mouth open as she laughed. She had to admit; it was an appealing picture.

"Adolfo!" She picked up the picture. "How in the world did you manage this?"

"How!" he scoffed, throwing his arms wide. "I am in the lighting, *mi amor.* My friends, they are the photographers, of course."

"You mean the camera guys?" she asked. "I haven't seen any of the crew yet."

"They come one day for the pictures that will appear in the papers and television."

"And you had them take a picture of me?" she asked, looking at him skeptically.

Adolfo smiled. "*No*. I will be liar if I tell you this. I choose this from many pictures they take."

She still looked at him skeptically, but his smile just deepened, and he lifted his shoulders, palms up. "You do not trust me?"

"No," she said with a laugh, but looked at the picture again. "This is really great, Adolfo. A little memento of the movie. It was really very sweet of you."

"For you, sweetheart, I do it. You must have this wonderful picture of you."

"Thank you."

"So now you will come to dinner with me, no?"

Leah laughed at his tenacity. "Maybe someday."

"Someday! When is this someday?" Adolfo whined, looking exceedingly charming nonetheless. "Is it this man again?"

"What man?" she asked coyly.

"The man, the man," he blustered, gesturing impatiently. "The bastard who does not deserve you. The bastard who makes your heart sad. *This* man."

"Oh. *That* man."

"*Sí, sí,* that man."

"Well . . ." she picked up the picture again and admired it. "It seems he gets around a lot." She peeked up at him. "He dates a lot of women." Adolfo lifted a dark brow. "A *lot*," Leah added emphatically.

"Ah," Adolfo said, and nodded. "I know this man. Let me tell you something. This man will promise you many things, but he will never give himself completely to you. Do you understand?"

"Better than you know."

"There, you see? I am the man for you. When will you have the dinner with me?"

"Maybe when we get back from Washington."

"As long as that!" he exclaimed, but then softened, took her hand in his once more and kissed her knuckles. "I shall wait, *mi amor*, I shall wait as long as you will torture me with this hope," he said, and let go her hand, smiled very sexily.

For some reason, the way he said it, the way his brown eyes seemed to sparkle through when he smiled, made her toes curl a little. She laughed a little, slipped the picture into the bag, and picked up her backpack. "Thanks again. And now, I have to go. See you, Adolfo," she said. She stood up, gave him a little wave with her free hand, and walked out of the commissary tent, almost colliding with a pole because she was too giddy to see it.

WHEN Michael showed up to work that morning, he looked at the package on the passenger seat and debated. This was stupid—he should have just left well enough alone instead of rifling through the little box that contained mementos from the few highlights of his life—a mathlete badge from the eighth grade, a Valentine's Day card a teacher had once given him. A cork from a rare bottle of wine he had shared with a European prince. A pair of panties he couldn't remember the specifics about anymore, but he figured it had to be good because he had kept them.

And a couple of other things, like Leah's phone number scrawled on a cocktail napkin, a playbill from one of the first plays he ever saw her in, before she even knew he existed. It was that stupid playbill he'd taken and had engraved and framed. The original playbill was yellowed with age and stained by a glass of wine he'd had with his date the night he'd seen Leah's play, a woman whose name he could no longer remember.

But that had been Leah's first Broadway play, and she'd been spectacular. He'd heard about it from the guy who had introduced him to Leah at a party, and he'd been so intrigued he'd taken his date to see Leah's play. His date never knew he was looking at Leah, that he was admiring her every move on stage. Even then he'd known there was something different about her. To think he'd contributed to ending such a bright and promising career filled him with grief.

And now—in light of what had happened between them in the last week, it seemed like a stupid extravagance. The day he had taken the playbill to the engraver, he thought they had a chance. Now, he wasn't so sure.

So he left the package in the trunk of his car, unwilling to bare his heart just to have her reject it. And he stayed in the office most of the day, working on the last-minute details before they moved the operation to Washington for filming.

At the end of the day, after the rehearsals and meetings had ended, the T.A. guys were all in the office finishing up when the door burst open and Marnie Banks, Eli's girlfriend, came barreling through. Her arms were full of wet gear, which she dumped on the floor between them before putting her hands to her hips and glaring at Eli. "Is that it? Because this gopher has a wedding to work this weekend and no time to be running all over town doing T.A.'s bidding."

Eli grinned, got up from his chair, sauntered over to Marnie, planted a big kiss on her lips, and said, "Thanks, baby."

Marnie instantly softened. "You're welcome," she said with a pretty smile, and cozied up to Eli, returning his kiss with one that prompted Cooper to tell them to get a room.

Marnie stepped back and surveyed the office. "This place is a pigsty," she announced cheerfully. "And who needs the wet suits, anyway? It's the hottest summer on record!"

"Tamara," Jack said with a weary sigh. "That chick carries more aggravation in one hundred pounds than all the women I've ever dated rolled up together."

"All the women *you* ever dated? Who's that, your prom date and this new girl Lindsey?"

Jack glared at Eli. "Thanks. Thanks a lot, Eli. Why don't you just borrow a bullhorn from the director and announce it to the entire cast?"

"What makes you think I haven't?" Eli asked stoically.

"Everyone knows it anyway, Jack," Marnie said with an airy flick of her wrist. "But what's this about Tamara? I thought Eli said the women were really working together as a team."

"They are," Eli confirmed. "They've really come around, and I think we've got a group of women that could really kick some ass. I'll be the first to admit I didn't think that was possible when we started this gig."

"You and me both," Jack snorted. "I've never had a worse crew to train in my life. Remember? There was all the talking and the phones and *whining*. Jesus, it was torture."

"Yep," Cooper said, leaning back and putting his hands behind his head, "we've definitely whipped this group into shape. Those women have probably never been in better shape in their lives."

"And they owe it all to you guys, huh?" Marnie asked, hands on hips. "T.A. has once again improved the lives of dozens just by showing up to work."

"Hey! We did get them in shape," Jack protested.

"They're professional actresses, Hercules. They are trained to adopt the persona of the roles they are going to play."

Before anyone could argue, Marnie whirled around to Michael, who immediately tried to look busy to avoid her gaze. There was one thing a person quickly learned about Marnie—if you got on her radar screen, it was hard to get off.

As if to prove his point, Marnie marched the two steps she needed to reach his side. "So, Romeo," she said, tapping his shoulder. "How's it going?"

"Great, Marnie. Great," he said, and tried to turn around to his computer, but Marnie plunked herself down on the desk, blocking his view of the screen.

"Really? You don't look so great. You look sort of grumpy."

Somewhere behind him, someone snickered.

"Okay," he said, smiling up at Marnie. "Someone around here has a big mouth. Based on what transpired earlier, I'm going to guess Eli," he said, slanting the cowboy a look. "But you don't need to worry about me, sweetheart. I've got it all under control," he said, and gave her a wink.

"Oh really? Well, then, I'll leave you alone. I won't tell you that she just stomped past the window here and didn't even look to see if you were inside."

Much to the delight of his partners, Michael instantly jerked around and craned his neck to see out the window.

"Well hell, I never thought I'd see the day the Extreme Bachelor would be the guy wondering what to do next," Eli drawled.

"Oh, honey, don't be so hard on him. Everyone needs a helping hand now and again," Marnie said, casually studying her cuticle.

Michael stood up, grabbed his bag, and slung it over his shoulder. "I'd love to stay and chat about how badly I've screwed this up, but I've got something I need to do."

"Wait!" Marnie cried, reaching up and brushing the hair from his eyes. "Oh *wow*," she sighed. "You are a handsome man."

Michael chucked her playfully on the chin and walked out as Eli protested that he didn't appreciate Marnie fawning all over Mike, while Marnie laughed and assured him that she loved only him.

Michael didn't hear the rest—he had to run a little to catch up to Leah, who was indeed stomping along at a clip. But he caught her, just before she went out the gate to the parking lot.

"Oh, hi, Michael," she said, and pushed a hand through her hair, but the blond locks just fell back again. "I didn't know you were here today."

"I'm here," he said, and pushed open the gate for her. "How was your day?"

"The usual. Lots of running around. How was yours?"

"Boring. Empty. Tedious."

Thankfully, Leah laughed a little.

"Maybe we could take a walk?" he suggested.

"Ah . . ." Leah paused, shoved a paper bag under her arm as she looked toward the parking lot, debating it. "I'm not sure . . ."

This was beginning to feel so heavy. Just like when he was a kid, a stupid little geek trying to the get the cute girl to look at him, almost to the point of begging. "No problem," he said instantly. "Just thought I'd ask." He smiled and started walking toward his car.

"Michael, wait," Leah said.

He slowed down and turned around so that Leah could catch up to him and walk beside him.

"I've been thinking," she said tentatively.

Thinking, dammit. Never a good sign.

"And I was thinking that maybe I should date other people. I mean, while I'm dating you. You know, just sort of date around and make sure . . ."

Her voice trailed off, and Michael stopped cold, midstride, to stare at her in disbelief. How had everything gone so far south so quickly? What the hell had he done, other than push Nicole away and do his friend Jack a favor? "Make sure of *what*?" he demanded.

"I don't honestly know what," she admitted with a light shrug. "I just think maybe it will help me get my head on straight."

Now she was just pissing him off. "Get your head on straight? I didn't realize there was a problem with your head."

"Why are you taking such a tone with me?"

"Why are you making such a big deal out of a couple of women with more imagination than common sense?"

"Okay," Leah said, shifting her weight to one hip, waving

her hand. "See, this is exactly why I think I should date other people. You are getting upset because I am not falling right into line with what *you* want, and the more I think of it, the more I think you have always been like that."

"Don't tell me what I've always been like," he snapped. "You didn't even know who I really was until a few weeks ago."

Leah gasped. "And whose fault was *that*?"

"So what—you, who claims to be dateless and sadly single for the last few years, are suddenly going to waltz out there and start dating?" he asked, throwing his arm at the *out there*.

"What the hell is that supposed to mean? Yes, I may start dating. I just happen to have one lined up, as a matter of fact."

"Right," he snorted. "Who is that? Brad?" he asked, knowing full well it was a low blow and not caring.

Her expression assured him that it was indeed a low blow. "What does it matter, anyway?" she snapped.

"It doesn't, Leah. But I guess since you know every woman I've ever dated or even thought about dating, it's only fair that I get to play that game, too."

"You have no right to be such an ass about this, Michael! You're constantly making moon eyes at some chick—for all I know, you've done *all* of them."

He was getting seriously annoyed with the conversation. "And you've been living in a convent?" he snapped.

"No," she said, her eyes narrowing. "Frankly, I don't owe you any explanation at all, but if you must know, his name is Adolfo, and—"

"Adolfo?" he all but shouted.

"Yes, Adolfo!"

Michael put his bag down. "Where is Adolfo from?"

"What?" Leah exclaimed.

"Mexico?"

A shout of incredulous laughter escaped her. "What—are you *prejudiced*?" she asked in disbelief. "You know, you're right, Michael—I *don't* know you. I always thought you were an enlightened kind of guy, and I never thought you'd be the type—"

"Come on, Leah. Is he American? Mexican-American? Mexican? Spanish, maybe?"

"I didn't ask him, because it doesn't matter! He's just a nice guy, and he's been very nice to me, and I may go out with him!"

Michael groaned, pushed his hands through his hair, turned full circle, then faced Leah again, his hands on his hips, his jaw clenched shut.

Leah stepped back.

"Okay. Do what you need to do," he said flippantly, and reached in his pocket, pulled out his keys, and pushed the remote button to open his car.

"Oh-kay," Leah said, sounding uncertain. "Thanks. I will."

He walked to the trunk, punched the button so it would pop open, and with no fanfare, he pulled out the gift bag and held it out to Leah.

"What . . . what is that?" she asked suspiciously.

"A gift for you, what else?" he said petulantly. "You can take it or leave it, whatever you want."

"Michael, please don't be like this."

He would be however he wanted to be. He was tired of trying to persuade her. "So do you want it?" he asked, shaking it impatiently at her.

Clearly exasperated, she thrust the sack she held toward him. "Hold it, will you?" she asked, and took the bag he held out.

Michael took the small sack in exchange. It felt like it held a picture frame. "What's this?" he asked, as she untied the bow around the handles of his gift bag.

"It's just a picture," she muttered. Michael opened the sack and took the picture out. "Hey!" Leah protested, but he ignored her and stared down at a framed picture of her smiling brilliantly, dressed in camouflage. It looked like some of the still shots the studio had done one day when they were fitting costumes.

"Where'd you get it?" he asked.

She snorted, yanked the handles of his gift bag apart. "Not that it's any of your business, but Adolfo gave it to me." She plunged her hand inside, pulled out the tissue-wrapped engraved playbill, unwrapped it, and studied it for a minute. "Oh my God," she said, a smile lighting her face as she stood up. "Oh dear God." She looked up at him, her eyes glimmering. "How did you get it?"

"I saw that play," Michael grudgingly admitted. "Before you even knew I was interested in you."

"Michael . . ."

But he was stung at the picture this Adolfo-character had taken, put in a very cheap and simple frame. Next to that picture, his gift looked like something a Casanova might come up with. Yet that's what he was—a Casanova. A guy who jumped from woman to woman, always surprised and delighted to be adored once again, never settling in for the work a true relationship required.

He suddenly felt like a fool. In frustration, he thrust the picture at her. Leah took it awkwardly, trying to hold it and the ridiculous engraved playbill. "Well, looks like you've got your course mapped out, Leah. Let me know if you ever figure out where I fit in."

"Hey, come on, Michael."

"Come on? You are the one who wants to date around, who can't trust me, who can't go back to what we had. Not me. I'm there. So the ball is in your court, baby," he said, and turned around, walked to the driver side of his car, and got in.

As he drove out of the parking lot, he caught a glimpse of Leah standing at her car, watching him. He looked the other way, pulled out on the road, and hit the gas.

He was reaching the end of his rope.

He just hoped that whatever happened between him and Leah, this Adolfo character was a decent guy and not dangerous like Michael's instincts were telling him.

Subject: 13 Months and Counting
From: Lucy Frederick <ljfreddie@hotmail.com>
To: Leah Kleinschmidt <hollywoodiva@verizon.net>
Time: 6:13 pm

Okay, at the risk of you causing my leap from the Empire State Building here, I have attached a very sexy halter dress in lavender. Surely you cannot have a problem with lavender. And lavender accents would look stunning on me with my dark hair. Don't write me back if you don't like it, because I do not want to be disappointed for the hundredth time.

So what's new with the Big Giant Loser (BGL)?

Subject: Re: 13 Months and Counting
From: Leah Kleinschmidt <hollywoodiva@verizon.net>
To: Lucy Frederick <ljfreddie@hotmail.com>
Date: 7:32 pm

Lavender is cool, altho I think I'd go with a softer pastel version instead of something that bold. But yeah, I can definitely do lavender.

So do you think I should go out with Adolfo? He brought me a picture of me in camouflage today, which I thought was sweet, but in a weird kind of way—I mean, I didn't know the picture was taken, so it had a stalking-ish feel to it. But he's really sweet and nice. Only he doesn't give me flutters in my stomach like I get when I see Michael, who, BTW, gave me an engraving of my first Broadway playbill. I didn't even know he went to that play.

Subject: Re: Re: 13 Months and Counting
From: Lucy Frederick <ljfreddie@hotmail.com>
To: Leah Kleinschmidt <hollywoodiva@verizon.net>
Time: 9:58 pm

You're kidding, right? This is your big cyber joke on me—
give me grief about the bridesmaid's dresses and then tell
me you're going to date someone else? Please tell me you
are kidding, because if you aren't, I'm not sure I can cor-
respond with you anymore. You're driving me nuts.

    P.S. The LAVENDER I picked out is the exact shade
of LAVENDER I want. So I guess that means you don't
like LAVENDER either.

Subject: Re: Re: Re: 13 Months and Counting
From: Leah Kleinschmidt <hollywoodiva@verizon.net>
To: Lucy Frederick <ljfreddie@hotmail.com>
Date: 7:04 pm

I'm leaving this week for Washington. Maybe we should
have this conversation when I get back. I know you are
really excited about your wedding, but its starting to get
to you and you're getting a little cranky, Luc. Whatever
color you decide is okay with me, I keep telling you that.
So just chill out, and I'll talk to you in a few weeks.

TWENTY-ONE

THE soccer moms, all bright-eyed and bushy-tailed, departed the next morning at the ungodly hour of crack-of-dawn-thirty—or at least an hour Leah previously had only seen sliding into from a party the night before—on a plane bound for Bellingham, Washington. In Bellingham, there was a big touring bus waiting to whisk them off to the tiny hamlet in the middle of the Cascade National Forest, where they would be camping for the next couple of days. After a couple of days of rafting, they would move back to Bellingham to begin filming.

The camping site, on the banks of a swift-running river, was absolutely beautiful. They were surrounded by mountains and towering pines and spruce. Carpets of green stretched along the side of the road, spotted with yellow, white, and purple wildflowers. Up the road from their campsite was a small hamlet with a grocery store and a couple of restaurants (Trudy said Mexican and Italian, although how she could possibly know that, Leah could not say), along with a place to rent area cabins and a river supply store.

Their campsite included four small cabins. In the area between the cabins, another dozen camping tents had been pitched. Between every couple of tents were big red Igloo coolers and camp chairs, and three fire rings spaced throughout the site.

As the bus unloaded, they were instructed to take their bags and select a tent—two women to a tent. "Ohmigod, this is absolutely gorgeous," Trudy gushed, dragging her incredibly large duffel bag along. "Who knew this was here?"

Anyone with an inkling of U.S. geography, Leah figured.

"Let's choose one close by," Trudy wisely suggested, after watching Tamara Contreras, who, predictably, shot ahead of everyone else to select the best tent.

Trudy squatted down in front of one and pulled the flap back, peering inside. "Not bad, not bad," she said. "There are two Sleep Number beds, a private bath, and a Jacuzzi . . . reminds me of the place I lost my virginity."

"Oh no," Leah said with a groan. "Please promise me you won't share that story."

"Don't be so squeamish," Trudy said cheerfully. "It happened when I was sixteen," she said, and crawled inside the tent, wiggling her butt as she tried to drag the giant duffel along with her, talking gaily about the time she lost her virginity in a voice loud enough for the entire campsite to hear.

As Yin and Yang settled into their tent for the weekend, a steady stream of people began to arrive. A camera crew showed up, and the rumor that spread like fire through the little camp was that the crew was filming a reality TV show—*The Making of a Movie*. Needless to say, it didn't matter who the cameras belonged to—there was a lot of preening for them regardless, and in fact, according to

Jamie, there was a little scuffle near the mess tent, when a couple of the Starlets tried to get the same close-up.

In addition to camera men ("You mean they are going to film us rafting?" Leah asked, horrified at the thought of anyone filming her drowning), there were various caterers, men with rafts and oars, and other official-looking persons who showed up, too. As the day slid into late afternoon, a party atmosphere had definitely invaded the campsite.

Fortunately for the soccer moms, a couple of the Starlets had discovered a booze locker near the cabin where rumor had it the T.A. guys would be sleeping. Apparently they'd dipped into it with a supersized ladle, judging by the shrieks of laughter coming from the banks of the river. Leah, who had taken it upon herself to do a reconnaissance mission for Trudy, Michele, and Jamie, detected a familiar scent in the air and traced it back to the tent of a couple of Serious Actresses.

"Pot?" Michele asked, her eyes lighting up. "How much fun would it be to go rafting stoned?" she asked, delighted, and toddled off to join in the fun by becoming a close, personal friend of a Serious Actress.

In the meantime, Trudy had pulled a silver flask from her bag. "Rick will never notice it's gone," she said confidently, and she and Jamie made up a concoction of vodka and diet sodas for the three of them. Red plastic cups in hand, the three women strolled around the campsite, taking it all in.

The cameras were everywhere, filming women with their arms wrapped around each other's shoulders, hamming it up for their big shot at reality television. Men with cameras walked around, filming candid shots of the soccer moms. The caterers were busy laying out what looked like a feast, and a bunch of guys, who Jamie instantly termed River Rats, were preparing the boats for the next day's rafting trip, but their eyes were definitely on the actresses.

When they were joined later by a slightly stoned Michele, the four women were comfortably buzzed, and set up camp chairs in front of the two tents they'd snagged, sipping more vodka drinks, remarking on how much of a vacation the whole thing felt like. Michele was reciting a list of clothes she had brought with her when a sleek Cadillac Escalade slid to a stop next to the campsite, and from its very plush interior, four men who looked like wannabe rock stars stepped out.

"Oooh, look at the eye candy," Jamie said.

Michael was the last to step out, looking so damn sporting in his hiking pants and boots, an all-weather shirt, and a baseball hat on backward.

"Oh my," Trudy drawled, checking him out over the rim of her strap-on sunglasses. "Look what the cat dragged in," she said, wearing a wolfish smile, as Michael, who had been intercepted by Ariel, smiled charmingly at her as he took whatever it was she handed him. "He's so pretty," she sighed.

Leah looked away. She wasn't really sure what she thought at the moment—other than she had the potential to be a total, locked-up whack job—and thought maybe that was better left unsaid. But she glanced back again, dying to know what he was doing—and Michael chose that precise moment to look up and around the camp, his gaze catching Leah's before she could look away. The pinprick of heat was suddenly a rash, spreading all over her skin.

But then Ariel returned to the scene. "*Her* again," Trudy said. "She never lets anyone else near him."

"Great," Leah muttered, and watched Michael and Ariel walk away, disappearing behind the cabin.

"Probably going for a quickie," Michele said with a dreamy smile. "You know how these co-ed trips can be."

"I'm going to get another drink," Leah said, standing up. "Anyone else?"

When she had drink orders, she wandered off in the opposite direction of Michael and Ariel and whatever they were doing. If they were doing anything. Part of her actually believed Michael. Another part of her wondered why, if he was not a big fan of Ariel's, he had to wander off with her at all. And then a third part of her—the chunk made up of equal parts bad judgment and just general idiocy—wondered if he would even seek her out, or whether she'd taken care of that by declaring she intended to date other people.

Later, after the food was served—and what a zoo that was, with half the actresses complaining about the cuisine— Trudy, Michele, Jamie, and Leah nabbed a fire ring before the Serious Actresses took them over and turned an otherwise pleasant evening into a long boring discussion of craft, which they'd heard them doing earlier.

Leah stuck close to Trudy, which turned out to be a huge mistake, because Trudy wanted desperately to keep an eye on Jack, because she hadn't quite given up on him yet. But when Jack wandered through the camp, he was waylaid by some Starlets who were wearing very skimpy little camisole numbers under their baby-doll jean jackets—seriously, the jackets were so small they looked like they'd been made for baby dolls. "Oh *hell* no, they are not going to win by dressing like sluts!" Trudy avowed, and went after them in tight velour pants.

With Trudy gone, Michele in a post-high funk, and Jamie telling her entire life story to one of the Serious Actresses, Leah kept her gaze steady on the fire, nursing yet another vodka drink. She had a better than average buzz, and frankly, in that slightly weakened state, she feared that if she looked at him, wherever he was, she'd find a reason to talk to him. And if she talked to him . . . Well. She just couldn't, not until she'd figured some stuff out for herself.

But she was so certain she was going to make eye contact or somehow unwittingly invite him back into her life that she left Jamie in the middle of her big crescendo on the life story (which was, apparently, getting this job), and turned in.

MICHAEL was thinking he was going to kick some serious Jack Price ass when this whole thing was over with, because he could not shake Ariel to save his life. He walked out of the T.A. cabin, and she was there. He got in line at the mess hall, and she was there. He walked around the camp looking for Leah, and who should he literally bump into, as in collide with when she darted out from behind a tent, but Ariel?

He finally resigned himself to it and let her lead him to a fire ring where Cooper was sitting between two very pretty Starlets, looking like a Greek god. He did, however, manage to lose Ariel when he at last managed to push her off on one of the camera guys that was ogling her, and stepped away, retreating to his cabin before she could discover he was missing.

It had to be a first, Michael thought as he crawled into a sleeping bag. A campsite full of beautiful women, and he could not have been less interested. He'd had enough of beautiful women to last a lifetime. For the first time in his adult memory, he really was just tired of having women hang around for the sake of hanging around. He wanted something more meaningful. He still wanted Leah.

HE and Eli were the first ones up the next morning, along with the caterers they'd hired, standing around in the chill of the morning, sipping coffee while most everyone else slept.

"This is going to be a long day," Michael said. "Never thought I'd be herding a bunch of women down white water."

Eli laughed a little and gave Michael a friendly clap on

the back. "Cheer up. This might just be the ride of your life."

Two hours later, as Michael looked around at twenty women stuffed into life preservers, he began to believe Eli was right. They were chattering like they always did, everyone talking at once, but miraculously hearing each other. Cooper and one of the four river guides were trying to talk, and while the women appeared to be listening, they were moving and whispering and looking around to see what each other was wearing. At least that was the way it seemed to the guys.

Michael swore not one of them understood what they were supposed to do if they fell in the water. He was certain none of them understood their left from their right. And as he exchanged a look with one worried river guide, he tried to smile. "Hey," he said, "we taught them how to wage war. They'll be alright."

The guide did not look convinced.

When it came time to split the women up into four groups—each of the T.A. guys taking a raft—Cooper made them all count one through four, then assigned the ones to a raft, then the twos, and so on. It turned out that Leah was assigned to Michael's raft—go figure—and he got a withering look for it, as if he had somehow managed to conspire with Cooper to get Leah to count off as a three. He held up his hands as she went marching by. "It was pure dumb luck."

"More like the luck of . . ." She frowned, trying to think of a comeback. "Whatever," she said with a toss of her head and followed their river guide, looking like a giant orange marshmallow in her life jacket.

The women climbed into the rafts with a lot of laughing and splashing, which was, Jack opined, the result of having too many cameras around. The four rafts—plus a fifth one holding a camera crew—were set. The guides and the T.A. guys pushed off, then scrambled onto the rafts. When Michael was seated, he glanced to his left and smiled a little. Once again, the guy gods were messing with him, because Michael was sitting next to Jill and directly behind Leah, who sat with her back ramrod straight, and oh goody, there was Ariel, too, sitting up front and grinning like a goon at him from the front of the boat. "This is so much fun!" she shouted at him.

How in God's name had *this* happened? So much for Guy Universe smiling down on him. This was karma alright—the bad variety.

Leah blasted an icy glare over her shoulder.

Michael smirked at her back until he felt someone staring at him and turned to his left. Jill was smiling, one brow cocked high above the other. "Trouble?" she asked sweetly.

"Eyes front," he said sternly, and she laughed and inadvertently dropped her oar in the water.

The ride of his life? More like the ride from hell.

The water was smooth where they put in, the day beautiful, and it wasn't long before the two front rafts—with Cooper and Jack leading the charge—began to splash and make various attempts to ram each other. And, as undoubtedly every river guide in the country knows, once the seed of hijinks is planted in the minds of novices, everyone is in on the act. In Michael's raft, Ariel was the first to fling water, and the game was on. The women were all screeching and laughing . . . all of them but Leah, whose paddle was dragging in the water.

He tapped her paddle with his. Leah jerked around. "Your paddle," he said. "Stay in the rhythm." That seemed to wake her up, and she grabbed her paddle and began to row, clashing with Ariel's oar in front of her. "Hey!" she shouted at Leah.

"Sorry," Leah said, and shot another glare at Michael over her shoulder for good measure.

They reached the first small rapid run, and they could see the first couple of rafts bobbing through, their shrieks of laughter echoing up the canyon walls. One paddle went flying out of the second boat, and a cameraman tried to stand to capture the mayhem just as their boat began to go through. He almost tumbled in, but some quick-thinking companion pulled him down.

"Forward!" the guide shouted at everyone in his raft, and the women began to row, their paddles clashing with one another in a riot of disorganization and lack of rhythm.

Michael groaned, and while the guide paddled on Jill's side of the raft—Jill was too intent on seeing the next raft go through to paddle—Michael began to paddle on his side and kept hitting Leah's paddle, which was constantly a moment behind everyone else. But they sailed through, soaring over rocks and water and screaming at the huge splash that soaked them in the end.

Jill laughed the loudest and turned toward Michael, her eyes and smile shining, and reached to wipe the water from his shades. He grinned at her and then inadvertently looked at Leah, who was looking at him as if he'd just grabbed Jill and laid one on her.

"What?" he asked, as Jill leaned forward to say something to the other women in the raft.

"Nothing!"

"Why are you staring at me?"

"I am *not* staring at you," she said, just as her paddle bounced off a rock and rattled her.

"Hey, Blondie, let's keep our eye on the river, okay?" the guide said to Leah. She snorted and began paddling again, almost knocking Michael's paddle out of his hands.

They hit calmer water, and the four rafts began to battle again, splashing each other with full frontal paddle assaults and ramming each other when they could. One of the soccer moms went over the edge of her raft, much to the delight of everyone else. Cooper caught her paddle first, then her, and pulled her back in like a man who had saved a million women before.

They hit a couple more fast runs before lunch, but nothing too spectacular. Nevertheless, the women seemed to think that they had seen some real white water when they stopped for lunch and were already trading war stories about who had almost gone over on what shoot.

Michael looked at the guide from his raft. "When does it get good?" he asked.

"Oh man, about an hour after the lunch break, we hit some *sweet* water," he said with a bob of his head. "You won't be sorry."

Easy for him to say.

The kid was right—an hour after lunch (during which Leah studiously managed to avoid him), they hit some great white water, which definitely made it worth the trip. Michael loved riding the water, loved taking the edge. His guide was down with it, and the women were inconsequential to the maneuvering of the boat.

The water was sufficiently fast enough that Leah didn't have the time or inclination to stare at him over her shoulder. Michael was pushing it, too—the thrill of the ride was helping him let go of some of the pent-up frustration he'd been feeling. The last good shoot of the day, aptly named Bones Canyon, was awesome. It looked like a drop of about forty feet overall, flowing hard through the shoot. The guide shouted at the women to ready their oars, and on his command, to go forward as hard as they could.

Everything was going great—they were flying—but then they hit a rock, and that slammed them up against the canyon wall. Leah went flying off the side, her paddle long gone. Michael grabbed her arm with one hand and maneuvered his paddle into the boat with his other hand. Her eyes were wide with terror as he manhandled her back into the raft while the guide shouted at the rest of the boat to *Move right! Move right! Move right!*

They managed to get off the rock and move on, everyone in the boat, their oars accounted for, save Leah's, and downstream, Michael could see Eli holding it up. Leah's knuckles were white; she gripped the rope on the raft tightly as if she was afraid she'd fall in again. But she looked back at Michael with gratitude in her eyes, and that one look, that single look of crystal blue eyes, pulled at his heart like nothing else.

The rest of the trip was uneventful. They were bussed back to camp, and after showers, several of them went into the little hamlet to dine on Italian food.

Leah went, Michael knew, because he watched her board the bus with Trudy. He and the rest of T.A. stayed behind. Tomorrow they were doing a harder arm of the river, and they wanted to chill out and get a good night's sleep. Eli had some excellent bourbon and cigars to put them down.

When Michael did drift off to sleep, it was Leah's wide-eyed look of terror that filled his mind's eye.

TWENTY-TWO

THE two restaurants in town were definitely hopping with what looked to be hungry campers from all over the Cascades. Fortunately for the ten actresses who had opted to come out tonight, the Italian restaurant had a little bar where they could all just barely squeeze in, much to the delight of all the men in the area.

And just so that no stone of this adventure was left unturned, the camera crew came along, too, squeezing in right behind the women. Trudy, who as of tonight had decided that Jack was beyond her ability to reach—"There are just too many chicks around," she complained—had her eye on someone new. One of the camera crew. "He's more attainable," she said to Leah as they sat at the back of the bar, sandwiched between the cigarette machine and waiter's station, sipping wine. "Plus, he's got a camera. That can't hurt."

"I'm not sure how it can help, but, whatever. What about Rick?"

"Thanks for reminding me," Trudy said with a snort. "I keep trying to forget him, and every time I do, you remind me."

"Sorry. It just doesn't seem fair," Leah said. "You already have a boyfriend and are trawling for one of the very few eligible bachelors in this group."

"You're one to talk," Trudy reminded her. "You have *the* bachelor wanting to make babies with you."

"Not really," Leah said, and turned her gaze in a new direction, hoping to nip the conversation in the bud. "But that's another story."

"So is Rick," Trudy said. "Here—" She shoved her wineglass at Leah. "Hold on to that for a moment, will you?"

Leah obliged her, and Trudy sat up, adjusted the teensy-tiny little halter top she was wearing, then brushed her black hair back from her face.

"How do I look?" she asked, pursing her lips for Leah's benefit.

Leah looked her up and down and nodded approvingly. "I'd do you."

Trudy smiled, took her glass from Leah. "See? That's why we're such great friends. Okay, wish me luck," she said, and narrowed her gaze on the cameraman, who was filming a couple of the actresses as they talked with a couple of guys in trucker hats and shirts with the arms cut out.

With a wink, Trudy left Leah sitting alone and sauntered forward, swinging her hips in her best slut fashion.

She would, no doubt, be victorious, Leah thought, and sipped her wine, watching as the little happy hour gained momentum.

The white-water rafting had been fun—except, of course, for the moment she almost drowned—but it also had been emotionally draining. Between Jill pawing Michael under the guise of wiping water off his shades, and Ariel practically screaming *watch me, watch me,* Leah had felt a sharp pang of jealousy she did not want to feel.

Oh, but she *was* jealous, and insanely so. As jealous as Marissa Pendergrast, the wallflower in sixth grade, had been when Leah had the audacity to hold hands with the round-headed kid named Zach. Zach had sweaty hands and thick lips, but there is no accounting for the way a heart leans, because Marissa had loved Zach and had been so incensed by Leah's actions that she'd pulled a wad of hair from Leah's head.

Leah was jealous on that scale, Marissa-jealous, wanting to pull a wad of hair from someone's head. What right did she have? None. Just like he had no right to be jealous. But she especially had no right, because she had moved on, had told Michael she wasn't hanging around to watch all the women fawn over him. *I am thinking of dating other people*, had been her famous last words.

How stupid could one woman possibly be? Of course, Leah wasn't certain what she was supposed to have said, because clearly, the man was not to be trusted. But she was pretty sure *I am thinking of dating other people* had been the absolute wrong thing to say, seeing as how she was having all these feelings whirling around in a friggin' blender inside her. She did not want to be jealous, but she was. She didn't want to see him, but the day felt so empty if she didn't see him. And she damn sure didn't want to want him, but she did, with every fiber of her body, with every smile, with every look, with every touch.

It was because her feelings were in such turmoil that she was very surprised and even relieved when she saw Adolfo sauntering through the crowd toward her, holding a bouquet of mountain wildflowers, tied together with a shoe string. When he finally reached her, he bowed, extended the flowers. "Beautiful flowers for a beautiful woman."

"Adolfo!" she exclaimed, taking the flowers. "What on earth are you doing here?"

"You will forgive my impatience, *sí*?" he purred with a warm, easy smile. "I could not wait so many weeks for your return."

"Oh," Leah said, grinning ridiculously as she admired the small, handpicked bouquet. "But I will see you Tuesday when we start filming."

"Days, weeks, they are the same when you are gone," he said. "Too long."

She could feel her grin broaden. "The flowers are beautiful. But how did you know where to find me?"

He winked and said, "The crew, they always know where to find the beauties."

Leah laughed.

"It warms my heart to see your smile," he said. "I shall buy you a drink, *sí*?" he asked, looking at her near-empty wineglass. "I shall bring you a Spanish wine that will make you sing."

"Please, no, I'm tone deaf. It's best that I not sing."

"But a good Spanish wine will give you new ears," he said, gesturing toward his head. "You will wait for me here, no?"

Like she could possibly shoehorn herself out of the packed bar. Like she'd even want to. "I'll wait," she said, and smiled back.

Okay, she was seriously going to have to reassess, she thought as he moved to the bar. Adolfo was wearing black slacks and a cool blue silk blouse. His black hair, slicked back, brushed over his collar. He was a very nice-looking man. *Very* nice. Okay, not as nice-looking as Michael—please, like anyone could compare—but he was pretty damn close.

Close enough that her spirits were picking up as Adolfo turned from the bar and headed back, still wearing that charming smile, holding two glasses in one hand, a bottle of wine in the other.

A whole bottle. She really wasn't that much of a drinker. "Wow," she said, laughing a little. "That's a whole bottle."

"A bottle yes, a bottle of fine Spanish wine for the most beautiful woman in all of the mountains and beyond."

"Applause, applause, Adolfo," she said. "Your lines are

improving all the time. I'm even beginning to believe them . . ." She glanced at the bottle, then squinted at the label. "But that isn't a Spanish wine, it's a California wine."

"Spain, California. It is all the same," he said, pouring a glass for her. "Now. The time for lines is gone," he said, handing her the glass and pouring another for himself. He set the bottle aside, then lifted his glass, touched it to Leah's. "Now is the time for honest *amor*."

The timbre of his voice sent a very delicious signal to her groin, and Leah blushed and looked at her glass. "Well, at the very least, it is time for wine," she said, and tasted the wine he had given her. "Excellent," she said.

"Of course it is excellent!" he said, sounding a little miffed, and took a rather big swig of wine himself. "Pity we are not in Spain now," he said, shifting closer, propping his arm against the wall beside her head. "For the Spaniards, we are lovers of fine wine, fine food, and fine women," he said. "You have the amazing eyes," he murmured.

There was the blush again. "Thank you. You have amazing cologne."

Adolfo chuckled and glanced at the wineglass she was holding. "Drink it, *mi amor*, drink it all, for wine is the elixir of life."

"And all this time I thought it was merely a complement to beef," she quipped. But she drank. Adolfo watched approvingly, and when she had sipped a couple of times, he tipped the bottle into her glass, pouring in a little more. "Drink, drink," he urged her again. "Let us celebrate the night, for the moon is full, and there is love in the air."

The wine was definitely making her feel mellow. "Did you learn to speak English from Broadway musicals?" she asked as she sipped from the replenished glass.

"Ah, Broadway," he said longingly. "I have spent many hours on Broadway."

"You *have*? Lighting?" she asked.

"What?" He seemed confused for a moment, then laughed. "*Sí, sí,* of course," he said, and began to tell Leah about the period of time he'd spent in the United States, working on Broadway and taking in as many Broadway shows as possible, because he was mesmerized by them. How funny, she thought, that she never ran across him when she was working on Broadway. Oh well. New York was a big city.

"What fascinates you?" she asked.

"The costumes, the singing. The joy."

"How about your parents? Do they ever come?"

Adolfo clucked his tongue. "They are gone," he said, and told her about a young boy, growing up in Madrid, longing to come to America, and how, as an adult, after his parents had passed away, he had come to the United States to pursue a career in filmmaking.

"One day I shall direct a great movie," he predicted.

"Welcome to the club," she said, clinking her glass to his.

Adolfo's eyes grew wide with surprise. "You, too?"

"In a way. I want to star in movies, not direct them. But look around, Adolfo Rafael. Almost everyone in this bar wants a piece of the pie."

"Ah, but you are the only one of them who could be a star," he said, signaling the waitress. "Tell me your story, Leah. Tell me how you come to Hollywood, like me."

"Well—"

He stopped her with a finger. "*Un momento,*" he muttered, turning to the waitress who had appeared and ordering another bottle of wine. Leah looked at her glass—it was half-full, and she was already feeling very light-headed. She couldn't possibly drink any more. But Adolfo turned back to her, all smiles, and before she could admit as much, he said, "Come and tell me now of your life."

"Oh. That," she said, rubbing her forehead a moment. "It's really not very interesting. I grew up in Connecticut. I studied acting, worked on Broadway, like you. And then

I met this guy in New York," she said, and glanced up at Adolfo. "You know . . . *that guy.*"

"Oh," he said breezily, "The bastard."

"Right, him," Leah agreed. "When he and I broke up— I mean, we didn't actually break up, but it was more like . . . well, okay, he dumped me," she admitted, and put her hand to her head again. She was feeling very woozy all of a sudden.

"And then?" Adolfo asked.

And then . . . there was so much. A shining career, a high-powered agent promising her fame and success. The huge crash and burn.

"And then I really didn't want to be in New York anymore. So I moved to L.A." That was all she could force herself to say. She smiled up at him; his face, she noticed, had softened. Or her vision had blurred. "Have you managed to find enough work?" she asked.

He nodded.

"That's great! What films?"

The question seemed to take him aback. "Films, *sí*. Here and there. Many films," he said again, then sipped from his glass.

Why was he acting so weird about it? Life came so much easier to men in Hollywood that she assumed he'd worked on dozens of films. Even Brad, who really wasn't that talented, had way more roles than she did. Granted, none of them were *good* roles—who wanted to be an extra Trojan in a cast of a thousand Trojans, for god's sake? But nevertheless, Brad still had more opportunities than Leah had been able to scrounge up. And now Frances, her agent, was telling her she was almost too old to work.

Leah was beginning to feel too old for anything, and for some insane reason, an image of Michael popped into her head—sitting around a campfire, cute and perky Ariel on one side, and pretty, younger-than-Leah Jill on the other side. Neither woman had come out tonight, so in all probability, they were sitting exactly where she imagined them.

Great. She hoped the three of them had a marvelous time together.

"No, no, what is this frown?" Adolfo asked, and tenderly touched two fingers to the corner of her mouth. "What has made you sad?"

Leah shook her head. "I'm not sad, I was just . . . just thinking of how long I have been in L.A."

"How long?"

She snorted, drank more wine, then shook her head. "A lifetime, pal. A thirty-four-year *lifetime*." She laughed at her own lame joke and drank more wine, and noticed, a little groggily, how Adolfo's eyes sparkled mischievously when he laughed, which he was doing right at that moment as he looked down at her, and how his lips seemed so full and kissable.

Kisses. She liked kissing, she thought, and propped her head, which was suddenly feeling very heavy, on her fist. She liked kissing a lot, but she would rather be kissing Michael than Adolfo. Not that there was anything wrong with Adolfo, no—lots of women would be killing themselves to kiss him. And she *might* kiss him, but really she preferred—

"Hey!"

Trudy's face was suddenly looming large in front of Leah's, startling her out of her wits and almost off her stool.

"What's the matter? You look drunk!" Trudy announced to all of Washington State.

"I'm not *drunk*," Leah said. Only . . . her head *did* feel a whole lot fuzzier than it had just a moment ago.

"Okay, so who is your *friend*?" Trudy asked, smiled at a smiling Adolfo. "He's really cute!"

"Thank you," Adolfo said with a bow.

"Oooh, and he has an accent," Trudy gushed. "Could this be Adolfo? *The* Adolfo?"

A camera lens suddenly appeared over Trudy's shoulder,

and it caught Leah off guard. Adolfo, too, apparently. He suddenly stood up and turned away.

"Excuse me," he said with a wink to Leah, and walked in the direction of the men's room.

"But wait! I didn't get to meet him!" Trudy pouted, plopping down on the stool Adolfo had vacated. "Girl, Adolfo is *hot*."

Leah moved to one side, away from the camera. "What is with this camera?" she demanded jabbing a thumb in the guy's direction. "Does he have to film us?"

"What? Oh! That's Chuck!" Trudy happily shouted to be heard over the din. "Don't worry. He'll make us look good. Right, Chuck?"

A man's head appeared above the camera, and he smiled a little leeringly at Trudy. "If you ask me nicely, baby," he drawled, and pointed his camera right at Trudy, who struck a kittenish pose and smiled seductively for a moment before turning her attention back to Leah.

"So that's the guy, huh?" she asked again.

"Yes, that's him, the lighting guy."

"I didn't know they were here," Trudy said, her brow furrowing a little. Until she realized the camera was still on her, at which point she instantly smiled, corrected her posture, and sucked in her gut. "Well, whatever," she said, tapping Leah's arm. "You're so not fair. Two hunks in one gig!"

"No, no, it's not like that," Leah insisted, her head in her hands now. "It's not what you think."

"Right, whatever," Trudy said cheerfully, and stood up. "Just don't do anything I wouldn't do—" She turned to the camera and in an imitation of Groucho Marx, added, "which pretty much gives you license to do whatever you want to do." She laughed, looked at Leah, and her smile faded. "Hey, are you okay?"

"I'm fine," Leah said, although her head felt as if it weighed one hundred pounds. "Just too much wine, I think."

"Don't drink too much. You won't want to miss out on

all the fun, right?" She laughed, and Chuck laughed with her. "Okay, girl, talk to you later. I'm going to take my camera around and show some of the Serious Actresses who I caught. They'll *die*. Are you ready, Chuck?" she asked, smiling at the camera.

"I'll follow you wherever you want to go, baby," Chuck growled.

"Well, now, *that* opens up a whole new world of possibilities," Trudy responded as the two of them went off.

As Leah watched her friend's figure turn watery, she decided that she'd definitely had too much to drink and needed to go outside for some air. This was weird. She wasn't much of a drinker, but she wasn't a teetotaler, either—she could usually hold her own. Maybe she was feeling so thick because she had drunk on an empty stomach. When Michael came back—oops, *Adolfo* came back—she'd suggest some food.

But when Adolfo came back, she found herself thinking about what he'd be like in bed instead of food. He was really sexy in that Spanish-pirate sort of way. He had nice, thick hands, which led to juicier, lascivious thoughts. But they were only thoughts—no matter that Adolfo was handsome and really smelled so good, and had those hands—she couldn't any more fall into bed with him than she could drink another glass of wine. She really couldn't fall into bed with any guy except one, and she'd probably spend the next five years trying to get over him *again*.

The thought sobered her a little, and she glanced down . . . and realized she had, indeed, drunk another glass of wine. How was that possible? What did that make, four glasses? No wonder her head felt like a bowling ball and her legs were so damn rubbery—

"*Mi amor*, you are funny in the face," Adolfo said suddenly, and leaned forward, cupping her face with his hand.

"Really?" she asked weakly. "I am feeling a little mushy inside."

"Mushy?"

She made a face and wiggled her fingers. "Mushy," she muttered, and felt, all at once, very flushed.

Adolfo was instantly on his feet. "Come then, you must take cold mountain air to be less mushy."

"Do you think?" she asked uncertainly. "Maybe if I just ate something—"

"Yes, of course, you must eat. But first, you must walk. Come, then."

"Okay," she said meekly. "Just let me find my feet."

That proved easier said than done, because her limbs felt so fluid. But she finally managed to put them down one after the other with Adolfo's help. He put his arm securely around her waist, held her tightly against his side, and led her outside, doing the walking for them both on the two occasions her feet refused to cooperate.

As they passed through a sea of nameless, swimming faces, Leah thought she should tell Trudy she'd be right back, but with a very sickly feeling burgeoning inside her, she just let Adolfo lead her out.

In the parking lot, the cold mountain air did indeed feel wonderful on her flushed skin, but it didn't make her feel any better inside, and if anything, she felt even fuzzier. She was only vaguely aware of Adolfo talking to her, asking her how she felt, if she could walk, if she could look at him. On the inside, however, Leah was panicking—she knew she'd had too much to drink, but she didn't think she'd had so much to be so suddenly incoherent and unable to move her limbs. Something felt seriously wrong with her body. This didn't feel like a drunk, this felt like a coma.

She felt the slide toward oblivion and could do nothing to stop it. The last thing she remembered was Adolfo's smiling face before her. "You will be fine, *mi amor.* I will look after you as if you were my own."

TWENTY-THREE

THE next thing Leah knew, it was daylight. At least she thought it was—it was hard to make out what was behind the yellowed and torn roll-up blind on the window. But whatever it was, she was slowly coming to the realization that not only was she absent from camp, she was in a strange, lumpy bed with musty sheets in a room that looked like it was built in the Stone Age.

How she had landed here was something that was not coming to her very quickly. Her first thought was Michael, but then she remembered that they were not exactly close at the moment.

She moved to sit up, but her heavy head was pounding, and she could only manage pushing up to her elbows to have a look around.

It was a cabin, a run-down, cluttered cabin bedroom. The paint on the walls and ceiling was peeling. The bedspread was threadbare chenille, and the sheets smelled of mothballs and Ben-Gay. There was a small vanity dresser with a tarnished mirror, the top of it stacked with papers and books and a couple of bottles that looked like Milk of Magnesia.

Great. She was in some granny's cabin.

With a moan, Leah closed her eyes. Her night out with the gang had left her feeling like her head was physically detached from her body. Her vision was blurred, and her mouth felt like a truck had run through it.

Wherever she was, she had to get out of here.

Leah blinked several times to clear her vision and sat up, and only then did she realize she was wearing nothing but a bra and panties. Well, if it wasn't clear what she'd done before, it certainly was now. But honestly, couldn't he at least have taken her to a nice hotel room or somewhere other than his granny's bedroom?

In answer to that question, Adolfo suddenly appeared, breezing into the small room wearing nothing but boxer briefs and munching on a section of an orange. "*Buenos días, mi amor!* How do you feel?"

This was the very reason she didn't drink to excess, because she always wanted to be dead certain she knew who she was in bed with, what she was doing, and if she at least enjoyed it. Her mouth dropped open, but no words came out. What did one say the morning after one did something she really wished she hadn't done, but wished she could at least remember—*hey, was it good for me, too?*

Jesus, how did she get out of this mess now? And speaking of getting out, she looked around for a clock. If she missed the all-call for the boats this morning, she'd be toast.

"You are pale. I will bring you orange juice, *sí*?"

"No thanks," Leah said, pulling the cover up around her neck. "What time is it, anyway?"

"Time." Adolfo chuckled, popped the rest of the orange section in his mouth, and wiped his hands on his boxers. "Time is irrelevant," he said with a smile.

"Oh-kay. But do you have a watch?" she persisted.

He plopped down in an old greenish-gold Naugahyde chair and grinned. "Perhaps I do."

One thing was certain—Leah was definitely not in the mood for post-coital fun and games.

IN the camp, Michael and Jack were gearing up for another day of rafting—actively separating the non-rowers from the rowers on a sheet of paper—when Trudy burst into their cabin looking so panic-stricken that Michael's first thought was that someone had drowned. Her dark hair was sticking up in really strange places, and she was wearing only a skimpy little sleep shirt that barely covered her butt, fur-lined boots that rose mid-calf, and dark aviator shades.

"Good morning," Jack said, obviously taking her bizarre appearance in stride. "Is something wrong?"

"Yes! No! I don't know—but I think something is really wrong!" she exclaimed through chattering teeth. She folded her arms across her body and held on tightly. "Leah didn't come back to camp last night!"

Michael felt his gut drop. He grabbed up a jacket and put it around Trudy's shoulders. "Calm down, Trudy. Are you sure she didn't come back? Maybe she's just in another tent."

"No, no, I checked," Trudy insisted, tears welling in her eyes. "The only other place she'd land is with Michele and Jamie, and they didn't see her last night, either. She didn't come back," she said again. Her bottom lip was starting to tremble, which was a sure sign that she believed something had happened to Leah.

Michael's heart began to pound. "When was the last time you saw her?"

"Last night, at the Italian restaurant in town," Trudy said as she pulled the jacket tightly around her. "She was drinking wine with Adolfo, the Italian guy."

Michael's stomach twisted. "Italian?" he asked. "Or possibly Spanish?"

"I don't know, I don't know! Maybe! He went to the restroom before I got to meet him, but he was really good-looking, and he had an Italian look. I think." She looked at Michael. "Maybe he was Spanish. I don't know!"

Now Michael felt absolutely ill.

Trudy was looking at him, waiting for him to speak. "I think maybe she hooked up with that guy. Only I don't know who he is, except one of the crew—"

"The crew?" Jack interrupted. "What makes you think he's part of the crew?"

"Leah said so. Lighting."

Michael and Jack exchanged a look. The crew was in Bellingham. It was possible one of them had come out, but he doubted it—they had too much to set up before filming began on Tuesday.

"What?" Trudy demanded, looking first at Jack, then at Michael. "Why are you looking at each other like that? You know something, don't you?"

"We don't know anything. But don't worry, we'll find her," Jack said smoothly. "You're right, she probably hooked up with the light guy and just needs a ride back to camp."

"I don't know," Trudy said uncertainly. "I thought so, too, at first. But Leah . . . Leah isn't like that."

Michael glanced at Trudy, but she wasn't looking at him; she was looking at the floor.

"I mean, okay, she's human, obviously, and the guy really was handsome . . . but of all of us, Leah is the least likely to just hook up with a guy she doesn't really know. That's why I'm so worried. But then again, like I'm saying, he was *really* handsome, and you know how that is."

Juan Carlo—if it was truly Juan Carlo as Michael feared—was not *that* handsome.

"Yeah," Jack said, and shrugged a little sheepishly when Michael narrowed his gaze.

"But Leah? I don't see it," Trudy reiterated.

While a regular guy might take a small measure of

comfort hearing that the woman he loved did not sleep around, it didn't give Michael any comfort at all. It just filled him with sick dread.

"Why don't you get dressed and ready for rafting, and we'll have a look around," Jack suggested.

"But she's not here, I already looked—"

"Right, but we'll look, too, and one of us will run into town and have a look around. In the meantime, you need to eat something and get ready," he said, ushering Trudy out the door.

"Maybe I should go with you," she suggested, but Jack already had her outside.

"You don't want to miss rafting, do you? Don't worry. It's a Podunk little town. It won't take more than half an hour."

"Okay," Trudy said, sounding very reluctant to let them go without her. "Just start at the Italian restaurant."

"We will," Jack promised her, and gestured her to go on. With one last look back at Michael, Trudy left.

When Jack closed the door behind her, he turned around to Michael. "You know something."

"No . . . well, maybe. Not really, it's just . . . hell, I don't know," he said with a sigh of exasperation.

"What's going on?"

"I can't really say," Michael said, hands on hips. "A friend of mine from Washington let me know that a guy I put away a few years ago—a Spaniard—was out and looking for me. They know he is in the States. They don't know exactly where, but they were fairly confident he wasn't on the West coast. At least not yet."

"What does this guy want with you?" Jack asked.

Michael's laugh was sour. "He wants me dead."

Jack's brows rose. "No shit? What'd you do, steal his girlfriend?"

Michael shook his head, thinking back to Spain, to those nights in Costa del Sol, to Barcelona, to Madrid, where he had lived and worked. "Worse. I slept with his wife, took his livelihood, and set up a sting that sent him to prison for what was supposed to be the rest of his life."

Jack whistled. "That's not good. How is he out?"

"Money, drugs, who knows?" Michael said with a shrug. "It happens." He rubbed the nape of his neck. "But how does he know about Leah? How could he have found her?"

"My guess is he found you," Jack opined. "And once he found you, it wouldn't take a genius to figure out she's important to you."

That was exactly what Michael feared. He picked up his cell phone. "Where can I get reception? I need to call a couple of people."

"Bellingham."

Michael picked up keys. "Go on without us. When I find her, we'll meet you back at camp."

"Are you sure?" Jack asked, following him to the door.

"No, I'm not sure about anything. But I don't know what else to do," he admitted honestly, and walked out, headed for one of the Jeeps they had rented. He had a sinking feeling there wasn't a moment to waste.

TWENTY-FOUR

THIS was an absolute nightmare, the worst thing that could happen, other than maybe a serious burst of cellulite—but Leah felt just that hopeless.

Adolfo had moved from orange to bread and cheese, which she wouldn't have any of, either, and refused to cooperate with her by telling her what time it was. He seemed to be enjoying her massive hangover.

She was sitting in the bed, her arms around her legs, pressing her forehead to her knees. "Shit," she said into her knees. "I cannot believe I did this!"

"Spanish wine is very powerful," he said, as if it was a proven, scientific fact.

"It was California wine, and I'm not talking about *that*," Leah moaned, and gestured wildly to the bed. "But *that*!"

"That?" Adolfo asked pleasantly.

Why did he have to be so obtuse now? "Yes. You know . . . *that*."

Adolfo blinked, and then he laughed. "You're a beautiful

woman, *mi amor*. But I do not take advantage of sleeping beauties."

Now Leah blinked at him. Several times. She could hardly see him her head hurt so badly. "Then why . . . ?" she asked, looking down at her underwear.

"You seemed to be not in comfort."

Oh dear God, that was a *huge* relief. Somehow, being a drunk was preferable to being a drunk and a skank. "Thank God," she breathed. "Oh thank God."

"Poor girl," Adolfo said sympathetically. "You want orange juice? We have orange and papaya juices."

No, she didn't want orange juice, she wanted to be dragged outside and shot. "No thanks. I think I just need to get my clothes and go, okay, Adolfo? I think our little flirtation thing," she said, gesturing at the two of them, "is over."

"As you wish," he said genially. But he didn't move.

She frowned at him. "Come on, what time is it?"

Adolfo smiled sympathetically. "It is as I said, *mi amor*. Time makes no difference to us now."

It did to her. Time would tell her, for example, how long she had been living this horrible drunk, and if she had any prayer of making the all-call for the rafting trip, or had to show up later when everyone would know—or guess—why she hadn't been on the raft in the first place.

She hated that. She wasn't like that, didn't go home with guys she didn't know. Frankly, she wasn't the type to go home with guys at all, and especially not drunk. Leah put her head down again and closed her eyes. Her head was spinning, her mouth incredibly dry.

"Have some orange juice, Leah," Adolfo said again. His voice startled her—it was suddenly very close. She looked up and instantly swayed backward. The man was standing over her with a glass of OJ shoved in her face. She recoiled at the sight of it. "Thanks . . . but I don't know if I can keep it down."

"You must try."

Leah shook her head and rolled away from him, to the edge of the bed. "Okay, all kidding aside now, Adolfo. Where are my clothes?"

"You don't need them here."

"I beg to differ." She needed them even worse than she needed liposuction on her thighs, and speaking of which, she had never intended to show those puppies to anyone. "I *really* need my clothes. I have to get back to camp or they will leave without me." And really, did she have to justify needing her clothes? Didn't everyone, eventually, get up and dress after they'd recovered from a dead drunk?

"Let them leave without you," Adolfo said cavalierly.

Clearly, Adolfo was not getting the message that she was regretting the whole thing, so she grabbed a sheet and stood up, testing her weight on her legs. When it looked as if they would hold, she turned around to look at Adolfo through the haze of a remarkably bad headache.

He was so relaxed. He was sitting in a threadbare upholstered chair, his feet propped on the end of the bed, sipping from one of two glasses of orange juice and casually checking Leah out. He was, she noticed through her haze, rather bold in his checking her out, nodding approvingly at her shape in that awful sheet, a wolfish grin spreading across his face.

Leah really did not care for that look—it was a little predatory for her tastes, and if he thought anything was happening now that she was conscious, he had another think coming. "Where are my clothes?" she demanded, a lot less nicely this time.

He shrugged. "Here. There. Everywhere. Come then, *mi amor*, have some orange juice," he said, and held up a glass. "Trust me, you will feel much better once you have had the orange juice."

What was it with him and the orange juice?

He was really beginning to annoy the hell out of her. So they'd had a fling that stopped short of completion due to her inebriation. Okay, she could accept it. Well, not accept it, really, but at least swallow the awful lump that accompanied the realization of how close she'd come. She could get used to the facts and maybe even believe that life would go on again after this spectacular mistake if she could only get the hell out of here! "Listen, I don't want any orange juice," she said sternly. "I just want my clothes, and I want to go home. Or at least to camp. So please show me where my clothes are, so I can get dressed."

Adolfo shrugged and nodded in the direction of what looked like a bathroom.

Leah stumbled in that direction, managed to make it inside and shut the door. She let the sheet fall away from her body, grabbed the edge of the chipped tile countertop, turned on the cold water, and stuck her face beneath the cold stream. A few minutes of that went a long way toward making her feel less foggy.

She stood up, glanced around the small bathroom, looking for a towel. Seeing none, she used the sheet. She noticed that the cute pale blue dress she had worn last night was draped over the edge of a pink tub. She grabbed it, pulled it on over her head, and struggled to zip it. But the thing wouldn't zip, and upon further examination, she saw that the zipper had been mangled.

Fabulous. It looked like it had been yanked apart. *"Don't go there,"* she muttered to herself, unwilling to think of how that might have happened. Whatever, the damn thing was unwearable, unless she wanted the whole world to glimpse just how badly she wore a thong as she walked down the street and tried to hail a cab.

With a sigh of exhaustion, Leah fell against the door of the bathroom and slid down to her haunches. Where *was* this place? She glanced up at the ceiling—stained and peeling in here, too, she noted. The rest of the bathroom looked like a seedy hotel. The linoleum on the floor was cracked, the mirror was tarnished, and a dark, rusty stain around the edge of the toilet made her shudder with revulsion.

She pushed herself up and looked around for something to put on. Finding nothing, she donned her dress with the ruined zipper—a dress she'd paid very good money for instead of buying it at a discount barn like she normally did. That really pissed her off. What sort of guy was Adolfo, anyway, that he'd ruin a dress someone worked to pay for?

She yanked open the bathroom door and marched into the small bedroom with the intent of giving Adolfo a piece of her mind. Except that Adolfo wasn't in the bedroom— she could hear him banging around in another room.

There was, however, a bag next to the chair in which he'd been sitting, and she bent over, peering inside. It was full of men's clothes. Apparently Adolfo was thinking of making a weekend of it. She squatted down, picked up a shirt lying on top, and stabbed her arms into it, tied the ends around her waist, looked around for her fabulous shoes, which were, thankfully, at the end of the bed, and picked them up before marching into the adjoining room.

Adolfo had donned a pair of jeans and a polo shirt and was at the kitchen sink, such that it was, cutting up an apple, munching as he went along.

There were a couple of brown paper bags on a counter cluttered with pots and pans and dishes, as if he'd just gone to the grocery store. "Ah," he said with a bright smile when she stomped in. "You found your dress. And my shirt."

"Yes. I'm sorry that I looked in your bag, but since my dress was ruined"—she paused there to glare at him for a moment—"I had to have something to cover it."

"Yes, that was regrettable, but necessary," he said. "Orange juice?"

What is with the orange juice? she screamed in her mind. And what the hell did he mean, it was *necessary*? Since when was ripping clothes off a comatose woman *necessary*? "Adolfo . . . we need to talk."

"Please," he said, gesturing to a scarred kitchen table.

Leah ignored that, and ignored him as he passed by and

set two glasses of orange juice on the table. "I am having an apple. Would you like?"

"No! I don't want any orange juice, or apples. Adolfo, please listen to me. I don't remember *anything* from last night," she said gesturing wildly.

Adolfo laughed, as if fooling around with a woman who didn't remember it was funny somehow.

"It's not funny!" she snapped. "Regardless of how we ended up here—and where is here, by the way?" she asked, looking around the dilapidated kitchen.

For some reason, Adolfo looked around, too, as if he had just noticed he was in a strange cabin. "A cabin of some sort," he said. "Perhaps it is for the holidays, although I cannot imagine who would want to holiday in such a place."

"Huh?" Leah asked, confused by his answer, but quickly shook her head. "Never mind. I guess what I am trying to say is that whatever happened, it happened, although I don't *how* it happened, but the thing is, I never intended for it to happen in the first place, and I'm sorry, but I guess I got really drunk, and you know how it is, you never know what you're doing when you drink, and who are we kidding—I *especially* didn't know it last night. But at any rate, I can't let it happen again. I mean, my head's not into it, and while it's been a lot of fun flirting with you, Adolfo, it should never have gone this far. Do you understand what I mean?" She paused to take a breath.

Interestingly, Adolfo did not seem upset. He seemed to mull over what she said and nodded thoughtfully. "*Sí,* if this is what you want." He smiled again. "Have some orange juice to feel better."

"That's it?" she cried, incredulous. "Have some orange juice? And will you *stop* with the orange juice already?" She fell into a chair at the table. "I'm glad you understand, Adolfo, but I thought there might be a little more reaction than that."

"Of course I understand," he said, seeming a little affronted that she thought he wouldn't. "It is clear to me. It is the bastard, no?"

"No!"

"No?"

"Well . . . alright, maybe a little," she admitted, and picked up the orange juice and took a sip. It tasted funny, like processed orange juice.

"*Sí, sí,* I know this for a very long time," Adolfo said matter-of-factly. "He has hurt your tender heart, yet you cannot get him out of it."

"Something like that," she admitted, and took another big sip of orange juice.

"I see this very often," he said, nodding sagely. He leaned up against the Formica countertop and pointed an apple slice at her. "My advice to you, *mi amor*, is that you get him out. He is like . . ." He tapped his chest. "*Poison* in there."

"You really think so?" she asked weakly.

"Yes," he said emphatically. "It is obvious."

It was obvious, and would be to her, too, if she would just think clearly about it. Leah sighed, drank more OJ, and pushed it away, had the thought that it was a little absurd to be having this conversation with a man she had almost slept with last night.

"Well," she said glumly, "be that as it may, I guess there is nothing left for us to say. I'm sorry if I gave you the wrong impression."

"*De nada,*" he said, flicking his wrist.

Why did he keep smiling like that? He was acting like he did this sort of thing all the time. Her head was beginning to ache again, and she put her knuckles to her temple and began to rub. "Will you at least tell me what happened to my dress?"

"The zipper, it was very stubborn," he said cheerfully.

"Did we . . . you know . . . do anything?"

He laughed at that. "You have a grand imagination."

Not really. "Can I borrow the shirt?" she begged. "I'll return it to you in Bellingham."

He nodded politely. Leah stood, and *whoa* . . . her knees were wobbly again. She laughed a little self-consciously. "I guess I really tied one on last night, huh?"

Adolfo smiled.

"So . . . you're going to give me a ride, right?"

"No, no," he said shaking his head.

Man, she felt bad. She put her hand on the table to steady herself. "Come on, Adolfo. I don't feel well, and I can't really walk through town dressed like this."

"No, that would not be good," he agreed.

Well all right then . . . why didn't he *move*? "I don't think you understand. I need a ride."

"No," he said, smiling brightly.

"Jesus, Adolfo, what is *with* you?" she cried with exasperation, the force of it making her feel extremely woozy. "What is your problem? I need to go, and I need you to take me!"

For some reason, Adolfo's smile faded. "But I cannot do that, Leah," he said, his pleasant voice belying the suddenly hard and very cold look in his eye. "I need you here."

Leah gasped. "What do you mean? Like a sex slave?" she almost whispered.

He chuckled at that, reached out and traced a line across her jaw. "That is an appealing offer, but put your mind at ease—I do not need you for that . . . not at this time," he added, his gaze flicking the length of her.

"I don't understand," she said, and had a very thick feeling that her brain couldn't absorb anything at the moment. "Look, I don't know what your deal is, but I am out of here," she said, and moved awkwardly for the door.

Adolfo caught her hand and turned her around, and Leah had to grab his wrist to keep from slipping to the floor, she was suddenly feeling so bad. "Leave me alone," she said sharply.

"But I cannot," he said, and reached behind his back,

into the waist of his pants, and when he brought his hand
around again, he was holding a black gun. A big, ugly
black gun that he held away from him, almost as if he was
afraid to touch it.

Leah shrieked and swayed backward, colliding with the
table and sending orange juice flying across the ugly linoleum floor. "What are you doing?" she cried.

"I need you here, *mi amor.* I need you so that the bastard
will come for you, and then I may kill him."

"What?" she shrieked. "*Kill* him? Kill *Michael*? Why?"
she exclaimed, and in her fogged mind, she meant to tell
him that he had no reason to kill Michael, that he was a
bastard, okay, but he didn't deserve to die for it. Yet all her
words were garbled, and the walls started to melt behind
Adolfo's smiling face as the floor rose up to meet her.

MICHAEL was able to get cell phone reception halfway to
Bellingham, and phoned Rex. "Well," Rex said after Michael
told him what had happened. "I think you've got your boy.
I'm on my way."

"I'm not waiting for you," Michael warned him. "I'm
going to kill him. I'm going to rip him in two."

"Don't go off and leave me nothing. I want a piece of
him, too," Rex said. "Why don't you leave all the killing to
me this time—I've got permission to do it and you don't.
I'll try and get a couple of guys out of Seattle to lend you a
hand. Just sit tight until they get there, okay?"

Michael couldn't promise that. He just told Rex to get
out there as soon as possible. And then he turned the Jeep
around and headed back for the little town and the Italian
restaurant where Leah had been seen last, and thought back
to the last time he'd seen Juan Carlo.

It had been a few years ago, at a party Juan Carlo had
thrown for his sister at his Costa del Sol mansion. Juan Carlo
loved a good party and that night had been amazing—the

pool had been filled with floating candles. Girls in skimpy bathing suits, high on coke, had walked around sharing liquor and cocaine with all the male guests.

Juan Carlo had been in fine form that night, dancing with his wife, Maribel (who complained to Michael in private that she couldn't bear his touch), flirting with all the girls, and clapping all the men on the back, sharing a joke, a cigar, or a drink. He'd told Michael that night that they were *compadres*, the closest of friends. "One day," he had said in English, "you will work with me. I will make you rich beyond your wildest dreams."

At the time, Michael had thought that was slightly amusing, because he knew the Spanish authorities would be paying an early morning call to Juan Carlo and that he likely would never see his mansion in Costa del Sol again. Juan Carlo—jovial, fun-loving, generous Juan Carlo—had made his millions from trading arms to terrorists who intended to use those arms against the United States. He was a ruthless arms supplier, crooked as the day was long . . . but he was nonetheless an affable, likable guy, and in a weird way, it had pained Michael a little to put him away for the rest of his life.

"You know how it is out there," Rex had waxed philosophically when he had told Michael that Juan Carlo was, surprisingly, out of prison and had been to see Maribel, roughing her up badly enough to put her in the hospital. "Money is a powerful corrupter."

Michael supposed so, and while he could have guessed Juan Carlo had wanted to kill him from the moment the federal agents had shown up and taken him down—there was no question in Michael's mind that Juan Carlo hadn't known immediately who set him up—he never would have guessed he would come to the United States to do it.

Frankly, he was a little blown away by it.

But the man had made a grave error when he'd touched Leah. Michael felt a fury boiling in his veins like he'd never felt in his life, a palpable energy coursing through him and dredging up every single drop of testosterone in his body.

He was seeing red, alright. And lucky him, he'd get to kill Juan Carlo with his bare hands, because he didn't have a gun on him, and Michael was honestly looking forward to breaking Juan Carlo's fucking neck.

TWENTY-FIVE

LEAH woke up once again, her head pounding and her mouth dry, lying on her stomach across the bed. She was still wearing the ruined dress, but Adolfo had taken his shirt back, the bastard.

With a groan, she pushed herself up and looked around through a curtain of hair. Adolfo was lounging in the old chair, the gun on his lap as he watched a small black-and-white TV. An old sitcom from the sound of it.

"You're an asshole, Adolfo," she said hoarsely.

He lazily turned his head toward her and smiled. "I have been called far worse."

She pushed her hair over her shoulder, rolled onto her back, and stared up at the ceiling, trying to focus. "It's the orange juice, isn't it? There was something in the orange juice."

"*Sí*," he answered readily, as if she was asking the ingredient in his special brownie recipe. "The same as was in the wine."

"What was it?" she asked in a near whimper. "Is it poison? Am I going to die?"

Adolfo clucked his tongue. "Not from poison. I do not want to kill you, Leah, I merely want to . . . how do I say it . . . make you not move."

"Incapacitate me," she said.

"*Sí, sí!*" he sang out, pleased that she knew the word.

"But why?" she cried. "Why are you doing this to me?"

"What are these tears?" he scoffed. "I have explained why, no? I need you so that the bastard will come to me."

Man, she had the distinct memory of having witnessed this very scene in a soap opera she'd watched between jobs once. A woman inexplicably captured and held in a remote mountain cabin—only it had gone on for months, and the woman had fallen in love with her captor. That was definitely not going to happen here, although Leah might fall in love with the men in white coats who came to get Adolfo.

"The bastard is not going to come," Leah said, swiping at a single tear from beneath her eye. "He's never going to find you here, and even if he does, he is so much smarter than you are. He won't walk into a stupid trap."

Adolfo chuckled. "First you despise him. Then you defend him. Which do you want, *mi amor*? To love him or to hate him?"

"Oh . . . just shut up," she said irritably.

"He will come. I left many clues, so even a man as *estúpido* as he will find us. And because I have you, he will arrive very soon, for he will be very afraid."

Leah sat up and glared at Adolfo. "You know, I used to think you were a nice guy."

He laughed again, inclined his head in acknowledgment. "It is a sad thing that you will know me only under these circumstances. I am very charming—many women have said so. In Spain, you would have adored me very much."

"Oh, right, you're a regular prince," Leah snapped. "So do I at least get to know why you want to kill him?"

He shrugged. "He is a liar. And he made love to my wife." Adolfo smiled coldly. "*Many* times."

Leah's heart sank a little—apparently, the Extreme Bachelor had gone international. She got off the bed, pausing only a moment until her head cleared a little.

When it did, she saw that Adolfo had sat up, had his hand on his gun. "What are you doing?" he asked, eyeing her suspiciously.

"The bathroom," Leah said, and ignoring him, she stumbled into the pit of a bathroom.

When she had availed herself of the facilities, such as they were, she emerged again, hands on hips, and glared once more at Adolfo, who was now on his feet, holding the gun with the ease of a man who had apparently done so many times before. He reminded her of one of the villains in a bad TV movie, holding it so carelessly.

"Can't you point that thing in another direction?"

He looked down at it and seemed surprised. He quickly pointed it toward the ceiling.

"What is the matter with you?" she demanded.

"*Ach,*" he said, flicking his wrist at her. "I do not care for guns. I have others use them on my behalf."

Leah's jaw dropped open. "You don't know how to use the gun you are holding?"

Adolfo shrugged.

Leah shook her head. "You ought to be ashamed of yourself."

He laughed, looked down at the gun he was holding. "You should mind your tongue when a man is holding you at gunpoint," he said, "especially when he does not know how to use it properly."

Excellent advice, but Leah smirked at him nonetheless. "Is there anything to eat or drink besides poisoned orange juice?" she asked, and walked past him, into the kitchen. Adolfo did not try and stop her, but followed her in, as if he, too, was interested.

"You will find small biscuits and canned foods," he

said, watching curiously as Leah opened a cabinet door.

"Wait a minute," she said, pausing to look at him over her shoulder. "Do you mean you planned to hold me captive without *food*?"

Adolfo laughed and took a can of tuna out of the dank cabinet. "I did not see the point of wasting good food on a woman who will soon be dead."

Leah gasped. His glittering brown eyes were hard as rocks, and she felt the pit of her stomach slide, woozy and sick, to her toes.

He was serious. Dead serious.

JUAN Carlo might as well have strewn his path with bread crumbs and cookies, or better yet, paint a big red arrow pointing up the mountain, he was so damn obvious about it. Michael started with the bartender, whom he had to rouse out of bed after coaxing his name from a waitress. The man wasn't very happy about it until Michael tossed a couple of twenties at him—then he remembered Juan Carlo very well. Juan Carlo had taken the time to have a long and memorable conversation with the man about cabins, and one in particular up the old Sunlight Canyon Road.

"Anything else?" Michael asked.

The bartender thought about it. "He was a nice guy, actually. A big tipper."

That was Juan Carlo, generous to a fault.

At the only real grocery in town, Juan Carlo had apparently proven once again that he was a consummate ladies' man. He had chatted it up for almost an hour with a middle-aged clerk with Brillo-pad jet-black hair who had added a thick slash of dark red lipstick across her mouth, perhaps in anticipation of a return visit by the dashing Spaniard. Whatever he'd said to the clerk had obviously kept her smiling into today.

"Do you know where he might be?" Michael had asked as he paid for some gum.

"I don't know for sure, but he was talking about making the drive up Sunlight Canyon Road."

"Up there?" Michael asked, feigning confusion. "I heard there wasn't much up there anymore."

"Oh there's not," the clerk agreed, confirming Michael's guess. "Just a couple of old family cabins. I know two of them have been empty for years, since the cost of heating fuel got so expensive. But there are a couple of nicer ones down by the main road. I'm sure that's where he's probably staying."

Michael was sure that's where he was *not* staying. He thanked the clerk, walked out to the Jeep. This was like finding an elephant in a haystack. All he had to do now was find the right cabin, which wouldn't be too hard, thanks to Juan Carlo's big red flags and pointers.

He got into the driver's seat and sat a moment. What was he going to do when he found him? Storm the cabin? Right. Juan Carlo was as crafty and cunning as any arms trader or dope runner could be and undoubtedly was waiting in the trap he'd set for Michael. Without backup—and Michael wasn't waiting hours for backup—he'd basically have to walk right into the trap if he was going to get to Leah.

He did not relish the thought of doing that, but he figured he had little choice. If she was still alive—and he couldn't even think of the other possibility—it was his only chance to get to her before Juan Carlo did something stupid. But once Juan Carlo had *him,* Leah would become secondary. Maybe he could negotiate her release in exchange for himself. He liked his chances much better on his own.

He couldn't even guess how this was going to play out, but first things first—he had to get Leah away from Juan Carlo.

AS he guessed, Michael found the cabin easily enough—it was just where he suspected it would be, high on the end of the old forest road, the last of a couple of run-down vacation cabins.

The car sitting out front of the cabin bore the familiar logo of a rental agency—it was a predictably high-end car and too nice for this particular area. It stuck out like a sore thumb. But Juan Carlo was the sort of guy who liked top of the line so that he could flash his wealth at every opportunity, even when he was in the hunt to kill a man. Stupid bastard.

Michael parked his Jeep at the bottom of the long road up, beneath a stand of spruce trees on an abandoned mining road. He tried to call out on his cell phone, but couldn't get a signal, and pitched it inside his Jeep. He'd already called Rex from town and told him what he knew. Once again, Rex had urged him to sit tight, that he'd have someone out from D.C. as soon as possible.

"D.C.?" Michael asked. "I thought you said Seattle."

"I did. But the FBI prefers we keep this below the radar. The president doesn't want any bad press over a known terrorist slipping undetected past our borders. If the media got hold of that, the administration would have to explain it. So just sit tight. I've got a plane—we'll be there in a matter of hours."

"Right," Michael said, but he and Rex both knew that he wouldn't wait. "Whatever you do, just be cool, man," Rex said before Michael hung up. Easier asked than done, Michael thought.

Outside of the Jeep, he took the lug wrench to carry with him for protection. He had never, in all the years he'd worked for the CIA, carried a gun. He had a deep cover, a businessman selling packing materials to people like Juan Carlo. He'd had no need of a gun. There was only one time he'd even wanted one—back when he was sleeping with Juan Carlo's wife and spent each night wondering if it would be his last. That, and today. He would have liked the feel of cold steel in his hand, would have liked to find Juan Carlo's fat face in its sites.

Unfortunately, there was no gun. There was a tire jack and a lug wrench. The lug wrench was almost useless as a weapon—Juan Carlo would kill him before he could do much damage—but he might be able to get one good lick in before Juan Carlo had that chance.

He started his trek up the slope of the mountain, tracking behind the cabin through a forest thick with spruce and pine trees. As he picked his way over fallen trees and rocks, which aggravated him by wasting his time, his fear of what was happening to Leah grew exponentially, and it occurred to Michael that he had, at last, formed a deep attachment.

It was weird to realize something that profound in this situation. But having spent years convinced he was incapable of forming an attachment, it felt huge—deep and inseverable. Thinking that Leah might be in any sort of danger—especially danger he had caused—felt as if someone or something had reached inside of him and wrung his heart clean of blood. He felt ill, unsettled, like his skin didn't exactly fit his body, like he needed to be doing something other than trekking through the woods.

To make matters worse, he had nothing to do but think on his way up, and knew that this would not have happened if he'd just been man enough to admit what he was feeling five years ago. Both of their lives would have taken a different track. But instead he had turned coward and had run. A change of scenery, that's what he thought he needed. Just like when he was a kid—as soon as he'd start to get close to someone, he'd always be moved to the next foster home. He always got a change of scenery.

How remarkable that a man could be thirty-eight years old and understand for the first time what a sick existence that was. How remarkable that he hadn't understood until now how much a person needed attachments. Back then, he hadn't understood it at all. He'd thought commitment meant he'd have to stay in one place, could not move to the next foster parent, or the next school, or the next life. Commitment meant he would die off in one place.

Now he understood that commitment meant freedom. It meant peace and a sense of belonging to someone at last.

He climbed up, stepping over logs and rocks, stoic and grim, the magnitude of the sea change in him weighing his steps. It took him more than two hours to climb through the debris of the forest before he caught a glimpse of the faded red paint of the cabin. He crouched down, tried to see through the brush. Nothing had changed since he had driven by earlier. The car was still parked out front, an old tattered wind sock still hanging from a flagpole. It actually looked as if nothing had moved. Not even the wind.

He moved quietly forward, to the edge of the tree line surrounding the house. There was a rickety old porch with three plastic chairs stacked in one corner. In the opposite corner was a pile of boards covered by a faded blue plastic tarp. One side of the cabin had nothing but the small square of a bathroom window. He moved to his right, saw that the other side of the cabin had a window looking out from the kitchen, through which he could see a cluttered table and countertop.

A rusted propane tank in the yard allowed him to get a little closer, and he used the cover of it to move to the back of the cabin, where an old chimney had been converted into a barbeque pit. There was a freestanding hammock, more chipped plastic chairs, and a couple of discarded beer bottles. Corona, Michael noticed. Juan Carlo used to have crates of the stuff trucked into Costa del Sol.

Moving from behind the propane tank to the cover of the forest again, Michael checked out the back of the cabin. There was a covered entry, but the door was boarded up with new lumber. There were two big windows overlooking what there was of a backyard, and in that window, sitting cross-legged on a bed was Leah.

Michael caught his breath, felt a rush of relief to see her alive, and squinted to see her better. It was difficult—there was nothing but natural light, and she was mostly in shadows. But when she looked up, he saw her face and thought she looked . . . perturbed?

Perturbed.

Not scared. Not furious. But irritated and tired, like she was babysitting a petulant child. Was it possible that she didn't know she was in danger? Was it possible that she thought she was involved in nothing more than a tryst with Juan Carlo? He swallowed down a lump of revulsion at that idea, and crept closer, straining to see through the dingy window into the shadowed room, until he saw her lift her hands.

They were bound together with rope.

His throat constricted; he felt the fury rise up in him again, hot and thick. He clenched his jaw, gripped the lug wrench and tried to control the anger. It was the first thing they taught you in the agency—never let your emotions take control.

They had a reason for teaching him that—because of his anger, he didn't hear Juan Carlo creep up on him until he said, "Welcome, *amigo.* I've been waiting for you."

Michael tried to rise up and swing out, but he was hit with such force on the back of his head that everything went very black and very still.

TWENTY-SIX

IF Leah ever got out of this mess, she was going to happily find a way to make Adolfo suffer before she killed him. The more she thought about it, the more she was really very incensed—first there'd been the drugs, then the gun he didn't know how to handle but insisted on waving at her anyway, then tying her up, her hands to her feet, and finally, dragging Michael inside and kicking him a couple of times before he gave in to her shouts to stop.

He was really turning out to be royal bastard.

With his arms folded across his chest, Adolfo glared down at Michael's still body. "Perhaps you are right," he said to her, panting heavily. "What is the point of hurting him? After all, I intend to kill him."

Leah shuddered at the calm, smooth way he said it. "Stop saying such ridiculous things, will you?" she insisted as he decided to drag Michael across the floor and lay him face down beside the bed. "You're not going to kill anyone,

Adolfo. You and Michael are going to sort out whatever is between you, like two calm, rational adults."

That made Adolfo laugh. "This cannot be, my sweet. Do you think I risk so much only to talk?"

Well, no, she didn't, but she was hoping he might see reason. As that seemed a lost cause—evidence: she was tied up, for Chrissakes—she leaned over and looked down at her fallen hero.

Poor Michael. He had an ugly gash on the back of his head. But he had come just like Adolfo said he would, and for some reason, that gave her a major feeling of warm pride. The man had put his life on the line for her. He really did love her, didn't he?

Adolfo trussed Michael's arms behind his back, chuckling to himself as he worked, muttering alternately in Spanish and English. When he had finished, he fell, exhausted, into the Naugahyde chair and smiled at Leah. "Here he is, the bastard. He's not such a very big man now, *sí*? Without the American government, he's a little cockroach, one that I will smash with my boot."

"Did you have to hit him so hard?" Leah asked, peering at the blood at the base of his skull. "He might be seriously hurt."

"What care do I have?" Adolfo exclaimed, then frowned at Leah's expression. "Don't cry! He's not dead, he is merely sleeping. I have not yet killed him!" He stood, looked down at Michael again, then abruptly squatted next to him. He tightened the rope that bound Michaels hands, and then—with a lot of grunting and grimacing—he hoisted Michael up, so that the upper half of his body was on the bed. He then grabbed Michael's legs and hoisted them up, too, so that Michael was lying next to Leah, his face in a pillow.

"At least move his face so that he can breathe," she insisted.

Adolfo rolled his eyes, sighed loudly, and with one big

hand, shoved Michael's face around, so that it was facing Leah. "There. You may gaze at your bastard and fill your mind with the memory of him before I kill him."

"Just *stop* it, Adolfo! No one is killing anyone here!" she exclaimed, and tried very hard to believe it. She leaned forward, put her bound hands to the gash at the back of Michael's head. "Ohmigod."

Adolfo laughed and turned toward the tarnished mirror and began to mess with his hair. "You do not understand. This man is no better than the dirt on your feet." He paused, leaned forward to examine his bangs a little more closely. "He deserves no better than to be slaughtered like a pig."

"Okay, I am asking you nicely to please stop saying things like that," Leah said, throwing up a hand. "It's really very upsetting."

Adolfo shrugged.

She was going to kill him, literally kill him with her bare hands, and she could, too. Cooper had taught them the hand-to-hand combat moves for the film, and had jokingly told them that with some real force, they could kill someone. If she could get her hands free, she'd cheerfully test that theory on Adolfo.

Leah turned away from Adolfo, who was preening in the mirror like he had a big date, and glanced at Michael. She leaned forward—and gasped softly. His eyes were open, and he was squinting up at her. His lips were pressed tightly together, and she had the distinct impression that he was trying to tell her to be silent.

Leah stole a quick look at Adolfo over her shoulder, who was now fixing the tuck of his shirt into his trousers just so, the goddam peacock. God, she hated him. But she hated even worse that she had fallen for his stupid lines and his easy charm. *Stupid, stupid, stupid.* She looked down at Michael, whose gaze was steady on hers, his jaw clenched tightly shut. She had the feeling again that he wanted her to do . . . *something.* But what?

Leah jerked her gaze to Adolfo, who caught her gaze in

the reflection of the mirror. "No, no, Leah. You must not have good feelings for him," he advised. "He is not a good man. He lies and he cheats and he steals. He pretends to be your friend and then he stabs you in your back. He is like a leech, creeping into your life and sucking the blood from you."

"Ewww," Leah said, wrinkling her nose.

Adolfo turned around and leaned up against the scratched bureau and flashed the charming smile that had sucked her in once upon a time. "I think we must change your binds of the hands," he said thoughtfully, gesturing to her hands. "I do not trust you not to untie him when he wakes, and I cannot watch you like a little bird. I have much to do." He studied her hands and her feet for a moment, muttered something to himself, then disappeared into the kitchen, returning a moment later with a wooden chair from the kitchen.

He put the chair near the bureau, then strolled to the bed, had a close look at Michael—whose eyes were closed now, his jaw slacked. Leah wasn't certain if he was faking it or if he'd passed out again. But then Adolfo grabbed the rope that bound Leah's hands to her feet and yanked it carelessly, jerking her legs, too. *"Ouch,"* she snapped at him.

"Oh, I am very sorry," he said with mock concern. But he untied her hands, then her legs. With a sigh of relief, Leah started to inch off the bed. Adolfo stopped her by grabbing her roughly by the arm and jerking her up into his chest. They stood nose-to-nose—well, forehead-to-chin, as Leah was shorter than him—and Adolfo laughed so darkly that a shiver of fear winged down Leah's spine. "Do not think to fight me, *mi amor*," he said with a cold smile, "for I have not yet decided if I will kill you, too."

"That's really . . . not very nice," she said through clenched teeth.

"I am not a nice man."

"I'm definitely starting to get that picture."

"Be good, and maybe I won't kill you," he said, and with another jerk, dragged her to the wooden chair while her head whirled around words like *decided* and *kill*. But when he pushed her to sit in the chair, natural instinct kicked in, and she struggled. Adolfo instantly grabbed the gun from his belt and shoved the nozzle up hard against her cheek. "What do you want, Leah? Do you want me to kill him now? Or do you want me to kill you?"

When she didn't answer, he pushed the gun even harder against her face. "I didn't hear you."

"Don't . . . don't, don't. You don't even know if the safety is on," she said through gritted teeth, trying her damnedest not to move.

It worked. He pushed her away, checked the safety, then stuffed the gun back into his trousers. But his point was made—he wrapped a long cord of rope around her, tying it tightly behind her back. When he had bound her, he stood back and admired his handiwork. One trussed up man on the bed, one trussed up woman in a chair. "Excellent," he said, nodding approvingly. "I think you will be good, you and him, until I return."

"Hey, wait!" Leah cried. "How long are you going to leave us like this? Michael could be seriously hurt!"

Adolfo didn't answer, just walked out of the bedroom. The next thing she heard was the front screen door slamming shut.

"Augh!" she screeched, and jerked her gaze to Michael, who had instantly rolled to his side to see her. "What in the hell, Raney? Who is this guy, and why did you sleep with his *wife*, you idiot, and now what are you going to do about us getting killed?" she shrieked in a whisper.

"All good questions," Michael said, and rolled to his back and managed, through sheer strength alone, to sit up. But he looked a little dazed.

"God, are you going to be alright?" she asked, her anger sliding into genuine concern.

He winced, tried to smile. "I'll be fine." He took a deep

breath and then managed to gain his feet. "What are you doing?" Leah asked frantically, and leaned back as far as her neck would crane, trying to see into the next room, which of course she could not do. "What if he comes back?"

"I am going to squat down behind you and try to loosen the knot. When you get free, untie me."

"And then what?"

Michael shook his head as if to clear it, then took a tentative step, testing himself. "Damn . . . he clocked me good," he said, seemingly impressed.

"Michael, what do we do when we get untied?"

"Let's just get untied first. We'll think of something then."

That did not seem like the best of plans to Leah, especially for Mr. CIA. "But we might be dead by then!"

"Don't worry," he said, hobbling toward her. "I have been trained for situations like this."

"You know, I don't find that terribly comforting at the moment," Leah shot back, as she tried to scoot the chair around to meet him. "When you told me you were CIA and pushed a lot of paper around, I had this image of you running an office somewhere, not actually taking on bad guys."

"It wasn't all paperwork. There was some fieldwork involved."

"Apparently," she said, frowning at him over her shoulder. "Fieldwork involving some guy's wife, it would seem. Just curious here—how many other guys are there out there holding a major grudge like this one?" she asked as Michael started to slide down behind her.

"Is that what he told you?"

"Yes!" she cried, and felt the tips of his fingers on hers and turned as far as she could to look over her shoulder.

"It's a little more involved than that," he said. He was squatting, holding himself up with the strength of his thighs as he fumbled with the knot at her back.

"I'm serious, Michael. What else do I not know?" Leah asked. "What else is out there?"

"Leah, baby," he said with a sigh, "Do you really think now is the time to have this conversation? I kinda need to concentrate here, and it's not exactly easy with the knot I have on the back of my head."

"I thought you were trained for situations like this."

"I am."

"Then . . . then why couldn't you sneak up without him finding you?"

"Do you mind?" he snapped, clearly irritated, as if this was somehow her fault, "Just give me some quiet a moment and let me do this."

"Well, hurry, will you? I don't feel like having my brains blown out today."

"And whose fault is that?" Michael asked irritably.

Leah gasped, tried to jerk around to see him, and wrenched her neck in the process. "What is *that* supposed to mean?"

"It's supposed to mean, why in God's name were you trying to hook up with a guy like Juan Carlo? He's a sleazy bastard that goes through women like water."

"Wait just a minute, mister! First of all, his name is Adolfo—"

"His *name* is Juan Carlo Sanchez. He is a highly successful arms dealer, and by that I mean he once armed most of the terrorists in the Middle East. I spent the better part of three years infiltrating his circle."

"Arms?" she squeaked weakly. "You mean like rifles?"

"Not exactly," Michael said, panting now. "I mean like rocket-to-ground missiles and rocket-propelled grenades. The sort of stuff you see on TV."

The sound of a car door shutting startled them both. "Okay," Michael said, popping up and managing to propel himself through air and land half-on, half-off the bed. "Whatever you do, keep him talking. The man likes nothing better than to talk about himself and impart his wisdom to everyone," he said. He got his legs up, held his body up for a moment to look at her. "And baby . . . nothing is going to happen. Trust me. Just stay calm. Help is on the way—Juan Carlo is too stupid to pull something like this off."

"Funny, he said the same thing about you," she muttered just as the screen door shut and the devil himself strolled in, looking very pleased with himself.

He held up a bottle of wine. "Spanish wine. The best in the world. I brought it from my home in Costa del Sol. Would you like?"

"You're not seriously going to serve wine," Leah said, incredulous.

"Yes, why not?" he asked with a bit of a shrug. "You should enjoy your last few hours on Earth."

Really, all the talk of dying and killing was seriously vexing. She smiled up at Juan Carlo as she felt for the knot at her hands. He had tied the rope tightly at her wrist, but Michael had worked to loosen it a little. If she could just get her fingers on one of the loops . . .

"I will find a straw," Juan Carlo offered. "Then you can enjoy it with me while we wait for him to wake."

"I know this will come as a big shock to you, since you obviously do this sort of thing all the time, but I don't want any wine," Leah said. "You don't have the best track record when it comes to serving drinks."

"But you must! It would not do to let your host drink alone, sí?"

"You're not exactly my host, pal. That would imply that I came here of my own free will instead of being drugged and dragged here."

"You *drugged* her?"

Michael's voice startled Juan Carlo. He whirled around and laughed tightly as Michael slowly lifted himself up.

"Sleeping beauty has joined us!" he said, and made a grand sweeping bow. "Welcome to the last place on this earth you will ever see."

"If you wanted me, why not just come after me?" Michael asked. "Why involve her?"

"It is true; I could very easily have killed you on the streets of Los Angeles. But you know the answer, my friend. You know you have something I want."

"Is this about Maribel?" Michael asked genially. "Because she was with *everyone*, not just me. Ricardo, Modesto, Pa—"

Juan Carlo roared, surged forward, and kicked Michael in the back. "Do not be coy, *señor*. You forget that I know you well. Just give it to me, and perhaps I will let your whore go."

"Hey!" Leah shouted.

"I don't know what you want, Juan Carlo," Michael said. "It's a mystery to me what you're talking about."

Juan Carlo frowned darkly. "Now you are *estúpido*. I want the key."

"A *key*? I don't have any key," Michael said, smiling. "And even if I did, do you think I would carry it on me to remind me of old times?"

"What key?" Leah asked, but both men ignored her.

"You are barking up the wrong tree."

Juan Carlo sighed, put his hands to his waist, and walked to the window. "Tell me where I will find it, and you will live another hour." He turned around, looked at Michael. "Play this silly game with me, and you will not live to even drink your wine."

Michael laughed as if that amused him. "I'm saying I don't know where it is. Maybe you should ask Maribel?"

At the mention of that name, Juan Carlo's face darkened and his smile faded into a sneer. He strolled back to where Leah sat—she froze, dropped her fingers from the working of the knot. Juan Carlo removed his gun from the back of his pants and casually held it up to Leah's head.

"Oh shit," she whimpered, and closed her eyes. This

was it. This was the end. She was never going to be a real actress, she was going to die in some mouse-infested stupid cabin because he didn't know anything about guns, and it was all Michael's fault.

"Juan Carlo, come on," Michael said, reading her fear. "You *hate* guns. Ironic for an arms dealer, I know, but true."

"Be careful, Michael Raney. You play with fire."

"Put the gun down. I don't have your damn key," Michael said again. "The last person to have it was Maribel."

Juan Carlo sighed and lowered his gun. Leah opened her eyes. Juan Carlo had moved to lean against the bureau, his legs crossed at the ankles, his arms folded across his chest, and the gun dangling from one hand. He was studying Michael closely.

Leah took the opportunity to ask, "Who is Maribel? Is that your wife?" Neither man so much as looked at her. "Listen, you two, you dragged me into this—the least you can do is tell me what the deal is with this key and who Maribel is and what is going on!"

Juan Carlo shifted his gaze to her and regarded her curiously. "Women," he said, shaking his head. "At the door of death, and still, she would have the gossip."

Okay, that was it. Leah started fidgeting with the knot at her back with a vengeance and looked at Michael, who actually scowled at her, as if she was bothering him with her questions. "Just relax, Leah. I'd rather not get into it right now."

"Of course not!" Juan Carlo bellowed, and suddenly stomped out of the room, into the kitchen, the gun swinging wildly with his gait. "You cannot admit to her the sort of man you really are!" he shouted from the kitchen as Leah frantically worked at the knot. "You would have her think you are a decent man, but you are not!" He reappeared in the bedroom, holding the wine, a gun, and three wineglasses. "That is the beginning of your problem, *sí*?"

he said to Michael. "You cannot be entirely honest with those you love."

The truth in that statement made Leah snort, and both men turned to look at her. "What?" she asked, and looked at Michael. "Well? It's true! You're not very good at telling the whole story."

"You're kidding me, right?" he asked incredulously. "We're not going to sit here and have a discussion about our relationship *now*, are we?"

"I'm just saying," Leah said.

Michael groaned, then inched his way into an almost sitting position and looked at Leah intently. "Putting aside, for a moment, that everything coming out of this asshole's mouth is a load of shit, Leah—let's keep it real here. Sometimes you don't make it very easy for me to be completely and totally honest."

"Me?"

"Ah, and the words coming from your mouth are pure, no?" Juan Carlo interjected with a snort of incredulity. "You are a liar and a thief!"

"Jesus, Juan Carlo, will you stop taking everything so personally?" Michael demanded. "Think about it—terrorists like you tend to have agents like me on your ass. That's our world. It's what we call business."

"You fuck my wife and call it *business*?" Juan Carlo bellowed.

Leah stretched her fingers wide for a moment. "See? You slept with his *wife*!"

"He took my wife to his bed *many* times to get close to me," Juan Carlo said with a wave of his hand. "She gave him all our money—" He suddenly whipped around and glared at Michael. "And she gave you a *key*. Where is the key, *señor*? Give me the key, and this one shall walk free, I give you my word."

"A key to what? Her heart?" Leah asked acidly, her own heart perilously close to sinking.

But Juan Carlo and Michael surprised her by snorting

simultaneously. "Maribel doesn't actually have a heart," Michael added.

Surprisingly, Juan Carlo nodded in agreement. "She is a hard woman, this is true."

"So what key?" Leah shrieked with frustration.

"A key to a safe," Juan Carlo clarified.

"What's in the safe?"

"None of your concern!" Juan Carlo cried. "But the key belongs to *me*."

Michael shrugged and lay down. "Ask your wife."

"I have asked her, and she told me you took it!" he roared, his face getting very red, the veins popping out. "You had no right to take it from me!"

"I had no right?" Michael shot back. "You were arming terrorists whose aim was to use those missiles to hit the United States! *That* gave me the right! Your own government gave me the goddam right!"

Juan Carlo clucked his tongue as if Michael was being petulant and smiled at Leah. "That is what he says. But who knows the truth? He is not honest even with you, and you do not sell arms."

Michael groaned and closed his eyes. "We're really going to do this, aren't we? We are going to use this opportunity to psychoanalyze me. Good torture technique, Juan Carlo. I give—let's just cut to the chase, okay?"

"I am a man who has had many relationships," Juan Carlo calmly explained. "Perhaps I can help you."

"Go ahead and put a bullet in me. I prefer that to any advice from you."

"But it's true," Leah said, because it *was* true. "You've never been entirely honest with me. In New York you weren't honest, and then in L.A. you haven't been completely honest. He's right—*I* haven't sold any arms to terrorists, so why can't you be honest with me?"

"He cannot," Juan Carlo opined. "He is not able to be honest. It is what we call a defect in the . . ." He gestured toward his torso.

"Character," Leah suggested, her fingers aching from working the knot.

"Character," Juan Carlo agreed.

"No, seriously. Just shoot me," Michael said, and fell on his side, looking entirely frustrated.

Great, Leah thought. When the going got tough, Mikey folded like a house of cards.

TWENTY-SEVEN

MICHAEL hadn't folded, but he'd definitely had enough. He didn't know if Leah was stringing Juan Carlo along, but he really was in no mood to examine their relationship with that asshole in the room, and when she said, "Excuse me, but I thought I deserved a little honesty in my final hour," he lost it.

"Excuse *me*, Leah," Michael said, struggling to sit up again, "but I was *painfully* honest when I saw you in L.A. I told you I'd made a huge mistake. I begged you to take me back. I laid it all out for you, bared my soul, and you couldn't handle it. You couldn't handle the fact that I had a past."

"Which past are we talking about, Michael? The past that earned you the name of the Extreme Bachelor? Or the past you failed to mention that involved guys like Adolfo, Juan Carlo, whatever his name is!"

"It is Juan Carlo," Juan Carlo, informed her. "Regrettably, also I am not a completely honest man."

Leah glared at him, and then glared at Michael, who all but had his tie undone. It was a shame, really. Juan Carlo was the son of a fisherman and should have been able to tie a better knot than this.

"You told me you weren't seeing anyone when you were," Leah was saying, ticking off all his sins. "You told me you pushed papers around when you were in the CIA, when you were *obviously* sleeping with other men's wives, and you made promises you couldn't keep!"

Promises? Granted, he'd made his mistakes, but he hadn't broken any promises. "What promises?" he insisted. "I keep my promises! I have kept every promise to you! *You* are the one who keeps dredging up the past, because you are suspicious and jealous and insecure! How can you not see all that I am trying to prove to you is *real*?"

"But that is your mistake, Michael Raney. You are trying to make her see this too hard," Juan Carlo calmly offered.

That certainly gave Michael pause—he looked at Juan Carlo curiously. "What? How do *you* know?"

"Leah has told me everything," he said cheerfully.

When they got out of here, he and Leah were definitely going to have a little chat. "Great," he drawled, turning a murderous look to her. "*Thanks*, Leah."

"Hey, *I* didn't know he was your enemy. You failed to mention that important piece of info, remember?"

"Why can't you just believe me?" he demanded. "Why can't you just accept that I love you and no one else?"

"I have tried to believe you!" Leah protested, looking dangerously close to tears all of a sudden. "But every time I do believe you, another woman shows up out of the clear blue, or I see you flirting with several of them, or a guy like Juan Carlo wants to kill me because you slept with his wife, and then there is Nicole Redding, who acts like she practically *owns* you—"

"She is this way," Juan Carlo said sagely.

"Wait . . . what?" Leah demanded.

Juan Carlo shrugged and held out his hand to study his cuticles. "I see it in the *Star* magazine. It has all of the informations about the movie stars. She is what you would call a *slut*."

Michael actually laughed at that as he worked the ties at his back.

"It doesn't matter," Leah snapped. "What I am trying to say is that I want to trust you, but you won't tell me everything, so how *can* I trust you?"

"Wait," Juan Carlo said, holding up his hand. "This is what is the problem. I see it very clearly." He paused for dramatic effect and to sip his wine. "Ah . . ." he said with a smile. "An excellent vintage." He put the wineglass down and looked thoughtfully at Leah. *"You,"* he said, pointing at her, "are too suspicious. A man does not like this distrust and accusations whirling about him," he said, making a whirling motion with his hand.

"When a man declares his love of a woman, he honors it. Does this mean he no longer looks at the other women? *No*," he scoffed. "Does it mean he does not occasionally sample the other women? No! Of course not! Men are creatures of the body. They must sample many women to be healthy. But that does not mean he *loves* another woman. It means only that he puts his love for her above all the other women and will honor her until the day he dies, and this, she must accept," he said, putting up his hand to stop any argument before it began.

"What he said," Michael quickly cut in. "But minus the sampling. On my life, I would never sample," he avowed. "That's a promise, Leah."

Leah rolled her eyes at him.

"Now *you*," Juan Carlo said, pointing to Michael. "You must be completely honest. It is how they say . . ." He paused, then said in Spanish, "That the women are the weaker sex and must be cared for properly."

"What?" Leah asked. "What did he say?"

Michael frowned. "That women are the weaker sex and can't take care of themselves."

Juan Carlo inclined his head. Leah gasped indignantly.

"This is exact," Juan Carlo said, waving her off. "I will not give you half-truths." He looked at Michael. "*You* must bare your soul to the woman you love. It is what they want, and you must give them what they want in order to have what *you* want."

"Well . . . in spite of the fact that we are getting advice from an international terrorist—and one who wasn't exactly faithful to his wife," Leah added, frowning at Juan Carlo. "I have to agree."

Oh, for the love of Christ. Juan Carlo was a fucking idiot, and she was *agreeing* with him.

This time, Michael managed to get completely upright and on his knees. "I *am* honest. I didn't intentionally keep anything from you," he argued to Leah. "Besides, we are focusing on the wrong thing here—you have no faith."

"What?" she screeched, almost coming out of her chair. "I have no faith? Ohmigod, I can-*not* believe you just said that! I had faith in you five years ago, and you dumped me!"

"Here we go," Michael said, his head lolling back, his hands free now, needing only the right moment. "Same song, same verse. *You dumped me, and therefore I must make everything as difficult as I possibly can.*"

"How can you *say* that?" Leah cried, incredulous and so furious that she was hopping forward in her chair until Juan Carlo stopped her with a hand to her shoulder.

"He says this because he is *estúpido*," Juan Carlo said soothingly. "He is a man who—pardon for my language—thinks with his cock. Not his heart. A Spaniard thinks with his heart."

"Thanks for your help, Juan Carlo, but I think I can handle this," Michael said irritably.

"My friend, you do not understand the mind of a woman," Juan Carlo pointed out as he strolled forward to look Michael in the eye. "A woman does not need the perfume and the expensive flowers. She needs to know how you *feel*," he said, tapping his fingers against his heart.

Leah made a little sound of surprise at that, and both Juan Carlo and Michael looked at her. "He's right," she chirped, but her eyes were suddenly as big as saucers. Michael didn't like the look of her wide eyes at all. She was up to something.

Juan Carlo smiled triumphantly and turned back to Michael. "You see?" he said proudly to Michael. "You must tell her how you feel with the small things. There is time for the big things later," he added, just as Leah pulled her hand free and waved it at Michael, grinning broadly, clearly pleased with herself.

He didn't so much as blink, but his whole body seized with fear. If she did something stupid, they would both be dead. Juan Carlo might not like guns, but he certainly wouldn't hesitate to use one. He barely spared her a glance.

"You must have a care for the heart," Juan Carlo said, continuing to advise. "You are too careless with the feelings of others, *amigo*. As with me," he said, gesturing grandly to himself. "We were friends. *Compadres*. I was very hurt by the spying and the seduction of my wife."

"Whatever," Michael said.

Juan Carlo abruptly turned around to Leah, who, thank God, had stuck her hand behind her back. "And *you*," he said sternly, "must open your heart and learn to accept his mistakes. Yes, this is very wise. Perhaps I should write it," he mused, and pulled the gun from his waistband and laid the nozzle thoughtfully alongside his nose, rubbing absently, considering it.

Michael noticed the rope was starting to slacken around

Leah and made a slight motion with his head. She looked down and blinked, but grabbed it behind her back and made it taut again.

"I think," Juan Carlo said, his eyes getting all squinty as he thought hard about it, "that you have been hurt in this life, Leah. Your heart has been broken, and it is not so easy to mend."

Leah forgot the rope a moment. "That's true."

Oh. *God.* Michael was now in danger of vomiting.

Juan Carlo went down on his haunches before her. "If you were not to die, I would urge you to trust more," he said, and put his palm on her cheek. "You cannot know great joy until you have known great pain."

"Oh, Ado—I mean, Juan Carlo. That's really profound."

"*Sí*, it is very wise. But hear this," he added. "You are too stubborn."

"Excuse me? Why does everyone think I should just blindly accept what Michael says?"

"You should not," Juan Carlo said. "But when he tells you things, it is not attractive to be stubborn. You look . . ." He glanced at Michael over his shoulder and said in Spanish, "like a bull."

"Bullheaded," Michael helpfully supplied.

"Oh!" Leah cried indignantly.

"Remember this." Juan Carlo smiled, patted her cheek, and stood up, tapping the nozzle of the gun against his arm as he turned toward Michael. "But it does not matter now, does it? Come now, Michael Raney. Give me the key."

Michael laughed. "The key won't do you any good, Juan Carlo. The safe is empty. It's all sitting in Swiss bank accounts with my name on it."

The tapping of the gun stilled. "Do not play games with me," he warned. "I will kill your love first and let you watch her die."

Leah's brows dipped into a V at that. She clenched her jaw and very quietly let go of the rope, judging by the way it slackened around her body. Michael kept his eye on Juan

Carlo, his eyes narrowed and his jaw clenched. "You want the key?" he asked.

"*Sí,*" Juan Carlo said with a bit of a bow as Leah managed to push the ropes down around her waist.

"Then I'll tell you where it is."

"Go on."

"Maribel has it."

Juan Carlo's laugh was cold. "Even if you do not produce the key, I will still kill you, Michael Raney. I have my honor to protect."

"Yeah, well, Maribel stomped all over your honor, *amigo.* She used that key like a red light," he said as Leah quickly pushed the rope down to her knees. "It was her ticket to good sex. That was her problem with you, you know. No finesse in the bedroom."

He would never know who moved first—Leah, or him, or even Juan Carlo. But as Juan Carlo lifted the gun to shoot him, Michael lunged at the same moment Leah rose up and clipped Juan Carlo in the back, just like Cooper had taught them in boot camp. When Juan Carlo doubled over on his side, Michael leaped to his feet and kicked him in the face, knocking him back.

The gun went flying out of Juan Carlo's hand, and he was forced around by the blow to his head. He fell against the bureau, and as Leah kicked him, Michael launched himself at Juan Carlo, landing on his body and crashing with him to the floor.

He didn't know how Leah fell, but when she scrambled to her feet, she was holding the gun by the finger loop, as far away from her body as she could.

"Leah!" Michael shouted. "Get the rope!"

She whirled around, saw that Michael had Juan Carlo's hands behind his back, but that Juan Carlo was struggling and cursing them in Spanish. She instantly put the gun on the bed, grabbed the rope—grappling with the chair for a moment—and then fell on Juan Carlo's legs, wrapping the rope around his feet.

In the meantime, Michael grabbed the other end of it and strove to get the rope around Juan Carlo's hands, who was frantically struggling now, his face red with his cursing. Leah scrambled up the side of Juan Carlo and grabbed his head, which caused a burst of blue Spanish and venom directed at her. Leah cringed, but Michael encouraged her. "Hold on, you're doing great."

She held on while Michael trussed him up, not only to himself, but to the bed. He jumped up with Juan Carlo screaming at him, grabbed the gun, and then grabbed Leah, pushing her out the door. "Go!" he said to her. "Get out of here!"

Leah ran.

Michael turned back to Juan Carlo, pointed the gun at his head. "You fucking bastard," he breathed.

Juan Carlo just laughed. "Kill me," he said easily. "Without the key, I am a dead man already."

As Leah reached the door, it flew open, and several men stormed in. She screamed; one of them grabbed her, clamped a hand over her mouth, and dragged her outside. "Jesus, lady, take a breath! We're here to help!"

She grabbed his hand and pulled it free of her mouth and then dragged a breath into her lungs. Several deep breaths, actually, until her heart stopped racing and her hands stopped shaking. And then she looked at the guy in the suit with the shades. "Who in the hell are *you*?" she demanded.

He smiled. "Hey, it's okay. Everything is okay."

TWENTY-EIGHT

JUAN Carlo was, as Michael very well knew, a very passionate man—but he'd never thought him stupid. Maybe a few years in Spanish prison had dulled his sharp senses, because he'd let passion get in the way of common sense, and his desire to see Michael dead lead him to some very bad decisions. Like coming to the United States, for example. And then tracking Michael down. And using Leah to draw him in.

But Juan Carlo was one lucky bastard, the recipient of a little divine intervention, because when Rex arrived, Michael had the gun barrel pressed against Juan Carlo's head and was debating whether or not he should kill him.

"Hey," Rex said breezily as he gingerly took the gun from Michael's hand. "I told you to let *me* kill him."

Juan Carlo snorted disdainfully, but Michael stepped back, put his hand to the back of his head where Juan Carlo had clocked him, and smiled maniacally at his foe, at the blood splattered on his expensive blue silk shirt, at his hands, now cuffed with steel. "Your ass is dead, Juan Carlo," he said, and Rex quickly put his hands to Michael's chest and pushed him back. "I'll see you dead before you lay another hand on anyone close to me."

"Michael," Rex said sternly, shoving him backward. "It's over. Shake it off."

Michael laughed and added in Spanish, "Keep an eye on your back, my friend, because I will never let this die."

Juan Carlo chuckled. "I would offer you the same advice."

"Okay, that's enough," Rex said, and shoved Michael hard into the kitchen, as another agent squatted down before Juan Carlo and began to ask him questions in Spanish. Predictably, Juan Carlo responded with colorful curses.

Michael shook Rex off and strode outside, pushing on the kitchen door with such force that it almost came off its hinges. He stalked off the porch and stood in the bright sunlight, his hands on his hips, taking deep breaths to calm himself down. On the other side of an overgrown yard, Leah was leaning against the trunk of a nondescript rental car, her arms folded tightly around her. There were dark circles under her eyes, her hair was a tangle of blond, and her dress . . . well, that dress just made his blood boil.

She was holding her arms tightly around her, staring at the ground as she answered the questions of agents, listened to them tell her not to speak of this to anyone until they said she could, which, of course, they would never do.

Michael turned away, his guilt at seeing her so exhausted and disheveled overwhelming. Rex had walked outside. "Let her go, get her out of here," Michael said.

"Sure," Rex said, and left Michael alone to collect his thoughts.

But a moment later, Michael heard an exclamation of frustration from Leah and turned around in time to see her striding toward him, her arms swinging, her eyes blazing. "You aren't going to pat my head and send me away after *that*," she said as she came to a halt in front of Michael, her chin tilted up defiantly, her hands on her hips. "Isn't there something you want to say?"

"Say?" he echoed dumbly. There were a million things he wanted to say. So many, he didn't know where to start.

Leah's eyes narrowed, and she rose up on her toes and leaned forward, so that they were almost nose-to-nose and said, "*Say*. For example, sorry this happened, Leah? I'm sorry I didn't tell you there was a crazy murderer lurking around and that you might possibly be in danger?" she added heatedly as they brought Juan Carlo out of the cabin. "Or how about, gee, it really sucks that you were poisoned and a gun was put to your head and you could have died!"

"It was not poison!" Juan Carlo shouted as two agents led him by.

"Oh, really?" Leah shouted after him. "Well, thanks to you I'll never drink orange juice again!"

Michael caught her arm, drawing her attention back to him. "I'm sorry, Leah," he said, assuming that was what she wanted. "I am so sorry this happened."

Dammit if tears didn't fill her blue eyes. It was one of those moments that every guy knows, a moment of total cluelessness as to what he'd said or didn't say to cause the tears. Inside, he groped in the dark, searching vainly for a lesson learned somewhere along the way that might fill him in.

And as he floundered, Leah choked on a sob as she hauled off and hit him in the arm as hard as she could. "Sorry isn't *good* enough!" she cried through her sobs. "You have used me and hurt me and humiliated me, and now you almost got me killed! *Sorry. Is. Not. Good. Enough!*" she said, hitting him with each word.

Michael stood there, stoic and unmoving, uncertain if she intended to hit him again, uncertain if he should just take it or make her stop. Leah raised her arm again, but then dropped it. Her shoulders sagged; she dropped her chin to her chest. "I want to go home."

"Okay, baby," he said low, and put his hand on her arm,

but Leah instantly shrugged it off and would not look up.

He looked at Rex, who put a hand on Leah's shoulder. "Let us take you back to camp," he said soothingly, and led a strangely dejected Leah away.

If Michael could have any moment of the day back, it would have been that one. He wished he'd never seen her expression—the weariness, the bewilderment. Part of him wished he'd never even run into her again so that he would have spared her all this turmoil. He'd been so intent on his own wants he had obviously failed to consider Leah's fully. He'd just been so certain they'd both want back what they'd lost years ago. It never occurred to him that the intervening years would rise up to stop him.

Leah didn't look back, just let Rex lead her away.

Michael felt about as low as he'd ever felt in his life.

After one of the agents took Leah back to camp, Michael spent the rest of the day with Rex ensuring that what had happened on Sunlight Canyon Road would not be discovered by local authorities or by the media—or whoever owned the rundown old cabin, for that matter. As far as the world outside the U.S. government was concerned, Juan Carlo Sanchez had never come to the United States, and government agents would make sure that his tracks were completely erased.

A nondescript white car pulled away from the cabin, whisking Juan Carlo away to some clandestine holding cell. As they watched it barrel down the gravel road, Rex asked, "So what's the deal with the key? Your boy won't stop talking about it."

"It fits a safe deposit box that was full of money and gold and a lot of blow at one time," Michael said with a snort.

"That explains some of it," Rex said. "We know he owes a lot of money to some really scary people."

"He won't find it in that box," Michael said. "And all this time, he thought I was the one to have cleaned it out, the stupid fool."

"Who did?" Rex asked.

Michael smiled wryly. "His wife. Who else?"

IT was late when Michael got back to camp, and the women were in rare form. As usual, they were divided into two main groups. The Starlets, as Leah called them, were sitting around a roaring campfire, obviously a little drunk, laughing and singing and calling out some surprisingly lewd suggestions to the camera guys milling around.

The cameramen, however, were not as interested in those suggestions—at least not professionally—because there was another group of women who were arguing over something that had happened on the rafting trip, and it looked as if it might come to blows.

"The girls are tired," Cooper said with a slight shake of his head. "They need a nap."

"What's going on?" Michael asked.

"A paddle accident," Eli said as he squinted in the direction of the squabbling women.

"A lost paddle?"

"Nope. One of them managed to hit another one in the back of the head through a chute, and wouldn't you know it, that opened up a whole other can of worms."

"About?" Jack asked.

Eli sighed, swiped the baseball hat off his head, scratched his scalp, and put the baseball cap back on before responding. "I'm not certain, but I think about shoes."

"Shoes?"

"*Shoes,*" Eli said emphatically. "Those two women and their friends almost killed each other over a pair of shoes."

"Now be fair, Eli," Cooper said. "It was a pair of Stuart Wiseass, or something like that."

"What does that mean?" Jack asked.

"Hell if I know," Cooper admitted.

The four men peered at the women, who were quite animated in their heated discussion about who had done what to whom, baffled by such strong feelings about shoes.

But when a petite brunette carelessly tossed a plastic tumbler at a buxom blonde and hit her in the knee, a screech went up that had Eli and Cooper moving quickly to break up what all of them feared could turn into a brawl.

"So how was *your* day?" Jack asked as he and Michael watched Cooper try to reason with women who were alternately pouting and arguing, while the rest of the women snickered about it.

"Not so great," Michael said truthfully.

"Where'd you find her?"

"You were right. She hooked up with someone." The lie rolled easily off Michael's tongue, just like the old days when everything he said had been a lie. It made him feel old.

Jack winced a little. "Sorry, bro. I know you've got a thing for her."

"Yep," Michael said. "But shit happens." And with that, he walked away, unwilling and unable to speak of it any further.

He walked along the edge of camp, far enough out where he wasn't easily noticed in the night, and therefore wasn't forced to talk to anyone, but close enough that he could see everyone in camp. He had a destination, of course.

Leah was sitting out around a small fire with Trudy, Jamie, and Michele. Leah was doing the talking for once— the others looked spellbound by whatever tale she was telling, her hands flying and punctuating the air with the sketches of her words. Michael wondered what she'd told them about her absence today, if she'd used the same lie he'd used. Rex had impressed upon Leah the need to stay silent about Juan Carlo's true motives until they had charged him. If ever.

He stood in the shadows, watching her for a long while, but all he could really see was her hitting him this afternoon, telling him sorry wasn't good enough. After all he'd put her through, Michael believed he now understood—he couldn't just pick up where they'd ended things. It just wasn't good enough anymore. He'd come around to his feelings far too late—the damage had been done, exacerbated by an absolutely surreal experience with Juan Carlo.

After a while, he turned and walked back into the shadows, away from that end of the camp, knowing that he really *wasn't* good enough for her—hell, he didn't even know how to talk about what had happened. He had no idea how to pick up the pieces. And frankly, he had his own shit to work through. At the moment, his relationship with the one woman he had ever really loved seemed like an insurmountable mountain.

THE next day, the group packed up and headed to Bellingham to get settled in before filming began on Tuesday. T.A.'s plan to unite the women and reward them with the rafting trip seemed to have worked—they were in good spirits, a tight group. For the first time since they'd begun training the women, the guys felt optimistic that they could and would pull off a war.

For two days since the incident at the cabin, Michael had not spoken to Leah. She hadn't spoken to him, either. It was as if some huge wall had suddenly been erected between them that neither of them could scale. On those few occasions their gazes locked, she glared at him. She was, he assumed, furious for what had happened to her, and he couldn't blame her.

As sorry as Michael was about it, he had reached a conclusion. He couldn't possibly apologize enough for who he was or what he'd done, and frankly, he didn't know if he should even try. Yes, he'd made mistakes with Leah, huge, colossal mistakes. But he wasn't sorry for his service to the United States. He couldn't have possibly predicted Juan Carlo would reappear, either. But that was the crux of the problem—he would never be able to erase the things Leah wanted erased. Maybe what he had always believed of himself was true. Maybe he was such a good spy because he never had been able to form deep, committed relationships. Maybe he was truly meant to be an extreme bachelor.

It was sobering, disappointing, and even a little heartbreaking for a man who'd had such high hopes.

But it was real.

TWENTY-NINE

IN Bellingham, the soccer moms were put up in a cheap hotel, two to a room. Of course Trudy and Leah took a room, and managed to finagle an adjoining room with Michele and Jamie. They thought it was funny that they had Starlets on one side, and Serious Actresses on the other side, who actually lived up to their moniker by posting times that everyone could run through their lines each night.

The first call sheet listed all the soccer moms, and when they arrived on set, the director explained that they wanted to do all the ensemble filming up front and as quickly as possible so they could send most of them back to L.A. and keep down costs. The schedule called for them to wrap up the big battle scenes in a week or so.

Michael, Leah noticed, was nowhere to be seen as they began to stage the first battle scene. And it wasn't until they started filming that she did catch a glimpse of him, standing behind the director, his hands shoved in his pockets as he watched the run-through.

Everyone was very excited about the start of filming. Charlene Ribisi handed out little gold soccer ball key chains to commemorate the event. The crew had swelled to dozens, and they surrounded the women and their battle-field. It was a moment Leah had looked forward to all her life, a moment she should have been absorbing through her pores.

But instead, Leah could hardly concentrate, because she kept looking at Michael across the way standing with the other T.A. guys, or laughing and smiling at some women, wondering why he hadn't tried to talk to her or at least try and apologize since they had come down off the mountain, as she had begun to think of it.

He should have at least had the courtesy to explain it all to her. She had spent a harrowing night and day in the com-pany of an international terrorist—perhaps not a very good one, but a terrorist nonetheless—and she deserved an ex-planation. If the roles had been reversed, and she had been in Michael's shoes, she would have at least apologized to him for his having suffered through it. And she definitely would have owned up to the issues between them, but *nooo*, Michael did nothing like that. Quite the contrary—he seemed to be avoiding her. *Avoiding* her! As if she was the problem! It infuriated her—she'd been through the greatest trauma of her life, no thanks to him, and he was treating her like she had the plague.

Damn him. Damn Michael J. Raney anyway!

She was so infuriated that when the director yelled *Places* for the first take, she scarcely heard him, and there-fore, missed her cue, started late, and ended up crashing into one of the Serious Actresses and muffing the stunt. Even worse, the Serious Actress took great offense to it and managed to elbow Leah in the ribs hard enough to knock her down before Harry called *cut*.

The T.A. guys trotted out to have a chat with the women who didn't get their stunts exactly right, and lucky her, it was Michael who appeared at Leah's side, his big hand on her elbow, pulling her up.

"Okay," he said, all businesslike, as if they had never been anything more than a trainer with his soccer mom trainee, "you remember the drills we did in boot camp? You want to do a one, two, and then a big leap to time the contact just right."

"I *know*," Leah said, shaking his hand off her elbow.

"Good. Then you ought to get it this take. No problem, right?"

"Yes! I will get it right," she said sharply.

Michael looked at her, his expression maddeningly calm and infuriatingly kind.

"Is there anything else?" she asked, her voice dripping with ice.

"Not unless you have a question," he said as the director yelled for everyone to take her place.

"Nope. No questions. It's all pretty clear to me," she said, nodding emphatically.

"Great," he said, and turned on his heel and walked off. Just like that. Just like nothing had happened.

Leah was still fuming when the second take was set into action, and took two huge enviable Superman strides. So huge, in fact, that she almost overran her target, colliding with the Serious Actress who had elbowed her, and spinning the woman around and into the bushes exactly as she was supposed to do. Perhaps a little too forcefully, but correctly nonetheless. When the director yelled *cut*, Leah high-fived Jamie and did a rooster strut off the battlefield.

By the end of the day, they had the first battle scene in the can. And Leah had not required any more instruction from the Extreme Bachelor, which was a good thing, as he and Nicole were sitting under the awning yucking it up.

This was it, she figured. He was done with her, moving on to the next conquest—not that anyone working this film thought that Nicole was any sort of conquest. But it was just exactly what she'd feared before the Adolfo–Juan Carlo thing, that he would eventually move on to the next woman, because that is what Extreme Bachelors do for a living.

"Good," she muttered to herself. "Good riddance." She stalked off in the direction of Trudy, who she knew would have something fun planned to take her mind off the extreme bastard.

Trudy did have something fun planned: an outing to Wal-Mart.

FORTUNATELY, the shooting schedule was so intense that the next few days flew by, and Leah had very few opportunities to even see Michael. Most of the time he was holed up with the T.A. guys, making last-minute changes to the stunt choreography. But sometimes she'd catch him talking to another woman, always in a deep conversation that made him smile beautifully, and that made the skin around his eyes crease in the way she loved.

But it wasn't until the last day of filming for her that she actually ran into him—literally, as it turned out. The director told them to take ten, and Leah was jogging back to the catering tent when she turned to shout at Trudy to keep her paint gun. That was when she collided with Michael, who had stepped into her path. He caught her by the arms and set her back. "Are you okay?"

"Yeah," she said, straightening her camouflage jacket. "Sorry."

"No problem. So listen, we were watching the last take, and we think you need to adjust a little to the left," he said, pointing to a line of fake trees. "What we want is for you to run and hit dirt right in front of that stand of trees, do the tuck and roll, and come up firing at Mary."

"Mary," she said.

"Right. Skinny brunette."

"I know who Mary is."

One of Michael's brows arched. "Okay. Cool. So do you want to go over the stunt before we do the next take?"

He had to be insane. "No, I don't want to go over it. I've been over it so many times that I can do it in my sleep."

The other brow rose up to meet the first. "Good," he said. "That's what we need." He moved as if he was going to walk away.

Leah couldn't believe this—almost a week had gone by since the nightmare she had lived, and he had yet to say a word to her. *"Michael!"* she cried before he could escape.

He paused. "Yes?"

He said it as if she were a lowly production assistant, not worthy of his time. No wait, scratch that—he spent more time with the P.A.'s than anyone.

"What is it, Leah?" he asked, clearly impatient to be on his way.

It was not an easy question to answer, because it was everything. "Where is Juan Carlo?" she demanded for lack of a good jumping-off point.

Michael took a quick look around before answering. "He's locked up. But don't worry—there is no way he can get out."

"And who were those guys who took him?" she asked, folding her arms.

He sighed, shoved a hand through his hair. "Leah . . . I think the less you know, the better."

"Were they CIA?"

"Some," he said, looking very uncomfortable. "All government."

"Can they just *do* that?" she asked, both hands slicing the air now.

"Do what?"

"Do *what*? Jesus, Michael, do you have to be so obtuse? Weren't you in the cabin with me, or did I just dream it? Can those men just sweep in and take someone away like that? Just take him off and lock him up?"

For some reason, that made Michael smile. "Apparently, they can."

Leah sighed irritably, punched her hands, encased in fingerless gloves, to her waist. "Just please give me the bottom line, can you do that?" she blurted. "I don't know what any of this means."

"You mean when the government steps in?"

"No, no," she said with great exasperation for his thick-headedness. "What it means for *us*. Assuming there was an *us* to begin with."

He didn't answer. He studied her, his eyes roaming her face and his expression—she'd seen that expression once before, a long time ago, and Leah felt her heart slip in her chest. *I'm leaving* . . .

"Honestly?" he said softly. "I don't know anymore."

Her heart plummeted, her breath left her. Whatever she thought, his response surprised her, stunned her. "So . . . ," she said, fumbling for words, fidgeting with her fingerless gloves. "Then . . . I guess that means it was too much to hope for, is that it?"

He shrugged, looked very uncomfortable. "Maybe it was."

Shit. As angry as she was with him, she realized immediately that was not what she wanted to hear. She glanced down at her hands, her fidgeting more frantic now. "Jesus, I don't know what to think anymore," she said weakly, feeling herself close to tears. "What was this all about, anyway, Michael? Were you just hoping you could finally commit, but realized you can't do it? Or do you fear that more strange men will suddenly appear out of the clear blue to terrorize your life?" She suddenly looked up. "Don't answer—you don't need to answer, because the truth is, I can't handle it. I can't handle the uncertainty with you, Michael. I can't handle the constant wondering, and the uncertainty and the fear—"

"I'm sure," he cut in, his eyes dark. "Just like I can't handle the constant need to apologize to you, or the need to prove to you that I'm not screwing around, or that every stranger who speaks to you isn't trying to kidnap you. I can't erase my past, Leah. It is what it is. I can't erase what happened in New York, or on Sunlight Canyon Road. I can't erase the fact that I have dated a lot of women. And I can't live my life with your . . . *constant* . . . uncertainty."

His response took her aback. "Are you kidding?" she asked. "Seriously, are you kidding?"

"Kidding?" He made a sound of disbelief. "Why in God's name would I kid about something like this? I don't know what else to say to you, Leah," he said angrily. "You are angry with me because I left you, but I can't change that, anymore than I can change my eye color. Jesus, I *love* you, I adore you, and I can't change that, either—I don't *want* to change that. But I am who I am, and if you can't be certain about me or what I say to you now, and if you will always wonder, then I don't know what else to say. I tried. I failed. I'm not going to be reminded of my failure day in and day out."

Her heart was reeling, her thoughts collapsing, her anger and frustration mounting. "Good, that's great," she said sharply, her voice betraying her hurt. "I'm glad to hear you say it, because I can't live with the uncertainty of you, I just can't. I can't live with the Extreme Bachelor or the ex–CIA agent with enemies or the worry whether you are being honest with me. It's too hard and too much and I don't want it! I want to be happy, not constantly fearing that this will be the day you break my heart to pieces again!"

He looked as if she had physically struck him. He blinked. Put his hand to his nape. "Okay," he said stiffly. "If that's what you want."

"It's what I want," she said firmly, yanking the stupid gloves from her fingers. But it was a lie, a stupid lie, because it *wasn't* what she wanted, it wasn't even *close* to what she wanted. Only it was too late—days, years, eons too late. And now that she'd said the words, had set them free to swell between them, she couldn't take them back.

Michael was already moving backward. "I wish you well, Leah," he said quietly. "Whatever you do, wherever life takes you, I wish you nothing but the best."

"Great," said, her voice damnably shaky. "You, too."

He smiled sadly, shoved his hands into his pockets. "Good-bye, Leah."

"Good-bye, Michael," she choked out, and watched the only man she would ever love turn on his heel and walk away.

Subject: Re: I'm Home!
From: Lucy Frederick <ljfreddie@hotmail.com>
To: Leah Kleinschmidt <hollywoodiva@verizon.net>
Time: 3:23 pm

I'm so glad you're back! There are soooo many things we have to decide, but the big one is the color of the bridesmaid dress, surprise, surprise. So now I'm thinking red, a rich, ruby red. You like red, don't you? Yes, you do. Remember that red dress you wore to my holiday party? Anyway, I attached another great halter dress to this e-mail. Tell me what you think.

Hey, did you get a chance to talk to Michael?

Subject: Re: Re: I'm Back!
From: Leah Kleinschmidt <hollywoodiva@verizon.net>
To: Lucy Frederick <ljfreddie@hotmail.com>
Date: 12:48 pm

I like the style of the dress. And the red is really pretty, even if most of your bridesmaids are blondes or redheads. I always thought red was a better color for brunettes. And BTW, I never wore a ruby-red dress to your holiday party. I wore black. Maybe a rich green would be a better idea. But hey, if you want red, that's cool, too. It's your wedding! I am here to serve.

I didn't talk to anyone. I mostly worked. I think I'm off guys for a while. And please don't give me the speech you always give me when I take a break from guys. I'm not being a hermit, I'm not wearing my feelings on my sleeve, I'm not doing anything but concentrating on my career, okay? In fact, Frances called me today and told me I have a shot at an HBO Original Series about pilgrims or something. Kewl, huh?

THIRTY

LEAH did manage to snag a role in the new HBO series, *Coming to America*, which was about the grueling reality the pilgrims faced in settling America. Leah had wanted the part of the trapper's daughter, but when she asked, Frances laughed so hard that she threw her back out. "You're not going to be the *star*, honey," she'd said, not unkindly, but as if it was obvious to the entire world, save Leah. "It's like I've been telling you—*character* roles."

Which is exactly what Leah got when they tapped her for the minor part of the wife of one of the settlement's elders. Essentially, that meant her on-screen time was devoted to slaving over a washboard, lifting giant kettles of water, or, conversely, stirring something in it, and looking after the five kids that supposedly she had given birth to while they eked out their meager existence, which no woman in her right mind would have done. In fact, it became a running joke between her and the other minor wives as to how in God's name their stinky pretend husbands could possibly be getting any action in bed, what with the life they led.

The only thing Leah liked about the role was the costumes, but even that got old after a bout of unusually warm weather and the soundstage heated up along with the rest of L.A. Wool was not Leah's first choice when the temperatures started hitting eighty-five degrees and higher.

Trudy dropped by the set a few times, always in stylish shades, ostensibly to check out the available guys, but really to bug the director, Ted, into giving her a part. Ted would never take the bait, so Trudy would do the next best thing—make Leah go out with her for drinks before she had to go pick up her kids at one relative's house or another.

Their favorite watering hole was a place on Sunset Boulevard, where the drinks were way too high for Leah to afford—she'd spent most of her *War of the Soccer Moms* windfall on a new car—but Trudy insisted it was a great place to see and be seen by all the right people.

"Who are the right people?" Leah asked once.

Trudy shrugged behind her John Lennon shades. "Directors. Producers. People like that. The next big thing is discovered in places like this all the time."

They both looked around at the other people in the bar. "Do you see anyone you know?" Leah asked.

"No, but that doesn't mean anything."

Exactly.

Leah drank water most of the time; Trudy drank Pink Ladies and talked endlessly about her kid (genius), her boyfriend (loser), and what she'd heard about the post-production work on *War of the Soccer Moms*. It had been three months since production wrapped, with a scheduled release date in another six months, to hit the summer rush.

"The film editing isn't going very well," Trudy told Leah one afternoon, nodding as if she was in-the-know, which she wasn't. But then again, she was an actress and liked the part.

"It isn't? How come?"

"Because there are a couple of divergent opinions about how it ought to be edited—one side thinks Charlene needs more screen time because she's the big draw, but get this—" Trudy paused, glanced surreptitiously about to see if anyone was listening in, then leaned forward and whispered loudly, "Apparently, Nicole was blowing the executive producer the whole time! And guess who is the exec's good golfing buddy?"

"Who?" Leah whispered.

Trudy inched forward a little more. "The *head* of the *studio*." She sat back, clearly pleased with her scoop. "So who do you think is going to get more screen time? Charlene?" she asked, thrusting one hand out, palm up, "or Nicole?" she finished, thrusting the other hand out in the opposite direction. "Do you *believe* that shit?"

"I don't know, and I'll be honest, Trudy—I don't care," Leah said. "All I care about is how much screen time *I* get. And with whom, of course."

With a snort, Trudy picked up her Pink Lady and took a healthy swallow. "You're not going to get enough screen time to make a difference to an ant, kiddo. With two stars like Charlene Ribisi and Nicole Redding, the rest of us poor bit players will be lucky to get a toe into a shot," Trudy said confidently. She suddenly sat up, her eyes shining. "Is Nicole a slut or *what*? She was blowing the exec producer the whole time she was trying to blow *your* guy!"

At the mention of "her guy," Leah almost choked on her water.

"What's the deal with him, anyway?" Trudy asked. "What happened to him?"

Leah shrugged and looked around the room, avoiding eye contact. "Who knows? It was just one of those production flings, anyway. You know, once it wraps, that's the end, and everyone is cool with that."

"Really?" Trudy asked, her brow wrinkling. "Are you cool with that? Because I thought he was so into you."

Leah shrugged again and pretended to be examining the drink menu.

"Okay, what about the lighting guy?"

"Who?" Leah asked, pretending not to know, hoping Trudy would drop it, knowing it was exactly the wrong thing to do.

So wrong, in fact, that Trudy actually laughed at her. "Don't give me that crap, girl," she said cheerfully. "So? Have you heard from him?"

"Oh him," Leah said flippantly. "No, I haven't. He went back to Puerto Rico, I think."

"I thought it was Spain."

"Spain, Puerto Rico," Leah said with a flick of her wrist as if they were practically the same country. She'd told so many lies about Juan Carlo the night she came back from the cabin that she couldn't remember what she'd said any longer.

"That whole thing was so weird," Trudy doggedly went on.

Leah glanced up over the top of the drink menu. "What was weird?"

"Just you and that guy," Trudy said thoughtfully. "It was so unlike you."

"Everyone has a one-night stand now and again," Leah retorted. "What about you and the sandwich guy?"

"Not the same thing," Trudy said with a shake of her head. "Because I *am* that kind of person, so it's no surprise when I do it. But when *you* do it, we all sit up and take notice."

Great, just what any girl wanted to hear. "It was a long time ago," Leah said, and ducked her head again. "I think I might try one of these martinis," she added, hoping to divert Trudy to one of her favorite pastimes—drinking.

But Trudy was having none of it. "Michael Raney, that was *really* weird," she said, squinting at Leah over her John

Lennon sunglasses. "I mean it—he was so *into* you. We all saw it."

"You guys saw what you wanted to see."

"Don't think so. And I don't think it was just a production fling."

"It was. Trust me," Leah muttered, refusing to make eye contact.

When she didn't play along, Trudy sighed irritably. "I guess you're right," she said. "I saw him the other day at the airport, did I tell you? I went to pick up my kid from his trip to see Grandma, and who comes striding down the Jetway out of first class like he owns the place?"

Leah looked up again. "From *Vegas*? You saw Michael get off a plane from Vegas?"

"Vegas!" Trudy reached over and bonked her on the shoulder. "What makes you think my mother lives in Vegas? She lives in Atlanta! And Handsome got off the plane from Atlanta! But he was just passing through. He said he'd been to Cairo to climb some pyramids or something like that."

"Cairo! As in Egypt? *That* Cairo?"

Trudy laughed. "Oh right, it was just a fling!" she cried dramatically. "You seem pretty interested to me."

"Shut up," Leah said, and ducked again.

"Fine," Trudy said with an exaggerated sigh. "So anyway, I picked up Barton that day, and do you know what my mother did to his hair?" she demanded, launching into a tale of her mother's lame ideas about child-rearing as Leah tried to process what she'd just heard.

Leah had wondered—oh, who was she kidding? She'd *obsessed*—about why he hadn't called her. Or if he would ever call her. And she'd assumed—in an obsessive manner again—that she had lost him twice in a lifetime. Really, what moron managed that? What sort of woman had *two* shots at the love of her life and watched them fall apart? She did not want to believe that it was really over, that a single day in a cabin with a madman could turn things around so completely. But it had.

Leah had done a lot of thinking about that day and the things she'd said after it was all over. She'd been hurt and frightened, and so damn angry that he hadn't fallen all over himself to apologize to her for it all that she'd lost sight of some of the stuff he'd said. Like how he couldn't live with her uncertainty, that he'd tried, and he'd been honest, but couldn't apologize enough for who he was to suit her.

And all she'd talked about was how "sorry" wasn't good enough.

Funny how crystal clear her thoughts were about him when he wasn't around to muddy the waters. Her thoughts were pretty crystal clear now that she didn't want to be without him. She loved him like she had never and would never love another man, she was certain. In spite of Juan Carlo, and all the women Michael had dated showing up everywhere, and even though he had left her so cruelly five years ago, she loved him.

After weeks of obsessing about it, it all seemed simple now. Her heart had finally won out over her fear of being hurt again. What she wanted, what would make her happy, had trumped the fear of the thing that would destroy her.

As Trudy talked, Leah remembered a time in New York, just a couple of months after she and Michael had started dating. She'd run into an old boyfriend—hard to believe that she'd been a dating fiend before she met Michael, but she had—and once, when she'd tried to remember them all, Lucy had to fill in some of the blanks.

Anyway, she'd run into John, and they had chatted a little bit, and he'd remarked that she looked great. Leah remembered very clearly what she was wearing—a black turtleneck sweater, black slacks, some killer Manolo Blahniks (an extravagance she couldn't afford even then), and a full-length camel coat. Her hair was pulled back in a ponytail, and she was holding a bag with two giant muffins, hoping to catch Michael before he went to work.

"Thanks," she'd said to John, beaming at the compliment. "You look pretty good yourself."

He laughed and shook his head. "I look like I'm going to a stuffy law office. You look . . . shiny. Very shiny. It must be a guy."

Leah had blushed a little, but laughed at his calling her shiny. "Okay, I'm busted, there's a guy. How'd you know?"

"Just a guess," he said, taking her in from the top of her head to the tip of her toes, "because you never looked that good with me. It's sort of corny, but my grandma used to say that the heart has a way of shining through when it's full. You know what I mean? You always looked good when we were dating, but you were never quite so shiny," he said with a laugh.

At the time, Leah hadn't understood exactly what he meant. But she did now.

She hadn't shined in three months.

THE following month, a new cast member was introduced to *Coming to America*. Nina Anderson was to play Meoma, a Native American woman who would become the love interest of one of the lead actors. She would make her debut in the last episode of the first season as a teaser leading in to the second season. Assuming there was a second season.

Leah liked Nina. She was mid-twenties, Leah guessed, petite with jet-black hair and luminous gray eyes. This was her first real break, and she was as excited as any young actress would be by the prospect.

When the series wrapped for the season, the director, Ted, and the producer planned a party at Ted's big rambling ranch house in Sherman Oaks.

Leah made Brad go with her so she didn't have to go alone. Brad was happy to oblige her—his last gig had been as a giant chicken (Leah thought he was a rooster, but Brad insisted he was a chicken) on a kid's show, and he was really getting desperate for some good roles. He even dressed in his best going out clothes—a tie-dyed tee and some baggy jeans.

Ted had a great place in Sherman Oaks, near Dixie Canyon, and had hired a valet to handle parking for the night. Leah wasn't crazy about that idea, because she'd just bought a slightly used T-bird like she'd wanted for so long. It wasn't blue, it was white, and it wasn't a convertible, it was a hardtop. But it was a T-bird, and it ran, and she didn't trust the pimply-faced kid who asked for her keys to treat it right.

But when she balked at valet parking, Brad had groaned. "You can be such an old lady sometimes," he said, and popped out.

Leah frowned at his back, but with a sigh, she got out, too, and gave the kid her keys. "You scratch it, and I will rip your head off," she warned him. Leah straightened the pale pink dress she'd found in the back of her closet, checked out the sparkly sandals Trudy had loaned her, and deciding that she looked okay, marched forward, into Partyville.

Partyville was in full swing, too—there were tons of people Leah had seen around the set and then some. There was a smell of pot in the air, and dance music was pumped into every room of the house. Tables of finger food were spread out through the cavernous living and dining areas, and then again on the flagstone patio that surrounded the in-ground pool. There were three bars, one of the cast members pointed out to her, tended by bartenders wearing pilgrim hats. Funny.

Brad abandoned her the moment they stepped in together. So Leah got a glass of wine and started working her way through the front room, speaking to everyone she knew, grabbing a couple of finger wraps to munch on. She found a couple of women who also played wives on the series, and they amused themselves for a while by making hilariously snarky comments about their characters.

When they had exhausted that series of gossip, Leah moved on, talked to a guy who was making independent films and thought she'd be perfect in his next one. It took Leah some doing to get away from him.

She had no idea how much time had passed when Brad, looking a little stoned, found Leah. "Great party!" he shouted over the noise.

"Yeah!" Leah shouted back.

"Hey, guess who I saw? That guy you like."

As she hadn't mentioned any guy she liked, Leah blinked.

"You know, the one with the flowers and perfume and shit."

Her heart twisted. Really, she could feel it twisting in her chest, knocking the breath from her lungs. *"Here?"* she shouted.

"Yeah, in there," Brad said, and pointed with a smoke and a full beer bottle toward the French doors that led into the living area. But when Leah looked in that direction, all she saw was Nina, who had obviously just come in. She actually felt relieved. She didn't know what she'd say to Michael after a couple of glasses of wine, and waved at Nina, who instantly glided over.

"Hey!" Nina said, happy to see her. "Have you been here long?"

"Long enough for a couple of these," Leah said, holding up her wineglass.

"Oooh, I'd love one of those. Where'd you get it?"

Leah turned and pointed behind her. "Pilgrim hat. You can't miss it."

"Okay, I'm going to get one. But listen, don't go anywhere. I want to introduce you to someone."

"I'm planted," Leah said, and smiled as Nina glided off to get her drink.

"Leah."

Her heart seized at the sound of his voice, just stopped beating altogether, and her tongue suddenly felt very thick and unusable in her mouth.

"Leah?"

He was closer. She squeezed her eyes shut, then turned awkwardly, gripping her wineglass like a gavel, and looked into those glimmering penny-brown eyes and smiled.

God, but he looked good. His black hair had grown a little, and he was wearing it in a ponytail at his nape. His jaw was covered with the start of a dark beard. He was wearing a black, collared cotton shirt tucked into white jeans and had a pair of really cool black sandals. "Oh. Hi, Michael," she said as cheerfully as she possibly could, given the circumstance. "How are you?"

"Good," he responded as his gaze flicked the length of her. He smiled, dimples creasing his cheeks. "You look great, as usual."

But I'm not shiny. "Thanks. So do you."

"How do you know Ted?" he asked, and his smile suddenly widened. "Hey, are you working on the HBO series?"

"Yep," she said, shifting her weight from one hip to the other and then back again. "I'm a . . ." She made a gesture with her hand. "A wife of an old guy."

He laughed. Leah didn't. "Oh," he said, smiling sympathetically. "I get it. Not a coveted role."

"Maybe by middle-aged character actors," she said with a smile. "I'm kidding. It's great work and fabulous exposure for me. If they'll just give me something I can sink my teeth into—" She caught herself. Now was really not the best time to discuss the stagnation of her career. "So, ah . . . what about you?" she asked. "What are you up to these days?"

"Pyramid climbing."

"Excuse me?"

He grinned at her look of confusion. "Scaling ancient pyramids. Don't laugh—it's a lot harder than it looks."

Leah had no idea how hard it looked—she'd never seen it or even imagined it. "I'm not laughing, I'm crying," she joked. "It does beg the question . . . *why* are you scaling ancient pyramids?"

She heard Michael's throaty laugh in spite of the loud music, and it drifted through her on a soft, slow wave. "Because it's there," he said with a wink.

"Ah." She couldn't think of a single thing she'd ever done, just because it was there. Maybe now was the time. Maybe today was the day she finally danced out on that fragile limb and jumped up and down a couple of times, just because he was here, just because she might never have this chance again. She had to do it. She had to tell him she'd made the mistake this time, and took a fortifying sip of wine. "So, Mikey . . ."

He raised a brow over his smile. "Yes?"

"I'm glad to see you. I've wondered about you."

His smile faded a little. "About Bellingham, you mean."

"Right, Bellingham." Except that wasn't right, and she looked at her glass of wine as someone pumped the music up. "No, not Bellingham. *After* Bellingham," she said, lifting her gaze again. "I've been thinking."

This was the moment she should say what she'd been thinking, but Leah couldn't get the words off her tongue.

Even worse, Michael couldn't hear her. He leaned forward and said loudly, "What did you say?"

"I've been thinking!" she said louder.

He nodded.

"And . . . and I've been thinking that you were right!" she shouted. "I was wrong, Michael, I was really wrong. I never gave you a chance, I jumped to conclusions, and I wasn't very open."

Michael blinked. He looked extremely surprised. Or was that mortified? Hell, there was no going back now. "I'm sorry for being afraid. I really did want it to work—I mean, I *still* want it to work. I do, Michael, I really do!"

Now he looked so stunned that she began to panic. What was she thinking? Shouting at him to take her back in the middle of a big party full of people she *worked* with? It was insane! Michael looked as if he wanted to crawl into a hole.

The panic swelled in her, and Leah was suddenly talking, her tongue, which wouldn't work a moment ago, now moving with lightning speed ahead of her brain. "I know what you must be thinking," she blurted. "That whole thing with Adolfo—"

"Juan Carlo."

"*Juan Carlo*. That whole scene was pretty weird, sure, and yes, I was upset—but then again, I'm not usually held hostage—"

"Whoa," he said, putting a hand on her arm with a laugh and uneasily looking around them to see if anyone heard.

"But I'm over it now! I am! I said some things I really didn't mean, and I'm sorry for that, and the only thing I can say is that I was sort of freaking out, but it's behind me, and I want it to be behind *us*."

He nodded, but still he said nothing, and his silence was killing her.

"Okay, you're going to force me to say it," she said moving closer. "The thing is, I don't feel shiny anymore, and—"

"*Shiny?*" Nina said from somewhere next to her, and Leah caught her breath, closed her eyes, and let her head drop back in sheer frustration. "What a weird thing to say," Nina laughed. "What does it mean?" she asked as she stepped in between Leah and Michael.

"Nothing," Leah said, trying to smile. "Just a joke. Sort of. Not really a joke, but a . . . saying."

Nina laughed and beamed a smile up a Michael. "So I take it you two already know each other?" she remarked, and slipped her hand into Michael's.

They were holding hands. *They were holding hands.* Leah couldn't stop staring at their hands, unable to speak or to think.

"We know each other," Michael said.

"You're kidding!" Nina cried. "That's great!" She smiled at Leah as she laid her cheek on Michael's shoulder. "Isn't my boyfriend cute?"

That remark made Leah forget she was holding a glass of wine, which she promptly spilled on the hem of her dress and all over Trudy's sparkly shoes. The heat of her stupidity and embarrassment began to bleed into her neck and face. "That's great!" she said, but she was looking at her dress. *Oh God, she could die, she could just die. Someone bury her here, right now, right away.* She felt like an old woman, an old, stupid, dull woman, and desperately grabbed the hem of her dress and lifted it slightly. "Will you look at what a klutz I am? I better go do something about this," she said, and forced a laugh.

"Get some soda water," Nina suggested.

"Yeah, I'll do that."

"Leah," Michael said, but she was already moving.

"Don't worry, I'll get it out," she said cheerfully, and walked away before she absolutely passed out from mortification and shame.

She hurried through the crowd in the living room thinking she had just played out the scene from every bad movie broadcast on *Lifetime*.

"Hey, Leah, where are you off to?" Ted called after her as she hurried past, headed for the door.

"I ah . . . I spilled some wine," she said.

"I've got some red wine remover. Let me get it—"

"No, really, I probably ought to just go," she said, opening the front door. "It's silk." As if that made a difference somehow. "Ted, the party was great. Thanks for inviting me."

"You're not leaving! We're just getting started," he exclaimed, following her out. "Why rush off? Try the stuff I have and see if that doesn't work."

She turned around to look at him, saw Michael making his way through the crowd after her.

"You know, I would, but I have an audition tomorrow," she said, lifting her hand.

"On a *Sunday*?"

"Yep. Gotta jet!" she said, and with a wave, ran down

the lawn, chanting *ohshitohshitohshit* in her head. She practically threw her token at the kid and asked for her car.

BEHIND her, Michael was aware that Nina was following *him* out, too—mainly because she kept calling out his name and trying to get him to stop. It was wrong, what he was doing, so damn wrong, but he couldn't make himself stop. He was being propelled by a force outside of his realm of control at that moment. He pushed through the crowd, finally making his way outside, right behind Ted, who was trying to coax Leah into staying.

It wasn't working, but Michael could have told him that—Leah could be very determined when she wanted to be. And there she was, standing on the curb, leaning far to her right to see around cars and up the street.

"Leah!" Michael shouted.

She jerked around at the sound of his voice, and he could see the panic and mortification in her eyes.

"What is going on?" Nina asked, bouncing to a stop next to Michael. "Did you guys have a fight or something?"

Michael didn't respond immediately—he was distracted by a few revelers who had come outside to see what was going on. "I just want to make sure she's okay," he said.

Nina looked at Leah standing on the curb and peering anxiously up the street for her car, and her brows dipped into a frown. "She looks okay to me, Michael."

Yeah, well, Nina didn't know her. Michael started forward again. "Leah, wait!"

"You know what this reminds me of?" he heard a woman say behind him. "*Sex and the City.* They're still running it on HBO."

He strode out of their midst. *"Michael!"* Nina angrily shouted after him, but he kept walking.

It was enough to get Leah's attention. She glanced over

her shoulder, saw Michael marching down the lawn, and turned around, apparently resigning herself to the fact that she was going to have to face him.

"Michael, I have to go," she said extending her arm to keep him at a distance. "Just . . . just go back inside with Nina," she said, fluttering her fingers in Nina's direction. "She's great. You'll be very happy with her."

"What did you mean when you said you weren't shiny?" he demanded, ignoring her order for him to leave.

Leah's mouth dropped open. Then closed tightly shut.

"What did you mean?" he demanded again, moving closer to her extended hand.

"I didn't mean anything—"

He wasn't letting her off that easy. He was going to hear it this time and no uncertainty or wishy-washiness from her was going to stop him. He needed to hear that she loved him before he could begin to think what to do. "Yes, you did. What did you mean?" he asked again, pushing her hand aside and moving and leaning forward, so that his face was directly before hers.

She recoiled slightly. *"Shiny,"* she repeated, waving one hand. "Bling-blingy." When he didn't bite, she anxiously ran a hand over her crown. "Just . . . shiny," she said again, only softer.

Michael leaned even closer, locking in on her eyes, her mouth. "Shiny as in sweaty? Or shiny as in your full heart shining through?"

Leah gasped. "How did you *know* that?"

"I *remember*," he said. "I remember it all, don't you know that by now?"

"Wait—what do you mean you remember?" Nina cried, having marched down after Michael. "Just how do you two know each other?" She grabbed Michael's arm, pulled him back from Leah.

But Leah didn't seem to notice Nina. Her gaze was locked on his, her eyes shining with regret and hope and something more. "I'm not shiny," she said again, and pressed a fist into her abdomen. "That means I'm empty. I'm devoid of life and love and . . . and *you*."

He knew exactly what she meant. It was the same feeling he'd been trying to fill up with a series of extreme sport outings over the last couple of months, looking for something, anything, to spark a fire in him. Nothing had worked. He went to sleep with Leah on his mind, woke up with her there, and filled most of the hours in between thinking of her, wondering what she was doing, who she was with, if she ever thought of him. If she hated him.

He'd endlessly debated calling her, alternating between needing her and not wanting to hear anything in her voice that even remotely sounded like rejection.

"What in the *hell* is going on here?" Nina cried furiously, wedging herself partially between Michael and Leah, glaring at Leah. "What part of *my boyfriend* did you not understand?"

"So what are you saying?" Michael asked over Nina's head, ignoring her, too.

"That I love you," Leah said firmly, and Michael felt his heart expand tenfold. "I always have. And I can't stop."

"This is unbelievable!" Nina shrieked.

"I know the feeling," Michael said, stepping around Nina. "I'm not shiny, either, Leah. I'm dull as a lump of lead without you."

"See, people? This is what I mean when I say *acting*," Ted announced to the growing group of onlookers, who had, apparently, walked down the lawn to hear the scene being played out. "You've got to put some *ummph* into it."

"Are they *acting*?" Nina asked Ted in a little-girl voice. "Is this a scene?"

The kid pulled up with a white Thunderbird, and Leah looked at it, then at Michael.

"Dunno," Ted said cheerfully. "If it's not, it oughta be."

"Leah, don't go," Michael said, and turned toward Nina. He regretted the audience, but he wasn't letting Leah get away. "Nina . . ."

"Oh no," she said, instantly stepping backward and colliding with Brad, who'd shown up to see what was going on. "You are *not* going to blow me off in front of all these people!" she hissed at him.

"I'm not blowing you off, sweetheart. But I want to take you home. We need to talk."

"I'm not leaving here!" she cried, stepping back again, into Brad's skinny chest. "You can go fuck yourself, Michael Raney!"

Michael looked at Brad. "Do me a favor, bro," he said, digging into his pants pocket for the token that would get his car from the valet. "Make sure Nina gets home okay, will you?"

Brad lit up like a Christmas tree. "Dude! Are you serious?"

"I'm very serious." He looked at Nina again. "Unless you want to come with me now, Nina."

"Get away from me you *bastard*!"

Brad instantly put an arm around her shoulder and squeezed. "That's okay, kid. Let him go. He *is* a bastard," Brad said with a wink for Michael.

Michael heard the car door open and close and jerked around. Leah was inside her car, about to drive away. "Leah!" he shouted, and took two deep strides toward Nina, grabbed her face between his hands. "You deserve to hate me all my days for this, Nina. But then again, maybe someday you will do something totally outrageous for love, and you will understand." He kissed her forehead and then ran for Leah's car as she started to pull away from the curb.

When Leah saw his hand on the door, she stopped, watched with wide eyes as he vaulted himself inside. "Drive," he said breathlessly.

"What—"

"Just *drive*," he said again, and glanced back at Brad standing next to Nina, whose arms were flailing as she said something to Ted. And there was a host of other people around watching Nina, then Leah's car as she put it in drive and sped away.

They drove in silence for the first few minutes, Leah winding through the streets like she knew where she was going. That was almost the worst thing he'd ever done, Michael decided. The only thing worse was leaving Leah five years ago. But he'd felt a moment of panic, that sick feeling he would never have the chance again if he didn't seize it then and there.

They came upon a park entrance, and Leah screeched to a halt, threw her hands over her face, dropped her head against the steering wheel, and her shoulders began to shake.

The waterworks. Great. He'd made her cry the last two times he'd seen her. And he still wasn't even sure what he was *doing*. But nina Leah suddenly lifted her face and turned toward him.

Only Leah wasn't crying. Leah was laughing.

She was laughing so that tears were running down her cheeks. "*Ohmigod*," she squealed, pressing a hand to her belly. "Could we possibly have made a more dramatic exit, do you think?"

Michael sighed with relief and shook his head. "I don't think so."

She squealed again, pressed both hands to her belly, and her head fell against the headrest. Through her laughter she said, "That . . . was the . . . most . . . *unbelievable* . . . scene *ever*!"

It was pretty spectacular.

She stopped laughing and slanted him a look as she tried to catch her breath. "How long have you been dating Nina?"

"It was our second date."

Leah gasped and looked at him, her crystal-blue eyes shining, and then howled again. When the laughter had finally subsided, she wiped the tears from her cheeks and smiled at him. "God, I love you Michael, I do. I don't ever want to be without you. I don't care how many other women there were, or how many Juan Carlos's, I don't care. I just want to be with you. I want to be shiny again."

That admission filled Michael with lightness of being and a connection that sank its tentacles deep, into his soul and heart. Leah would always be his. He would always have somewhere and someone to belong to.

"I love you, too, baby. That's all I've wanted, is to hear you say you love me, too."

She reached for him at the same moment he reached for her, their mouths seeking each other, their hands groping for each other.

Until Leah began to laugh into his mouth again. She pulled away and grinned up at him. "I won't be able to show my face on the set again. Did you hear Ted point out the *ummph* in our acting skills?" she asked, and they both burst into laughter.

THIRTY-ONE

Subject: Re: Re: Re: Wedding Recap
From: Leah Kleinschmidt <hollywoodiva@verizon.net>
To: Lucy Frederick <ljfreddie@hotmail.com>
Time: 10:04 am

No, I didn't hear anyone talking about how bad the veal was, Lucy. I think that is all in your head. The veal was fine. Everything was beautiful. You were beautiful. Even the stupid red dresses, which I so will NOT wear again, were beautiful. I think you can finally put this obsession with your wedding behind you and go on to something else, like what you're going to name your first kid.

P.S. I TOLD YOU Michael was a great guy! You were practically drooling all over your wedding dress!

Subject: Re: Re: Re: Re: Wedding Recap
From: Lucy Frederick <ljfreddie@hotmail.com>

To: Leah Kleinschmidt <hollywoodiva@verizon.net>
Date: 1:12 pm

I KNOW the red dresses were beautiful, you moron! That's what I've been telling you for like two years, but you never listen! And I'm sorry, but I think the veal was a little gamey. I am writing my wedding coordinator, because I don't think she should use that caterer again. That was a lot of money to spend on gamey veal. We've got our pictures back from Fiji, BTW. I have attached several.

Yeah, yeah, okay, Michael was great. He really was. I am glad I finally got a chance to spend a little time with him, because I would hate to show up to your wedding and not like the groom. And yes, I would to be happy to be your matron of honor! Gawd, Leah, I can't believe you are actually getting married! Yiii-ippppeeeee!

Subject: Re: Re: Re: Re: Re: Wedding Recap
From: Leah Kleinschmidt <hollywoodiva@verizon.net>
To: Lucy Frederick <ljfreddie@hotmail.com>
Time: 10:23 am

I know, I can't believe it either! I have a new friend here who is going to coordinate it (she did the big Olivia Dagwood and Vincent Vittorio wedding that fell through—remember, the one where they got stuck in the mountains and it was all over the news?). Anyway, Marnie said I need to pick out my colors so we can start working on a theme. So, I have attached some colors and dresses I sort of like for the bridesmaids. Since you like red so much, what do you think of rose? Don't hold back. Tell me what you really like and don't like.

    P.S. I'm so excited!!!!!!

*   *   *

Subject: Re: Anniversary Party
From: Michael <michael.raney@thrillsanonymous.net>
To: Jack <jack.price@thrillsanonymous.net>
  Eli <eli.mccain@thrillsanonymous.net>
  Coop <cooper.jessup@thrillsanonymous.net>
Date: 2:13 pm

Hey guys, thanks for the info on a really ridiculous plan for an anniversary party on a private island to include volcano and waterfall hiking. Yeah, right. Maybe it's just me, but I don't see a bunch of New York real-estate moguls hiking their fat asses up a waterfall or an active volcano. What I see is a lot of drinking and screwing around, but hey, that's an extreme sport in and of itself. Unfortunately, I will not be able to join in on the planning for this treat, because I will be on my honeymoon in Paris. Fortunately, as I did not draw the short straw when we decided who would take the lead on this thing, I feel perfectly comfortable showing up just in time for happy hour when the gig begins. And, Jack, I can't tell you how it warms my heart to know that you will be leading this. Paybacks are a bitch, dude. You can't say I didn't warn you.

First in the all-new contemporary romance series featuring men who find love the most extreme sport of all.

From National Bestselling Author
Julia London

Wedding Survivor
0-425-20631-9

Survivor meets *Bridezilla* in this all-new series about a members-only adventure service that caters to the rich and famous. In this captivating opener, one of its founders is about to embark on the thrill ride of his life—meeting a woman he can't live without.

"Sprightly and fresh...
A gifted and versatile writer."
—*Publishers Weekly*

"Writing that sparkles with sexy, sassy charm."
—*Booklist*

Available wherever books are sold or at
penguin.com